FIGH

Clint drew swiftly and fired at Lanigan. The bullet shattered Lanigan's right collarbone, numbing his arm so that the gun dropped from it.

Myles had his gun out, but Goodnight was firing, and although his shots were going wild, they were enough to attract Myles's attention. Clint took advantage of the situation and fired at the man. His bullet struck Myles square in the chest, punching right through his breastbone and driving all of his breath out of him . . .

DON'T MISS THESE
ALL-ACTION WESTERN SERIES
FROM THE BERKLEY PUBLISHING GROUP

THE GUNSMITH by J. R. Roberts
Clint Adams was a legend among lawmen, outlaws, and ladies. They called him . . . the Gunsmith.

LONGARM by Tabor Evans
The popular long-running series about U.S. Deputy Marshal Long—his life, his loves, his fight for justice.

LONE STAR by Wesley Ellis
The blazing adventures of Jessica Starbuck and the martial arts master, Ki. Over eight million copies in print.

SLOCUM by Jake Logan
Today's longest-running action Western. John Slocum rides a deadly trail of hot blood and cold steel.

THE GUNSMITH

144

WEST TEXAS SHOWDOWN

J. R. ROBERTS

JOVE BOOKS, NEW YORK

WEST TEXAS SHOWDOWN

A Jove Book / published by arrangement with
the author

PRINTING HISTORY
Jove edition / December 1993

ISBN: 0-515-11257-7

A JOVE BOOK®
Jove Books are published by The Berkley Publishing Group,
200 Madison Avenue, New York, New York 10016.
JOVE and the "J" design are trademarks belonging to Jove Publications, Inc.

PRINTED IN THE UNITED STATES OF AMERICA

10 9 8 7 6 5 4 3 2 1

THE GUNSMITH

144

WEST TEXAS SHOWDOWN

ONE

When Clint Adams rode into Lubbock, Texas, he was tired. He had ridden his big, black gelding, Duke, hard through much of New Mexico over the past few weeks, and all he wanted from Lubbock was a rest stop before he continued on to Labyrinth, Texas.

He put Duke up at the livery, with instructions to the liveryman for special care.

"Don't worry, mister," the man said, "an animal like this *deserves* special care."

Duke was getting on in years, but he was an impressive beast, nevertheless.

Clint only wished he could say the same thing for himself.

"You can't be serious about this, Charles," Fred Canby said.

"I'm very serious, Fred," Charles Goodnight said.

The two old friends were sitting at a table in

1

the Americana Saloon, enjoying a glass of whiskey and a cigar each.

"But bringing in more wire . . ." Canby said, shaking his head.

"The wire is necessary, Fred," the cattleman insisted.

"Maybe a *fence* is necessary, Charles," Canby said, "but *barbed* wire—"

"You've been reading too many horror stories, Fred," Goodnight said. "Barbed wire is not the scourge of the West, as the Eastern newspapers have been making it sound."

"Perhaps not," Canby said, "but there are enough of your neighbors who think it is. Hell, you've already had encounters with Sessions and Taylor," Canby said, naming two of Goodnight's closest and biggest neighbors.

"Frank Sessions is a fool," Goodnight said. "He thought he could abuse my hospitality, and he tried it once too often."

"You and Frank used to be friends, Charles," Canby pointed out. "Since the wire—"

"It's *not* since the wire," Goodnight said, jabbing at the air with his lit cigar. Goodnight was a big, barrel-chested man with dark hair going gray in streaks. At the moment he was wearing a three-piece gray suit, but he was more at home in his trail clothes.

"My dispute with Sessions started when he got greedy," Goodnight explained. "He started to abuse the use of my land, and the water that I was allowing him to use. It's because of that abuse that he and I are at odds, *not* because of the wire."

"If you took down the wire," Canby said, "rather than putting up more—"

"Forget it, Fred," Goodnight said. "My wire is up to stay, and I've brought more in. It'll be going up as soon as I get it back to Palo Duro Canyon."

Goodnight's ranch sprawled throughout the Palo Duro Canyon, between Lubbock and Amarillo. He had neighbors, but none of them had as much land as he had. For years he had allowed his neighbors to graze on his land, until men like Frank Sessions began to abuse the privilege.

"You're asking for more trouble, Charles," Fred Canby said, shaking his head. "More trouble than you need, believe me. . . ."

Goodnight pinned his longtime friend with a hard stare and asked, "Is that a threat, Fred?"

"Oh, not from me, Charles," Canby said. "It's not a threat, it's . . . a warning . . . or a prediction, if you prefer. I only wish you'd listen to reason—"

"Fred," Goodnight said, leaning forward in his chair, "I know you don't like the barbed wire. In fact, I recognize that you are an ardent detractor of it, but don't let that put us on opposite sides."

"Believe me, Charles," Canby said, "the last thing I want to do is end up on the, uh, opposite side of the fence from you."

"Good," Goodnight said. He stood up and looked down at his friend. "I have to get going. I've got miles of wire to string."

Canby watched sadly as his friend left the saloon.

• • •

As Clint walked past the general store, he saw a buckboard out front. It appeared to be loaded with rolls of barbed wire. Clint had not been following the controversy over the wire, but he was well aware of its existence. Curiosity caused him to cross the street to get a better look at it.

Standing by the buckboard, he touched the hard, sharp ends of the short wire points. He could see where the points could tear up a cow—or a man. He could also see, however, where the wire would act as a deterrent.

"Can I help you?" someone asked from behind him.

He turned and saw a man standing there, staring at him, possibly as curious about him as he was about the wire. The man was in his late thirties, wearing worn trail clothes. He wore a gun, but Clint had the feeling he was much more at home with a lariat.

"No," Clint said, "sorry, I didn't mean to—I was just curious, that's all. I really haven't seen the wire up close before now."

"You a cattleman?" the man asked.

"No, no," Clint said, "I just got into town and was on my way to the saloon. I saw the wire and I'm afraid my curiosity got the better of me."

"This here is Mr. Goodnight's wire," the man said. "He don't want nobody messin' with it."

"Fair enough," Clint said, putting his hands up. "I was just looking. I'll be on my way."

"That's a good idea, mister," the man said.

Clint waved and walked away from the buckboard. The last thing he needed was to get into some sort of confrontation just moments after arriving in town.

That was when he heard the first shot.

TWO

Clint turned and saw two men. One was the man he had just spoken to. He was no longer standing, but lying on the ground.

The other man was wearing a suit with a vest. He was crouched behind the buckboard with a gun in his hand. It only took Clint a moment to realize that no one had shot at him, but at the man he'd been talking to. As two more shots rang out, he saw that the man in the suit was now the target.

Clint drew his gun and tried to locate the source of the shots. When two more shots were fired, he saw where they were coming from. Somebody was on the roof of a nearby building, using a rifle to fire down at the man by the buckboard.

The man in the suit fired back, but his aim was off. He struck the front of the building, but that was all. Clint decided to lend a hand because he hated bushwhackers.

He ran to the side of the man in the suit and said, "I'll cover you. Get your man to safety!"

The man looked at him for a moment, as if trying to decide what his stake was in the matter.

"Pull him to safety!" Clint shouted, and then fired up at the man on the roof. His shot came considerably closer than that of the man in the suit, and the bushwhacker ducked down for cover.

"Now!"

The other man moved quickly, grabbing the fallen man beneath the arms and pulling him to safety behind the buckboard.

The man with the rifle stood to fire again, but Clint dissuaded him with another shot. He thought he heard someone cry out, and then the man disappeared from view.

"How is he?" Clint asked.

"He doesn't look too bad," the other man said, "but he needs a doctor."

"Then get him to one," Clint said. "I'll check the roof."

"All right."

Clint left the cover of the buckboard, but the rifleman on the roof did not reappear.

Clint quickly located the building the man had been firing from and ran inside. He found himself in a woman's clothing store. The clerk, an attractive young woman with black hair, looked at him, startled. The customer she was waiting on actually cried out and put her hand to her mouth. She was considerably older than the clerk.

"I'm sorry," he said, "but someone is firing shots from your roof. How do I get up there?"

The clerk reacted immediately, shrugging off her surprise in a way he admired.

"Through here," she said, indicating a curtained doorway behind her, "and up the stairs."

"Thanks."

He hurried behind her counter, brushing against her as he passed. He went through the curtained doorway and found the stairs.

He was fairly certain he had hit the bush-whacker on the roof, but since he didn't know whether the man was wounded or dead, he ascended the stairs carefully. When he reached the second floor, he looked for a hatch in the ceiling and found it easily because it was open. There was a chair just beneath it, which made it obvious how the man had gotten up there. The question now was—was he still there?

He stood on the chair and had to holster his gun in order to reach up and pull himself up. He knew he was putting himself in a vulnerable position, and took a moment to wonder why before hauling himself up and through the open hatch.

When he was through, he rolled on the rooftop, clawing for his gun at the same time. He came to a stop with the gun held out ahead of him and quickly scanned the roof.

He was alone.

The shooter was gone.

He took a moment to examine the roof and

found some bloodstains by the front, where the man must have stood while firing. Satisfied that he *had* wounded the man, but apparently not badly enough to keep him from getting away, Clint started back to the street.

THREE

Clint was coming out from the curtained doorway when a man with a gun entered the store. In a split second he saw the man's badge and managed to put his hands in the air, holding his gun in his right.

"Take it easy!" he called out.

He didn't want to get shot by a nervous or overzealous lawman.

"Just keep your hands up!" the lawman shouted.

"They're up."

The female clerk was standing off to one side, watching the two of them with wide eyes. She did not, however, look frightened.

"Sheriff," she said finally, "I think you're making a mistake."

"We'll see about that, Miss Garfield," the man with the badge said. "Drop that gun," he told Clint.

"I'm going to lay it down," Clint said. "Dropping it could do some damage to it or cause it to go off."

"Just set it down real easy," the man with the badge said.

At that moment, as Clint was setting his gun down, the man dressed in the suit came in.

"No, no, Sheriff," he said testily, "not *that* man. He's the one who helped me."

The sheriff looked confused.

"I . . . didn't know . . ."

"I tried to tell you," Miss Garfield said.

"Sheriff, you'd better go out and try to find that shooter," the other man said.

"You might try around back," Clint said. "He might have dropped down from the roof. I wounded him, so you might also look for some blood."

"Well, Sheriff?" the man said.

"I'm goin'," the sheriff said.

The lawman went out the door, and the man in the suit looked at Clint.

"He's useless," he said. "Pick up your gun, mister. I'm beholden to you."

Clint picked up his gun and said, "I just have a habit of poking my nose where it doesn't belong."

"Lucky for me," the man said. "My name is Goodnight, Charles Goodnight."

Clint frowned.

"The Goodnight who blazed the Goodnight-Loving Trail?" he asked.

Goodnight looked embarrassed and said, "My partner and I did that, yes."

"Well, it's a pleasure to meet you," Clint said, shaking the man's hand.

"Would you let me buy you a drink?" Goodnight asked.

"I don't see why not," Clint said. "Just let me talk to the young lady a moment."

"I'll wait outside," Goodnight said.

When Goodnight was gone, Clint turned to the woman and took a good look at her. She was extremely pretty, wearing a white lace blouse with a high collar and a long black skirt.

"Ma'am, I'd like to apologize if I frightened you," he said.

"That's all right," she said. "I gather from what I heard that you saved Mr. Goodnight's life."

"That's possible," he said. "There's no telling what would have happened if I had minded my own business."

"I don't think you'll convince Mr. Goodnight of that," she said.

"May I ask your name?" Clint said.

"Alicia Garfield."

"I'm Clint Adams, Miss Garfield," he said. "I'd like to do something to make up for the intrusion."

She looked surprised and said, "Sir, are you . . . asking me to . . . to . . . "

"Go to dinner with me, yes," Clint said. "It will be my way of apologizing."

"As I said before," she said, "there is no need."

"But you do eat dinner, don't you?"

"Well . . . yes," she said, looking amused.

"Then perhaps we could eat it together?" he said, pressing the issue.

Looking even more amused, she said, "I . . . hardly know you."

"Then we'll have a long dinner," he said, "and

by its end we'll know each other a lot better. What do you say?"

"Well . . ."

"Good," he said, "I'll call for you here. What time do you close?"

"At seven."

"Then I'll be here," he said, and left before she could protest.

Outside he found Charles Goodnight waiting for him.

"Might I ask your name, sir?" Goodnight said.

"Clint Adams, Mr. Goodnight."

Goodnight stared at him and said, "You mean . . . the Gunsmith?"

"I've been called that, yes," Clint said.

"Well, sir," Goodnight said, "this is a pleasure. Come, I'll take you to the finest saloon in town for the libation of your choice."

He'd hardly been in town half an hour and already he'd been involved in a shooting, made the acquaintance of a rather famous man, *and* a lovely young lady.

Lubbock was turning out to be much more than he'd bargained for.

FOUR

Goodnight took Clint to the saloon he had just left Fred Canby at, the Americana. It was more than a saloon, really. It was a full-fledged gambling hall, with enough gaming tables to entertain the whole town—or so it seemed to Clint. The ceilings were high, and the bar was polished mahogany. Once upon a time you only saw establishments like this in San Francisco or New Orleans. Now they were spreading all over the West, to Lubbock, El Paso, Dodge City, Tombstone, and Virginia City.

As they entered, Clint thought Goodnight was looking around for someone, but he didn't comment.

In truth, Goodnight was checking to see if Fred Canby was still there, and was satisfied to see that the man wasn't.

"Let's get a table," Goodnight said. "One of the girls will bring us a drink. What'll you have?"

"Just a beer," Clint said. "As a matter of fact, I

just rode in under an hour ago, still haven't had anything to cut the trail dust."

"The beer's cold here," Goodnight assured him. "You'll enjoy it."

They sat at a back table, and as Goodnight had predicted, a saloon girl came over and asked what they would like. Clint had the feeling he would not have gotten such service had he not been in the company of Charles Goodnight.

"Two beers, Brenda, please," Goodnight said.

"Yes, sir," she said, and for a moment Clint thought she might execute a slight curtsy.

"You, uh, don't own this place, do you?" Clint asked Goodnight.

"Oh, no—you mean the service?"

"And the respect."

"Well, I'm in here quite a bit when I'm in town," the man said. "They know me here."

Clint didn't know if he meant at the saloon, or in the town, but then decided that both probably applied.

"You don't live in town, then?"

"Oh, no," Goodnight said, shaking his head. "I have a spread in the Palo Duro Canyon, north of here. It's between here and Amarillo. I have some property in New Mexico and Colorado, as well, but my primary concern these days is the Palo Duro spread."

"I noticed the wire—" Clint said, and then stopped when Brenda returned with the drinks.

"Will there be anything else, Mr. Goodnight?" she asked suggestively. "For you *or* your friend?"

"Not right now, Brenda," Goodnight said. "We'll

let you know if there is, though."

As Brenda walked away, Goodnight watched her and then said to Clint, "Not what you'd call pretty, but fetching as all hell, wouldn't you say?"

"I would," Clint said. He had noticed that the blond Brenda, though not particularly pretty as Goodnight had pointed out, did indeed have a "fetching" quality to her. Clint was a firm believer that women did not have to be beautiful to be attractive or sexy. Brenda seemed a perfect example of the type.

However, the woman in the store, Alicia Garfield, was another matter entirely. . . .

"Drink up, Mr. Adams," Goodnight said, lifting up his mug. "I'd like to drink to the health of the man who saved my bacon."

Clint raised the mug in return and then took a healthy drink.

"I was saying I noticed the wire," Clint went on. "Talked to your man, in fact, just moments before the shooting. How is he, by the way?"

"I'll check on him when we're through here," Goodnight said. "I think he'll make it, although he won't be doing any work for me for a while."

"Was the shooting related to the wire, do you think?" Clint asked.

Goodnight put his mug down and eyed Clint with interest.

"Why do you ask that?"

Clint shrugged.

"It was a bushwhacking," Clint said, "pure and simple. That means someone with a grudge. I understand that this barbed wire has been known to bring the worst out in some people."

"That it has," Goodnight said. "Some of my neighbors have exhibited some bad feelings about my using the wire myself."

"You think this was one of your neighbors' doing?" Clint asked.

"I didn't see the man who was doing the shooting," Goodnight said, "not that it would have mattered if I had. He was probably just a hired gun."

"Probably."

"You hit him, you say?"

"I did," Clint said. "There's some blood up there on the roof."

"Well, maybe you slowed him down enough for that good-for-nothing sheriff to catch up to him," Goodnight said sourly.

He was playing with his beer more than he was drinking, turning the mug around in circles over and over again. Some of the beer had sloshed over onto the table and his hand, but he didn't seem to notice.

"Don't think much of the local law, I gather?" Clint asked, taking another long sip from his beer after the remark.

"Humph," Goodnight said, snorting in disgust, "there's an election coming up soon, and I'll be backing a man against him."

Clint didn't say anything. It seemed to him that with a man like Goodnight behind him any man would be able to get into office rather easily. He'd been to many towns where the sheriff was in some rich rancher's pocket. He wondered if Goodnight was the kind of man who wanted *that* kind of a sheriff.

"Say," Goodnight said, leaning forward, looking at Clint with keen interest now, "you wouldn't be interested in a job, would you, Clint? It's all right if I call you Clint, isn't it?"

Clint frowned across the table at the man, considered both questions, and wondered which of them he should answer first.

FIVE

"I'm not really looking for a job, Mr. Goodnight," Clint said, "and of course you can call me Clint."

"And you have to call me Charles," Goodnight said. "Don't misunderstand me, please. I was not offering you the *sheriff's* job. What I was referring to was you coming to work for me, on my ranch."

"I'm not much of a ranch hand."

"No, no," Goodnight said, "I'm still not making myself clear."

"Charles," Clint said, very slowly, "I don't hire out my gun."

Goodnight studied Clint for a few moments, and then sat back. He took his hand away from the beer mug he'd been playing with.

"Let me change directions here, Clint," he said finally. "I'm certainly not trying to offend you in any way. If I have, I'm sorry."

"It's all right."

"Do you mind if I ask what you're doing here in Lubbock?"

"Passing through," Clint said. "I just stopped here so my horse and I could get some rest."

"Excellent!" Goodnight said, obviously pleased.

"I'm sorry?"

"My ranch is a perfect place for you to rest," Goodnight said. "I'd like to invite you to come out . . . as my guest, naturally."

"Well," Clint said, "that's very generous, Mist—I mean, Charles, but—"

"May I point something out here?"

"Please do."

"The chances of you getting any rest here in Lubbock are very slim."

"Why is that, Charles?"

"Well, as you said, you were hardly here an hour and already you've managed to take sides."

"I didn't take any sides."

"I'm sorry, but you did. When you stood beside me out there, you took sides."

"That's absurd."

"I agree," Goodnight said, "but how do you think the rest of the town will look at it? First you help me, and then we come to the saloon together—not that I planned this, Clint!" the man hurriedly added. "I'm simply pointing out how it must look."

Clint saw that the man was right.

"Keep going."

"Whoever sent that gunman after me is also going to think that you've sided with me," Goodnight said. "They might be after you next, wanting to get you out of the way before they come after me again."

Another point well-taken, Clint thought.

"Well then . . ." Clint said, "I could just leave town."

"Exactly what I'm proposing," Goodnight said.

"I mean leave and head south."

"To where?"

Clint hesitated a moment, then said, "To wherever I was headed."

"All right," Goodnight said, "never mind where you're headed. That's none of my business. Finish your beer. Would you like another?"

"No," Clint said. "I think I'd like to check into the hotel and get some rest."

"Of course, you're right," Goodnight said. "Look, when I leave here I'm going to check on my man and then head back to the ranch."

"Alone?"

"I have other men here in town."

"I see. . . ."

"I'll leave you directions to my ranch," Goodnight said. "If you change your mind, you can ride out and you'll be welcome. How's that?"

"That's fine," Clint said.

"Good."

They left the saloon together and stopped on the boardwalk outside.

"I want to thank you again, Clint," Goodnight said. "You did me a service today I will not soon forget."

"I was glad to help."

"I won't shake your hand," Goodnight said. "Not out here, anyway, with people watching—"

"Don't be an ass," Clint said and put out his hand.

Goodnight beamed, accepted the hand, and pumped it vigorously.

"I hope to see you soon," Goodnight said. "If not, then sometime in the future. You'll always be welcome."

"I appreciate it, Charles."

They parted company there, Goodnight walking back toward his wagon and Clint headed for the hotel.

Clint knew Goodnight was right. Anyone who had witnessed his assistance of the man would take that as a sign of a side taken. Their public handshake just now would also foster that impression. There was nothing he could do about that, though. He decided not to worry about it, that there was no reason for him to put himself on guard.

He spent his life that way, anyway.

SIX

Fred Canby regarded the wounded man with an annoyed expression on his face. They were in Canby's office, on the second floor of the brick City Hall building. The man had entered through the rear door, so that no one would see him. Even though he'd done that, Canby was incensed that he had come to the building. More than that, though, Canby was angry that the man had failed to do what he was being paid to do—kill Charles Goodnight.

"You're an idiot!" he snapped. "I should have known better than to hire you."

"Mr. Canby," the man began, holding his wounded arm. Blood seeped through his fingers, but Canby ignored that totally. "The other man—" he tried to continue, but Canby cut him off.

"I don't want excuses," Canby said. "You were hired to do a job and you didn't do it."

"I got the other man—"

"A ranch hand," Canby said, "and you didn't

even kill *him*. He's recovering. In other words, Murphy, you're a total failure."

Murphy frowned, more at Canby's words than at the pain in his arm.

"Does that mean I ain't gettin' paid?"

"Oh, you're getting paid, all right," Canby said bitterly. "You're getting paid to get the hell out of town—and out of Texas! Don't ever come back, either."

"What about my arm?" the man said. "I need a doctor to look at—"

"You'll live until you get out of Texas. Find a doctor in Oklahoma, or New Mexico."

Canby took an envelope out of his desk drawer and handed it to Murphy. It was the money he was supposed to have been paid to kill Charles Goodnight.

"I don't care which direction you ride in, just get the hell out of town and out of Texas. Do you understand?"

"Sure, Mr. Canby," Murphy said, taking the envelope in his good hand. It immediately soaked up the blood from his wound. "I understand."

"In case you don't," Canby said, "let me make it clearer. If you come back to Texas, I'll have *you* killed."

"S-sure, Mr. Canby," the man stammered, "I under—"

"Get out!" Canby said. He turned his back on the man to stare out his window at the main street below.

He heard the door open and close and the echo of the man's footsteps as he walked away. Moments later he heard the door open and close again, but he had heard no approaching footsteps. That always amazed him about Hank Lanigan.

He turned and saw Lanigan standing in front of his desk, looking as taciturn and impassive as ever. He employed Lanigan because the man never let emotion get in the way of his job. In fact, Canby had never seen Lanigan exhibit emotion of any kind.

"Follow him," Canby said. "When he's far enough out of town, kill him and get my money back."

"Right."

Lanigan turned and started for the door. He stopped with his hand on the knob.

"What is it?" Canby asked.

"What about Goodnight?"

"Don't worry," Canby said. He turned to look out the window again. "I have other plans for Charles Goodnight."

Clint walked to the hotel, entered, and checked in. He was on the steps to the second floor when it hit him.

If Charles Goodnight had more men in town, where were they while the shooting was going on?

"Damn it!" he said.

To the surprise of the desk clerk, Clint ran back down the stairs, out the front door, and headed for the livery stable.

SEVEN

When the buckboard carrying the barbed wire stopped, Goodnight frowned. He had been riding behind it while one of his men drove the wagon and the other two flanked it. Now that they all had stopped he rode on ahead.

"What's wrong?" he asked. "Why have you stopped?"

"Sorry, Mr. Goodnight," one of the mounted men said. Goodnight was shocked to see that the man was pointing a gun at him.

"What's going on?"

"Just sit your horse easy, Mr. Goodnight," the other man said.

Goodnight turned and saw that the second man was pointing a gun at him as well.

"Traitors!" he said, understanding what was happening. "How much were you paid?"

"A lot of money," said the man on the buck-board. His name was Ayres. On Goodnight's right was Fenner, and on his left, Holcomb.

"I'll double it," Goodnight said.

"No you wouldn't," Ayres said. "You'd never forget this, and you'd hold it against us."

To Goodnight's way of thinking, none of these men had worked for him for very long.

"Well, at least you've worked for me long enough to know that," Goodnight said. "So, which one of you will it be?"

"Which one of us will . . . what be?" Ayres asked.

"Which of you will pull the trigger and kill me?" Goodnight said.

Ayres looked puzzled. He had yet to produce his own gun.

"We're not gonna kill you, Mr. Goodnight," he said. "We're only supposed to take you someplace—you and the wire."

"And I'll be killed there."

Ayres didn't say anything.

"Or are you naive enough to think that I wasn't going to be killed at all?" he asked the three men. "Come on now. You men must know that you are to be, at the very least, a *party* to murder. Accomplices!"

The three men exchanged uncertain glances.

"Well, I won't wait for that," Goodnight said, "so you had better be ready to use your guns now."

"Mr. Goodnight," Ayres said, "don't do anything foolish. Take out your gun and drop it on the ground."

"I'll do no such thing," Goodnight said. "In a moment I'm going to draw my gun and shoot the lot of you—that is, unless you shoot me first."

"Don't force us—" Ayres said.

"Take him!" Holcomb shouted.

Goodnight heard shots even as he went for his gun, even as he knew he'd be too late, but he was damned if he'd go meekly to his death without taking *somebody* with him.

Odd, though, that he hadn't been shot yet. . . .

Clint rode hard until he saw the wagon and the men around it. Two of them were pointing guns at Goodnight, and if he read the man right he wasn't about to go anywhere willingly.

He heard one of the men shout and, cursing, he drew his gun and started firing.

To Goodnight's surprise, Holcomb, the man who had shouted, fell from his saddle. Goodnight had his gun out by then, and as he turned to look at Fenner, the man went flying from his horse as if he'd been yanked off from behind.

Goodnight looked at Ayres, who was going for his gun.

"Don't, son."

Ayres ignored him. He grabbed for his gun, and Goodnight fired. His bullet took Ayres in the face and knocked him from the buckboard.

Goodnight turned as he heard a horse behind him and was surprised to see Clint Adams approaching him, gun in hand. It was only then that he realized what had happened to Holcomb and Fenner.

"Saved my bacon again, huh?" Goodnight asked.

"We'd better check them," Clint said, dismount
ing.

He went to each man and examined them, sat-
isfying himself that they were dead.

"They all work for you?" he asked Goodnight.

"They did."

"For how long?"

"Not very long."

"They say who hired them?"

"No," Goodnight said, "only that they were paid
a lot of money."

"To kill you?" Clint asked.

"They said no," Goodnight replied. "They said
they were supposed to take me someplace—me
and the wire."

"The wire," Clint said, nodding.

"What brings you out here to save my life again?"
Goodnight asked.

"I got to thinking," Clint said. "I remembered
you said you had other men in town, and I was
wondering where they were when the shooting
was going on."

"So you assumed they had been paid off?"

"It seemed a safe bet," Clint said.

"And you figured I'd never get to my ranch
alive," Goodnight said.

"That also seemed a safe bet."

"Well," Goodnight said, "as it turned out, *they*
didn't make it. I'll have to go it alone from here."

"No," Clint said, "I'll ride along with you."

"You'll work for me?"

"No," Clint said, "I'll *ride along with you*, and
maybe take you up on your offer to rest at your

place for a while—but that's all."

"That's enough," Goodnight said. "Let's get started."

"No," Clint said again. "Tomorrow."

"Tomorrow?" Goodnight repeated. "Why tomorrow?"

"Because you may not have much respect for the lawman in Lubbock," Clint said, "but we still have to have some respect for the law. We'll have to take these men back to town and explain what happened to the sheriff. After that, we can head for your ranch."

"Very well," Goodnight said reluctantly. "I suppose you're right."

"I know I am," Clint said. "Now, you want to step down and help me collect these bodies?"

EIGHT

Clint drove the wagon back into Lubbock, with Goodnight riding alongside. Trailing behind were Duke and the horses belonging to the dead men. There was one dead man slung over one horse and two on the other.

They went directly to the sheriff's office and found the man behind his desk.

"Did you find that son of a bitch who shot at me?" Goodnight demanded as they entered.

The sheriff leapt to his feet, almost knocking his chair over.

"I found some blood behind the building, like this fella said," the lawman said, "but I wasn't able to find anybody."

"Well, we've got three somebodies outside for you," Goodnight said.

"What?"

"Outside," Goodnight said, staring at the man.

Goodnight and Clint went outside with the sheriff trailing behind curiously.

"What the hell—" the man said when he saw the bodies on the horses. "Who were they?"

"My men," Goodnight said. "Some son of a bitch paid them off."

"Who?"

Goodnight gave the man a disgusted look.

"If I knew that, I would have told you," he said impatiently.

"Unfortunately," Clint said to the sheriff, "we weren't able to keep one of them alive so he could tell us."

The sheriff looked at Clint and said, "Say, just who are you?"

"His name's Clint Adams, that's who he is," Goodnight said. "He's going to be my guest for a few days."

"Adams?" the sheriff said.

"Are you still checked in at the hotel?" Goodnight asked Clint.

"I am."

"Well, I guess I better take a room."

"You're stayin' in town tonight?" the sheriff asked Goodnight. The man looked surprised.

"We'll be getting an early start in the morning, Sheriff," Goodnight said. He turned to Clint and asked, "Will you take the wagon to the livery?"

"Sure," Clint said, reasoning that he had to take Duke back over there anyway.

"I'll see you at the Americana later," Goodnight said, "after I check in."

"Charles," Clint said, "don't you think you should keep a low profile for a while? I mean, there have been *two* attempts on your life in the past couple of hours."

"I know that," Goodnight said, "but I'll be damned if I'm going to hide my head."

"I'm not saying you have to hide," Clint said, "just don't go walking around by yourself."

"What do you suggest?"

"Check in at the hotel and wait for me there," Clint said. "We'll go to dinner."

Goodnight thought a moment, then nodded and said, "All right."

"And you're buying," Clint added.

Goodnight laughed, slapped Clint on the back, and said, "I *insist* on buying!"

Goodnight went off, still laughing, leaving Clint with the sheriff.

"Who killed these men?" the lawman asked.

"I killed two, and Goodnight killed one," Clint said. "They didn't leave us any choice."

The sheriff looked at Clint curiously.

"How long have you worked for Mr. Goodnight, Adams?" he asked.

"I don't work for him," Clint said. "If you heard him, he said I was his guest."

"How long have you known him?"

"A couple of hours."

"You make friends fast, don't you?"

Clint smiled at the man and said, "I'm just a friendly guy, Sheriff."

He untied the two horses bearing dead men from the back of the wagon.

"That ain't the reputation I know," the sheriff said.

Clint handed the reins to the man and said, "Then don't believe everything you hear, Sheriff."

Fred Canby spent many of his days staring out his window. In his youth he had spent most of his days in the saddle but, unlike Goodnight, he had moved onto other business endeavors. Some days, however, when he was just looking out the window, he wished he was back in the saddle once again.

Canby was looking out the window when Clint Adams and Charles Goodnight rode back into town, bringing with them three dead men. He stared at them, shaking his head.

It looked as if he was going to have to take more drastic measures to achieve his goals.

First, though, he was going to have to find out who the hell that other man was.

NINE

Clint found Charles Goodnight waiting impatiently for him in the hotel lobby.

"Did you get a room?" Clint asked.

"I did," Goodnight said. "Are you ready to eat?"

"As soon as I put my saddlebags and rifle in my room," Clint said.

"Well, get to it, then," Goodnight said. "I'm famished."

"It'll just take me a minute," Clint said.

"Go, go, go," Goodnight said impatiently.

When Lanigan returned to Fred Canby's office, his face was as impassive as ever. Canby knew that Lanigan could have returned from killing a family of five and he would *still* look that way.

"Is it done?"

As his answer Lanigan produced the envelope of money Canby had given Murphy. It was smeared with blood. He dropped it on the man's desk, where Canby allowed it to stay.

"All right," Canby said. "Goodnight is back in town."

"How?"

"He brought three dead men in with him, that's how," Canby said.

"Goodnight killed all three men himself?" Lanigan asked.

"No," Canby said, "he had help."

"Who helped him?"

"That's what I want you to find out," Canby said. "Tonight."

"All right."

"Don't *do* anything, Lanigan," Canby said. "Just find out who the man with Goodnight is, and let me know. After that, I'll tell you what to do. Understood?"

"Understood."

"All right, then," Canby said, "go."

Lanigan was the perfect employee, Canby thought. The man was like a gun. You pointed him and he went off when you pulled the trigger—and he *never* asked questions.

TEN

Goodnight took Clint to a small restaurant he would never have found on his own. The man was greeted the same way he seemed to be everywhere in town, as if he owned the place.

"Respect," Goodnight said, but Clint had to wonder if it really was respect, or fear.

They were shown to a table by a waiter who asked Goodnight if he wanted beer.

"Yes," Goodnight said, "we both do . . . and the beef stew."

"Yes, sir."

As the man walked away, Goodnight said, "They don't serve beer here."

"So how are we going to get it?" Clint asked.

"They'll send someone to the saloon for it," Goodnight said.

"Because they respect you so much."

"Right."

Clint nodded to himself.

"I hope you don't mind that I ordered for both of us," Goodnight said, "but the beef stew is exceptionally good here."

"That's fine."

"Besides," Goodnight added, "I want you to have the best. You saved my life not once, but twice today. Would you consider accepting some sort of reward?"

"No."

"Money, or—"

"No, nothing."

"I was going to say, perhaps a horse? I have some fine stock—"

"I have a horse."

"Yes," Goodnight said, "I couldn't help but notice. It's a magnificent beast. Too bad it's a gelding. Was it difficult to handle? Is that why you gelded it?"

"He was already gelded when I got him," Clint said. "I don't know why."

"Probably difficult to handle," Goodnight said. "It's the most common reason."

"Tell me about the barbed wire," Clint said suddenly.

Goodnight looked surprised.

"What about it?"

"I don't know," Clint said. "Its history, the different types."

Goodnight spoke briefly about the beginning of the wire, then went off on a long discussion of the different types. Clint heard names like Ellwood Ribbon, the Winner, Corsicana Clip, Split Diamond, Knickerbocker, Burnell's Four

Pointer, Necktie, Tack-Underwood, Brotherton Barb, Brink Flat, and Buckhorn.

Basically, there seemed to be two types, two-point and four-point.

"I prefer a four-point wire myself," Goodnight said. "It's the most effective, and it's difficult to unwind. My preference is the Brotherton Barb. That's the one in my wagon now."

"You seem to have made quite a study of the wire," Clint said.

"I think it's an important invention," Goodnight said, "and when I decided to use it, I wanted to make sure I got the best."

By now they had their beer and their dinner and were almost done with both. Goodnight called the waiter over and asked for two more beers.

"He doesn't have to do that," Clint objected. "We can go to the saloon after this and have one."

"All right," Goodnight told the man, "forget it. Just clear away the dishes."

"Yes, sir. Coffee?"

Goodnight looked at Clint, who nodded.

"Yes," Goodnight said, "for both of us."

The waiter brought a fresh pot and two cups and poured for both of them.

"Tell me something about yourself," Goodnight prompted.

"There's not much to tell."

"What about your reputation?"

"What about it?"

"Is it warranted?"

Clint hesitated. He didn't like talking about himself, but he was to be a guest in Goodnight's house, and the man seemed interested.

He talked briefly about his earlier days, when he first discovered how good he was with guns— not only shooting them, but taking them apart, putting them back together, fixing them, modifying them.

"Wait a minute," Goodnight said at one point, holding up his hand. "You're telling me that you came up with the double-action weapon before Colt did?"

"I suppose."

"My God! You could have been rich if you'd patented it!"

"I suppose," Clint said again.

"Aren't you—doesn't that bother you?"

"No," Clint said.

"Are you telling me that you don't want to be rich?" Goodnight asked.

Clint thought a moment, then said, "I suppose I wouldn't turn down the opportunity if it was offered to me, but I don't have any regrets."

Goodnight shook his head, but simply said, "Go on."

Clint talked about being a lawman for a while, and then of becoming annoyed at the way townspeople looked at their local lawmen. Finally, he told Goodnight about outfitting his own gunsmithing wagon and riding around the country for the past several years.

"So, you actually work as a real gunsmith?" Goodnight asked.

"Sometimes."

"Where's this wagon now?"

"It's in Labyrinth, Texas," Clint said. "I didn't need it this trip."

Goodnight nodded, digesting the information as he poured them each another cup of coffee.

"So . . . what about all the stories?"

"What stories?"

"About the men you've killed."

Clint hesitated, and then said, "I've killed men when it was necessary. I suspect the same is true of you."

"Yes, but I don't have a reputation for that."

"You do have a reputation though, right?"

"Yes."

"Is it totally deserved?"

Goodnight studied Clint for a few moments, then said, "Hmm, I see what you mean."

ELEVEN

Lanigan entered the sheriff's office without announcing himself with a knock. The sheriff looked up from his desk and stared at him. He knew Lanigan was a hard case who sometimes worked for Fred Canby, who was a big man in town. The lawman wasn't necessarily afraid of Lanigan, but he *was* afraid of Canby—and so, by extension, he was *leery* of Lanigan.

"Lanigan," he said, nodding.

At first Lanigan had intended to go to the hotel to find out who the man with Goodnight was, but since the man and Goodnight had returned to town with dead bodies, that meant they had talked to the sheriff. This seemed a more direct course of action.

"Sheriff," Lanigan said, "I notice Goodnight came back into town toting some bodies."

"That's right."

"Had some help killin' 'em, did he?"

"He did."

42

"I was wonderin'," Lanigan said, "who that help came from. You know, who that other fella was?"

The sheriff hesitated a moment, then said, "Who was wonderin', Lanigan, you or Mr. Canby?"

Lanigan shrugged.

"What's the difference, Sheriff?" he said. "I'm doin' the askin' now."

They matched stares, and the sheriff was the first to avert his eyes, damning himself for doing so.

"His name's Adams," the man said finally, "Clint Adams."

"Clint Adams," Lanigan repeated. "You mean, the Gunsmith?"

"That's right, Lanigan," the sheriff said, looking back at the man now to see his reaction, "I mean the Gunsmith himself."

If the sheriff was expecting Lanigan to appear frightened by the news, he was disappointed. The only look that came over Lanigan's face was one of interest.

"Well," Lanigan said finally, "what do you know about that?"

"You find that interestin'?"

"Sheriff," Lanigan said, moving toward the door, "I find that *very* interestin'."

"You think Mr. Canby will find it—" the sheriff started, but before he could finish his question, Lanigan was out the door and gone.

TWELVE

After they finished their coffee, Clint and Goodnight went once again to the Americana Saloon. It was crowded now, in full swing, but Goodnight still managed to find an empty table in the back. Brenda, the saloon girl from earlier, was at their side as soon as they sat.

"What'll it be, gents?" she asked.

"Beer," Goodnight said. She looked at Clint, and he nodded.

"Comin' up."

As she walked away—watched closely by Clint, Goodnight, and every other man close enough to watch—Goodnight said to Clint, "She likes you."

"That's nice to know."

"She's available, you know," Goodnight said. "All the girls here are."

"That's okay," Clint said. "I don't like paying for a woman."

Goodnight chuckled and sat back in his chair.

"Don't have to, eh?" he said. "You do all right for yourself?"

"I don't get lonely much," Clint admitted.

"Me," Goodnight said, "I've got a wife waiting for me at home. I get lonely when I'm away from her."

"That's nice," Clint said.

"Ever thought about getting married?" Goodnight asked. The question surprised Clint, caught him off guard.

"Once."

"What happened?"

"She got killed."

"Oh," Goodnight said, "I'm sorry."

"It was a long time ago."

"Still," Goodnight said, "it's a bad memory."

"That it is," Clint said.

Brenda returned with the two beers, set them on the table, then looked at Clint and gave him her best and brightest smile.

"Anything else?"

"Not right now," Clint said.

"You'll let me know if there is?"

"First thing," Clint promised.

She put her hand on his shoulder for just a fleeting moment, said, "Good," and walked away.

"Woman like that," Goodnight said, "she knows when she's being watched."

Clint nodded.

"Yep," Goodnight said, lifting his beer, "she likes you."

• • •

They talked about a lot of things that night. Some more about barbed wire, some about politics, gambling, women, the "old" days.

After several hours—and more than several beers—Goodnight sat back in his chair and said, "Well, time for this fella to turn in. I'd like to get an early start in the morning. That all right with you?"

"I have no objection," Clint said. "Let me walk you back."

"Oh, no," Goodnight said, waving him away. "That's nonsense. I don't need my hand held."

"There were two attempts on your life today, Charles," Clint said.

"Which you don't have to remind me of," Goodnight said, "but with two failed attempts, what are the odds there will be a third one tonight? I think it's more likely they'll lay low for a while before they try again."

"Well," Clint admitted, finding logic in what Goodnight was saying, "you have a point there."

"Good," Goodnight said, "then I'll see you at first light, in the lobby."

"Right."

Goodnight stood up and said, "You can keep drinking all you want. It will go on my tab."

"Thanks," Clint said, "but I'll probably finish the one I have and turn in myself."

"Suit yourself," Goodnight said. "I'll see you in the morning."

Clint watched Goodnight wend his way through the crowd until he went out the door. He picked up his beer to finish it when someone sat down across from him.

It was the saloon girl, Brenda.

"Well," she said, eyeing him boldly across the table, "I thought he'd never leave."

THIRTEEN

On the way to his hotel Brenda made it quite clear to Clint that she expected no money from him.

"If you offer me some," she said, holding onto his arm, "I'll get very insulted. I'm not doing this for money."

"Why are you doing it?" Clint asked.

"Isn't that obvious?" she asked. "I like you. Isn't that a good enough reason?"

He smiled and said, "It always has been for me."

She entered his room ahead of him and then turned and came into his arms even before he could close the door. They groped at each other's clothes, removing them frantically, and then fell onto the bed in a tight embrace, arms around each other, bodies pressed together, kissing passionately. She moaned as his hands moved down her back to cup the smooth flesh of her buttocks.

Her hands roamed all over him knowingly,

touching him lightly beneath his testicles, cupping him firmly, and then stroking him until he was incredibly hard. That done, she slithered down between his legs and began to work on him with her talented mouth. He rolled onto his back to make it easier for her, and she crouched there between his legs, sucking him and stroking him at the same time. When she sensed that he was near exploding, she stopped, straddled him, and took him inside of her. She rode him that way while he reached up to touch her breasts and her nipples, and before long she moaned out loud, a moan that escalated into a near scream as he exploded inside of her. . . .

Later, as she was lying on her left side, he pressed himself against her, sliding one hand around to touch her belly and her breasts. His penis, hardening, lengthening, fit very nicely into the cleft of her buttocks. When he reached down between her legs to touch her, she quickly became wet. His fingers manipulated her expertly until her eyes were shut tightly and she was groaning, her body growing taut.

She reached behind her then, found his penis, spread her legs, and guided him into her from behind. She lifted her right leg high, draping it over his hip, and he moved inside of her that way, slowly at first, and then faster, his hand still stroking her in the front. The dual stimulation soon drove her over the edge, and he followed closely. . . .

• • •

Later, they talked while lying side by side. . . .

"Are you friends with Mr. Goodnight?" she asked.

"I wouldn't say that."

"Working for him?"

"No."

"Then . . . what?"

"I just happened to be in the right place at the right time, Brenda . . . twice," he explained.

"Will you be staying in town?"

"Tomorrow I'll be going back to Goodnight's place with him."

"To work for him?"

"No," he said. "Just to see that he gets there safely, and to stay as a guest for a few days."

"And then?"

"And then," he said, sliding a hand over her flat belly, "I may be back through this way."

"May be?" she asked, as his finger slid into her and made her wet.

"Yes," he said, "maybe."

As his fingers moved over her, she arched her back and said, "Oh God . . . I guess maybe will have to be good enough . . . for now!"

FOURTEEN

The next morning Fred Canby awoke in his large house at the southern end of town. He had this house, and he had a ranch on the outskirts of town. The ranch was not nearly the size of Charles Goodnight's, but Canby knew that it could be if he wanted it to be. He had other interests, though, aside from ranching, which was what separated him from Goodnight. It was what made him the better man.

At the ranch he also had a wife, a woman he had grown increasingly more tired of over the past few years. For that reason he spent most of his time in town, at this house, with a variety of young women warming his bed for money. Oh, he had no illusions about that. He was in his fifties, he was not an attractive man, and there was no way any of these women would be in his bed were he not Fred Canby, with the power and money that he had.

The girl in bed with him this morning was all

of twenty-five. Lying on her back with the sheet gathered around her waist, she seemed to be all pear-shaped breasts and tousled black hair. Luckily, with this one he had been able to perform, and perform quite well, even if he did say so himself. Of course, having her on her hands and knees, with her impressive butt hiked up in the air, pleading with him to "give it to her" had helped a lot.

At his age he often needed extra added incentive.

Clint awoke first, with Brenda lying on his left arm. He flexed the fingers of that hand experimentally and knew that he still had some time before it began to grow numb. At that point he'd have to try to slide it out from beneath her without waking her. For now, he was content to lie there with her head on his arm and the length of her body pressed against his. He put his other hand behind his own head and stared at the ceiling.

He was having second thoughts, not only about riding out to his ranch with Goodnight, but about then remaining as a guest. Granted, he was somewhat curious about what the ranch would look like, but he'd gotten himself into all kinds of trouble in the past trying to satisfy his curiosity.

Still, what else did he have to do? If he didn't go with Goodnight, he would simply ride back to Labyrinth, Texas, and wait for another good reason to leave there. Most likely, he'd end up bored and start back out on the trail *looking* for reasons.

And he'd gotten himself into all kinds of trouble in the past in the name of *not* being bored, hadn't he?

It all boiled down to keeping his word to Goodnight, and at least seeing that the man—and his wife—got safely to his ranch.

Canby slid from the bed without waking the woman. He pulled on a dressing gown and went downstairs. He could smell the coffee in the kitchen, and he knew that the cook would be working on his breakfast now. Canby was confident that he had the best cook in Texas working for him, even if it was a man.

He entered the kitchen and saw Miraflores standing at the stove.

Raphael Miraflores was forty-six years old and had worked for Canby for many years. How many, each man had forgotten. As far as Fred Canby was concerned, Miraflores was the only person in the world he could trust, besides himself.

"Good morning, Raphael," Canby said as he entered the kitchen.

"Good morning, sir," Miraflores said. He spoke English with only the faintest hint of a Spanish accent. Miraflores was from Spain, and not from Mexico, so when he spoke Spanish it was true Castilian Spanish.

"What's for breakfast?" Canby asked.

"Flapjacks, sir," Miraflores said, "made with honey, and bacon."

"Very good."

Miraflores turned to face his employer. He was a

slight man with slicked down black hair parted in the center and a very carefully tended mustache—so carefully tended that it was hardly noticeable.

"Will the lady be staying for breakfast, sir?" Miraflores asked.

"I doubt it, Raphael," Canby said. "I doubt it."

Miraflores poured a cup of coffee and handed it to Canby.

"Thank you, Raphael," Canby said. "I'll go upstairs and wake the young lady and send her on her way."

"By the time you return," Miraflores said, "breakfast should be ready."

"Good," Canby said, "very good."

Clint stepped out of his room, closing the door gently behind him. He'd inform the desk clerk that Brenda was asleep inside and was not to be disturbed. He'd pay an extra day for the room so she could sleep.

As he started down the hall, the door to Goodnight's room opened and a woman stepped out. She had red hair, still disheveled, and the front of her dress was not quite closed. Clint was able to see the cleavage between her creamy breasts. She noticed him, giggled behind her hand, and hurried down the hall to the stairs.

Clint stopped at Charles Goodnight's room, put his ear to the door, and listened. He heard movement inside, probably the man getting dressed.

So much for being a married man and lonely for his wife.

Canby sat at the kitchen table and ate his breakfast. He knew that Goodnight and his new crony, Clint Adams, would be leaving early for Goodnight's ranch in the Palo Duro Canyon. He did not have to be in his office, looking out the window, to know that. Very soon now they'd leave their hotel and be on their way. If Lanigan had done his job right, someone would be trailing them, keeping an eye on them for him until he decided what to do.

He had no problem with allowing the wire to reach the ranch, but he was not about to let Charles Goodnight string it. No sir, before that happened he'd come up with a plan and put it into effect successfully—Gunsmith or no Gunsmith.

Clint waited down in the lobby for Goodnight, who appeared in ten minutes. He was impeccably dressed, with every hair in place.

"Good morning," he said.

"Morning," Clint said. "Sleep well?"

"Very well," Goodnight said, "which is a surprise, since I hate being away from home."

"And your wife?"

"Especially my wife," Goodnight said. "A wonderful woman."

"I'm sure," Clint said.

He decided not to tell Goodnight that he had seen the woman leaving his room.

"Are we ready to get under way?" Goodnight asked.

"As soon as we get to the livery, get the team hitched up, and my horse saddled," Clint said.

"Well, then," Goodnight said, "let's get to it. I'm anxious to get back home."

FIFTEEN

The ride to Goodnight's ranch was a one-day trip on horseback. With the wagonload of wire, it was a two-day trip, at best.

The first day passed uneventfully, which was a welcome change from the day before.

"We'll camp over the next rise," Goodnight said as early evening approached. "There's a water hole there. We can water the horses, fill our canteens, and wash up."

Since Goodnight had made the trip many times before, Clint did not question the man's choice of campsites.

They topped the rise, and Clint saw the water hole. There were indications around it of old camp fires.

Goodnight was driving the wagon, with Clint riding alongside on Duke. They went down to the water's edge and stopped. Goodnight applied the brake and dropped down to the ground.

Clint dismounted and said, "I'll scout up some firewood."

"I'll get the coffee out," Goodnight said. "Since we're only to camp one night, I'm afraid all I brought to eat is beef jerky, but there's plenty of coffee."

"Sounds good enough," Clint said.

"Besides," Goodnight said, "there'll be a fine meal for us when we get to the ranch. Count on that."

"I'll get the wood," Clint said, "and then tend to the horses."

"I'll unhitch the team in the meantime," Goodnight said. "Have to do my part, right?"

Clint had the feeling that Goodnight didn't often do much around a campsite except give orders. Of course, he could have been wrong. The man couldn't have built up the ranches that he had without doing some hard work. Maybe he was just far removed from those times.

Clint decided to give him the benefit of the doubt.

"We've got company," Clint said when they were seated around the fire, each with a cup of coffee in one hand and a piece of jerky in the other.

The horses had been taken care of, with special attention given to Duke. Once he had been sure that the black gelding was well taken care of, he had gone to join Goodnight at the fire.

"What do you mean?"

"Someone's been following us all day," Clint said.

"How do you know?"

"Well," Clint said, "first I could feel it, and then I spotted him."

"When?"

"About midday."

"And what's he doing?"

"Just following us."

"Alone?"

"Yes."

"What do you think he wants?"

"Well, since he's alone," Clint said, "I don't think he's going to come after us. I mean, if he was intending to kill us, he's had a clear shot many times."

"So if he's not out to kill us, then what?" Goodnight asked.

Clint shrugged.

"I suppose he's just keeping an eye on us," Clint said.

"For who?"

"That's a good question," Clint said. "One that maybe you can answer."

"I have a lot of enemies, Clint," Goodnight said. "I've made many over the years."

"What about now?"

"Now?" Goodnight asked. "You mean, right now?"

"I mean the wire," Clint said. "Who doesn't want the wire to go up?"

"Most of the people around here don't," Goodnight said, "but I think that's because they can't afford to put it up themselves."

"Why are you putting it up, Charles?"

"Because," Goodnight said, "it's an idea whose time has come. The open range is a thing of the past, Clint. These days you have to take land and make it yours, and the way to do that is to keep others off of it."

"And so, the wire."

"Yes," Goodnight said, "the wire."

They finished their meager meal and put on a fresh pot of coffee.

"So what do we do?" Goodnight asked. "About the man on our trail, I mean."

"Nothing, for now," Clint said. "He knows where we're going. That's no secret, so there's no harm in letting him follow."

"We could grab him and find out who he works for," Goodnight said.

"If we tried that now, he'd see us coming," Clint said. "We'd never reach him."

"You're good with a gun, right?" Goodnight said. "Couldn't you just . . . pick him off from here?"

Clint gave Goodnight a stern look.

"Never mind," Goodnight said, "forget I said it. We'll just let him follow us. What harm can he do if he's just doing that?"

"Right," Clint said. "Sooner or later we'll find out who he works for—that is, if you can't figure it out yourself before then."

"We?"

"What?"

"You said sooner or later *we'll* find out who he works for."

"Oh," Clint said. "Well, that's just my curiosity talking."

"Oh?" Goodnight said. "And how much trouble has *that* gotten you into before?"

"Tons," Clint said, rolling his eyes.

"And haven't you learned better by now?"

Clint hesitated a moment and then said, "Obviously not."

"Well," Goodnight said, "very few of us learn from our past mistakes, do we?"

"No," Clint said, "we don't."

SIXTEEN

They made good time the next day, even with the wagonload of wire. As they came to within sight of Goodnight's spread, Clint stopped to take a look at it from a distance.

"It's very impressive," he said.

"Yes, it is," Goodnight agreed, "even from this distance. Wait until we get even closer, though. Then you'll really be impressed."

Goodnight was right. The closer they got, the more impressed Clint became. The house, when they finally reached it, was one of the largest he'd ever seen outside of a Southern plantation. The barn was the biggest he'd ever seen anywhere. The corral, in front of the barn, held some of the finest-looking horseflesh he'd ever laid eyes on.

As they rode up to the house, with Goodnight driving the wagon, they drew a crowd of ranch hands, one of whom stood out. He was a big man, standing about six four, with broad shoulders, a deep chest, and massive arms. He was blond and appeared to be in his early thirties. He was the one who spoke when they reached the house and the men who had grouped in front of it.

"Mr. Goodnight," the big man said. "We were starting to get worried. We expected you back yesterday."

"I know, Carl," Goodnight said, stepping down from the rig. "I ran into some trouble."

"Where are the others?" Carl asked. "Terry, and the rest?"

Clint had learned from Goodnight that Terry Lester was the man who had been injured during the first attempt on Goodnight's life, the man who had initially warned Clint away from the barbed wire.

"Terry was wounded, Carl, when somebody took some shots at me."

"Shots?" Carl said, looking and sounding concerned. "Are you all right, sir?"

"I am, thanks to this man," Goodnight said. "Uh, Carl, why don't you get the men back to work? Have someone take charge of this wagon and of my guest's horse."

"Yes, sir."

Carl turned and barked some orders at the men. Two of them stepped forward. One climbed atop the rig to drive it away, and the other man advanced on Clint and accepted Duke's reins.

"Take extra good care of that horse," Goodnight said.

"Yes, sir," the man said, and walked Duke away.

The other men dispersed, casting curious

glances back at Goodnight and at Clint. Obviously, they were wondering who he was.

"No reason for the other men to hear this yet, Carl," Goodnight said.

"Hear what, sir?"

"First, let me introduce the two of you," Goodnight said. "Carl Rivers, meet Clint Adams. He saved my life twice in Lubbock."

"Twice?" Carl asked.

"Clint," Goodnight said, "Carl is my foreman."

"Good to meet you," Clint said, and the two men shook hands briefly.

"Mr. Goodnight, you say he saved your life twice?" Carl said. "I don't understand. Where are the other men you took with you?"

"I want to talk to you about them, Carl," Goodnight said. "Let's go into my office, shall we? Clint? Would you come with us?"

"Of course."

Carl was looking at Clint and his boss with a bewildered look on his face.

"Come on, Carl," Goodnight said, putting his hand on his foreman's huge shoulder, "I'll tell you all about it inside."

In Goodnight's office Carl Rivers listened to his boss's story of the incidents that took place in and around Lubbock, and the part that Clint played in them. When Goodnight was done talking, Rivers was shaking his head.

"I can't believe it," the big man said. "I hired those men, Mr. Goodnight, all three of them. I can't believe that they all tried to kill you."

"Kill me or kidnap me, it really doesn't make much of a difference."

"When did you hire them, Carl?" Clint asked.

Carl looked at Clint, and then at his boss.

"Answer him, Carl."

"I'm not sure, really," the foreman said.

"Did you hire them all at the same time?"

"No," Carl said, "all three were hired separately. I don't even think they knew each other until they met working here."

"That could be," Clint said. "They could have been strangers and all been bought off separately."

"Or you're thinking that they could have been planted here one at a time," Goodnight said.

"I thought of that, yes."

"Which would mean that this thing was planned well in advance."

"Sessions," Carl said. "Do you think it was Frank Sessions, Mr. Goodnight?"

"Who's Sessions?" Clint asked.

"My nearest neighbor."

"Is he going to suffer the most from the wire you're going to put up?" Clint asked.

"Probably," Goodnight said. "We were sharing grazing land and water holes for a while, but he got too greedy. That's when I decided to fence it off."

"And he doesn't like it," Clint said.

"He hates it," Carl said. "And he especially hates barbed wire."

Clint looked at Goodnight and said, "Well, he sounds like a good number one suspect, Charles."

"Except for one thing," Goodnight said.

"What's that?"

"If Frank Sessions wanted me dead," Goodnight said, "he'd kill me himself. He's that kind of man."

"You seem fairly certain of that," Clint said.

"I am," Goodnight said.

"How?"

"I know him well," Goodnight said. "We used to be partners."

"What happened?"

"What usually happens to drive two men apart," Goodnight said.

"A woman?"

Goodnight nodded.

"We both fell in love with the same one."

"And?"

"And I married her," Goodnight said.

SEVENTEEN

After Carl Rivers left, Goodnight told Clint to close the door of his office.

Just before Carl left, though, Goodnight reminded him to have someone go to Lubbock the next day to see about bringing Terry Lester back.

"I'll take care of it, sir."

The big man threw Clint an unreadable glance and left the room.

"How about a glass of sherry?" Goodnight asked, when Carl was gone.

"Sure, why not?"

Goodnight poured sherry into two crystal glasses from a similar decanter and handed one to Clint.

"After this I'll introduce you to my wife," he said, raising the glass. "I think you'll be as impressed with her as you were with the ranch."

"What about Rivers?" Clint asked.

"What about him?"

"Do you trust him?"

"He's my foreman."

"Yes," Clint said, "but do you trust him?"

There was the slightest hesitation before Goodnight said, "Yes."

"How long has he worked for you?"

"About six years," Goodnight said. "He's been foreman for two."

"Who was foreman before him?"

"A man named Harley Rose. Harley had been with me a long time."

"And what happened?"

"Somebody killed him."

"How?"

"A bar fight, over a woman, or a fifth ace, I believe," Goodnight said. "Maybe both. Harley was a gambler *and* a ladies' man."

"And then you made Rivers the foreman?"

"That's right," Goodnight said, "and he's done a fine job ever since. Are you saying that you suspect Carl of having something to do with this?"

"Well," Clint said, "he *did* hire the three men who tried to abduct you."

"He's hired a lot of men over the past two years, Clint."

Clint shrugged and said, "Hey, you know the man. If you trust him, then I suppose he's all right."

They finished the sherry, and Goodnight set aside the two glasses.

"Let's go and find my wife, Annie," Goodnight said. "After you've met her, I'll have you shown to your room so you can get cleaned up for dinner."

"Fine."

They left the office and Goodnight led Clint to a parlor. He'd expected the inside of the house to be lavishly, perhaps even outlandishly furnished, but instead it was done quite tastefully and in muted colors that, to Clint's way of thinking, did not fit Goodnight's personality.

"Don't think I had anything to do with it," Goodnight said, as if reading Clint's mind. "Annie bought all the furniture. If I had, there'd be a lot more overstuffed chairs in red and yellow. Have a seat, and I'll go and see where she is."

"All right."

Goodnight left the room, and Clint sat down rather than pace around. He thought a bit about Carl Rivers. If the other three men had been planted in advance, couldn't Carl Rivers also have been planted? No, that didn't make sense. Who would plant someone six years in advance? If you were going to start thinking that way, you'd have to suspect every man employed by Goodnight as being a possible plant. That was just too much to think about.

And so he decided not to.

He had finally taken to pacing, occasionally peering out the window, by the time Goodnight returned with his wife on his arm.

"Clint Adams," Goodnight said, making the introduction proudly, "this is my wife, Anne Goodnight."

Clint was stunned. Anne Goodnight was a statuesque redhead with clear, creamy skin and green eyes. As she smiled at him, he could have sworn that she was the same woman he had seen leaving

Goodnight's hotel room the morning they left, but he quickly realized that she was not. Although that woman had had similar hair and skin and had been of comparable age—perhaps late twenties—she was nowhere near as beautiful as this woman was.

It seemed that even when Goodnight cheated on his wife, he did so with look-alikes.

"Mr. Adams," she said, extending her hand.

He took it and found her handshake surprisingly firm—firmer than that of many men he had known.

"I have to thank you for saving Charles's life, not once but twice," she said. She released his hand and took hold of her husband's arm. "We're very grateful."

At a loss for words momentarily Clint finally said, "I was, uh, just glad to be able to help, Mrs. Goodnight."

"And I *am* so glad that you've consented to be our guest for a few days," she said. She turned to her husband and said, "Darling, I'm going to go and tell the cook to plan an extra special dinner."

"Dear," Goodnight said, "I'm sure Olivia has already started dinner—"

"Well, then," Anne Goodnight said, "she'll just have to start again. After all, how often do we have a very special guest such as Mr. Adams?"

"Please," Clint said, "don't go to any trouble."

"I'll go to as much trouble as I please, Mr. Adams," she said, with a smile that took away any sting her words might have had. "After all, it is my home, isn't it?"

"Yes, ma'am," Clint said, "that it is."

"Now, Charles," she said, "you make sure Mr. Adams is *very* comfortable, do you hear?"

"I hear you, dear," Goodnight said, "but since Clint *is* to be our guest for a while, I think it would be all right if you called him by his first name. Don't you think so, Clint?"

"Of course," Clint said, "I insist."

"Then you must call me Anne," she said.

"Or Annie," Goodnight said.

"Oh, darling," she said, "no one calls me Annie but you."

"Then I'll call you Anne," Clint said.

"That's fine," she said. "Now, if you gentlemen will excuse me? I'll see to dinner."

They both watched her leave the room, and then Goodnight turned to Clint.

"Well? Impressed?"

"Very," Clint said. "She's . . . lovely."

"She is much more than that," Goodnight said. He looked, for all intents and purposes, like a man head over heels in love with his wife.

Which made the incident with the woman leaving his hotel room even more puzzling.

"Come on then, Clint," Goodnight said. "I'll show you to your room myself."

EIGHTEEN

Goodnight showed Clint to the second floor and his room, which was furnished in a similar fashion to the rest of the house that he had seen so far, tastefully, in muted colors.

"Make yourself comfortable," Goodnight told him. "I'll send someone up to get you when dinner is ready."

"I'd like to take a bath, if I can," Clint said.

"Of course. There's a tub in the room. I'll send someone up with water. Hot or cold?"

"Hot, please."

"I'll see to it."

"I'll also need my saddlebags—"

"And rifle," Goodnight said, cutting him off. "I'll see to it, Clint. Just make yourself comfortable."

Clint looked around the room and said, "I don't think I'll have a problem doing that."

"Good, good," his host said. "I'll see you for dinner, then."

Clint nodded. Goodnight backed out of the room

and closed the door. Clint turned, surveyed the room briefly, and then went to sit on the bed. The mattress was lush and, for most people, would have been extremely comfortable. Clint, however, was used to sleeping on the ground, or on mattresses that were no thicker than a folded blanket. In a bed like this he'd feel lost.

Of course, a mattress of this sort would be fine for lying with a woman. . . .

"Now that we've greeted our guest," Anne Goodnight said to her husband when he joined her in the kitchen, "tell me about what happened."

"I've told you already, dear," Goodnight said. "He saved my life twice."

"And once from your own men?" she asked, appalled. "How could that happen, Charles?"

"Annie, you never know if the men you hire are going to be dependable until you do hire them," Goodnight explained. "You know that."

"But to expect them to kill you? That's not something you can just accept. You had better talk to Carl Rivers about his hiring qualifications."

"I'll talk to him, Annie," Goodnight said, trying to soothe her. "Right now I have to see to our guest's needs. He wants a bath, and his belongings must be brought to him."

"You see to his belongings," Anne said, "and I'll see to his bath."

"But what about dinner—"

"I've already talked to Olivia about dinner," she replied. "I'll see that he gets his water."

"All right," Goodnight said. "He wants a hot bath, not a cold one."

"I'll see to it," she said, using a statement she had heard her husband use many times.

"All right," Goodnight said. "I'll send you a man to lug the water."

Anne Goodnight watched her husband leave the house by the back door, then turned and folded her hands in front of her face, as if in prayer, resting the tips of her fingers against her lips. She was thinking about Clint Adams sitting in a hot bath.

Clint was stripped to the waist, still wearing his jeans, when there was a knock at the door. Assuming that it was either a man with his belongings or a man with his hot water, he opened the door.

It was not a man, it was Anne Goodnight— *Mrs.* Charles Goodnight, he reminded himself as he took in her beauty once again.

"Oh," she said, eyeing his bare chest with obvious pleasure, "I'm sorry. I didn't mean to disturb you."

"You haven't," he said. "I'm waiting for my things, and some hot water."

"Yes, I know," she said, raising her eyes from his chest to his face. "Charles is seeing to your things, and I've arranged to have your water brought up. Did you locate the tub?"

"Uh, yes, I did—"

"It's over here," she said, boldly brushing past him into the room. She crossed the room to show him the tub, which stood behind a standing screen.

Deliberately leaving the door wide open—as wide as it could possibly go—Clint turned and faced her.

"Yes, Mrs. Goodnight," he said, "I managed to locate it myself."

"Oh," she said, folding her hands in front of her, waist high. "Of course. It wasn't hard to find, was it?"

"No, it wasn't."

She raised her eyebrows and said, "I thought we had established that you would call me Anne."

"Did we?"

"Yes, we did."

"Well," he said, "that was downstairs, not when we're alone in my room."

"Oh," she said, suddenly looking around her, "we are alone here, aren't we?"

"Yes, we are," Clint said. "If I may say so, I don't think it's proper."

"Well," she said, walking across the room toward him, "I'll leave then. I don't want to make you nervous. After all, you are our guest."

"Thank you for your concern," Clint said.

She went past him, and he noticed that she was a tall woman—and a sweet smelling one. She was wearing a green dress that went well with her red hair, but he found himself wondering what she'd look like in riding clothes, with a belt cinched tightly around her waist.

"The water will be here soon," she assured him. "I will see you at dinner."

"Thank you, Mrs.—uh, I mean, thanks, Anne."

She gave him a little wave and went out the door, which he closed after her—tightly. He was uncomfortable, not because he found her extremely attractive, but because he thought that she felt the same way about him. That was not the way to start up a new friendship, by sharing a mutual attraction with your new friend's wife.

NINETEEN

Clint was fresh from the bath when there was a knock on his door. It was the fourth knock since his arrival. The first had been Anne Goodnight, followed closely by his belongings, and finally the water for his bath. He wrapped a towel around himself and hoped that he would be opening the door to Anne Goodnight again.

It was not his host's wife, however, but the man who had brought him his water.

"Mr. Goodnight says dinner will be served in fifteen minutes," the man said.

"All right," Clint said, aware that he was dripping on the floor, "thank you. I'll be there as soon as I dry off and dress."

He closed the door and proceeded to get ready for dinner.

When Clint came down for dinner, the Goodnights were already there. Charles Goodnight was wearing a jacket and tie, making Clint feel somewhat underdressed.

Anne Goodnight looked stunning. Once again she was wearing green, but this time the dress was low-cut, revealing creamy flesh and ample cleavage. She was a well-built woman, full-breasted, broad-shouldered, and wasp-waisted.

"Sorry I didn't have something more fancy to wear," Clint said as he sat.

"Don't worry about it," Goodnight said. "I hate this dressing for dinner, but Annie insists on it."

"It's the only civilized way to eat dinner," Anne said.

Goodnight was seated at the head of the rectangular table, and Anne Goodnight was sitting right across from Clint. He found her cleavage disconcerting, to say the least. Goodnight did not seem to notice.

"I think you'll be very satisfied with dinner," Goodnight said. "It'll certainly be better than what we had last night."

"Better than anything you've had in some time, I hope," Anne Goodnight said. "Olivia is a wonderful cook."

Clint sniffed the air and said, "I'm sure it'll be wonderful."

"How long do you think you'll be staying with us, Clint?" Anne asked.

The question surprised him, especially since it had come from her. Or perhaps it shouldn't have surprised him. Not after her seemingly innocent visit to his room.

"Oh, just for a few days I'm sure," Clint said. "No more."

"Well," Anne said, "maybe I'll have some company on an early morning ride while you're here. My husband is usually too busy to accompany me."

"You know I have to be up early, my dear," Goodnight said.

"So do I, darling," Anne said, "but not to work. What do you say, Clint? Would you ride with me in the morning? I understand from Charles that you have a beautiful horse. I'd love to see him."

"Well, I don't—"

"Oh, ride with her, Clint," Goodnight said, "or I might never hear the end of it."

He reached out and put his hand over his wife's, smiling at her.

"All right," Clint said. "I'd be happy to ride with you, Anne."

"Good!"

At that point a woman entered with a man behind her, bearing a tray of food. Clint assumed that the woman was the cook, Olivia. The man with the tray was the same man who had brought him his bathwater and then called him to dinner.

Clint watched as Olivia served dinner and noticed that the cook and the host's wife were not exactly on the best of terms. Clint wondered if that was simply because he was there and Anne Goodnight had invaded the kitchen, or if it was their usual relationship.

Speaking of relationships, all through dinner

Clint found himself wondering about the marriage of Charles and Anne Goodnight. They spoke to each other with affection but rarely seemed to touch. He had also been witness to a woman coming out of Goodnight's room at the hotel. Then there was the odd visit to his room by Anne Goodnight. Now the invitation for a morning ride, which may or may not have been an innocent one. Either way, the invitation was supported by her husband.

The dinner was delicious, as promised, but the rest of the situation was puzzling, to say the least.

TWENTY

After dinner Goodnight invited Clint into his study for a glass of sherry. Anne Goodnight did not accompany them. In fact, Clint had no idea where she went after dinner, or whether or not he'd see her again. It was still early, and she had not yet bid him goodnight.

In the study Clint said, "The meal was wonderful."

"As I promised," Goodnight said, handing Clint a glass of sherry.

"And the spread is unbelievable."

"Well, you'll see more of it tomorrow when you go riding with Annie," Goodnight said. "By the way, I appreciate your agreeing to do that."

"No problem," Clint said. "I'd like to see some more of the place."

"Well, she'll show it to you," Goodnight said proudly. "She knows the place like the back of her hand, she's been back and forth over it so many times."

"She, uh, seems to be taking the news of the attempts on your life pretty well."

Goodnight's face sobered and he looked at Clint.

"Not as well as she would like us to believe, I'm afraid," Goodnight said. "She's quite frightened by it. That's another reason I'd rather not have her riding around alone."

Not afraid enough to go with her himself, Clint observed. He refrained from voicing his thought.

"You know," Goodnight said, "I wish you'd reconsider working for me."

"Charles—"

"I'd make you foreman, at a handsome salary," Goodnight added quickly.

"What about Rivers?"

"Well . . . Carl just might be in over his head in the job, Clint," Goodnight said.

"It's taken you two years to notice that?" Clint asked. "Or would you simply fire him in order to hire me?"

"Well, you have to admit," Goodnight said, "you would be the better man for the job."

"I doubt it," Clint said. "I've never ramrodded a major outfit, Charles. It's a little bit outside of my line of work."

"Well," Goodnight said, "take the next few days to think it over. I could use you here."

Clint thought that Goodnight was probably still thinking about him more as a gun than as a man. He could think all he wanted over the next few days, but Clint wasn't about to change his mind.

TWENTY-ONE

After the sherry, Clint said he'd like to go outside for a walk.

"Feel free," Goodnight said. "You have the run of the place. I'd join you, but I have some paperwork to catch up on. I'll be in my office, though, if you want to talk about anything."

"All right," Clint said. "Thanks."

"Uh, do you always wear that?" Goodnight asked, indicating the gun on Clint's hip.

Clint looked down at it, and then back at his host.

"Sorry," Clint said. "Sometimes I forget that it's there."

"No problem," Goodnight said. "I can understand where a man of your . . . stature would have to wear it. It's okay, really."

"I *could* take it off while I'm here—"

"No, no," Goodnight said, holding up one hand. "I wouldn't think of asking you to do that, not if it would make you uncomfortable. Besides, I'd actually rather you did wear it, especially when you're around Annie. Forget I even brought it up. I was just . . . curious."

They left the study together and separated in the entry foyer. Goodnight went to the back of the house, where his office was, and Clint went out the front door.

It was brisk outside, but he decided not to go back inside for a jacket. He only intended to walk a bit, and when he got too cold he'd go back to the house.

Dinner had been a late affair, and it was already dark out. There were a few men roaming about, probably seeing to last minute chores, but for the most part he was alone, walking unnoticed.

Or so he thought.

When he reached the end of the house, furthest away from the barn and corral, he became aware that someone was standing there. He turned and saw Anne Goodnight. She was wearing a wrap, and her arms were crossed in front of her, as if she were trying to keep herself warm.

"Hello," she said.

"Anne," he said. "You shouldn't be out here."

"Why not?"

"It's cold."

"Is that the only reason?"

"What other reason would there be?"

She moved up alongside him and said, "Let's walk. You *were* taking a walk, weren't you?"

"Yes."

"Do you mind if I join you?"

"No, of course not."

They started walking, close together but not touching.

"Are you worried that someone might try to kill me, the way they did Charles?"

"Not really."

"It's a possibility, though, isn't it?" she asked. "That they might try to kill me, or abduct me? Perhaps to get at Charles?"

"Yes," he said, after a moment, "it is a possibility, Anne."

"I thought so," Anne said. "Charles is trying to tell me that it's not."

"Well, I don't want to contradict him—"

"You're not," she said. "He's trying to keep me from worrying. You're telling me the truth, which is the way I'd much rather have it."

They were getting further away from the house than he wanted to be with her. It was almost like being alone in his room.

"Anne," he said, stopping, "it's cold—"

She turned to face him and said, "You're afraid of me, aren't you?"

He stared back at her and said, "No."

She raised an eyebrow and said, "Wary, then?"

"Yes," he admitted, "wary."

"I won't bite you." She put her hand on his chest and said, "I feel safe with you around."

He stepped away, breaking the contact.

"What's wrong?"

"I just remembered something."

"What?"

"I had a dinner date with a woman in Lubbock two days ago."

It was true. He had just recalled asking Alicia Garfield to have dinner with him. In the wake of the second attempt on Charles Goodnight's life he had totally forgotten about it—until now.

"Oh?" she said. "With whom?"

"A woman named Alicia Garfield."

"Alicia," she said. "I think I know who she is. Dark-haired, works in the dress shop?"

"That's her."

"You know her?"

"Not really," he said, "and after this I doubt that I ever will."

"Pity," she said. "Well, shall we go back to the house?"

"Yes," Clint said gratefully, "yes, I think we should."

"Don't forget our date to ride tomorrow."

"I won't," he said. "How early?"

"Oh, I'm a *very* early riser," she said. "I'm usually up before the sun."

"Then I'll meet you at the barn at first light," he proposed.

"That would be fine."

When they reached the house they stopped and she turned to face him.

"Well, thank you for the walk, Clint . . . and the conversation."

"Don't mention it."

"I'll see you in the morning."

She started up the stairs, then turned and looked down at him.

"Aren't you coming in?"

"In a while," he said. "I just want to walk a bit more."

"Well, be careful," she said. "It's cold."

"I know," he said. But it was the oddest thing. As he watched her walk up the stairs to the front door and then enter, he didn't feel cold at all.

TWENTY-TWO

The man standing in the barn watching Clint Adams had almost stepped from his cover to follow as Clint walked to the other end of the house. He stopped short when he saw a second figure join Clint, and then he recognized the second person as Mrs. Goodnight.

As Clint and Anne Goodnight walked away from the house, the darkness seemed to swallow them up. The man in the barn was sorely tempted to leave his cover and follow, but abruptly the two people stopped and walked back. He watched as they conversed in front of the house, and then Mrs. Goodnight went up the stairs and back inside.

Funny, he had only seen Clint Adams come out of the house. The woman must have come out from a door at the rear of the house.

Since the man's job was simply to watch, he did so as Clint started to walk, this time in the opposite direction. It was a few moments before the man realized that Clint Adams was now walking toward him!

The man panicked for a moment as he realized that Adams might be coming to the barn to check on his horse. He looked around, though, and realized that there were plenty of hiding places in the barn, if he needed them.

He was standing behind the barn doors now, peering out from a crack as Clint Adams continued to advance toward the barn. The man was just about to bolt from his present position to seek a hiding place when Clint changed direction and walked to the corral.

The man remained where he was, and watched.

Clint stopped at the corral. There were only a few animals left inside, and they were all fine-looking specimens. If these were any sample of the stock Goodnight was raising, then the man was very good at what he did.

One of the horses trotted over to where Clint was and nuzzled him.

"Looking for sugar?" Clint asked. "Sorry, I haven't got any." He pushed the animal's head and said, "Go on, go away."

Somebody on the ranch was probably in the habit of giving sugar to some of the horses, or maybe this particular one was a favorite. This was a young colt, probably not even broken yet. He watched as the animal trotted to the other side of the corral and stood with his back to Clint.

"Insulted?" Clint asked aloud. "Well, I'm sorry,

but I'm not in the habit of giving sugar to strange horses."

He turned away from the corral, briefly toyed with the idea of checking on Duke, then decided he could do that just as well in the morning. After all, he *was* meeting Anne Goodnight early—*very* early.

As he walked back to the house, he realized how tired he was. He'd been on the go virtually from the moment he'd first arrived in Lubbock—and his aim when he had arrived in town had been to rest.

He decided to make an early night of it.

From his position behind the barn door, the man watched Clint Adams walk back to the house, go up the steps, and enter. He came out of the barn and walked over to the corral. The same young colt who had nuzzled Clint for sugar came over and did the same to this man.

"Okay. Okay, boy," the man said, putting his hand in his pocket. "I've got your sugar for you."

TWENTY-THREE

The next morning Clint rose before dawn, feeling refreshed. Turning in early the night before had been the right thing to do.

As he'd feared, though, he'd had to drag himself out of that comfortable bed. Sleeping in a bed like that night after night could get to be a habit—a bad habit.

He washed himself, using a basin and pitcher that were on a table near the now dry bathtub, then dressed and went downstairs. As far as he could see, there was no one moving about in the house. Maybe he had gotten up before Anne Goodnight.

He was about to leave when he did hear some sounds of activity from the kitchen. Probably the cook preparing to start breakfast. He thought about popping his head in, but if the woman resented Anne Goodnight invading her kitchen, how would she feel if *he* did it?

He went outside and walked toward the barn

instead. When he reached it, he heard someone moving around inside. As he went inside he saw Anne Goodnight, saddling a handsome bay mare.

"Good morning," he said.

She turned to face him, smiling.

"Well," she said, "you're up earlier than I thought. I barely beat you."

He had been right to wonder what she'd look like in riding clothes. She was wearing trousers and boots and a white shirt that looked like silk. The sleeves were big, even billowy. Her wide, shiny black belt made her waist seem even more impossibly slim than the night before. Her hair was down, hanging past her shoulders, and there was a green ribbon in it.

She looked incredible.

"I tried to saddle that beast of yours," she said, "but he wouldn't let me near him."

"He's like that sometimes," Clint said.

"He's beautiful, though, isn't he?"

"Don't let him hear you say that."

"Do you think he'd mind if I watched while *you* saddled him?"

"I think we can work that out," Clint said. "Come on."

"After all," she said, following Clint to Duke's stall, "you are the master, aren't you?"

"That's where you're wrong." They reached Duke's stall, and Clint reached out to touch the big gelding's huge head. "You see, neither of us is the master. We're partners."

"I see. Then he doesn't belong to you?"

Clint set about saddling Duke and said, "No, I

don't consider that I *own* him, not the way I own my . . . my gun, or my gun belt."

"You have an interesting relationship, then," she said while she watched.

"I suppose you could say that," Clint said. "We've saved each other's lives so many times that I've lost count. I don't even know who's up on who."

"I don't think it matters," she said. "Look how gentle he is while you saddle him. Are you the only one he trusts to let touch him?"

"Usually," Clint said.

"Fascinating."

Once Duke was saddled, Clint led him from the stall and over to where Anne's bay stood.

"This is Lindy," Anne said, stroking the white blaze on the mare's face. It extended from between the horse's eyes down to her nose.

"She's pretty."

Anne turned to look at him and said, "I notice you do what I do when you refer to horses."

"What's that?"

"Call them him or her rather than it, as Charles does."

"You don't like the way your husband does it?"

"No," she said, shaking her head, causing her hair to bounce nicely, "it's so cold and impersonal."

"Well, for your husband, horses are a business, Anne," Clint said. "It's understandable that he'd want to be impersonal where his business is concerned."

"I suppose so," she said. "He *is* good at what he does, isn't he?"

"So I understand," Clint said. "Shall we ride?"

"Yes," she said, her eyes sparkling. She obviously enjoyed riding. "Let's."

Not only did Anne Goodnight love to ride, but she loved speed. They galloped a bit until they were well away from the house, and then she suddenly kicked her heels into her horse's sides and off they went.

Clint urged Duke into a run, but kept the big gelding well within himself, allowing Anne to remain ahead of them. He knew he could have overtaken her anytime he wanted, but decided not to push Duke.

Eventually, she stopped and waited for him to catch up. When he did, he noticed that her color was high, she was breathing hard and—if possible—looked even more beautiful than ever. With a jolt he realized that she looked like she had just had sex—and wonderful sex, at that. He felt his own body responding to that.

"Do you think you could have caught me anytime?" she asked.

"Yes, I could have."

"Why didn't you?"

"I didn't think that was the point," he said, "for me to catch you. I thought we were just out riding."

"I like riding," she said, "but what I really want to do is race. I *love* speed."

"That's obvious."

She patted and rubbed the mare's neck and said, "She's the fastest horse on the ranch."

"She's pretty fast," he agreed.

She stared at him, eyes wide, and said, "I would love to race her against your horse."

Clint had raced Duke before, and the gelding had never been beaten. In fact, he had literally raced other horses into submission. Some of those animals had never been the same again. He would hate to see that happen to Anne's mare, Lindy.

"Uh, I don't usually race Duke."

"Why not?" she asked. "Afraid he'll be beaten?"

The sting he felt from her question was illogical—but it was there.

"He's never been beaten," Clint said, before he could stop himself.

"Well," she said, "there's always a first time. Want to race now?"

"No." He was angry with himself for allowing her to bait him.

"All right, 'fraidy cat," she said. "We'll just ride, then."

She started away, then turned in the saddle and shouted at him, "But I'll try not to run the poor old boy's legs off!"

She rode off laughing.

TWENTY-FOUR

As Clint Adams and Anne Goodnight left the ranch for their morning ride, a man came out of the bunkhouse and saw them.

"Damn," he said, and started walking quickly toward the barn.

He actually wasn't sure what he was supposed to do. His job was to keep an eye on Goodnight and Clint Adams, but now Adams was riding off without Charles Goodnight. He was, however, with Goodnight's wife.

The man decided that Clint Adams took priority over Goodnight, simply because he was the man who had already saved Goodnight's life twice before. The man who was paying him didn't want Adams to be around for the third time.

He was almost to the front door of the barn when he heard someone call his name from behind. He turned and saw that it was the foreman, Carl Rivers.

"Where are you headin'?" Rivers asked.

"Just wanted to, uh, take a look at my horse, boss," the man said.

"Well, while you're looking at him, saddle him up," Rivers ordered.

The man asked, "Uh, am I goin' somewhere, boss?"

"Yeah," Rivers said, "you're goin' to Lubbock."

"What for?"

"To bring Terry Lester back," Rivers said, and then added, "that is, if he's in any shape to come back."

"Uh, that's a long ride, boss," the man said, trying to do something he just wasn't equipped to do—think fast.

"I know it," Rivers said. "That's why *you're* makin' it, and not me."

"Uh-huh," the man said.

"Well . . . get to it!" Rivers said. "I want you back here in three days, tops."

"I hear you," the man said.

He turned and walked to the barn. He had two employers, Charles Goodnight and the man who had hired him to keep an eye on Goodnight and Adams. It would take him the length of time it took him to saddle his horse to decide which of his employers' instructions it would be wisest to follow.

TWENTY-FIVE

"Do you know what I'd like to see?" Clint said
to Anne Goodnight.

"What?"

The look she gave him was a bold one, and he
thought he knew what she was thinking. It wasn't
something a married woman should have on her
mind, either—unless it was with her husband. Of
course, he could have been wrong. . . .

"The wire."

"What?"

"I'd like to see some of the barbed wire that's
already up."

"For God's sake, why?" she asked.

"I've never seen it," he said. "I saw it all coiled
up in the back of your husband's wagon. I think
I'd like to see it strung."

"It's disgusting!" she said.

"You don't approve?"

"I don't . . . but that's my husband's business."

"You haven't told him of your disapproval?" he asked her.

"No," she said, shaking her head. "He never asks me about his business, and I don't butt in. It's the way he wants it."

"Look," he said, "if you don't want to—"

"No, no," she said, tossing her hair over her shoulder, "if you want to see it, I'll show it to you. We're not far from a stretch of it now. I was going to turn back, but we'll go on ahead."

"Anne—"

"Come on," she said. "It's not far."

She rode off and he followed. Had he known how much she disliked the wire he wouldn't have asked, but now that he had he was looking forward to having his curiosity satisfied.

"There it is." she said.

They had just topped a rise and she was pointing downhill. He looked ahead of them and saw that the wire was strung out as far as he could see in both directions.

"Whose land is on the other side?" he asked.

"That's part of the Sessions spread," she said. "Frank Sessions."

"I understand he and your husband were once friends," Clint said.

"Yes," she said, and then looked at him and added, "and I suspect you know why they are no longer friends, don't you?"

"It had something to do with you, I believe," he said. It was another subject—like the wire—that he now wished he hadn't brought up. "I'm sorry," he said, "I spoke without thinking."

"It's all right," she said, looking down at the wire. "Not talking about it is not going to make it go away, is it? They both fell in love with me, and it made enemies out of two men who were once friends." She looked at him and added, "I'm not proud of it, you know."

"I don't think it's your fault," he said. "You shouldn't feel proud or ashamed."

"Oh," she said, "I don't feel ashamed. I didn't say that. I just said I wasn't proud of it. Truthfully, I think they were both silly about the whole thing."

She looked away from him, back at the wire, and said, "Well, there it is. Why don't you go down and take a look at it? I'll wait here."

He was going to protest, but finally said, "All right." He really did want to see it up close. "I won't be long."

She looked away from him and the wire and said, "Take as long as you like."

He stared at her for a moment, but when she kept her face averted he urged Duke on down the hill toward the wire.

About a mile on the other side of the wire Sam McCallum, the foreman of the Sessions ranch, and several of his men were attempting to round up some stray cattle.

"How many we got?" McCallum asked a man named Harvey Dunn.

"About a dozen, boss."

"There should be a few more," McCallum said. "Why don't you and the men take these back. I'll scout up ahead and see what I can find."

"Why not take a man with you?" Dunn asked. "I don't need all the men to take these strays back."

"Okay," McCallum said. "Tell Webster to ride with me, and the rest of you head back."

"Okay, boss," Dunn said.

As Dunn went to tell Webster, McCallum looked off in the distance. He knew he was about a mile away from Charles Goodnight's wire, and he had a strange feeling of dread about it.

God, he hated that wire!

Clint rode Duke up to the wire and stared down at it without dismounting. It looked benign enough to him. Of course, you could see what damage it *might* do under the proper circumstances, but just *being* there the way it was, it seemed more a deterrent than something . . . malevolent. It did not seem to him something that someone should kill over.

He dismounted to touch it, rather than ride Duke too close to it.

"Stand easy, big boy," he said as he released Duke's reins and walked up to the wire.

He looked up at Anne once, but she was still not looking his way.

He walked to the wire then and touched it. He could see that it was strung very tautly, and the points of the wire were very sharp. In fact, had he not been extra careful he might have actually cut his finger.

He turned and looked up at Anne once again, and found it odd that she was not there. He looked right and then left and saw her riding away at a fast gallop. Had she succumbed to some basic fear of the wire and decided to run away from it? No, as he watched he became positive that she was not running *away* so much as she was running *to* something.

He did not know what she had seen, but whatever it was, it had been enough to make her rush to it.

He mounted Duke, swung him around, and started after her.

TWENTY-SIX

Anne heard him coming and turned to look at him. Her eyes were streaming with tears, and her hands were covered with blood.

"Help him!" she cried.

She still had her hands on the bleating—and *bleeding*—calf, who had somehow gotten himself tangled up in the barbed wire. This, then, was what she had seen that had sent her off in such a rush.

Clint dismounted and went to her side. It was then that he saw that all of the blood was not the calf's. In fact, she had cut her hands on the wire in her attempt to free the helpless animal.

"All right," he said, taking her wrists and firmly pulling her hands away, "let me do it. You're just making your own cuts worse."

She allowed him to pull her hands away, and then he went back to look the situation over while she tried to calm the calf. The more the poor beast struggled, the worse the situation got.

"If I had something to cut the wire with—" he said.

"Oh, do something, Clint! Please! He'll die if we don't get him out."

It was true. If the calf kept struggling, the bleeding would get worse and he would die.

"All right," he said, "there's only one thing I can see to do."

He drew his gun. Anne's eyes went wide.

"No!" she shouted.

"I'm not—" he started, but he was cut short by the sound of a shot.

"Holster your gun, mister," a voice said. "You ain't shootin' that calf."

Both Clint and Anne looked at the two men who were sitting their horses on the other side of the fence.

"Mr. McCallum," Anne said, "we're trying to get this animal free. Is he one of yours?"

"Yes, ma'am," McCallum said, "and I can't see how you can help it by killin' it."

"I'm not planning on killing him," Clint said.

"Then why the gun?"

"I can't untangle him from the wire if I can't cut it," Clint said. "Do you have something to cut it with?"

"No," McCallum said.

"Then let me do it my way, before he bleeds to death," Clint said.

McCallum still wasn't sure what Clint had in mind, obviously, but he holstered his own gun—and waved his man to do the same. Then he said, "Go ahead, mister."

"I'll need your help, since you're here," Clint said.

"Why should I help you?"

"It's your calf, isn't it?" Clint asked. "Besides, Mrs. Goodnight isn't strong enough for what I want."

The two men exchanged glances, and then McCallum nodded and they both dismounted.

"What do you want us to do?" McCallum asked, as they both approached the fence.

"Hold on to the animal," Clint said. "When I fire he might try to bolt, and he'll cut himself even worse."

The two men exchanged glances again, then crouched by the animal and took hold of him.

There were three strands of wire. Clint held the barrel of his gun to the first strand and fired. The bullet severed it cleanly. The calf cried out and tried to bolt, but the two men held him fast.

Anne Goodnight and Sam McCallum finally realized what Clint's intention had been with the gun. Against his better judgment, McCallum felt admiration for the man's ingenuity. Anne Goodnight simply felt foolish that she had misinterpreted his intention.

Clint fired twice more, and when the three strands were cut, he and the other men were able to unwind the wire from the calf and free him.

Clint, Anne, and McCallum watched while the other man examined the calf's wounds.

"How bad, Webster?" McCallum asked.

"Could've been worse, boss," Webster said. "We treat his cuts, he should be all right."

"Good," McCallum said. He looked at Clint, and then at Anne. "We're obliged for your help, but the fact remains, Mrs. Goodnight, that your husband's wire is responsible for this."

"Mr. McCallum," Anne said archly, "if you could control your cattle, this would not have happened."

McCallum gave her a calm look and said, "Strays are strays, ma'am. It happens."

McCallum looked at Clint and said, "What's your name, mister?"

"Clint Adams."

"Mine's McCallum," the man said, "Sam McCallum. I'm the ramrod of the Sessions outfit. That was pretty smart what you did. I'm sorry I drew down on you."

"That's all right," Clint said. "You had no way of knowing what I was planning."

While he spoke, Clint ejected the spent shells from his gun and replaced them with live ones. McCallum watched every move.

"Well, we better get this calf back to the ranch and treat his cuts. Again, much obliged for your help."

McCallum put his hand out and Clint shook it briefly. The Sessions foreman tipped his hat to Anne, and then he mounted his horse. The other man, Webster, lifted the calf and handed him up to McCallum, who draped him over his saddle in front of him. He was unmindful of the blood he was getting on his hands and clothes.

Webster mounted up, and the two men rode away.

Clint turned and looked at Anne, who also had blood on her clothes and hands, some of it hers.

"Let me see your hands."

"They're all right," she said, but she couldn't seem to close them.

"Is there any water nearby?"

"There's a water hole. . . . It's about half a mile away," she said.

"Let's get over there and wash those cuts, and then I'll bind them."

"It can wait—"

"No, it can't," Clint said. "Come on."

He helped her into her saddle, then mounted Duke and took hold of her reins. She kept her arms folded in front of her, her hands palms up, while he led her horse to the water hole.

TWENTY-SEVEN

When they reached the water hole Clint helped
Anne down from her horse and sat her down on
the ground at the water's edge. He then pulled
his shirt out of his pants and tore three strips
from it.

"Put your hands in the water," he said.

She did so.

"It hurts," she said, "and it's cold."

"Good," he said.

He took one hand out of the water, leaving the
other in. Using one of the strips he'd torn from
his shirt, he tried to clean the wounds. She had
three cuts in the palm of this, her right hand. Two
seemed superficial, but one, right in the center
of her palm, seemed fairly deep. Once he had it
cleaned as well as he could, he bound it, making
sure that he did so tightly, to staunch the flow of
blood from the bad cut.

"Give me your other hand."

She did, and he examined it and cleaned it.

This one had four cuts in it, but none of them were serious.

"You knew those men?" he asked while he worked.

"Only McCallum, because he's Frank Sessions's foreman. The other man was just a hand."

"How does your husband get along with McCallum?" Clint asked.

"He doesn't deal with him."

"What about Rivers?"

"What about him?"

"Does he know McCallum?"

"I'm sure he does," she said, "but I have no idea how well."

He bandaged the hand less tightly than he had the other. She was able to flex the left hand, but not the right.

"Can you ride?" he asked.

"I can direct the horse with my knees, if need be," she said. "I'm an excellent rider."

"I know you are."

She stared at him and then said, "I'm sorry. I'm being too sensitive. Thank you for taking care of my hands—and for freeing that calf."

"Well . . . you were obviously distressed about it," he said. "I had to do something."

"Are your hands cut?" she asked.

"Not badly," he said, and showed her. He had a cut on each hand, but they were both superficial.

"I'm sorry," she said.

She took his right hand in hers so she could look at it, then brought it closer to her face. Before he knew what she was doing, she had pressed her mouth to it. He felt almost helpless as she ran her tongue over the cut.

"Anne—"

She looked at him, then got to her knees, leaned close to him, and kissed his mouth. For a moment he responded, opening his mouth so that her tongue had free entry into it. Abruptly, though, he took her by the shoulders and pushed her away without releasing her.

"This isn't right," he said.

"I know," she said, but her eyes were shining. He could see that although she agreed with him, she really didn't care whether it was right or wrong.

He released her shoulders and stood up.

"We should get back and tell Charles what happened," he said.

She smiled and got to her feet.

"Everything that happened?" she asked.

He frowned at her, then turned and mounted Duke, leaving her to mount up on her own. As he watched her climb atop her horse without much difficulty, he thought that he could still feel her tongue on his hand, and her kiss on his lips.

Maybe it was time for him to leave the Goodnight ranch.

TWENTY-EIGHT

When they got back to the ranch, Goodnight was still out with some of his men.

"You'd better go inside and wash those hands again," Clint said, as they both dismounted. "I'll take care of the horses."

"Come up to the house when you're finished," she said. "We can have something to drink."

"Anne—"

"And talk."

He frowned, but said, "All right."

"Maybe my husband will be back by then."

He watched as she turned and walked toward the house, and hoped that Charles would indeed be home when he got there.

He knocked on the front door, and when there was no answer he tried the doorknob and found the door unlocked. Against his better judgment, he opened the door and went inside.

"Anne?" he called.

There was no answer.

"Charles?"

When there was still no answer, he went into the dining room and through to the kitchen. He opened the kitchen door and stuck his head in. The cook, Olivia, turned her head and glared at him. She was a big woman, with powerful-looking arms. He didn't think he'd ever want to be the object of her anger.

"Yes?"

"I'm sorry," he said. "I was looking for Mrs. Goodnight."

"Well, she ain't in here," the cook said, with obvious approval.

"I, uh, see that," he said. "I'll, uh, I'll just look elsewhere."

"Fine."

He backed away and let the door close. When he turned, he saw Anne Goodnight standing there looking at him.

"She doesn't like people in her kitchen, does she?" he asked.

"You noticed that?"

He looked at her hands and saw that she had put proper bandages on them.

"How are your hands?"

She looked down at them briefly and then said, "They're fine."

"That's good."

They stared at each other awkwardly for a while. She had changed from her riding clothes into a simple dress in solid blue. It buttoned all the way up to her neck.

"Come along with me," she said, "and we'll have something to drink. Charles is not home, yet, and may not be for some time."

He was following her from the dining room through the entry foyer when there was a knock on the door. They stopped, and he watched as she went to the door. When she opened it, Carl Rivers stepped in.

"Mrs. Goodnight," he said, respectfully removing his hat.

"Carl."

He looked down at her hands, at Clint, and then at Anne's face.

"One of the boys told me he saw you and Mr. Adams ride in," Rivers said. "Said something looked funny. What happened to your hands?"

"There was an accident," she said, putting her hands behind her, out of sight, as if she had done something wrong and was trying to hide them. "With the wire."

"The wire?" Rivers asked, frowning.

"A calf was caught up in the wire," Clint said. "Mrs. Goodnight tried to free it without my help."

"I see," Rivers said. He did not look at Clint, but chose to continue staring at Anne Goodnight. Clint had the feeling that there might be more going on here between the two of them than immediately met the eye. "Whose calf was it?"

"It was a Sessions calf."

Rivers nodded.

"Two men happened by while we were trying to free it," Clint offered. "Their names were, uh, Webster, and Sam McCallum."

"McCallum," Rivers said. Now he looked at Clint. "Was there any trouble with them?"

"No," Clint said, "no trouble. In fact, they helped us free the calf, and then took it with them."

"I see," Rivers said. To Anne Goodnight he said, "Do you need a doctor?"

She started to say, "No—" but Clint interrupted and said, "It wouldn't be a bad idea. Do you have to send to town for him?"

"There's one in town," Rivers said, "but old Doc Handley lives near here. He used to be the town doctor until he retired."

"Will he come?" Clint asked.

Rivers looked directly into Clint's eyes and said, "I'll send someone to get him."

"Send someone to *ask* him to come, Carl," Anne Goodnight said firmly.

Rivers looked at Anne Goodnight and said, "Yes, ma'am. As you say. I'll take care of it."

Now there was an awkward moment there among all three of them before Rivers nodded, put his hat on, and left the house.

Anne turned and looked at Clint.

"I really don't need a doctor."

He smiled at her and replied, "Just as I said, it wouldn't be a bad idea."

She still had her hands behind her back when she said, "Come on, I think I need a drink."

TWENTY-NINE

They went into the parlor where Clint had first met Anne, and she walked over to a sideboard to pour some brandy.

"Want some?" she asked Clint.

"Too early for me," he told her. "You go ahead."

"For the pain," she said. "Please sit."

He sat at one end of the sofa, and she chose to sit at the other, with a single cushion between them. She held the glass in her less injured hand.

"I'm sorry," Clint said suddenly, "but I notice some things going on here."

She lifted her chin and asked, "Like what?"

"Like . . . what was going on between you and Carl Rivers just now?"

She elevated her chin just a fraction higher and asked, "What do you mean?"

"I think you know what I mean, Anne."

She hesitated a few moments, killing the time sipping her brandy, and then she said, "Nothing's going on . . . now."

"But there was, at one time, wasn't there?"

"Yes."

Now he waited, watching her to see if she would continue.

She used her free hand to smooth her dress in her lap, and then looked at him.

"My husband . . . works very hard, Clint. He has to, in order to build the kind of empire he wants. I admire him for that."

He remained silent.

"It does, however, leave me alone quite a bit," she said. "We're not—he is a very sweet man, really . . . but Charles is not the most . . . romantic . . . of men . . ."

He saw how much difficulty she was having with this and decided to take pity.

"Look, Anne," he said, interrupting her, "I'm sorry, I was out of line—"

"No, no," she said. "You deserve to know. I mean, I don't want you to think that I'm a . . . tramp, or anything—"

"I don't think that."

"There have been other men, Clint," she said, "at other times. . . . Nothing very serious, you understand . . . and my husband knows nothing about . . . about any of them. . . ."

"How serious was it with Rivers?"

She compressed her lips and said, "Not very serious . . . on my part . . . and with Carl it was . . . a mistake."

"How long . . . uh, how long ago was—"

"Carl?" she said. "It's been over four months."

"It must be difficult. . . ."

"More so for him, I fear," she said. "I told him in the beginning that there could be nothing . . . serious, nothing *permanent* between us. He said he understood . . . and yet . . ."

"He fell in love with you."

She nodded.

"I suspect that many men fall in love with you, Anne," he said. "Your husband, Frank Sessions, Carl Rivers . . ."

She looked at him boldly and asked, "And you?"

"No," he said, shaking his head, "not me. I don't make it a habit of falling in love with other men's wives."

"I see," she said, lowering her eyes now. "That's probably . . . wise."

"Of course," he added, "I haven't known you that long. . . ."

She looked up at him then and smiled, and he could see how men fell in love with her. There was something between them, even now. Not love, certainly not that, but an attraction was undeniable. It had been so ever since they first met, and Clint could not understand how Charles Goodnight could not see it. He also could not understand how a man could neglect a wife like Anne Goodnight.

It caused them both to start when they suddenly heard the front door close. Neither of them had heard it open.

Abruptly, Charles Goodnight came striding into the room.

"Ah, good, you're both here," he said. He was slipping a pair of black leather gloves from his hands. Clint wondered if he just liked the way they looked, or if they were necessary for handling the wire. "We were stringing some wire in Parson's Meadow when we ran into Sam McCallum and some of his men."

Goodnight went immediately to his wife's side and fell down on one knee. He took her free hand in his.

"McCallum told me what happened with the calf, and the wire. Are you all right?"

"I'm fine, Charles."

Goodnight looked at Clint, who said, "Rivers is sending for Doc Handley."

"Doc Handley," Goodnight said. "All right, that's good, that's very good."

"Did anything happen between you and McCallum's men?" Anne asked.

"We were stringing the wire and some of McCallum's men rode up. It was fairly tense, and I thought that something would happen, but then McCallum came along. The man has a cool head, I'll say that for him. He kept anything from occurring."

"I had the impression he was . . . formidable," Clint said.

"He is," Goodnight said. "He worked for me once."

"Really?"

"Yes," Goodnight said, "before he left to work for Frank Sessions."

"I see."

"Dear," Anne said to Goodnight, "why don't you go and wash up? Clint and I will wait here."

"Actually," Clint said, putting his glass aside and standing up, "I'd like to get cleaned up myself."

"Of course," Anne said.

Goodnight fronted Clint and said, "McCallum told me how you handled the wire."

Clint braced himself, thinking that maybe Goodnight was going to take him to task for severing the wire.

"It was smart," Goodnight said instead, "very good thinking."

"Thank you."

"Of course," he said, "I've sent some men out there to restring it."

"Of course," Anne said.

"Well," Goodnight said, "perhaps I will clean up, then."

"I'll wait here," Anne said to both of them. "Doc Handley should be here shortly."

"I'll be back before he arrives," Goodnight said. He leaned over and kissed his wife's cheek. "I'm glad you're all right."

"I'm fine," she said. "Clint kept me from being too badly cut."

Goodnight looked at Clint and said, "Then that puts me further in your debt, sir."

Clint would have protested, but he knew it would do no good. He simply nodded, and both men left Anne Goodnight there to go and get cleaned up.

On the way up to his room Clint thought back to their meeting with Sam McCallum. At the time he had not noticed anything going on between

Anne Goodnight and McCallum, but then he *had* been fairly preoccupied. Now he found himself wondering if McCallum was one of those many men who had fallen in love with her.

THIRTY

When Clint came back down, his own cut hand cleaned, his clothes fresh, there was a white-haired man in the parlor with Charles and Anne Goodnight. As he entered, he saw that the man was sitting next to Anne on the sofa, ministering to her injured hands. There was a glass of whiskey close at hand. Clint wondered why so many doctors he had known drank so much. Was it because they dealt so much with other people's pain?

"Ah, there you are, Clint," Goodnight said. He was standing by, watching the doctor work. "This is Doc Handley. Doc, this is Clint Adams."

Handley did not look away from his work.

"Good to meet you, Mr. Adams," the doctor said. "I've heard a lot about you."

Clint couldn't be sure if the doctor was talking about his reputation in general, or simply that he'd heard about him from the Goodnights.

"I understand," the man went on, bandaging

Anne's hands, "that your own hands were injured by the wire, as well?"

"Not really," Clint said. "A few minor cuts, is all. Nothing to concern yourself about."

"Well," Handley said, "my guess is you been cut or injured a time or two before, so you must know what you're talkin' about."

"I do."

"Fine, then," Handley said. He finished Anne's hand, then reached for his whiskey.

"Done, Doc?" Goodnight asked.

"I've done all I can," Handley said after a healthy swallow of whiskey. "They'll heal just fine. Cleanin' 'em up right away was a good idea."

"That was Clint's—Mr. Adams's idea," Anne said. "He insisted."

"Good thing he did, too," Doc Handley said. "Kept any chance of infection to a minimum."

Handley finally looked up at Clint, and Clint was surprised to see that the old man had to be in his eighties, at least. His face was so heavily lined it looked like some sort of map. His eyes were blue, liquid, almost faded, and yet they betrayed the fact that the mind behind them was still sharp.

"That damned wire . . ." Doc Handley said to no one in particular.

"Come on, Doc," Goodnight said, "I'll have someone take you back home. What do I owe you?"

Handley, staring into his glass, said, "A bottle of this fine whiskey would do nicely."

"You've got it," Goodnight said.

He assisted the doctor to his feet, and they walked from the room together.

"How do your hands feel?" Clint asked Anne.

"They're fine," she said. "Time for everyone to stop making such a fuss over me."

"If that's what you want."

She looked up at him then and smiled.

"Oh, what woman really wants that, right?" she asked him.

"None that I've known," he said. "Women like being fussed over, don't they?"

"I'll bet you know that for a fact," she said to him. "I bet you've known a lot of women, Clint Adams."

"A few."

"Was there ever someone . . . special?"

"There was . . . once."

"Once?"

He gave her a wan smile and said, "She died."

"I'm sorry," she said. "And now?"

"Now?" he said. He thought briefly of the ladies he'd known. He shook his head and said, "No. No one special."

"You travel quite a bit, I bet."

"Yes."

"Why is that?"

He shrugged.

"I guess I just never found one place I'd like to stay in forever."

"Do you think you ever will?"

"I don't know," he said. "No, that's not true. The answer is no. I don't honestly think there is a place out there like that for me."

"Really?" she said. She was silent for a moment, and then she said, "I think that's sad."

He thought about it for a moment as well, wondering if he thought so, too.

THIRTY-ONE

If Charles Goodnight noticed any awkwardness between Clint and his wife, Anne, he certainly didn't show it at dinner. He talked away about the length of wire they had strung that day, and how much they would be stringing the following day and the rest of the week.

"Before long," he said, "I'll have every foot of my property fenced and wired, and then let the bastards complain."

"Do you have that much wire, dear?" Anne asked, with something less than real interest.

"Not yet," Goodnight said, "but I will, soon."

"Charles," Anne said, "what do you intend to do about the attempts on your life?"

"What can I do?"

"You can find out who it was."

"Who it was?" Goodnight repeated. "I know who it was, Annie."

"You do?" she asked.

"Well," he said, hedging, "I have a pretty good idea, don't I?"

"You mean . . . Frank Sessions?"

"Who else?"

"You do have other neighbors who object to the wire, Charles," she pointed out.

"No one who objects as much as Sessions does," he told her.

"And then there are the people who simply don't like the wire."

Goodnight shook his head.

"There is no one who is as against it as Frank Sessions is."

Anne looked across the table at Clint, probably for support, but since Clint did not know Frank Sessions at all, there was nothing he felt he had to offer.

"Well, then," she finally said, "if you're so sure, why don't you do something about it?"

Goodnight gave Clint an amused look, as if to say "Isn't she cute?" and then looked at his wife.

"What would you suggest, dear?"

"Go and talk to him."

"To Sessions?"

"Of course, to Sessions."

"About what?"

"About the attempts on your life!" she said, exasperated.

"Why should I talk to him about the attempts on my life?" Goodnight asked. "He *knows* about them. He was *behind* them."

Once again Anne looked across the table at

Clint, imploring him to say something.

"This doesn't sound like a bad idea, Charles," Clint said.

The look on Anne's face clearly said, "Thank you!"

"What?" Goodnight said, looking at him. "What are you saying, that you agree with her?"

"Sure," Clint said. "Why not talk to Sessions? Are you a hundred percent sure he was behind the attempts on your life?"

"Well . . . no," Goodnight said, backing off a step now that Clint had taken up Anne's cause, "I'm not one *hundred* percent sure—"

"Then why not go and talk to the man and find out?" Clint said.

"You mean . . . just ask him?" Goodnight asked incredulously.

"No, you don't have to come right out and ask him," Clint said, "but you can talk to him, and watch his face, and be able to tell if he was behind any of it."

Goodnight looked at his wife, who nodded to him and then back at Clint.

"Let me get this straight," Goodnight finally said. "You've done this before? Looked into a man's face and been able to tell if what he was saying was the truth?"

"I have."

Goodnight hesitated, then exploded.

"Excellent!" he said, with enthusiasm.

"Then you'll do it?" Anne asked.

"Of course I will, dear," he said, "if it will put your mind at ease."

She smiled and said, "Oh, it would, Charles."

"Fine, then," he said, patting her hand. He looked at Clint and said, "We'll leave for the Sessions ranch first thing in the morning."

"What?" Clint said. "What do you mean, *we*?"

"Well, you're coming with me, naturally," Charles said. "Otherwise, how am I going to tell if he's telling the truth or lying?"

"I just told you—"

"You told me that *you* can tell by looking at a man," Goodnight said. "*I* don't have that ability, Clint, you do. So, I'll need you to come with me."

"Charles—"

"Please, Clint," Anne said, cutting him off. "Go with him and keep him out of trouble."

Goodnight beamed at his wife, then looked at Clint and asked, "How can you turn down a face like that?"

Clint stared across the table into Anne Goodnight's face—her lovely face—and he knew that he was being manipulated.

"All right."

"You'll do it?" she asked.

"Yes," he said sourly.

"Excellent!" Goodnight said again.

"But tell me something, Charles," Clint said, looking at his host.

"What?"

"If it isn't Sessions who was behind the attempts, what will you do then?"

"That's easy," Goodnight said. "We can go and talk to all of my neighbors, and you can pick out the guilty man for me."

"Now wait—"

"I don't know how to thank you for your help, Clint," Anne said.

"Listen," Clint said, "the two of you have gotten the wrong idea—"

"I'm kidding, Clint," Goodnight said. "If you think Sessions is not my man, then maybe Frank himself will have some ideas about who is."

"You'd work with Sessions?" Clint asked.

"Hey, if he would work with me, why not?" Goodnight said, and then added, "But I mean on this. I don't mean that we'd become partners again."

"Of course not," Clint said.

"So whether he did it or not, we'll deal with that when the time comes. Agreed?"

Clint looked at Charles Goodnight, then back to Anne's eager face, and finally said, "All right, agreed."

THIRTY-TWO

"Okay, tell me again, what happened?" Frank Sessions said.

Sam McCallum was standing in front of Sessions on the porch of the man's house. He had just finished relating to him all of the occurrences of the day. It was what they usually did at this time of the evening, the foreman reporting to the employer.

Only this time, there was more interesting news than usual.

McCallum took a deep breath and then told Sessions again about the calf, Anne Goodnight and Clint Adams, and then about interrupting what was about to become a battle between Goodnight and his men and Sessions's men.

"Are you sure the man said his name was Clint Adams?" Sessions asked.

"Positive, boss," McCallum said. "He told me his name was Clint Adams."

"The Gunsmith."

"He didn't say that."

"He didn't have to," Sessions said. He was a tall man, taller than McCallum, but not as young and not as well-built. "If he said his name was Clint Adams, then he's the Gunsmith."

"That's what I figured."

"You know what that means, don't you?" Sessions asked his foreman.

"What?"

"Goodnight has gone and hired himself a gun," Sessions said.

McCallum frowned and said, "That wasn't the impression I got."

"What makes you say that?"

"Oh, the man's actions," McCallum said. "If he was a hired gun, I think he might have tried to take the two of us."

"Well, you're lucky he *didn't* try, because he probably would have succeeded."

"You think so?" McCallum asked, with a wounded look.

"Come on, Sam," Sessions said. "You're not a gunman, and you know it."

Grudgingly, McCallum said, "Well, maybe not, but I'm no slouch."

"Besides, you don't get paid enough to go up against a man like the Gunsmith," Sessions said, "and neither does anyone else around here."

"That's true enough."

"So," Sessions said, rubbing his long jaw, "maybe what we need around here is someone who does."

"You mean . . . hire your own gunman?"

"Why not?" Sessions said. "Goodnight's opened the door now, hasn't he? If this erupts into some kind of a range war, it will be his doing, won't it?"

Shaking his head, McCallum said, "I told you before, boss, I don't think Adams is here as a gunman."

"What other reason could he have for being here?" Sessions asked.

"Well . . . he was with Mrs. Goodnight, maybe Goodnight hired him as her bodyguard."

That stopped Sessions for a moment.

"Why would she need a bodyguard?"

"Well, somebody tried to kill Goodnight—twice! Maybe he's worried about his wife."

"Maybe," Sessions said, rubbing his jaw again.

"Maybe what we—uh, you should do is try to find out what Adams *is* doing here."

"And how would you suggest I do that?"

McCallum shrugged and then said, "Ask him?"

THIRTY-THREE

Early the next morning Clint came down for breakfast and found Charles Goodnight waiting for him.

"Thought I was going to have to come up and wake you," Goodnight said amiably.

"I'm not a rancher," Clint said, "so I don't rise as early as you do."

"That's okay," Goodnight said. "I've got Olivia making some eggs for us, and then we can get started."

"Get started?"

"Have some coffee," Goodnight said, indicating a pot that was already on the table.

"Thanks."

As Clint poured himself a cup, Goodnight said, "Yes, we have to go see Frank Sessions, remember? You're going to read his mind."

Clint sat down with his coffee and shook his head slowly.

"I tried to tell you and Anne last night that you

had the wrong idea about what I was saying," Clint tried to explain.

"That's all right," Goodnight said. "It's a sound idea anyway, to go and talk to him. In fact, I know Frank pretty well; I'll probably know if he's lying or not."

"Doesn't Anne usually have sound ideas?" Clint asked him.

"She's a smart girl," Goodnight said, "but she doesn't usually get involved in my business."

"Maybe she should."

Goodnight gave him a look.

"She's a woman," he said, as if that explained it all away.

Clint opened his mouth to speak, but at that moment Olivia came in from the kitchen bearing a big plate of bacon and eggs.

"I'll bring out the biscuits," she said.

"Does she ever smile?" Clint asked, when she'd left.

"No," Goodnight said, "but who cares? She's a good cook. Go on, help yourself."

Clint did so, taking heaping portions of food, and then a couple of biscuits when Olivia brought them out. By the time Olivia left the room and he had enough food in front of him, he decided to mind his own business where Charles and Anne Goodnight were concerned.

Goodnight, however, had other ideas.

"She's never shown any inclination to get involved in my business before," he said.

Clint didn't reply. He didn't think he had to. It appeared to him that Goodnight was talking as much to himself as he was to him.

"Then again," the man said, cocking his head to one side, "I've never asked her to, have I?"

No answer. Clint kept his mouth busy chewing bacon, eggs, and biscuits.

"Well," Goodnight said, "maybe it's something to think about . . . later. Meanwhile, I've got something I want to talk to you about."

"What's that?"

"Work."

"Again?" Clint said. "Charles, I thought we settled that—"

"This is a different kind of work, Clint," Goodnight said.

Clint hesitated, then asked, "What did you have in mind?"

"I need someone to look after Annie."

"Look after her? How?"

"I mean protect her," Goodnight said. "Until I find out who wants to kill me, I think she needs a bodyguard."

"Are you offering me the job?" Clint asked.

"Yes," Goodnight said, "and I'll pay you well. She's very important to me. Money is no object."

Clint remained silent and thought about it. First of all, he hadn't intended to stay around for so long, and who knew if and when they'd find out who was behind the attempts to kill Goodnight. Secondly, being around Anne Goodnight all the time—without her husband—didn't seem like that good an idea to him. The attraction between them was too strong, and he didn't think he'd like to test his willpower in that fashion. It would be like taking a man who had stopped drinking and making him work in a saloon.

But then there was Goodnight's last statement, about money being no object. That did have a nice ring to it.

"Well?" Goodnight said. "What do you say?"

Against his better judgment, Clint said, "I can stay a few more days, Charles, but beyond that I'd have to recommend someone else."

"If you did that," Goodnight said, "recommend someone, I mean, would you stay until that person got here?"

Clint frowned.

"Let me think it over, see who I can come up with and when they can get here," he said after a few moments, "and then I can answer that better."

Goodnight nodded and said, "Okay, fair enough. Meanwhile, eat up, then we'll go and introduce you to my neighbor."

THIRTY-FOUR

By the time they finished breakfast, Anne Goodnight still had not come downstairs. They left the house and Goodnight sought out his foreman, Carl Rivers.

"Carl, Clint and I are going over to talk to Frank Sessions."

"Give me a minute and I'll get some men together," Rivers said immediately.

"No," Goodnight said, "Clint and I will ride over alone."

Rivers frowned and said, "That doesn't sound like a good idea to me, boss."

"Maybe not," Goodnight said, "but Clint's done all right by me so far, hasn't he? I feel safe riding over with him. Meanwhile, there's something else I want you to do for me."

"What's that?"

"Keep an eye on Annie for me, will you?" Goodnight said. "Don't let her stray too far away from the house alone."

"I can do that," Rivers said. "I'll watch over her myself."

"Fine," Goodnight said, touching the man's arm, "I knew I could count on you."

Remembering what Anne had told him about her and the foreman, Clint thought that this might be sort of like sending the fox to guard the chicken coop.

Clint and Goodnight went to the barn, saddled their horses, and then rode out. Goodnight was slightly in the lead as he led the way to the Sessions ranch.

Frank Sessions stepped out onto his front porch and took a deep breath. The plan was for him and his foreman, McCallum, to ride over to the Goodnight ranch this morning to talk to Charles Goodnight. Sessions wanted to find out for himself just what the Gunsmith's role—if he had any—was going to be in the ongoing situation that existed between him and Goodnight.

It was odd how you could be friends with someone for so long, and then that person could quickly become an adversary. Initially, of course, their falling-out was over Anne Perry, who eventually became Anne Goodnight. That soon faded, though, at least for Sessions. He realized that Anne had to choose one or the other, and she made the choice that she thought was the best for her. How could he possibly fault her for doing that— or fault Goodnight for taking her?

Now, however, there was the wire. Sessions *hated* barbed wire, and Charles Goodnight was trying to ring his land with it. Sessions just didn't think he could take that lying down. He had to try to take some action to keep Goodnight from putting up the wire. He knew that some of their neighbors felt the same way, but he also knew that even if he combined his land with that of his neighbors, Goodnight still had the bigger spread. Goodnight had the biggest spread in the state, and while Sessions may have run second to him, it was by a large margin.

Sessions became aware that McCallum was walking toward the house from the barn.

"The horses are saddled, boss."

"Good," Sessions said. "Let's get started then. I want to catch Charles before he starts stringing wire for the day."

Together they started walking toward the barn, but they were intercepted by another man.

"What is it, Styles?" McCallum asked.

"Riders comin', boss."

"How many?" McCallum asked.

"Two."

"Do you know who they are?"

"One," the man said, "but not the other."

"Well," Sessions said impatiently, "who is the one you recognize?"

Styles looked at Sessions and said, "Charles Goodnight, sir."

Sessions was surprised, but then he looked at McCallum and said, "Well, it looks like Charles has gone and saved us a ride."

Both men moved to a point from where they could see both riders.

"Recognize the other man?" Sessions asked McCallum.

"Yes, sir," McCallum said, "that's Clint Adams."

"The Gunsmith," Sessions said, and McCallum thought he heard something odd in his boss's voice.

Was it awe?

"Should I get some of the other men?" McCallum asked Sessions.

"No," the rancher said, "I don't think they're riding in here to try anything. They're probably just coming to talk."

Both Sessions and McCallum were wearing guns, but Sessions knew that individually or together they would be no match for the Gunsmith.

"Take off your gun," he told McCallum.

"What?"

"I said, take off your gun belt," Sessions said, unbuckling his own.

"What are you doing?" McCallum asked.

Holding his gun belt in his hand, Sessions said, "I don't want to give Adams any reason to think he has to use his gun. Now take yours off."

McCallum did as he was told, and Sessions draped both gun belts over a nearby corral fence, in plain sight. He had just stepped away from both guns when Goodnight and Clint Adams reached them.

THIRTY-FIVE

As they approached the two men, Clint noticed two things. First, they were unarmed, and second, their gun belts were hanging on the corral fence. Neither man was close enough to the guns to get to them in less than five or six steps. Clint was sure that this was by design.

They knew who he was.

Clint recognized one of the two men as Sam McCallum. He assumed that the other man was Frank Sessions. Sessions was both bigger and older than McCallum, but Clint thought that McCallum was the man in better shape.

"Good morning, Charles," Sessions greeted.

"Frank," Goodnight said.

"You saved me a trip," Sessions said. "I was just on my way out to see you."

"Is that a fact?" Goodnight asked. "About what?"

"Why don't you step down from your horses and we'll talk?" Sessions suggested.

Goodnight and Clint exchanged glances, and then Goodnight said, "Why not?"

He and Clint dismounted. Goodnight walked his horse over to the corral and tied the animal off. Clint simply grounded Duke's reins, allowing the animal to stand on his own.

"Got a lot of faith in that horse, don't you?" Sessions asked.

Clint shrugged.

"He'll go or stay, as he chooses."

"Beautiful animal," the man said. He turned to Goodnight and asked, "What did you want to talk to me about, Charles?"

"What about you?" Goodnight asked. "Why were you coming to see me?"

"Well," Sessions said, "since you saved me the trouble, and technically you're my guest, why don't you go first, huh?"

Goodnight considered the suggestion and then nodded.

"All right, then. There were two attempts on my life recently," Goodnight said.

"So I understand," Sessions said. "Do you know who was responsible?"

"There are a lot of possibilities," Goodnight said, "including you."

"Me?" Sessions said. "Is that why you came? To ask me if I tried to have you killed?"

"That's right."

Sessions stared at Goodnight for a moment and then said, "You've got a lot of nerve coming here and asking me that, Charles."

"Why?" Goodnight asked. "Are you going to tell

me that the thought never entered your mind?"

"No, I'm not going to tell you that," Sessions said. "As a matter of fact, the thought has entered my mind many times."

Goodnight waited for the man to go further and when he didn't, he said, "So?"

"So what?"

"Come on, man!" Goodnight snapped. "What are we talking about here?"

"We're talking about two attempts on your life," Sessions said. "Let me ask you something."

"What?"

"Even if I was responsible, do you think I'd tell you?" Sessions asked.

"I don't know, Frank," Goodnight said. "Would you?"

Sessions thought the question over for a few moments and then said, "You know what? I don't know. I truly don't know if I'd tell you or not."

"So then what you're saying is," Clint said, "that you had nothing to do with the attempts on Mr. Goodnight's life?"

Sessions looked at Clint and said, "Yeah, that's what I'm saying."

"Well, all right, then," Goodnight said. "All I wanted was a straight answer."

"You got it," Sessions said. "That's as straight an answer as I can give you."

"It didn't sound so damned straight to me," Goodnight mumbled.

"I've got a question for you now, Charles," Sessions said.

"All right," Goodnight said, "ask it."

"This man," Sessions said, pointing to Clint.

"What about him?"

"Do you know who he is?"

"Of course I know who he is."

"Does he work for you?"

"No, he does not."

"Then what's he doing here?"

"Mr. Adams is a guest in my house," Goodnight said, "and he simply offered to keep me company on the ride over here."

"Then he's not your hired gun?" Sessions asked.

"No," Goodnight said.

"I'm nobody's hired gun," Clint added.

"So then he's just a friend?"

"That's right, Frank," Goodnight said, "he's just a friend. Not an old friend, but a friend, nevertheless."

Sessions stared at Goodnight for a few moments, flicking his eyes at Clint every so often. Clint knew what was going through his mind. It was very likely that Frank Sessions was dwelling on one of Clint Adams's own most disliked words—coincidence.

As if he had been reading Clint's mind, Sessions said, "That's a little bit of a coincidence, Charles, don't you think?"

"Why do you say that, Frank?" Goodnight asked. "Do you think I was *looking* for a hired gun and Mr. Adams just happened into town?"

"No," Sessions said, "but it is quite a coincidence, isn't it, that he just *happened* to come into town in time to save your life?"

Goodnight nodded and said, "It sure was. It was

a *fortunate* coincidence that he got here in time to save it not once, but twice."

"And did you really think I had something to do with those attempts, Charles?" Sessions asked.

"You have to admit, Frank," Goodnight said, "that you would benefit if I were killed."

"Why? Would that keep the wire from going up?" Sessions asked. "Wouldn't Anne just go ahead and continue, in your memory?"

Goodnight smiled.

"I really can't say what Annie would do in my absence, Frank."

Maybe Goodnight couldn't say what Anne would do, but Clint thought he could. He knew how Anne disliked the wire, and he doubted that she would continue with it if her husband were killed. In fact, she might even—at that point—take down the wire that had already been strung.

"Are we clear on all of this, then?" Goodnight asked Sessions.

"On what?"

"I didn't hire Clint Adams as a hired gunman, and you didn't have anything to do with somebody trying to kill me," Goodnight explained.

Sessions paused a moment, then nodded shortly and said, "That sounds clear."

Goodnight looked at Clint and said, "Well then, I guess we'd better be going."

Both Goodnight and Clint walked to their horses and prepared to mount. As Goodnight put his foot in his stirrup, Sessions called his name.

"What?" Goodnight asked. He paused in that position, but did not turn around.

Clint had already mounted and was watching Frank Sessions and his foreman very carefully.

"Can we talk about the wire again while you're here, Charles?" Sessions asked.

"No," Goodnight said and proceeded to mount his horse. He looked down at Sessions and said, "We've talked enough, Frank. Nothing either of us says is going to change the other one's mind. We both know that."

"So where does that leave us?" Sessions asked.

"The same place we've been for the past several years," Charles Goodnight said. "Going our separate ways."

THIRTY-SIX

During the ride back to the Goodnight spread from the Sessions ranch Clint was wondering if someone was still following them. They had been followed during the ride there. It felt to him like they were being followed, but that could have been due to the fact that he was expecting to be followed.

"Are we still being kept an eye on?" Charles Goodnight asked him.

"I'm not sure."

"I wonder who it is," Goodnight said, "or was."

"If we knew that," Clint said, "maybe we'd know who was trying to have you killed."

"What should we do?"

Clint thought a moment. He could break off from Goodnight and try to ride back, but the route between the two ranches was largely flat. There was not that much opportunity for cover. Whoever was trailing them would see him in time to be warned. He could try to chase the fellow down, but even with Duke the other man might have enough of a head start to elude him.

"There's not much we can do at this point," Clint said. "But next time . . ."

"What about next time?"

"I don't know," Clint said, "I'm still thinking about it."

In point of fact, the man who had followed them before, and who had followed Clint and Anne Goodnight during their ride, was indeed following them now. When he was sure that they were headed back to the Goodnight ranch, however, he veered off and rode the other way. It was time for him to keep a prearranged meeting with the man who had hired him, to make a report on what he had seen so far.

When Goodnight and Clint returned to the ranch, they were met on the front porch by Anne, who had been sitting out.

"What happened?" she asked.

They dismounted and handed their horses off to one of the ranch hands.

"What's that?" Goodnight asked, indicating the pitcher next to his wife's chair. It was filled with an amber liquid and ice cubes.

"Iced tea," Anne said. "Would you like some?"

"I'd like something a little stronger," her husband replied.

"I'll have some," Clint said. Goodnight looked at him. "It's cold, it's wet, and it will cut through the dust as well as anything else."

Goodnight seemed to think it over for a moment and then said, "All right, I'll have some, too."

Anne poured them both a glass and handed one to each of them. She took her seat again, and her husband sat on the bench next to her. Clint leaned against the front wall of the house.

"So, what happened?" she asked.

"Frank denied that he was behind the attempts to kill me," Goodnight said.

"Did you believe him?"

"I think the question is," Goodnight said, "did Clint believe him?"

"No," Clint said, "I think you should answer the question first."

Goodnight frowned, then took a moment to think. He drank half his iced tea while he was doing so.

"All right," he said finally, "yes, I believe him. I think he was telling the truth."

"So do I," Clint said.

"Then if it's not Frank Sessions," Anne said, "who is it?"

"I don't know," Goodnight said, shrugging. "It could be . . . anyone."

Clint drank his tea thoughtfully. He didn't agree that it could be *anyone*. It had to be someone who would definitely benefit in some way from Goodnight's death.

"I think we have to talk," he said to Goodnight.

"About what?"

"I don't know," Clint said. "Just talk, and see what comes out. Whoever is behind this has something to gain. If you talk about everyone you know, or have done business with, maybe it will become obvious."

"About *everyone*?" Goodnight asked.

Clint looked at him and nodded. "Everyone."

"That could take all day," Goodnight said, "and half the night."

"Maybe," Clint said, "but maybe that means that by morning we'll have an idea who the culprit is."

"He's right, Charles," Anne said.

Goodnight looked at her, and then at Clint.

"So what do we do now?" he asked.

"That's easy," Clint said. "You start talking."

THIRTY-SEVEN

Lanigan waited impatiently at the prearranged place for the man he'd hired, using Fred Canby's money. It seemed to him that he had been waiting a lot lately, and he was not the kind of man who could do that easily. He preferred action.

He preferred killing, because that was what he did best. Also, it was what Fred Canby paid the most for.

Lanigan wanted Canby to send him after Charles Goodnight and Clint Adams, but the old man wouldn't hear of it.

"I might send you against Goodnight alone, Lanigan," Canby had said, "but not against Adams. Just be patient. I'll get you some help, and then when the time comes, you'll kill one or both of them. We'll see."

Lanigan didn't like that phrase. It seemed to him that was all he used to hear when he was a kid. His mother or his father would say that to

151

him all the time. "We'll see . . . we'll see . . ."

Lanigan didn't want to *see*, he wanted to *do*.

The man riding to meet Lanigan was named Harlan Michaels. Michaels had been working for Goodnight for a few months, but a ranch hand didn't make a lot of money. When he was approached by Lanigan to spy on Charles Goodnight, he agreed. Lanigan was paying him more than twice what he was earning working on the ranch. Taking money from both sides meant he was now making three times as much money as he had before.

He saw Lanigan waiting for him as he approached on his horse, and he got that feeling in the pit of his stomach. Lanigan scared him, because Lanigan had a killer's eyes. Michaels had seen eyes like that before on other men who were killers. Cold, emotionless, expressionless eyes. He figured he'd keep taking Lanigan's money for a while, and when he had enough of a poke saved up, he'd just light out. He didn't want to work for Lanigan much longer.

You never knew with a killer when he'd turn on you and kill *you*.

Lanigan watched Harlan Michaels dismount and walk over, leading his horse.

"What have you got for me, Harlan?" Lanigan asked. His voice was expressionless.

"Not much," Michaels said, then went on to explain how he had followed Adams and Mrs. Goodnight. He told about the incident with the calf and Frank Sessions's men, and then about how he had tailed Goodnight and Adams to the Sessions ranch just that morning.

"That's all?"

"That's it," Michaels said. "Do you, uh, have my money?"

"No," Lanigan said.

"What?"

"You haven't given me anything that's worth money, Harlan," Lanigan said. "In fact, I don't think I need you anymore."

"What?" Michaels said. And as Lanigan drew his gun, the man cried, "Wait, wait, I can get more—"

The sound of the shot drowned him out, and the impact of the bullet in his chest cut him off. He wanted to say something else, but suddenly he couldn't breathe, and he couldn't talk, and then he couldn't see or feel anything at all anymore. . . .

Lanigan rode back to Lubbock and reported to Fred Canby in his office. The older man listened with great interest, especially to the part where Goodnight went to see Sessions.

"I guess he thought Sessions was behind the attempts," Canby said.

"I guess."

"Maybe Frank convinced him that he wasn't," Canby went on. "If that's the case, he'll start looking somewhere else."

"I guess so."

"About Michaels . . ."

"Yes?"

"Did you have to kill him?" Canby asked.

"Yes."

Canby decided not to question Lanigan any further on the subject.

"All right, then," Canby said, "someone came to town today that I want you to meet."

"Who?"

"You'll meet him later today," Canby said. "He's over at the hotel now, resting up. He rode long and hard to get here because I offered him a lot of money to back your play."

"And when do I make my play?"

"Soon," Canby said, "very soon."

Especially if Goodnight was going to start looking elsewhere for the culprit, Canby thought. How long would it be before his old friend realized that he, Fred Canby, had a lot to gain by keeping the range open and free of the barbed wire?

Goodnight and Adams were going to have to be taken care of before that could happen.

THIRTY-EIGHT

At some point during the night, Clint and Goodnight left the porch of the house and moved into Goodnight's office. They also switched from iced tea to something stronger.

Clint did not try to match Goodnight drink for drink. It occurred to him that the drunker Goodnight got, the looser his talk got. Clint decided that one of them had better be sober enough to remember what Goodnight was saying.

Along around three A.M., Goodnight suddenly stopped talking. Clint had been staring at the floor, listening to the man drone on. When the voice stopped, he looked up and saw that Goodnight's chin had fallen down to his chest. The man had either nodded off or passed out. Either way, Clint decided to carry him up to his bedroom.

He was standing over Goodnight when he realized that carrying him upstairs would mean waking Anne Goodnight, who had turned in some time ago. He decided instead to put Goodnight on one of the sofas in the parlor.

He hoisted the man up onto his shoulder, carried him from the office to the parlor, and set him down gently on a sofa. As soon as he did that, the man began snoring. The sound made Clint realize just how tired he was, as well. He didn't know at that point if Goodnight had said anything of great value, but he decided that morning would be time enough to go through it all again, weeding out what was useless and what was useful. At the moment his brain was just too tired to deal with it.

He left Goodnight where he was and went upstairs to his room.

Clint had just gotten into bed when there was a light knocking at his door. He got out of the bed and, clad only in his underwear, padded barefoot to the door. He opened it a crack and looked out into the hall.

"May I come in?" Anne Goodnight asked.

She was wearing a nightgown—a low-cut nightgown, and he couldn't take his eyes off her breasts.

"I, uh, don't think that's a good idea, Anne," Clint said.

"Why not?" she asked, leaning close. He could smell her now, and his body was reacting of its own accord. "Charles is asleep downstairs, isn't he? Or rather, he's passed out drunk. He's not going to wake up for hours."

"Anne—"

"Please, Clint," she said. "I want to come in and . . . talk."

He hesitated, then said, "All right. Let me get something on."

He left the door ajar and turned to walk to the bed for his pants, but then he heard her enter the room behind him.

"Anne—"

"You don't have to put anything on, Clint," she said, closing the door. "For what I have in mind you don't need to be dressed."

He turned to argue with her and was just in time to see her nightgown fall to the floor in a heap around her lovely ankles.

He opened his mouth to say her name, but no sound came out. She was completely naked, and he couldn't help but drink in the sight of her. Her breasts were full, almost pear-shaped, and the nipples were dark and erect. She had a small waist, which made her hips seem even wider than they were. Her thighs were full, and her calves firm. She was a big woman, all right, as he had suspected each time he saw her dressed. Now, naked, there could be no doubt.

And there was also no doubt about what it was she had in mind. He didn't want to do it, but his body was not listening to his mind—and she knew it.

She walked across the room to him and put her hands on his bare chest.

"You want me, don't you?" she asked.

She slid her hands down his torso, over his belly, and then reached between his legs.

"Yes," she said, "I see you do want me, just as I want you."

"No," he said, but she did not believe him.

"Yes," she said, "oh yes . . ."

She was almost as tall as he was, and she only had to lean up a little to kiss him. As she did so, she slid her hand inside his underwear to take hold of him. He growled into her mouth, deciding that if this was what she wanted, then she might as well get it—and he might as well enjoy it. He'd worry about the consequences afterward.

He put his arms around her and pulled her to him, kissing her deeply. His tongue entered her mouth and she moaned. Using both hands she slid his underwear down until it fell to the floor and there was nothing between them. She moaned again as he slid his hands down her back to cup her buttocks.

Squeezing her marvelously firm and smooth butt in his hands, he turned her and pushed her back toward the bed. When the backs of her thighs struck the mattress she fell onto it, taking him with her.

On the bed he began to explore her body with not only his hands, but his mouth as well. Her moans and cries increased in volume, but neither of them worried about that. Charles Goodnight was well beyond hearing them.

He worked his way down her body until he was nestled between her legs, his mouth and tongue working avidly.

"Oh my God, yes!" she cried. "Oh please, oh yes, Clint . . . yes!"

She began to buck beneath him as waves of pleasure flooded over her, and then he raised himself above her and plunged into her. He groaned as her heat surrounded him. He had his knees outside of her legs, and she seemed incredibly tight as he worked himself in and out of her.

She reached down with one hand to press against his leg, and he thought he knew what she wanted. He lifted one knee, and then the other, until he was now kneeling inside her thighs. He drove into her more deeply that way, and although she wasn't as tight in this position, she was still very hot and wet. She brought her legs up, then, to wrap them around his waist, and also encircled him with her arms. She brought him tightly against her, so that her mouth was right against his ear as she moaned and cried out. They moved together, the tempo increasing until they were both grunting and sweating with the effort.

He felt the rush building up inside of him, as if it was welling up from his ankles, through his legs and thighs into his groin. He knew he was going to explode inside of her, and he didn't want to, not just yet. He controlled it and continued to move with her until her cries became such that he knew she was very near her climax . . . and that was when he released the control he had over himself and allowed his explosion to happen. . . .

THIRTY-NINE

"Well," Clint said later, "this was a mistake."

Lying next to him, exhausted, Anne Goodnight asked, "Do you really think that?"

"Yes," Clint said. "Oh, I'm not saying it wasn't wonderful, Anne, but it definitely was a mistake. Aside from that it was just plain wrong."

"That's the way you look at it," Anne said. "To my way of thinking, it was just right."

"How do you figure that?"

She stretched, and he was glad that the sheet was covering her. He knew he wouldn't be able to resist her now any more than he had the first time. Actually, he was wishing she'd get dressed and go back to her own room.

"I needed this, Clint," she said. "I needed you, here, tonight. It doesn't mean I don't love my husband, and it doesn't mean that it will ever happen again."

"Oh, it won't," he said. "I can promise you that."

"Really?" she said. Suddenly her hand was on

160

him, and he was swelling again. "Never again?" she asked as she stroked him gently.

"No," he said, turning and reaching out for her, "never . . . not after tonight."

In the middle of the night Fred Canby suddenly sat up in his bed. The move was so abrupt that it woke the young woman who was sleeping next to him. She was still there, despite the fact that he had been unable to perform with her. He had told her that he still wanted her to sleep with him, and she didn't mind. She was still getting paid, and she didn't even have to service him.

"What is it?" she asked.

"Nothing," he said. "Go back to sleep."

He swung his feet to the floor, reached for his robe, put it on, and left the bedroom. He went to his office and poured himself a drink.

He wasn't sure what had awakened him. He didn't think it had been a dream. At least, he didn't remember any dream. All he knew was that he had awakened with the sudden knowledge that today was the day that Charles Goodnight and Clint Adams had to be taken care of. In the morning he would call for Lanigan and give him his instructions. He and the new man would go out and kill both Goodnight and Adams today. By nightfall, both men had to be dead, and business as usual could go on for Fred Canby. He had open range to claim and then sell, which he could not do if Goodnight's wire was in the way.

First he'd get rid of Goodnight, and after that the damned wire would come down.

• • •

Anne Goodnight left Clint's bed at about four A.M. and went back to her own room. She seemed very content, and not regretful in the least. He, too, was physically content, but mentally he was somewhat less than that.

He had slept with his host's wife. He wasn't sure yet that he and Goodnight were friends, but that still did not excuse his behavior.

He stood up, walked to the window, and looked out at the grounds in front of the house. He truly wished that he had never stopped in Lubbock, but now the damage was done. Besides, if he hadn't stopped in Lubbock, there was a good chance that Charles Goodnight would now be dead. He shook his head. There was no way to change this. He certainly would not trade Goodnight's death for this not to have happened. He was just going to have to deal with it.

He went back to bed, wondering how Anne would feel in the morning. Would she regret what had happened? Would she be unable to meet his eyes with hers? Would Goodnight notice that something was amiss?

Clint decided that maybe tomorrow was the day he should leave—and when he did, he would ride *around* Lubbock as he headed south, not through it.

FORTY

Fred Canby watched Lanigan and the new man, whose name was Myles, Douglas Myles. He preferred to be called Myles, though. Canby marveled at how alike the two men were. Both preferred to be called by their last names. Both were quiet, seemingly emotionless men— and both were killers.

Myles had a reputation for getting the job done, which was why Canby had sent for him.

The main difference between the two men was physical. Lanigan was very tall and thin,— bony. Myles was under six feet, stocky, easily outweighing Lanigan by fifty pounds.

When the two men had met in the saloon the day before, they had studied each other warily. Canby knew that Lanigan and Myles would never be friends, probably never even like each other. That didn't matter to him. All they had to do was work together for a day or two, and then they could go their separate ways once more.

Canby was of the opinion that, left in the same place too long, one would most certainly kill the other. It was simply their nature.

"All right," Canby said, "today is the day."

"Today?" Lanigan said.

"That's right."

Lanigan frowned. If it was to be today, they would have to ride hard to get there. A man on a horse, riding nonstop, could make it by late afternoon. It was only when you were burdened—the way Goodnight had been with the wagonload of wire—that it was an overnight trip.

"All right, then," Lanigan said. "Today it is."

"Well, good," Myles said around a wooden match. "I was afraid I was gonna have to stay here longer."

"You don't like it here?" Lanigan asked.

Myles gave Lanigan a heavy lidded look and removed the match from his mouth.

"No, I don't."

"What's wrong with it?"

Myles smiled humorlessly and said, "I don't much like the people."

"Anybody in particular?" Lanigan asked, bristling.

"That's enough . . . gentlemen," Canby said. "As long as I'm paying you, I'd prefer that you do your bickering on your own time."

Myles still smiled, but he placed the matchstick back into his mouth and looked at Canby.

"You're the boss," he said. Then he added, "For now."

"That is correct," Canby said. Neither man

frightened him exactly, but he felt uncomfortable in their presence.

"Where do you want it done?" Lanigan asked.

"I don't care where or how," Canby said, "I only care that it be today."

"You want both of them?" Myles asked.

"I want Goodnight," Canby said. "I don't much care what happens to Adams. He's yours if you want him."

"That'd be a feather in my cap," Myles said, "killing the Gunsmith."

"Who says *you're* gonna kill him?" Lanigan asked.

Myles looked at him and said, "You sayin' you can take him?"

"You think I can't?"

"Gentlemen," Canby said, "if you please. I'd prefer that you don't kill each other until after you have taken care of my business?"

Lanigan and Myles both looked at him, and Canby squirmed in his seat, wondering if he had gone too far.

"He's got a good point," Lanigan finally said.

"Yes, he does," Myles said.

"Let's get to it, then," Lanigan said.

They both stood up and headed for the door. Canby held his breath as they reached the door together, wondering if they were going to argue over who would go through it first. They did not. Lanigan opened the door and allowed Myles to precede him. As the door closed behind them, Canby expelled a sigh of relief.

FORTY-ONE

That morning at breakfast Clint was very surprised at Anne Goodnight's behavior. She chattered away with her husband and with him, and not once did Clint see any hint of discomfort on her part. As for him, he had come downstairs with feelings of dread, but it soon became clear to him that they were unwarranted.

Goodnight himself was another surprise. For a man who had drunk as much as he had the night before and passed out, he was surprisingly chipper.

"All right," he finally said at one point, "enough idle chatter. Tell me, Clint, did my drunken ramblings last night reveal anything?"

It was odd, but that morning when he had awakened, Clint realized almost immediately that Goodnight had indeed said something that was of value.

"Who is Fred Canby again?"

"Fred?" Goodnight said. "He's a local businessman. Owns a small ranch, mostly for show."

"Is that all?"

"Well, no . . . he has some political ambitions, Fred does. Why?"

"Is he a friend of yours?"

"I consider him, a friend, yes," Goodnight said. "I've known him a long time."

"How does he feel about the wire?"

"He's against it," Goodnight said.

"How strong is his opposition?"

"Fairly strong, I guess, but see, he's not a rancher, so his opposition is moral."

"Is it?" Clint asked.

"What do you mean?"

"What if his opposition was political?"

"I don't understand."

"What if 'Open Range' was his platform for running for office?" Clint asked.

"Clint, do you know much about politics?"

"Very little."

"Then you don't understand that the people who would support Fred are the big ranchers, the cattlemen. Like me," Goodnight explained.

Clint frowned.

"Then I *really* don't understand politics," Clint said. "If he needs your support, why would he oppose you on the wire issue?"

Now it was Goodnight's turn to stop short.

"I don't know," Goodnight said.

"In your opinion," Clint asked, "are the big ranchers going to be largely in favor of the wire, or will they be against it?"

"I think Frank Sessions will be in the minority,"

Goodnight said. "The big ranchers are going to want to fence off their land, and the barbed wire is the perfect way to do that and be sure that no one is going to trespass."

"Then I'll ask you again. Why is Fred Canby opposed to it?"

Goodnight frowned and said, "I don't know."

"This is just a theory," Clint said, "but what if Canby is buying up land around here?"

"I'd know about it."

"Not if he had someone doing it for him," Clint said.

"Are you leading up to accusing Fred of trying to have me killed?"

"I don't know what I'm leading up to, Charles," Clint said. "It just struck me as odd that someone who would be after your support would be opposing you on an issue as important as this."

"Now that you mention it," Goodnight said, "it does seem odd. Maybe we should ride into Lubbock and ask him, huh?"

"Maybe we should," Clint said.

"Then we'll do that right after breakfast."

"There's something else," Clint said.

"What?"

"From Lubbock I'll be continuing on," Clint said. "It's time for me to leave."

That drew him a look from Anne, one which Goodnight did not see.

"Well," Goodnight said, "I think I've done everything I can to get you to stay. I've offered you every job I have to offer."

"I appreciate the offers, Charles," Clint said,

"but it's time . . . that's all."

"I understand," Goodnight said. "When I was younger, I was that way. You just stay in one place too long and you get the urge to move on. I appreciate everything *you've* done for *me*, Clint."

"I was glad to help, Charles," Clint said, feeling a great surge of guilt over what he had done last night.

"We'll be sorry to see you go, Clint," Anne said, looking right at him. "Now who will ride with me in the mornings?"

"I think Charles should," Clint said.

"If I only had time—" Goodnight started, but Clint cut him off.

"Make time, Charles," he said. Goodnight looked at him sharply and Clint added, "You've got a lovely wife. Make time for her. She's the one who's going to support you no matter what."

Goodnight stared at Clint, then turned his head and looked at Anne, who smiled at him. Suddenly, Goodnight covered his wife's hand with his.

"You might have something there, Clint," the man said. "You just might have something there."

FORTY-TWO

Clint Adams and Charles Goodnight left the Goodnight ranch on horseback at the same time Lanigan and Myles left Lubbock. It was destined, then, that they would meet halfway.

"I was just thinking about what you said this morning," Goodnight said.

They had been riding at a good clip for a few hours and were almost at the halfway point between the ranch and Lubbock.

"About Canby?"

"Well, that too," Goodnight said, "but I was thinking more about what you said about Annie."

"Oh."

"I think you're right," Goodnight said. "I haven't given her enough attention. In fact, at times I've just downright neglected her."

"Well," Clint said, "she's still there for you, isn't she?"

"Yep, she sure is," Goodnight said, "but it's tak-

170

en you to make me realize it. Tell me, what makes you so smart all the time?"

"I'm not smart *all* the time," Clint said. "In fact, I don't think I'm too smart *most* of the time."

If he was, Clint thought, he wouldn't keep getting himself in these kinds of messes.

"I say we take Adams out first," Myles said.

"He's not the target," Lanigan argued.

They had been riding along, pushing their horses for quite a while, and were now approaching the halfway point between Lubbock and the Goodnight ranch.

"Maybe not," Myles said, "but he's the one who's gonna be the hardest to handle."

"Still," Lanigan said, "he ain't the one we're bein' *paid* for."

"Maybe not," Myles said, "but he's the one who can *keep* us from gettin' paid."

"Okay," Lanigan said, after a moment. "Okay, so if they're together, we'll have to take him first. That makes sense."

"I know it does."

"But if they're *not* together, then we'll take care of Goodnight first," Lanigan said. "I want to make damned sure I do what I'm gettin' paid to do."

Now Myles took a moment to think, and then said, "Sounds fair."

Lanigan looked over at Myles, who was looking straight ahead. Lanigan didn't trust the other man. He thought that Myles was in this for more than just the money. He was in this for the glory that killing the Gunsmith would bring him.

Lanigan's first and only allegiance in this life was to money. If killing Clint Adams brought him more recognition, he'd simply be able to command more money for his services. He did nothing just for the glory of it, and he felt that men who did were dangerous.

Myles was dangerous. Lanigan wouldn't put it past Myles to try to kill him after they finished with Goodnight and Adams.

That meant that Lanigan was going to have to kill Myles before Myles could kill him.

That was something that was going to have to be timed just right.

FORTY-THREE

"What's that?" Goodnight asked.

Clint peered into the distance and said, "If I'm not mistaken, it's a body. Let's take a look."

They rode up to it, and as they approached, they could clearly see that it was indeed a body.

They dismounted, walked over to it, and turned the corpse over.

"Know him?" Clint asked.

"I sure do," Goodnight said. "He works for me. His name is—or was—Harlan Michaels. Carl told me he sent this fella into Lubbock to see if Terry Lester was well enough to ride back."

Clint studied the body.

"He must have been bushwhacked," Goodnight said.

"He was shot at close range from the front, not the back," Clint said. He checked the ground and said, "There was someone here with him. Look here."

Goodnight took a look and saw a horse's hoofprint with a half-moon cutout in it.

"What are you thinking?" Goodnight asked.

"Just that maybe he was meeting somebody here to talk to them, give them some information."

"About us?"

Clint nodded.

"You're thinking that this is the man who was tailing us, keeping tabs on us for . . . for who?"

"For whoever," Clint said. "Besides, he wasn't the first of your men to be bought, was he?"

"Jesus," Goodnight said, passing his hand over his forehead, pushing his hat back on his head, "maybe I ought to start paying my men more."

"Maybe," Clint said, "or maybe you should be more careful about who you hire."

"You want to bury him?" Goodnight asked.

Clint wasn't listening, though—not to Goodnight, anyway.

"What is it?" Goodnight asked.

"Riders coming."

"I don't hear—"

"Listen!"

Goodnight listened, and then suddenly he heard them. Horses were approaching at a gallop.

"How many?" he asked.

"Two, I think," Clint said.

"What should we do?" Goodnight asked. "Take cover?"

"No," Clint said. "Let's just stand our ground and see who it is. It may be nothing, but spread out a little, anyway." He pointed and said, "They'll probably come over that rise. Let's be ready for anything."

As they approached the rise, Lanigan suddenly realized that they were near the place where he had met and killed Harlan Michaels.

He and Myles topped the rise, and where Lanigan expected to see Harlan Michaels's body instead he saw the body—and two men.

"Hold it!" he shouted to Myles, who reined his horse in hard.

"What is it?" Myles asked.

"Those two men."

"I see 'em," Myles said. "Who are they?"

"That's Charles Goodnight and Clint Adams. Adams is on your left."

Myles looked surprised, then pleased. He licked his lips, the way a man facing a big dinner might.

"Well," he said, "it looks like they're gonna make this easy for us. Have they ever seen you?"

"Goodnight has, around town."

"Does he know you work for Canby?"

"I don't know," Lanigan said. "I can't be sure."

"Well, they're starin' up at us and we're starin' down at them. Nothin's gonna get done this way."

"What do you suggest?" Lanigan asked.

"I say we ride down there nice and easy like, and then throw down on them."

"That's the Gunsmith down there, Myles," Lanigan reminded him.

"So?" Myles said. "We both take him first, that's all."

"He might get one of us," Lanigan said.

Myles smiled and said, "That'll mean that one of us will get paid and one of us won't. You worried it might be me and not you?"

"The hell with it," Lanigan said tightly. "Let's go do it."

"They're coming down," Clint said. "Do you know either one of them?"

"I can't be sure from this distance," Goodnight said, "but the one on the left looks like a man I've seen in town."

"Who?"

"His name's Lanigan."

"What's he do?"

"Not much," Goodnight said. "He's just always around. Works for people here and there."

"Has he ever worked for Canby?"

Goodnight hesitated, then said, "You know, I think he has . . . as a matter of fact, I'm sure of it. Lanigan came into the Americana Saloon once, and Fred commented that the man had his uses."

"Well," Clint said, "remembering that might have just given us the edge we need, Charles."

"I'm not a gunman, Clint," Goodnight said. "I mean, I'll back you, but I just want you to know that."

"When the shooting starts, hit the ground and

roll," Clint said. "If you're moving, it'll be harder for them to hit you."

"And just about impossible for me to hit them."

Clint looked at him and said, "Just do it, leave the rest to me."

FORTY-FOUR

The two riders approached, and Clint kept his eyes on both of them. Luckily, they were riding close together. When they started to move apart, it would signal that they were ready to make their move. He only hoped that Goodnight wouldn't give in to nervousness and do something stupid.

"Looks like you fellas have had some trouble," Lanigan said.

"Not us," Clint said, "this fella. We just found him that way."

"Gonna bury him?" Lanigan asked.

"No," Clint said. "Maybe you want to."

"Why would I?"

Clint decided to take a wild shot and said, "Maybe because you killed him."

The other man moved his horse away from Lanigan's as Lanigan said, "Shit," and went for his gun.

"Now!" Clint shouted at Goodnight.

Goodnight hit the ground and rolled to his left, clawing for his gun.

Clint drew swiftly and fired at Lanigan. The bullet shattered Lanigan's right collarbone, numbing his arm so that the gun dropped from it.

Myles had his gun out, but Goodnight was firing, and although his shots were going wild, they were enough to attract Myles's attention. Clint took advantage of the situation and fired at the man. His bullet struck Myles square in the chest, punching right through his breastbone and driving all of his breath out of him.

Lanigan, his right arm useless, was having trouble with his horse, which had been spooked by the shots. Suddenly the horse reared and Lanigan fell off, dropping backward and hitting the ground with his back. He lay there motionless, unable to move because of the pain in his arm and the fact that all of the breath had been knocked out of him.

"Easy!" Clint shouted to Goodnight, who was staggering to his feet. "It's all over."

Clint walked over to Myles and checked him to make sure he was dead. After making certain of that, he walked over to Lanigan, who was still breathing. The man was lying on his back, and his eyes were open, but he didn't seem able to move.

"Keep an eye on him," Clint said to Goodnight.

"Right."

Clint rounded up the two men's horses and checked their hooves. Sure enough, the horse that Lanigan had been riding had a half-moon shape cutout in the hoof of his left foreleg.

"Well," Clint said, "we can be pretty sure he killed Michaels. Now let's find out for sure who he works for."

Clint hunkered down next to the injured man, who was just beginning to breathe normally.

"Hurts," the man gasped at the pain in his shoulder from the shattered collarbone.

Clint inspected the wound and saw shards of white bone showing through the skin.

"Looks bad, all right," he said. "You need a doctor."

"Doctor—"

"Nearest one's in Lubbock, I guess."

The man closed his eyes, and for a moment Clint thought he had passed out, but then he opened them again.

"We can get you to the doctor, Lanigan," Clint said, "but there's a price."

"W-what . . . price?"

"The name of the man you work for," Clint said. "The name of the man who sent you to kill Charles Goodnight."

There was a pause, and then the man said, "Can't. . . ."

Clint reached down with his hand and touched the tip of a bone that was protruding. He hardly touched it really, but the pain that it caused must have been considerable. The man gasped, arched his back, and almost passed out.

"The name, Lanigan, and we'll get you to a doctor," Clint said.

Lanigan closed his eyes, and Clint waited. He had either passed out or was trying to decide what to do. Finally, he opened his eyes.

"C-Canby," he said weakly, "F-Fred Canby. N-now . . . doctor. . . ."

"Sure, Lanigan," Clint said, "we'll get you to a doctor."

He stood up and looked at Goodnight.

"Goddamn!" Goodnight said. "Fred Canby?"

"I guess we better get Lanigan into Lubbock, and then we can get the sheriff and have Canby arrested. Then you can ask Canby why."

Goodnight was shaking his head.

"It doesn't much matter why, Clint," he said. "It's enough that he tried to kill me. The why of it really isn't that important."

"Well," Clint said, "with Lanigan still alive, we can prove that it was Canby, so I guess you can stop looking over your shoulder."

"No," Goodnight said sadly. "After this I'll be looking over my shoulder even more, at my men, my neighbors, my friends. . . ."

"Well," Clint said, realizing that he had lived most of his life that way, "it never hurts to be too careful, does it?"

Watch for

GILLETT'S RANGERS

145th novel in the exciting GUNSMITH series
from Jove

Coming in January!

A special offer for people who enjoy reading the best Westerns published today.

WESTERNS!

NO OBLIGATION

Mail the coupon below

To start your subscription and receive 2 FREE WESTERNS, fill out the coupon below and mail it today. We'll send your first shipment which includes 2 FREE BOOKS as soon as we receive it.

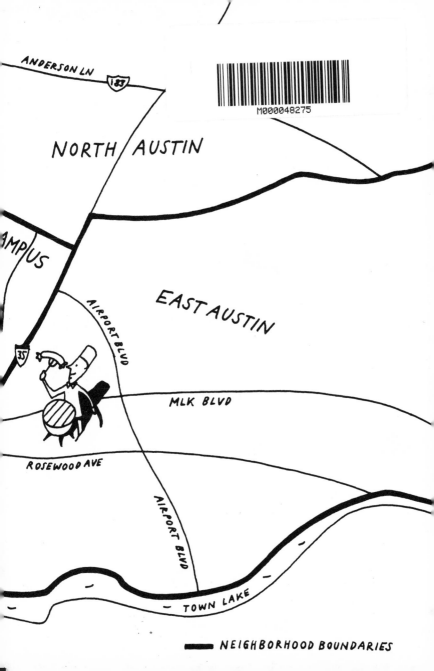

ANDERSON LN

183

NORTH AUSTIN

M000048275

CAMPUS

EAST AUSTIN

AIRPORT BLVD

35

MLK BLVD

ROSEWOOD AVE

AIRPORT BLVD

TOWN LAKE

━━━ NEIGHBORHOOD BOUNDARIES

austin

a u s t i n

by Margaret Moser and
Andy Langer

with maps by Ingo Fast

Longstreet
Atlanta, Georgia

edge guides

Published by Longstreet Press
A subsidiary of Cox Newspapers,
A subsidiary of Cox Enterprises, Inc.
2140 Newmarket Parkway
Suite 122
Marietta, Georgia 30067

Printed in the United States of America
First Printing, 1998

book design by Sue Canavan

A Balliett & Fitzgerald Book
editors: Rachel Aydt, Vijay Balakrishnan, David Downing
production editor: Sue Canavan
copy editor: Meagan Backus
proof reader: Donna Stonecipher
associate editors: Kristen Couse, Aram Song, Mike Walters

ISBN 1-56352-518-6
Library of Congress Number 98-066368

table of contents

introduction   1
plus: pronunciation guide... 2

downtown   6
eating/coffee... 13, bars... 27, music/clubs... 32,
buying stuff... 44, sleeping... 49,
doing stuff... 52, body... 58
plus: bats... 10, your five pre-sets... 21,
kings and queens of clubs... 38

campus/central   60
eating/coffee... 65, bars... 76, music/clubs... 78,
buying stuff... 81, sleeping... 94,
doing stuff... 96, body... 105
plus: why an armadillo?... 78

north   108
eating/coffee... 112, bars/music/clubs... 125,
buying stuff... 128, sleeping... 133,
doing stuff... 135, body... 139
plus: swimmin' nekkid... 137

south 140

**eating/coffee... 144, bars/music/clubs... 159,
buying stuff... 166, sleeping... 175,
doing stuff... 177**
plus: seven musicians you must know... 162,
austin for next to nothing... 180,
south by southwest... 185

east 186

**eating/coffee... 190, bars/music/theater... 195,
buying stuff... 196, sleeping... 198,
doing stuff... 200**
plus: the portable austin... 199

west 202

**eating/coffee... 206, bars... 214,
music/clubs... 215, buying stuff... 216,
sleeping... 223, doing stuff... 224, body... 227**
plus: hometown heroes... 218

off the edge 228

phone numbers 235

austin calendar 237

index 239

introduction

"There's a freedom you begin to feel the closer you get to Austin . . . it's a great place to live."

— Willie Nelson, genuine Texas legend

"Don't Move Here!"

— T-shirt slogan from the Wannabes, a genuine Austin punk/pop band

A living, breathing contradiction? Welcome to Austin.

When you come to this booming burg, one thing you can absolutely count on, even more than being hit up for change on the Drag or getting stuck behind a two-toned '82 Ford pickup on South Lamar, is that you'll quickly meet someone happy to tell you how much better things were before you got here. But take heart: Texans are a friendly lot; we're just a bit perturbed that folks keep moving here who insist on shopping at Whole Foods instead of eating chicken-fried steak. But we're glad to have you. Really.

Of course, none of us are from Austin either. "Austinite" might as well be the name of a rare gemstone found only in this part of Texas, because finding a real one around here is harder than finding a parking spot by 6th Street on a Saturday night. As of April 1995, Austin was the second-fastest growing city in the U.S., and as the capitol of the biggest state in the lower 48, it rightfully claims its share of bragging rights typically associated with the Lone Star State: The University of Texas' Jester Dormitory is so large it has its own zip code and two polling precincts; as home to the film *Slacker*, Austin is the organic heart of Gen X; Dell Computers—begun in a dorm room at the University of

pronunciation guide

Austin-speak has its own peculiarities, and nothing distinguishes a newcomer more than inept pronunciation. It's not hard to tell when you've stepped into linguistic limbo, because your utterances will be frequently followed by bemused looks on the faces of locals, particularily if you come asking for directions to "Hwah-duhloopay" Street. (If you speak Spanish, please disregard proper form and just play along. This is Texas.)

Buda: BYOU-duh
Bowie: BOO-wee
Burnet Road: BURN-it
Conjunto music: cun-HOON-toh
Guadalupe Street: GWA-da-loop
Koenig Lane: KAY-nig
Lake Buchanan: buk-KANN-un
Lavaca Street: la-VAHK-uh
Manchaca Road: MAN-shack
Manor Road: MAY-ner
Mueller Airport: MILLER
New Braunfels: Noo BRAWN-fulls (be prepared to hear "Noo BRAWNS-fuls" also)
Pedernales River: PURD-in-AL-iss
Tejano music: tay-HAH-no

Texas—is one of the world's major players in the high-tech field; the internationally famous music scene is closely followed by a thriving, growing film industry; and in four hours by car you can be in another country. And judging by the amount of construction going on these days—especially on the north and south ends of town—people just keep coming and coming and coming. And who can blame them? Everyone who comes here seems to think they've discovered their own private slice of heaven, until they go to the cool waters of Barton Springs one July afternoon and find out everyone else has, too.

Austin's weather is probably the main reason this town has such a reputation as Slack Capital of the Free World. Most of the time, it's simply too hot to do anything besides crash on the couch in your underwear or go swimming. The rest of the time, it's too gorgeous to even think about anything resembling work. But the sad truth is, keeping pace with the skyrocketing rents often necessitates two or three jobs.

Austinites, especially young ones, also have to work hard to keep their pockets lined with disposable income. Lone Star tallboys and cockroach races get old pretty quick, but there's plenty to do once the paycheck comes in. Austin is most assuredly a nocturnal city—again, mostly because it's so hot during the day—populated by thousands of people who love nothing more than to seek out a nightclub and get their groove (and their drink) on. If they're not partying on 6th Street or being swingers on 4th with martinis, cigars, and Sinatra impersonators, they could be raving at the Red Room or two-stepping at the Broken Spoke. Mostly due to the large population of students

hanging around (except for summer, when internships
and ski trips call them elsewhere), Austin is one of the
major stops on the college/indie circuit, meaning the
Electric Lounge, Emo's, and Liberty Lunch are usually
good for at least a dozen solid roadshows a month. Versus,
Tortoise, Modest Mouse, Girls Against Boys, Curve, and
Los Fabuloso Cadillacs all make their way through town.
And wonder of wonders, Austin has finally discovered hip-
hop in the past couple of years. But despite its continuing
flirtations with up-and-coming genres, Austin's musical
heart belongs to blues and country. Anyone with an interest in musical development knows how closely related the
sounds are at root, and how much they have to do with
rock 'n' roll. That's why Fastball and the Butthole Surfers
are Austin's most popular exports, but Willie Nelson and
Stevie Ray Vaughan are still the gods.

Contrary to what is written in the Slacker Manifesto,
there are other things to do here besides drink and listen
to bands. Austin has a symphony, ballet, lyric opera, art
galleries, and museums, but then it's had lofty aspirations
ever since it was founded in 1839, with an unfortunate
European namesake. The name was changed to Austin
when it became apparent that "Waterloo" maybe wasn't
the best choice in a place where folks still remembered
Napoleon all too well—to say nothing of the Mexican
general Santa Ana, sometimes known as "The Napoleon of
the West" for his attack on the Alamo. (But the old name
lives on in several businesses, including what has to be
one of the finest record stores in the world—Waterloo
Records.) As the population grows, Austin has even come
up with its own honest-to-God pro (if minor league)

sports team, surely one of the few hockey teams in North America that plays its games in an iced-over rodeo arena.

Austin today is much different from the Austin of 25, 15, or even five years ago. As ground zero for a good deal of the current technological revolution (only Silicon Valley employs more cyber heads), the city appears poised to continue its growth spurt well into the millennium. Thanks to the efforts of state government, local business, and the universities (there are four besides U.T.), 60 percent of the city's population makes use of computers and the Net, making this the most computer-literate city in America. Even so, this town is still full of God-fearing folks who listen to both kinds of music (country and western), proudly make a living with their hands, and wouldn't think of eating anything they couldn't smother in cream gravy. But Austin also offers the full range of choices—everything from batter-dipped chicken-fried steak and the ubiquitous *migas* (Mexican scrambled eggs), to haute vegetarian and exotic wild-game cuisine. Everything from hippie to hippy and back again.

So far, Austin has been pretty successful at striking that balance between old and new, lo-fi and high-tech, fiddling and sampling, Bubba and Buffy. Yes, we do have our differences: indie Tamale House vs. Taco Cabana chain; Cosmic Cowboys vs. club kids; Ann Richards vs. George Bush, Jr.; tree-huggers vs. developers; and so on. But what makes it such a great place is that you can actually choose both, which makes living here—or visiting—a breeze. And as cities go—especially for those growing from adolescence into adulthood—it has nothing to prove. Or hide. Welcome to Austin. And quit talking like that.

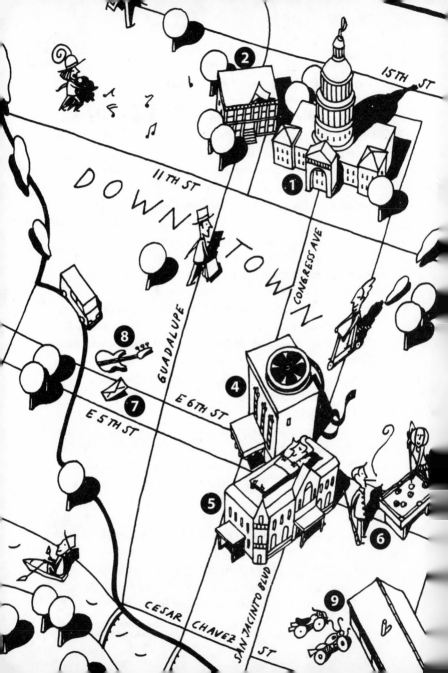

MLK BLVD

③

N

11TH ST

RED RIVER

35

downtown

Recently, Austin's largest advertising firm, GSD&M, moved its headquarters to Downtown and, in celebration of the move, launched a campaign that attempted to give a singular name to both their new building and to Austin itself. "Idea City" is what they came up with. "Idea City," indeed. It's a term too cheesy for most Austinites to use themselves, but the irony is that for the moment, anyway, ideas themselves—too many of them— seem to be Downtown's problem: Every mayor-wannabe seems to have a different idea about what's best for Idea City.

turn page for map key

Throughout the '90s, political wars have been waged among interest groups trying to shove their particular panaceas down the throats of the populace. For every party looking to increase the area's residential options, there are developers equally determined to double Downtown shopping space. For every well-intentioned soul dedicated to building shelter for Austin's burgeoning homeless population, there's a civic-minded opponent who swears that government-sponsored housing will spark the type of urban decay Downtown Austin has so far avoided. Add to these ideas those of musicians and Downtown club owners—who fear that proposed changes in everything from zoning laws to noise ordinance regulations threaten the vitality of Austin's now-legendary club circuit—and GSD&M's "Idea City" becomes a damningly accurate moniker.

"Everyone's got an agenda for Downtown, and nobody's fighting just to maintain the status quo," says one city council insider who believes that today's Downtown will be barely recognizable in five years.

For better or worse, the status quo of Downtown is already overwhelming to many Austinites—it's something of a victim of its own success. Though Downtown itself is a relatively small area—bordered by Martin Luther King Boulevard to the north, the Guadalupe River to the south, I-35 to the east, and Lamar Boulevard to the west—it's the hub of state and local government and the center of

map key		
	1 Texas State Capitol	6 Lovejoy's
	2 Governor's Mansion	7 Post Office
	3 Erwin Center	8 Babe's
	4 Paramount	9 Club Deville
	5 Driskill Hotel	

the city's multimedia, hotel, and restaurant scenes. The majority of the tens of thousands of yearly visitors who come Downtown (it's only an $8 cab ride from the airport) for an event at the Convention Center never leave here, and why should they? After all, Downtown's 50-plus nightclubs (more per capita than Los Angeles, New York, or Chicago) make it internationally famous as the "Live Music Capital of the World." It's also pedestrian-friendly, gay-friendly, and well-policed. (But, should you see mounted police coming to break up a drunken late-night brawl, get far away. The horses will step on you and the officers will mace indiscriminately.)

Equestrian tramplings notwithstanding, another symptom of the cramped conditions is the lack of affordable housing: Those lucky enough to secure one of the 2,000 residential units Downtown pay the highest rents in all of Texas. But even with aggressive plans that call for 1,000 new residences by the millennium, rents—and demand—are expected to stay high. Other problems facing Downtown include how best to accommodate the city's largest congregation of homeless—many of whom use the huge Salvation Army outpost or wait around for day labor opportunities—and what to do with the equally large congregation of automobiles: Parking, like housing, is one of the area's scarcest commodities.

What all this amounts to is that walking remains the best mode of transportation for two reasons: (1) the area is suitably compact and flat, and (2) the mostly one-way streets make driving about as easy as drawing a circle on an Etch-A-Sketch. But for every move the city council considers that would help alleviate traffic congestion—like turning several major Downtown arteries into two-way streets—it simultaneously considers proposals that would only compound the problem (decisiveness not being one of democracy's strong suits). The latest? A proposal to build a huge marketplace at 5th Street and Lamar Boulevard, long considered one of West Austin's worst intersections. But

bats

Drive across the Congress Avenue Bridge before sunset and you'll see full moons lined up from north to south. Actually, it's just the butts of all the tourists waiting to watch America's largest urban bat colony depart on its evening quest for food.

This local phenomenon developed quite by accident. When the Congress Avenue Bridge was widened from two to four lanes in 1980, its redesigned underbelly became home to Mexican freetail bats (*Tadarida Brasiliensis*) who had previously lived around the Capitol dome and other high-flyin' Downtown and University area roosts. Their presence wasn't readily apparent until the mid-'80s, when the colony seemed to have grown up overnight.

Today numbering well over a million, the bats roost under the downtown bridges from roughly March through November. Their nightly treks attract hundreds to this bridge as well as lakeside bars and restaurants for good reason: It's fascinating to watch. Sometime around sunset, the bats awaken and set out on their evening quest for dinner—the remember—this is Idea City. A more ambitious plan to fill Waller Creek (named after the guy whose big idea it was to make all those one-way streets) and create a shopping district upon its banks could actually decrease traffic by making it possible to walk from the University of Texas straight to Downtown. If the plan sounds suspiciously like

many insects and crop-threatening pests that populate Austin and the Hill Country. A single night's outing might net up to 30,000 pounds of food for the decidedly non-vampire bats, whose numbers peak in August and September.

Besides the bridge, there's an observation area on the southeast shore of Town Lake, just below the bridge. The metal sculpture of a large purple bat plunked in the traffic island where Barton Springs Road meets Congress Avenue gives you a clue you're at the right spot (there is also another observation area on the north banks of Town Lake at the Four Seasons Hotel). It's a grand view of the awe-inspiring scene, but if the wind is blowing toward you, so is the acrid smell of bat piss and guano. The bats darken the sky before sunset, ascending in groups of tens of thousands and forming undulating ribbons that stretch for miles. Bat Conservation International watches over the critters, and if you call their Bat Hotline (512/416–5700), you can get an estimate of what time they'll be taking off that night. Little carts at the end of the bridge sell lots of overpriced tourist-trap novelties: bat videos, bat T-shirts, rubber bats .... It'll make you batty.

San Antonio's River Walk, it's because it is—only with an earth-friendly twist. Whereas the River Walk is essentially along a cement pond, Austin's plan would maintain the creek's natural bottom. Score another one for environmentalists—and natural-bottom-lovers—everywhere.

Although some are counting on Waller Creek to revitalize Downtown by day, the area doesn't have any trouble attracting nighttime crowds: Downtown's 6th Street and the Warehouse District are Austin's two primary points of nightlife. The stretch of establishments along 6th Street has become the hub of Downtown nightlife since Clifford Antone opened his blues club (Antone's) in 1973, inviting dozens of imitators/competitors to the strip.

With more than 75 music venues, clubs, and restaurants on the street, 6th has its share of soulless karaoke nights, frat-boy-on-a-bender dives, and cheesy piano bars. Fat Tuesday's and Tropical Isle are the worst offenders of the bunch, as are a headache of a joint called "Bob Popular" and a couple of faux New Orleans Bourbon Street watering holes. Watch out, too, for some of the cigar-and-martini bars in what's being called the "adult" (no, not that kind of adult) 6th Street—the Warehouse District—as they can be just as cloying. (Technically, the Warehouse District falls between 4th and 6th, and Lavaca and Congress.) That said, the plentiful live music is worth fighting the crowds for, and for every loser of a bar there seems to be a cool alternative lounge—like Lovejoy's or Casino El Camino—nearby. This is one of the pluses of having so much nightlife crammed into one small area—you're never too far from a better option. And never far from food, either, as Downtown sports dozens of restaurants with diverse menus and fair prices.

No matter how much Downtown changes, it's hard to imagine that grabbing a bite and ducking into a live-music venue will cease to be part of Austin's routine nightlife. Then again, even people with aversions to bars or music do well Downtown, by visiting The Paramount, a '20s-era movie house that shows classics, or the State Theater Company for smart drama. In fact, it's so easy to fill a night in Downtown Austin that it's easy to forget the politics and not worry much about whether the bar or poolhall you just hung in will survive the post-millennium restructuring. Guilt-free, Downtown fun: There's a real idea.

eating/coffee

If New York's most celebrated professional hybrid is the actor/waiter, then Austin's best-known resident is the musician/waiter. Locals contend that the quickest way to secure better service is to casually inquire about your waitperson's band. (And if you look like you're from New York or Los Angeles, they might even slip a demo tape into your doggie bag.) Most of the 150 or so Downtown eateries are regular, rather unspectacular joints—good ol' fashioned hamburgers and Mexican food dominate the scene. But it's the half dozen or so upscale restaurants catering predominantly to businesspeople and conventioneers (and their expense accounts) that get the most attention. Most Downtown diners during the day and early evening are filled with workers and students looking for cheap lunches and inexpensive dinners; they easily find what they're looking for.

Cost Range per entree
$/under 10 dollars
$$/10–15 dollars
$$$/15–20 dollars
$$$$/20+ dollars

bagels... Unless you count the bagels Fed-Exed in from New York by homesick transplants, there are no great bagels in Austin. Instead, there are good rolls that pass as decent bagels, which is what you'll have to settle for at **Hot Jumbo Bagel** (307 W. 5th St. 512/477–1137 $), the best, and longest-running, Downtown bagelry. For what it's worth, Hot Jumbo lives up to its name, in that they still appear to care more about making fresh bagels than fancy designer cream cheeses. And for a dimly lit joint that used to have the nerve to post two prices (one to go and a slightly higher one to dine in), Hot Jumbo has nonetheless managed to amass a loyal following. So much so that it survived Austin's Bagel Invasion when the Brugger's chain actually had the chutzpah to move in next door. Brugger's has since retreated, and Hot Jumbo once again has the lock on the bagel, so to speak.

barbecue... Although you might expect an abundance of barbecue joints catering to the Convention Center crowd's curiosity for authentic Texas cuisine, there are only three Downtown hot spots—all dependable, none spectacular. In this crop, **Stubb's Bar-B-Q** (801 Red River St. 512/480–8341 $) is the obvious standout, not so much for their meat as for their sauce: It's become so popular that it's now bottled and sold in groceries nationwide. (Texas-grown tomatoes and spices make other brands seem like watery ketchup.) The restaurant is a tribute to C.B. Stubblefield, a West Texas legend whose place in the original Lubbock location became famous for offering Joe Ely, Stevie Ray Vaughan, Muddy Waters, and Willie Nelson the chance to play for supper. Although this spot, in a converted '30s-era house, opened only in 1995, it has proved itself one of the city's best live-music venues [see **music/clubs**], and struck Sunday morning gold with a fantastic gospel brunch. Plus, they still offer Twinkies and Ding Dongs for dessert.

The Iron Works (*100 Red River St. 512/478–4855 $*) doesn't sell its sauce in stores, but they'll ship food anywhere in the world (which is good to know if you ever need an authentic brisket plate in Brunei). The building itself is a historic monument and the enclosed patio is an okay enough spot for dinner, but the oh-so-Western motif and the fact that it's connected to the Convention Center make it feel a bit too touristy. In contrast, it takes a more adventurous tourist to gamble on **The Pit** (*501 E. 5th St. 512/478–1166 $*). It's generally pretty dingy inside and out, but the barbecue, freshly smoked outside, is a consistently good bet.

chinese... Although locals like to rave about the selection of vegetarian dishes at **China on the Avenue** (*908 Congress Ave. 512/474–0137 $–$$*), the best Chinese restaurant Downtown (maybe in all Austin) is **Pao's Mandarin House** (*800 Brazos St. 512/482–8100 $–$$*). It's hidden in a nondescript office building two blocks off 6th Street, where the lower rent allows for a huge dining room to accommodate its brisk business-lunch crowd. Usually there's no wait at night, the service is attentive, and the typically Mandarin dishes are generously portioned and moderately priced. The scallion pancakes melt in your mouth.

coffee... Surprisingly for a college town, finding a good cup of coffee in Downtown Austin is difficult. The real estate pinch has inflated the cost of Downtown retail space, so mom 'n' pop coffee shops would have to sell a ton of coffee just to cover the rent. **Starbucks** (600 Congress Ave. 512/499–0250 $), with its volume buying and fairly expensive lattes, seems to have no trouble setting up shop on pricey real estate, so their presence at Congress Avenue's busiest corner (6th) shouldn't come as a surprise. Nor should it come as a surprise that flaky city planners keep rejecting plans for **Little City** (916 Congress Ave. 512/476–2489 $) to expand its two window seats into a full-on sidewalk cafe. And it's too bad, because although all the funky art-deco trappings and drop-clothed chairs inside make it a bit claustrophobic, it's a great spot for people-watching.

    Ruta Maya (218 W. 4th St. 512/472–9637 $), on the other hand, is a fully politicized coffee experience worthy of a National Public Radio feature: It serves 100 percent Arabica coffee beans grown by cooperative farmers in the highlands of Chiapas, Mexico. The farmers, in turn, receive a portion of the profits, which also fund educational studies of the Maya and the printing of local-language educational books for Guatemalan use. None of this would make you feel so warm and fuzzy inside if the coffee sucked, but it doesn't. In fact, their medium, dark, and espresso beans are roasted and packed daily, making Ruta

Maya Austin's standard for both in-house drinking and take-home beans. People also swear by both their Cuban sandwiches and hand-rolled Cuban-seeded cigars (found in their adjoining smokeshop). The international bent continues with nightly world-music performers, whom you can enjoy as you sip your Ruta Maya Negra Lager Beer imported from, yes, El Salvador. Ruta Maya is perhaps the friendliest and least pretentious spot in the entire Warehouse District. Incidentally, if you're on 6th Street and not in the Warehouse District but still need a cup of coffee at night, try **Lovejoy's** *(604 Neches St. 512/477–1268)*. See the bar section for why they're a great bar, but know that they also happen to serve the best coffee sold in a bar in town.

Jake's Coffee *(827 W. 12th St. 512/499–8828 $)* may specialize in organic coffee and fruit smoothies, but it feels like a real bar anyway. A cast of regulars lines up at the counter for political conversations and a collective read-through of the newspaper each weekday morning. And because it's housed inside a popular used bookstore (12th Street Books), is close to the courthouse, and is directly across from Austin Community College, it attracts a mixed bag of professors, students, lawyers, defendants, musicians, and government retirees.

french... The folks at **Chez Nous** *(510 Neches St. 512/473–2413 $$–$$$)* are half right when they call them-selves "one of Austin's best-kept secrets." The building is no secret—it's a half block away from the heart of 6th Street and nearly impossible to miss. But the tiny French bistro's lace curtains create a kind of mystery and intimacy that drives Chez Nous' ultra-loyal following. In fact, the whole affair is low-key, from the decor (where a crude Montmartre mural shares space with flower-filled aperitif bottles) to the prices ($17.50 for the three-course dinner). While Chez Nous remains the Downtown restaurant of choice for French expatriates (the "French Embassy," as some call it), **Jean-Luc's French Bistro** (*708 Colorado St. 512/494–0033 $$–$$$*), with a menu similar to that of Chez Nous and a slightly more affordable wine list, has quickly achieved the culinary buzz Chez Nous has spent 16 years without. Both restaurants offer friendly service that flies in the face of stereotype, but politicized Austinites say that Jean-Luc's commitment to natural chicken, hormone-free beef, and organic field greens (all from Central Texas) gives the newer bistro a slight edge.

hamburgers...
Both **Babe's** (*208 E. 6th St. 512/473–2262 $*) and **Casino El Camino** (*517 E. 6th St. 512/469–9330 $*) make great hamburgers [see **music/clubs** and **bars** respectively], but locals generally give the nod to **Hut's Hamburgers** (*807 W. 6th St. 512/472–0693 $*), which has been in business since 1939 and in the same building since 1969. Not only do they have over 20 burger variations, from the Ritchie Valens to the Theta Special, but not one of them is over $5. The dining room, which still sports some original splotches of '50s-era wallpaper near the door, is full of Austin-oriented memorabilia that would make the Austin Convention and Visitor's Bureau jealous.

healthy...
If **Mars** (*1610 San Antonio St. 512/472–3901 $$–$$$*) isn't one of the best Downtown restaurants, as

many claim, it's certainly the most unique. Within a converted house near both Campus and the Capitol, Mars serves a combination of Asian, Indian, French, and Mediterranean food. Surprisingly, they do each as well as any specialty restaurant in town. The hummus and baba ganoush are popular, and the hottest dish on the menu is a spicy Thai-style stir-fry offered both vegan-style or with chicken, shrimp, or steak. They'll also mix 'n' match just about anything to your liking, which pleases both locals and visiting celebs (no less a star than Drew Barrymore ate here every night of a recent three-month movie shoot). The split-level deck is a smoker's paradise, with heaters in the winter and one of the town's few misting fans in summer.

The HighLife Cafe (407 E. 7th St. 512/474–5338 $) isn't quite as upscale, but for the 6th Street area, it's just as unique. In a storefront surrounded by dance clubs, they've achieved a nice homey feel with several small dining rooms, both smoking and nonsmoking. Vegetarians come here for the salads and hummus, but the all-day breakfast is even better, with excellent French-press coffees, espresso, machine-steamed eggs, and hearty wheat waffles.

italian... One's lively, the other's romantic, but both **Mezzaluna** (310 Colorado St. 512/472–6770 $$–$$$) and **Carmelo's** (504 E. 5th St. 512/477–7497 $$–$$$) are among the best upscale Italian restaurants Downtown. Mezzaluna, in the heart of the Warehouse District, specializes in Northern Italian. Like the Brick Oven, another popular Downtown spot for Italian, the dining room is built around a brick oven that turns out fresh breads and designer pizzas, and a large concrete bar that jumps with crowds. As good as the food is, Mezzaluna is still as much a scene as a restaurant. It's best early in the evening for wine, appetizers, and finding a date for the rest of the evening. On the other hand, Carmelo's is a better bet if you've got a date to impress. In a restored 19th-century hotel, Carmelo's specializes in Sicilian fare in a setting straight out of a bad Mafia flick. Yet, despite a run of recent expansions, it remains intimate and romantic. The service is excellent and there's hardly a better place near 6th Street to kick off a date, business meeting, or family reunion. This has become such a traditional spot for students to have dinner with their parents that reservations are highly recommended for any weekend with a U.T. football game, visitor's day, or graduation.

japanese... Downtown you have one choice: **Kyoto** (315 *Congress Ave., Ste.* 200, 512/482–9010 $$–$$$). You know the drill—shoes off, credit card out, sushi in. Even so, it's consistent; you can't go too wrong with the combination plates of shrimp and vegetable tempura, chicken teriyaki or charbroiled salmon, beef, or seafood kushi on rice, or a sushi combo. Call ahead, not just for a seat, but because some items have three-hour preparation times.

late night... **Katz's Deli & Bar** (618 *W. 6th St.* 512/472–2037 $–$$) isn't bad, but it's not quite the New York deli they like to pretend it is either. So while they can take credit for introducing the blintz, knish, and matzoh ball to the Austin marketplace, it's like McDonald's introducing the hamburger to Russia: If it's all you know, it's good enough, comrade. In fact, nobody in town offers a

your five pre-sets

1. **KGSR (107.1 FM)**—Of all of Austin's commercial stations, KGSR sports the most eclectic and challenging playlist. They not only go from Sheryl Crow to Tom Waits and back to the Beatles in an average set, but are also the most Austin-centric of the local stations, feverishly playing Alejandro Escovedo, Lucinda Williams, Kacy Crowley, Joe Ely, and Kelly Willis.

2. **KUT (90.5 FM)**—U.T. owns and operates KUT, but this ain't no college radio station. There is no playlist, and diehard life-long music fans like it that way. And although its NPR programming takes up a good chunk of the day, its evenings and overnights are long-running deejay-driven free-form programs covering jazz, blues, alt rock, R&B, and country.

3. **KLBJ AM (590 AM)**—This AM talk outlet faithfully carries Dr. Laura, Rush, and Bruce Williams. But it also has the city's best local news team, who generally break stories faster and more accurately than their better-paid television counterparts.

4. **KAMX, a.k.a. The MIX (94.7 FM)**—If you hit town and couldn't care less about local music, the MIX is the place for you. They've got all the hitmakers packaged in a small playlist that virtually guarantees you can get in the car and hear your favorite Dave Matthews, Jewel, or Alanis Morissette tunes.

5. **KASE (100.7 FM)**—If you're in Texas and want to do as the Texans do, tune into KASE's paint-by-numbers country music. The ratings are huge, as are the laughs on their down-home morning drive show *The Sam & Bob Show*.

broader selection of equally bland food at higher prices. But sometimes you have to pay for convenience, because as they say, "Katz's Never Kloses." Plus, it's just a few blocks down 6th Street, and beyond the Warehouse District, which means it's the area's default post-party eatery. It also means there are long waits after 2 a.m., which somehow never seems to be a problem at the **International House of Pancakes** (*707 E. Cesar Chavez Blvd. 512/478–1188 $*), also 24–7, south on Red River and across from the Convention Center. While Katz's is constantly trying to turn over tables, the service at IHOP is slow. But if you're out past 2 a.m., what's your hurry—it's not like you're headed out to work at the crack of dawn.

Early in the evening, those trying to rush to a show, put a little something in their stomachs to drink on, or catch a bite before heading home often have just two 6th Street options—vendor carts or pizza by the slice. The former, parked up and down the street, serve lukewarm hot dogs and fajitas—hardly worth a repeat performance. And although the 6th Street pizza joints seem like disguised cardboard outlets, the best of the lot is **Hoak's** (*320 E. 6th St. no phone $*), a small storefront stand next to the Ritz. The crust is a bit thin and bubbly, but they're generous with the toppings and offer more pie combinations than Austin has unemployed guitarists.

mexican... Most tourists hover like bees around their hotel hives and the Convention Center during their stay, which is why so many visitors buzz off thinking all Austin has is a slew of Mexican restaurants and some trained bats [see **bats sidebar**]. Truth be told, there *are* more than two dozen restaurants in Downtown that serve some sort of Mexican entree, so it's more than possible to start each day of your visit with *migas* and end with a late-night enchilada (though your gastroenterologist might not agree). For breakfast tacos, **BB's** *(616 Nueces St. 512/472–8646 $)*, a small cafe hidden at 7th and Nueces streets, is the place for your morning fix. Not only do they offer dozens of generous breakfast taco combinations, but the tortillas and the guacamole rank among the freshest in town. They serve lunch too, but close at 4 p.m. (which is why MTV's short-lived "Austin Stories" series frequently shot in this otherwise undistinguished shop).

If you long for *migas*, try **Las Manitas** *(211 Congress Ave. 512/472–9357 $)*, the rare restaurant that's become famous yet managed to keep its character. You'll wait in line, but you'll also do some quality people-watching: Folks like *Lonesome Dove* author Larry McMurtry, Ann Richards, Shawn Colvin, Joe Ely, and Lisa Loeb slum here often. The beat-up lunch counter, mismatched tables, and postered walls are funky, but the kitchen's clean (which you know because you walk through it to get to the covered patio).

Manuel's *(310 Congress Ave. 512/472–7555 $$)*, a slick leather-laden pad that's only half as expensive as it looks, has a Sunday brunch with live music and stellar eggs and chorizo that rivals Las Manitas'. But lunch and the happy hour are the real drawing cards. At night, the stylish lighting and house specialties like blue crab nachos, grilled (not fried) flautas, and chile rellenos smothered in cream sauce (rather than cheese) are creative departures from the run-of-the-mill-Mexican food experience.

Creativity is one thing, but longevity is another. Perhaps

because it's been serving Mexican fare in the same brick shack for more than 60 years, **Jaime's Spanish Village** (*802 Red River St. 512/476–5149 $*) is nothing short of an institution. That said, Jaime's (pronounced HY-mees) is basic, cheap Tex-Mex—no more, no less. And while it still serves as a middle ground between the government and campus contingencies, lately it's become popular as a margarita pit stop for folks headed to or from Stubb's [see **barbecue** above] across the street. In fact, the frozen margarita (topped with a blood-red splash of sangria) draws people from **Serrano's Symphony Square** (*1111 Red River St. 512/322–9922 $–$$*), the popular restaurant in a limestone-lined arts complex and amphitheater just down Red River. It's not unusual to see people eat at Serrano's (more basic Tex-Mex), pass on the post-dinner drinks, and then duck into Jaime's before they hit 6th Street proper.

Closer to the Warehouse District, there's **Miguel's La Bodega** (*415 Colorado St. 512/472–2369 $–$$*) and **Calle Ocho** (*706 Congress Ave. 512/474–6605 $*) which have two things in common—average food and great dancing. The former leans a bit more toward the upscale, although neither menu is anything exceptional. The latter has a small luncheonette downstairs and a big dance floor upstairs, where free salsa and merengue lessons are offered on Thursdays and Fridays. Miguel's charges $5 each for similar classes Wednesday through Saturday, most enticingly "Merengue Madness" and "Sexxy Salsa with Barbara." The restaurant's club side has earned a reputation for hosting the city's best salsa bands—thereby inviting a legalized form of bump 'n' grind. Unfortunately, it's become something of a late-night carne market.

seafood... The name might imply TV dinners or cocktails served in coconuts, but **Gilligan's (407 Colorado St. 512/474–7474 $$)** is a popular spot for sophisticated Caribbean cooking. Many credit (blame) its 1992 arrival for the beginning of the Warehouse District's boom in upscale eateries. Good word-of-mouth among locals has made both the Atlantic salmon and tuna fettuccine big hits. The building itself is the topic of much discourse as well: a 100-year-old warehouse that's had former lives as an auto garage, refrigerator repair shop, and office of the Department of Welfare. The "tropical warehouse," as it's now called by locals, is also oddly quiet for a Downtown spot that does this much business.

It may be a coincidence, but about the same time Gilligan's opened its doors, **City Grill (401 Sabine St. 512/479–0817 $$–$$$)**, another seafood restaurant in a converted warehouse, launched an aggressive coupon campaign that continues today. Almost every weekly newspaper or hotel concierge has the popular two-for-one coupons, so if you're paying full price at City Grill, you're paying too much. Even so, the trout and shrimp come in generous portions and are well-prepared, and the large dining room and deck are undeniably classy.

"Classy" ain't the word most Austinites would use to describe **The Boiling Pot (700 E. 6th St. 512/472–0985 $–$$)**; "inexpensive" or "family" would be more accurate. Rather than the linens you'll find at Gilligan's and City Grill, The Boiling Pot simply offers butcher paper and bibs. You'll need them for the Cajun Combo, an option that combines blue crab and a half pound each of shrimp and sausage with new potatoes and corn; it feeds two, and is a bargain at $13.95. Get a cup of their chunky gumbo just to make sure. If you want some atmosphere with your gumbo, head down 6th Street to the recently expanded **Jazz** (214 E. 6th St. 512/479–0474 $–$$). It's a Cajun/Creole mainstay that's big on pastas, crawfish, catfish, blackened filet mignon—and live jazz. It's the only Bourbon Street theme joint on 6th Street where the concept doesn't feel forced.

stir-fry... Don't let the name mislead you: **Mongolian BBQ** (117 San Jacinto Blvd. 512/476–3938 $–$$) is straight and simple stir-fry. You choose your meat, vegetable, and sauce from a huge buffet line and they fry it. It's right next to the Convention Center and is clearly the informal answer to Benihana: cheap, easy, and the best lunch or ultra-casual dinner in the Downtown area.

truly upscale... There are a host of restaurants in Downtown, but only a handful qualify as upscale. Of those, both the culinary elite and the upscale scenesters tend to declare **Sullivan's** (300 Colorado St. 512/495–6504 $$$–$$$$) the best. At this relatively new, simply decorated spot, customers don't seem to mind paying big prices for big steaks. And at 20 ounces, the house specialty Kansas City strip ($24.95) is a good deal. Unfortunately, everything else is à la carte, so you can tack on at least another $10 for salad and potato. Many opt to skip dinner and take their chances in the large bar up front, where singles on the prowl simply lie and say they're waiting for a table.

Louie's 106 (106 E. 6th St. 512/476–2010 $$–$$$) also has a popular bar and cigar room, but despite its traditionally upscale crowd, "casually elegant" dress code, and wood-paneled interior, it's not nearly as expensive as you'd think. The tapas are a cheap fill and the char-grilled salmon filet will set you back only $8.95. Also check out Louie's terrific collection of more than 300 wines.

Primarily because it's close to The Four Seasons, has a private party room, and attracts a business-lunch crowd, **The Shoreline Grill** *(98 San Jacinto Blvd.* 512/477–3300 **$$–$$$)** has become one of the more dependable but boring upscale eateries Downtown. Simply put, it's a corporate-feeling spot that caters to businesspeople and unadventurous visitors. The seafood and steak options are reliable, but not as good as Sullivan's. Shoreline's is recommended only between late spring and early fall, when patio seating overlooking Town Lake and the Congress Avenue Bridge offers the best bat-watching in town.

bars

The only part of Downtown life that may be harder to track than the live-music scene is the bar scene. At any time there are well over 50 Downtown bars to choose from. Nowhere do bars come and go more quickly than along 6th Street. The rapid growth of the Warehouse District has also created its own share of overnight sensations and quick flops. Broadly speaking, 6th Street bars are popular with college students and musicians, while the Warehouse District has thrived by catering to upscale crowds looking to get away from said college students and musicians. Downtown also serves as the social center of the local gay community, although it's almost devoid of lesbian bars. Other than that, there's a drink for virtually everyone.

Scholz Garten (*1607 San Jacinto Blvd. 512/474–1958*), established in 1866, is the oldest operating restaurant-bar-*biergarten* in Texas. It has seen every kind of political and campus activity imaginable because it's so close to both the Capitol and U.T. Unfortunately, with all the Downtown competition, it's not as vital as it once was, except on fall Saturdays when U.T. has a home football game. Scholz's is still ground zero for Longhorn football celebrations, so alumni/alumnae may rest assured that this is still the best place in town to not-so-randomly run into old classmates.

For '90s U.T. students and a lot of the music scene, **The Dog & Duck Pub** (*406 W. 17th St. 512/479–0598*) has become one of the better near-campus-but-not-6th-Street hangouts. It's accessible, without the parking headaches and attitude that 6th Street can have. There is an active pool and dart room as well as a collection of comfortable pub couches. Imported brews are the specialty here, particularly those from England and Ireland. They complement British pub food such as shepherd's pie and bangers and mash. The Dog & Duck is also the site of a giant can't-miss St. Patrick's Day party.

Waterloo Brewing Company (*401 Guadalupe St. 512/477–1836*) calls itself "Texas' Oldest Brewpub," but real Austinites know that's a dubious superlative, since brew-pubs were only legalized by the state in 1993. Nonetheless, Waterloo was the first to cash in and has also become the city's most consistently popular brewer. Despite three floors of food, pool, and darts, Waterloo has always felt like an oversized neighborhood bar. Unlike most bars in the Warehouse District, it's rarely too crowded. Waterloo's has become famous for its seasonal brews, from the cleverly named Stout By Stoutwest to Sam Houston's Austin Lager.

Across the street at **The Bitter End** (*311 Colorado St. 512/478–2337*), the idea for an upscale version of Waterloo has been usurped by a focus on food (as opposed to beer). The bar is always busy, but mostly as a waiting area for a table. None of this is to say that the Bitter End's five regular taps and selection of rotating specialties aren't worthwhile. In fact, many claim EZ Wheat is the best light beer in town.

Across town, and just off 6th Street, lies another popular brewpub, **The Copper Tank** (*504 Trinity St. 512/478–8444*). It's hardly worth fighting off the amateurs for, although these particular amateurs have an excuse—they've just turned 21. Yep, The Copper Tank is part sports bar, part frat house. You can forget about bellying up to the bar on a weekend night, although early weekdays aren't too crowded to grab a Big Dog Brown Ale, a nice chocolatey English-style ale. But there's something suspicious about their Raspberry Ale—a concoction one recent beer poll called a cross between Dimetapp and Kool-Aid.

If local brews aren't your thing, chances are that **The Gingerman** (*304 W. 4th St. 512/473–8801*) carries whatever is. They have over 80 beers on tap, so if you're homesick, this might be the best place to find your hometown hero.

The Austin branch of **Fadó Irish Pub** (*214 W. 4th St. 512/457–0172*), on the other hand, is either everything that's wrong with the Warehouse District or a sign of everything it could hope to be. A small army of owners reportedly spent millions constructing an "authentic" Irish pub, importing all the interior wood, bars, and furniture direct from the motherland. Not only do they have all the Guinness you can drink, but they also have imported farmstead cheeses and a staff with actual Irish accents. Admittedly, the place has enough nooks and crannies to hang out in comfortably, but it's somehow all so Disney (which shouldn't be surprising, since Fadó is, for all its posturing, a chain). This is Texas, not Ireland, and when you're there sober for more than two minutes, that begins to look obvious.

The Speakeasy (412 *Congress Ave.* 512/476–8017) may be the club most responsible for pushing the Warehouse District fully upscale. With dark hardwood floors, brick walls, and a snazzy people-watching mezzanine, the club has a faux 1920s Prohibition-era look. But like Fadó, it's attempting something that's tough to replicate in Texas, so the whole affair comes off as one of those insidiously trendy Los Angeles lounges. To that end, it features an alley-only entrance, velvet ropes, and doormen with Secret Service-style ear pieces. And lo and behold, there's even an in-house Hollywood celebrity director, Robert Rodriguez. He co-owns a private film editing/screening room upstairs that brings the occasional director, actor, or actress downstairs. But even celebrity-stalkers don't deserve having to endure a joint this smug.

Lucky Lounge (209-*A W. 5th St.* 512/479–7700) hasn't been open long, but it's already been adopted by the Speakeasy elite who are bored and looking for something new. But there's hope for Lucky's after the upscale crowd moves on to the next-big-thing. It's a simple, nondescript spot with not much more than a bar, some chairs, a few couches, a small upstairs, and a surprisingly classy collection of rubber-lined walls. In fact, it will probably adapt best to the neighboring Antone's crowd, or to any number of scenesters who are loyal to Matt Lucky, one of the bar's co-owners and the city's only bona fide celebrity bartender. For some reason, Lucky has acted as a magnet—making all the bars he's worked at the happening scene.

Lucky actually used to be the only charming thing about **The Iron Cactus** *(606 Trinity St. 512/472–9240)*, a giant three-level monstrosity on the corner of 6th and Trinity streets. It has high ceilings and a dependable southwestern kitchen, but it's also brimming with party-hearty college kids and muscle-bound thugs with bad pick-up lines. The only reason to stop in is that the deck has a spectacular view of Downtown. If people try to steer you to the deck at **Maggie Mae's** *(325 E. 6th St. 512/478–8541)*, it's a good sign they don't get out much. The deck does have a good view, but the bar itself is a cover-band wasteland. Every college town has one of these holes: It's perennially crowded, but mostly because it's where the weekend warriors go.

Let's just say **Lovejoy's** *(604 Neches St. 512/477–1268)* is everything Maggie's isn't. Not only is it one of the last bastions of hipness on 6th Street, but it was also one of the first bars in town to draw the live-music crowd without actually providing live music. What they do provide are $2 pint specials, 20 different drafts, 120 brands of bottled beers, and a staff that knows about each and every one of 'em. But the real appeal for the rock 'n' roll set is that Lovejoy's is the bar equivalent of alternative rock, with comfortable couches, mix 'n' match tables, pool tables, and rotating original art displays. Long before Timothy Leary and Ministry frontman Al Jourgenson shared a beer here, Lovejoy's called itself the "the leader of the new, new revolution." It's 6th Street's only real can't-miss.

The folks that run **Casino El Camino** (517 E. 6th St. 512/469–9330) spent so much time hanging at Lovejoy's that they decided to build their own tribute to it right up 6th Street. It doesn't quite have the same ineffable coolness, but its popular "Brutal B-Movie" showcase of slasher flicks challenges patrons to keep down what many consider to be Austin's best hamburgers. Plus, it may well have the best jukebox in town, with everything from Tom Waits to local heroes like the Butthole Surfers.

The extra-large outdoor patio at **Club Deville** (900 Red River St. 512/457–0900) doesn't need a jukebox, because the laxative jazz from its obnoxious neighbor, the Caucus Club, often oozes in over the rock walls. But despite the Muzak, it's made quick headway toward becoming a classic Austin bar. The design is simple: a small indoor lodge area resembling a ski resort, plus two patios filled with thrift-store lawn accessories. From there, it's anybody and anything goes. No Downtown bar draws a more diverse bunch—think of the bar scene in Star Wars—but nobody feels uncomfortable, and everyone gets treated well.

music/clubs

Every piece of city letterhead officially declares Austin "The Live Music Capital of the World," and Downtown is undeniably ground zero. On 6th Street, Red River, and within the Warehouse District, there are so many nightclubs that feature live music nightly that many establishments actually cater to clubgoers trying to get the hell away from live music. But even in those rooms, the jukebox is more than likely to kick out tunes by folks playing live down the street, be it Don Walser, the Derailers, Storyville, or Jimmie Vaughan. In truth, Austinites are spoiled by their live-music scene. Folks like Jimmie Dale Gilmore, Joe Ely, and Alejandro Escovedo may be popular touring attractions elsewhere, but here they routinely play modestly sized Downtown venues like La Zona Rosa, Antone's, or Stubb's. (The exception is Shawn Colvin, whose infrequent local performances make her more of an Austin homeowner than an Austin musician.) In fact, until just three weeks before Fastball's "The Way" shot up the national radio charts in 1998, the band was playing for as few as 50 people on a Wednesday at the Electric Lounge. It wasn't that people didn't like Fastball, it's just that there are so many choices. Competition means cover charges are reasonable and the big names often look for an edge by playing on off-nights.

Because so many touring musicians like to spend their downtime in Austin checking out the music scene, the city sees more roadshows than similarly sized markets. Downtown plays host to the city's four largest venues for touring acts: the Austin Music Hall, Liberty Lunch, Stubb's, and La Zona Rosa. While those venues play significant roles in South by Southwest (SXSW), the annual music conference that brings thousands of industry professionals to Austin for nearly a thousand showcases, the conference also highlights just how many other stages Austin has and how easy it is to jump among dozens of Downtown clubs in a night. Add to the equation the growing popularity of happy-hour gigs and early shows, and it's not hard to see three or four artists a night at as many clubs, SXSW or not. They don't call it The Live Music Capital of the World for nothing.

If you visit only one Downtown club, make it **Antone's (213 W. 5th St. 512/474—5314)**. As advertised, it's "The Home of the Blues." Since 1973, Clifford Antone has been a blues missionary, bringing legends like Muddy Waters and Albert Collins to Austin and providing a stage for local legends like the Fabulous Thunderbirds and the late Stevie Ray Vaughan. You'll find purists who gripe that the club lost its gritty soul when it moved back Downtown in 1997, but frankly, they're wrong: Antone's has actually moved twice before, from its original 6th Street location to North Austin, followed by a 15-year run on Guadalupe Street. Each successive location has proven that the soul of Antone's lies in the owner's grasp of the blues and the booking legacy he and his sister Susan share, not in the rooms themselves. But the current incarnation is their most user-friendly location yet—it's the biggest of all of their previous rooms (1,200 capacity), there's not a bad view of the stage anywhere, and the bars are long and easily accessible. Best of all, the musicians themselves have stayed loyal to the club, which means folks like Jimmie Vaughan, Ian Moore, and Charlie Sexton are just as likely to pop in on the Monday night blues jam as they ever were.

Unfortunately, few of Antone's neighbors in the Warehouse District are anything to write home about. **Ruta Maya (218 W. 4th St. 512/474—9637)**, with its coffee and showcasing of singer/songwriters, is generally credited with bringing nightlife and commerce to the area, but **The Cedar Street Courtyard (208 W. 4th St. 512/495—9669)**, a mediocre jazz club, deserves the blame for first turning the area into a playground for the cigar-and-martini set. The narrow indoor bars that surround the courtyard itself are very stylish, but the atmosphere is too uptight for comfortable lounging. For what's mostly an outdoor venue, it's horribly stuffy: If Antone's is the Home of the Blues, this is the Home of the Three-Piece Suit and Implants. But none of it's nearly as irritating as the jazz itself, geared on weekends towards Fuzak fans who prefer Kenny G. to Coltrane. Luckily, weekdays are a bit better, although local jazz heavyweights like Martin Banks and Elias Haslanger seem to prefer playing ringside at **Sullivan's (300 Colorado St. 512/474–1870)**, another upscale jazz venue, this one attached to a steakhouse. It's smaller and quieter, but the marble floors, wood paneling, and above-bar stage make it a better showcase room than hangout. Plus, it's about the only venue in town where you'll feel stupid in jeans and a T-shirt, which may say as much about local jazz fans as it does about the neighborhood itself. And despite both being excellent rooms for traditional jazz, neither **The Elephant Room** (315 Congress Ave. 512/473–2279) on Congress Avenue nor **Top of the Marc** (618 W. 6th St. 512/472–9849) above Katz's is any more casual.

Music is all you'll get at **Liberty Lunch** (405 W. 2nd St. 512/477–0461), the mid-sized concert venue on the outskirts of the Warehouse District at 2nd and Guadalupe streets. It's little more than a warehouse with a long bar, a stage, partially detachable roof, and garage doors that open up to a large patio. Only the beach mural on the back wall hints at the club's 20-year history, a run that has gone far beyond its original focus on reggae. For the last decade or so, the booking policy has been wholly egalitarian, ranging from Nirvana and NRBQ to De La Soul and Danzig. It's often voted "Best Place to See Music" in *Austin Chronicle* polls, which is no small feat considering the stiff competition.

The Austin Music Hall (208 *Nueces St.* 512/495–9962), an equally plain but substantially larger venue within walking distance of Liberty Lunch, hosts artists too popular for the Lunch. But unlike the Lunch, which has some kind of mysterious charm, the Music Hall seems soulless. Because most shows are general admission (no seats), the experience often feels like a cattle call. Even when seats are occasionally added for shows that cater to older rockers, it's no better, really—only more crowded and harder to get to the bars. On the other hand, it's the only indoor venue with the capacity to hold acts like the Foo Fighters or Marilyn Manson, or to host intimate shows with big guns like Bob Dylan, Eric Clapton, or Ozzy Osborne. In that respect, the Music Hall serves its purpose.

The same folks that own the Music Hall have done a better job with **La Zona Rosa** (612 *W. 4th St.* 512/472–2293), a renovated mid-size room that competes directly with Liberty Lunch, Antone's, and Stubb's. It's the most comfortable of the mid-size rooms, with ample air conditioning and a garage-door system that allows the room to shrink or grow, although the sound system is mysteriously bad. While it regularly hosts local bands with strong college followings like Vallejo, Sister 7, and Robert Earl Keene, it's generally a room for touring acts from Ray Davies and David Byrne to No Doubt and Johnny Lang.

The Electric Lounge (302 *Bowie St.* 512/476–3873), is

unbelievably friendly for an alternative-rock club. It's become quite the center for all things alternative, from local lo-fi acts to raucous poetry readings. The club ambitiously books developing national acts and generally features popular local bands with national profiles (Spoon, Wannabes, Hammel On Trial). It also hosts a long-running Wednesday night gig featuring Asylum Street Spankers, the popular and unamplified retro-'20s outfit. In fact, despite the club's name, the Spankers' anti-electric stance actually fits in well here; an electrical fire set the lounge ablaze a few years back. The offending fusebox now hangs on the wall for art/posterity, but the lounge still has a huge neon sign above the stage that doubles as house lights, casting an eerie fire-red glow over the bands.

The glow at **Babe's (208 E. 6th St. 512/473–2262)** is usually on folks' faces when they first see Don Walser, the 65-year-old yodeler often hailed as the "Pavarotti of the Plains." Despite his national emergence, he still plays this intimate hamburger joint most Monday nights. When he's not there, the club's roster of up-and-coming blues and country acts is still worth a peek, as are the club's tabletops covered with vintage baseball cards. Despite a recent face-lift, the attached **Babe's Stageside (208 E. 6th St. 512/473–2262)** is still the best Downtown room for '80s-style hard rock. It's an amusing curiosity, but hardly a vital stop.

The Black Cat (309 E. 6th St. no phone), which started as a biker bar and still sports its share of hogs parked outside, is at any given point either the most or least popular club on 6th Street. Its residency system—whereby bands attempt to develop a following by playing a set night every

kings and queens of clubs

You may be wondering why this town attracts such a vibrant array of talent. One answer is that the club owners and managers take their business seriously. Step into any one of the following places on any night and you're likely to be greeted by the owners and managers, whose presence is part of why their venues are the crème de la crème of nightspots.

Clifford & Susan Antone, Antone's—She books the acts, he presides like chairman of the board, and the brother-and-sister team have worked to bring blues into a country music–lovin' town for almost 20 years. That's Susan with the camera; Clifford looks his role as the Godfather of Austin Blues.

Danny Crooks, Steamboat—In the '90s, the affable Crooks turned this nightspot around from being a spot for old-school singer-songwriters into a nonstop funkfest. Watch for him decked out in outrageous print pants and running the sound.

Eric Hartman, Emo's—Looking like a former football tackle player has its advantages, and the blond, friendly Hartman is a highly visible presence as the owner of Austin's premier punk/alternative venue.

week for more than a year—has created some of the biggest bands in town, including Ian Moore, Sister 7, Soulhat, and the Ugly Americans. But getting those bands to catch on has proven tricky, so the club falls victim to cycles of popularity. When they do, there's no better scene

Mike Henry, Electric Lounge—He's the unassuming guy with the black, or possibly bleached blond, hair and the Buddy Holly glasses who may be booking the next big alternative act into his super-popular club on the edge of Downtown's entertainment district. You may also find him coaching a team of slam poets.

Tim O'Connor, Austin Music Hall, The Backyard—One of Willie's boys, O'Connor has overseen numerous musical venues, but none as successful as this AMH/BY combo.

Mark Pratz & J-Net Ward, Liberty Lunch—These two well-scrubbed-looking partners worked day jobs as public-school teachers, and Pratz still does, which might explain their reps as good guys in a business with few of them.

Debbie Rombach, Hole In The Wall—Rombach began as bartender, moved up to manager, is now buying the place, and is, well, still bartender. She sometimes works the door of this West Campus fixture as well.

Steve Wertheimer, The Continental Club—The dapper, white-haired clubowner is not above grabbing a mop when a toilet blows.

in town. Eight hundred people will pack into this 400-person room twice a week and jam so hard the rafters and floor actually shake. But even a downtime is no reason not to go, because it's still one of the funkiest no-frills, cheap-beer, no-phone-ownin' bars on 6th Street. At least part of its popularity is because it's one of the few venues that allows underage patrons ("All ages all the time").

Just down the street, **The Bates Motel** (317 E. 6th St. 512/480–8121) has become the latest pitch-black, sweaty punk dive to catch on. Expect to see local punk bands at The Bates Motel, and then expect very little else. Also popular with the Bates crowd is the giant downstairs pool hall of **The Ritz Lounge** (320 E. 6th St. 512/474–2270). The Ritz was once a 1930s movie theater that later went on to host shows by both the Dead Kennedys and the Clash. Now the music has moved upstairs to what was once the balcony, and the place has become a lounge for the groovy swing set, with a small dance floor and great stadium seating. Most of the musicians are folks you'll find at Miguel's or even Cedar Street, but this is clearly the least pretentious venue to see them in. The swing-dance set dress to the nines, but nobody is considered underdressed and the emphasis is still on the dancing, not the drinks or cigars.

Steamboat (403 E. 6th St. 512/478–2912) has been on 6th Street for more than two decades and is the block's live-music can't-miss. What was once the preeminent club for cover bands, with the occasional Stevie Ray Vaughan, Christopher Cross, or Eric Johnson show thrown in, has spent this decade nurturing original local music. Not only was it the club of choice for the ARC Angels (Charlie Sexton's collaboration with Stevie Ray Vaughan's Double Trouble), but it still regularly features shows from guitar heroes like Chris Duarte, Ian Moore, and Breedlove (featuring Jimmie Vaughan's son, Tyrone). The cover charge here is usually more than at other venues, but that's because the owners believe in paying musicians fairly. They also have a policy against drink specials, as they believe a sloppy-drunk crowd is a less attentive crowd. That said, Steamboat is refreshing, the last bastion on 6th Street where music is the main focus.

At **The Mercury Lounge** (503-A E. 6th St. 512/457–0706), the crowd doesn't seem as drunk as it does high. But what can you expect from a club that started as a tribute to the Grateful Dead (complete with happy-hour bootleg-tape trading parties) called The White Rabbit? Since changing names and owners, the Mercury has settled into a groove thing, with local funksters and touring soul bands turning the place into the kind of room P-Funk or Maceo Parker would play if only it were big enough. For all its hipness and genuine soul, the Mercury is too small to be an effective dance club and too cramped and smoky to be much fun for too long. Its neighbor, **The Flamingo Cantina** (515 E. 6th St. 512/494–9336), fares slightly better because most of the regulars congregate on a deck above the stage, leaving room for people to dance to the weekend's reggae offerings. During the week there's an emphasis on young punk outfits.

With the Flamingo and Bates now attempting punk showcases, punk (in all its subtle '70s, '80s, and '90s variations) and alternative rock have become the dominant form of music on 6th Street. But those clubs, musicians, and clubgoers have **Emo's** (603 Red River St. 512/477–EMOS) to thank for trailblazing. The club, on the corner of Red River and 6th, is an offshoot of the legendary Houston venue of the same name and once offered free cover for all its shows, including roadshows from folks like L7 or the John Spencer Blues Explosion. Now, it's still all ages, and the cover is a straight $2. It's also still a bargain, considering this is the punk venue both local and touring musicians prefer to play. And while the club had its scary period, when piercing and tattoos seemed mandatory, it's chilled out nicely over the past few years to the point where the club's patrons actually embrace the occasional alternative country or hip-hop show—just don't expect to see any Dockers quite yet. Emo's is so proud that Johnny Cash played there during a SXSW, that the stool he sat on hangs above the bar. Even better, Emo's has also become something of an alternative art gallery, with original Frank Kozick paintings and dozens of his posters gracing the walls.

Another piece of art hangs above the indoor stage at **Stubb's (801 Red River St. 512/480–8341)**, the Red River barbecue emporium: a sculpture of a tastefully naked woman that looks a lot like Janis Joplin, but isn't. (Incidentally, during the club's Sunday Gospel Brunches they cover her with a T-shirt, so as not to offend the churchgoing crowd.) The model was actually a homeless woman the Stubb's owners met when they first went out to survey the land. Legend has it she blessed the grounds, and they bought the site shortly thereafter. The blessing must have been effective, because Stubb's has become one of the best venues in town. The indoor stage may be somewhat small, but it's big enough to host a dizzying array of musical styles from one night to the next. It's not unusual for Stubb's to cover blues, metal, country, punk, ska, and singer/songwriter terrain within a given week. As such, it's one of the few clubs that's always crowded, but never with the same people. And by building a 3,000-capacity outdoor venue out back and alongside Waller Creek, Stubb's has also become the mid-size venue of choice.

gay clubs... Over the last year or so, **The Forum** (408 *Congress Ave.* 512/476–2900) has become a prime spot for alternative cruising. This multilevel bar and dance club offers a peek at a good cross section of Downtown's gay scene, from preps to club kids. Big crowds and narrow thoroughfares make it a bit hard to really mingle, but there's a giant upstairs patio with a great view of both Congress Avenue and the Warehouse District. You'll also find the requisite go-go boys, a pseudo-leather room, and a small dance floor. Since the club has both a predominantly male crowd and dance music in a slightly upscale setting, it's begun pulling clubgoers away from what was Austin's most popular and well-dressed nightspot catering to a gay clientele—**Oilcan Harry's** (211 *W. 4th St.* 512/320–8823). But the Oilcan's large dance floor is still full, with plenty of preppy guys and their gal pals grooving alongside the club's male dancers; locals claim that the deejays rival the best San Francisco or New York have to offer. Unfortunately, Oilcan's gay clientele has to put up with gawking straight couples who wander in from the Warehouse District—as well as a strict "No Drag Queen" rule.

On the other side of the drag queen coin is **Charlie's** (1301 *Lavaca St.* 512/474–6481), a seedy dance club that does some of its best bar business during its Sunday night drag shows. Famous for being Austin's "wildest gay bar," Charlie's all-inclusive atmosphere (mostly men), darts 'n' pool, and amateur strip shows bring in scores of patrons looking for Mr. Right (or Mr. Right Now). But while Charlie's prides itself on inclusion, **The Chain Drive** (504 *Willow St.* 512/480–9017) caters to a distinctly leather set.

In fact, it's Austin's only real leather bar. Despite being a stone's throw (ouch!) from the Convention Center, it's isolated from the other gay clubs; the anything-goes attitude draws both more regulars and stay-all-night patrons than any other Downtown gay nightspot. At its best, it's actually wilder than Charlie's. At its worst, it can feel more dangerous.

Although **The Rainbow Cattle Co. (305 W. 5th St. 512/472-5288)** draws more lesbians than any other local gay club, it's still predominantly male. But what sets it apart is its country motif—with all the wood paneling, wagon wheels, and neon beer signs you'd expect at any local country bar. There's a fairly strict diet of country music—with perhaps a few disco spins after-hours for cheap thrills—free line-dancing lessons on Tuesdays, and one of the biggest raised dance floors in town.

buying stuff

Almost every plan for Downtown revitalization includes incentives for retailers. That's because even the local politicians realize the dismal current state of Downtown shopping. In truth, shopping's always been a tough sell in Downtown because most folks come to the Downtown area to work, and parking limitations make it tough for shoppers from other areas to make the trip in. As such, there are a few decent gift shops and clothing stores, but not much more outside the thriving gallery scene. And many of the stores worth recommending aren't in strip malls, on 6th Street, or in the Warehouse District, but instead in stand-alone buildings closer to West Austin or Campus/Central. If you're stuck Downtown without a car, just take a short cab ride west, down to West 5th and 6th streets, where you'll find the budding retail strips [see **west austin**] that Downtown only wishes it could lay claim to.

clothing/accessories... Anytown USA with a skateboard scene probably has its equivalent of **Blondie's** (*510 Rio Grande St. 512/472–7343*), but in Austin the notion of a large skater shop is still pretty new. There's tons of stuff here—from gear to clothes—but very little of the merchandise is unique. Even so, Blondie's is where adults go to buy cool weekend apparel—skater-oriented T-shirts, shorts, etc.—and where parents go to drop off their kids for a few hours of semi-supervised fun, hanging out, and skateboarding. The best time to shop by far is on weekend nights, when the store's surprisingly large indoor stage hosts some of the best free punk showcases in town.

If skateboard chic is just a slice of pop culture, then **Atomic City** (*1700 San Antonio St. 512/477–0293*) is the whole freakin' pie. It's a converted house full of eye-catching merchandise, from clothes to imported Japanese toys and action figures. It's always been cluttered, but the infinite mass of one-of-a-kind items and the massive shoe collection have kept its clientele loyal. Their commitment to selling shoes you can't find anywhere else once led them to discontinue (with a high-profile half-off sale for hundreds of pairs) their most popular and profitable line—Doc Martens—only because they had become too common.

Lush Life (807 W. 12th St. 512/476–8381), another converted house full of funky clothing, is sort of the women's middle ground between Atomic City and Blondie's. It also prides itself on unique product lines for cosmetics and apparel, many from upstart local designers. Best bet for club kids are the baby-T's, belts, and jewelry. It's also a popular spot for on-the-rise (or -prowl) musicians looking for outrageous stage clothes to land that elusive contract (or date).

galleries...

At the center of what's recently become known as the Uptown Arts District is **ArtPlex** (1705 *Guadalupe St. 512/474–7799*), a giant collective of galleries and studios that feature works by local painters, photographers, sculptors, potters, and neon artists. These galleries all adopt a bare-bones approach, so visiting feels like you're simply peeking in on the artists' actual studios, which in many cases you are. Many of the spaces display avant-garde work seen nowhere else in Austin. ArtPlex has also become the home of Pro-Jex, Austin's best gallery for photography, with collections on display from both local and non-local photographers. The Artist's Coalition of Austin, whose home office is located within the ArtPlex, has a good-sized gallery downstairs featuring some of its members' most accessible work.

Next door is the "gallery without borders," **Galeria Sin Fronteras** (1701 *Guadalupe St. 512/478–9448*). In a very simple but well-lit setting it houses sculpture, mixed media, traditional drawings, and paintings from nearly 100 Latino and Latina artists. In the same block is another popular specialty gallery, **Women & Their Work** (1710

Lavaca St. 512/477–1064). As you might guess from the name, this nonprofit gallery displays contemporary and folk art from women artists and has a great gift shop with prints, postcards, and trinkets. Next door to it is perhaps the city's best-known gallery, **Lyons Matrix** *(1712 Lavaca St. 512/479–6118)*. Although the art itself is generally more conservative than what you'll find in the rest of the area, the gallery floor is the largest in Downtown and features more traveling and local exhibitions from established and emerging artists than anywhere else in town.

gifts... **Wild About Music** *(721 Congress Ave. 512/708–1700)* is one of those only-in-Austin kinds of places: a large Downtown space where every item is music-related, from a gallery with paintings, sculpture, and mixed media to a gift shop with home furnishings, jewelry, and stationery. Not only is it the best place in town to pick up *Austin City Limits* and Stevie Ray Vaughan memorabilia, but here you'll also find ceramic guitar-and-amp teapot sets, or cheesy Paul Shaffer–style lounge vests. The gallery displays works from local musicians who moonlight as artists—like Joe Ely—some of whom you might also find shopping in the store. Shopkeepers like to repeat the now-infamous episode when Charlie Sexton expressed an interest in a crude oil painting without realizing it was supposed to be of him. (Does that say more about the artist or the subject?)

Sabia *(500 N.Lamar Blvd., No. 150, 512/469–0447)*, an aromatherapy superstore hidden between GSD&M's Idea City offices and Whole Foods, has become a part of Austin counterculture. Product inventory is based on a world view described as "future < nature" (whatever that symbol means), but most customers seem to be there for a chance to drop a ton of money on aroma-, sea-, and clay-therapy kits, as well as skin and body care products, natural extracts, and take-home spa treatments. At first glance it may seem only like a hyped-up version of your local mall's bath and body shop, but what's really cool about Sabia is that you walk in clueless about this stuff and they'll educate you without talking down to you.

Bydee Arts & Gifts (412 E. 6th St. 512/474–4343), a small art gallery/gift shop buried between 6th Street shot bars, has become something of a multicultural phenomenon. African-American artist and Bydee owner Brian Joseph has created a world of Bydee People that live within the unique prints, posters, T-shirts, postcards, and books the store produces and sells. The characters in this other world are all African-American, and the simple, colorful images and accompanying poetry have universal appeal.

You'll find all things Latin American at **Tesoros Trading Company** (209 Congress Ave. 512/479–8377), a small Congress Avenue shop specializing in arts and crafts from religious paraphernalia to wooden toys (safe for tots) from Mexico, Guatemala, and Peru. Of the dozens of folk-art merchants in town, this should be your first stop: The inventory is diverse, the prices are reasonable, and the help is knowledgeable. It's also the best place to kill time while waiting for a table at Las Manitas [see **eating/coffee**].

music/books... As it turns out, the best record store and the best bookstore in Downtown are both specialty shops. Even if most people believe Waterloo [see **west austin**] is the best place in town to buy local music, it

would be a mistake not to check out **Local Flavor** (305-
B E. 5th St. 512/472–7773) also. It's more of a classic record
shop than a modern record store, in that it carries mostly
CDs and cassettes from local bands, many of whom release
their product independently and trust the shop on a consignment basis. This mom 'n' pop store's owners, Sue and
Mike Donahoe, know local music like Siskel and Ebert
know movies: Offer a vague, nameless description about
the band you saw last Saturday night, and they'll tell you
the name—and most likely have their CD in stock, too.

The staff at **Adventures in Crime and Space** (609-**A
W. 6th St.** 512/473–2665) will probably be equally helpful
if you can't remember the name of a recent guest on Art
Bell's syndicated radio program for fans of the unex-
plained. As the name might suggest, it sells only crime and
science-fiction books. But for a relatively small enterprise
the store carries a large stock, with new titles sharing shelf
space with rare, autographed, and first-edition books. The
shop attracts its share of conspiracy theorists and comic-
book-convention nerds, but it's generally a friendly place.
In fact, the bookstore's regular science-fiction reading
group, sponsored by FACT (Fandom Association of Central
Texas), advertises online for new members.

sleeping

At first glance, it seems as if there's a hotel on every Downtown corner. But apparently, there just aren't enough rooms
Downtown to meet the demand. And as you'd expect, the
convenience of staying near the Convention Center or a

stumble away from 6th Street doesn't come cheap. Still, although Downtown room rates ($100 average per night) may be slightly more expensive than San Antonio, they're an average of $20–$30 less than comparable lodging in Dallas or Houston. For that reason, city planners say Austin's been a hard sell to developers interested in building new hotels in the Downtown area. The Convention and Visitor's Bureau itself has said that some larger conventions don't consider Austin because there aren't enough large hotels to accommodate them. Also, because Austin is becoming a popular tourist destination in its own right, Downtown occupancy rates have increased faster than the number of available rooms. But there are also plans for a hotel boom: close to 1,000 new rooms near the Convention Center, another 100 at 6th and Guadalupe streets, a renovation of the old Stephen F. Austin Hotel on Congress Avenue, and a nearly 200-room expansion of the Radisson on Town Lake. Boom or not, rates are expected to stay relatively high. If top dollar (even if it's only Texas top dollar) is a problem, you might want to stay elsewhere and rent a car.

> **Cost Range** for double occupancy per night on a weeknight. Call to verify prices.
> $/under 50 dollars
> $$/50–75 dollars
> $$$/75–100 dollars
> $$$$/100+ dollars

Everyone in Austin knows **The Driskill (604 Brazos St. 512/474–5911 $$$$)**, a historic luxury hotel that's been the cornerstone of 6th Street since 1886. It's played host to almost every notable visiting politician—LBJ had a suite here—and is the favorite of entertainers and executives stopping in Austin. Oil baron Jesse Driskill built the edifice to rival the luxury hotels in New York and Chicago, placing a bust of himself and his two sons over the entrance to proclaim his accomplishment. The busts, the arched doorway (the largest in Texas), and the cavernous lobby and ballrooms are still the hotel's main attractions. Despite several serious fires and extensive renovations, the Driskill's elegance has been faithfully preserved by both original 19th-century furnishings and awesome reproductions. In fact, the rooms are the only ones in town where you'll find handmade desks and custom antique art alongside in-room fax modems and vaults. And speaking of vaults, some say the fifth floor of the Driskill houses the ghost of a 19th-century guest, who reportedly flirts with female guests (including the rock group Concrete Blonde) and occasionally calls for the elevator. If you're not buying the ghost story, or even a room, you can't miss with the free walking tour or a visit to the upscale but low-key piano lounge.

Once you've seen The Driskill, the rest of Austin's Downtown hotels are just . . . well, the rest. The Driskill may have hosted the 1888 legislative session while the Capitol was under construction, but **Austin Marriott at the Capitol** (701 E. 11th St. 512/478–1111 $$$$) and **La Quinta Inn** (300 E. 11th St. 512/476–1166 $$$–$$$$) are both decent hotels within a shorter walking distance of the Capitol itself. The Marriott has a gorgeous pink granite exterior and very plush rooms, but unless someone else is springing for the bill, the La Quinta is a better, if less glamorous, deal. A longtime favorite of musicians from the Psychedelic Furs to Cowboy Mouth, La Quinta is just a short jaunt from Stubb's and 6th Street. **The Omni Austin Hotel Downtown** *(700 San Jacinto Blvd. 512/476–3700 $$$$)*, a 340-room hotel housed in a futuristic looking glass atrium, is closer to 6th Street and has become the default luxury hotel for the hoi polloi not connected or lucky enough to swing a room at **The Four Seasons** *(98 San Jacinto Blvd. 512/478–4500 $$$$)*. The rooms at the latter are decorated in Southwestern decor and have lovely Town Lake views. Because it's become the hotel of choice for visiting stars working on their latest projects, the lobby bar is one of the hottest people-watching spots in Austin. In fact, bubbly Jennifer Aniston was recently reunited with her lost puppy in the bar (it wasn't a "Friends" episode, either), and John Travolta graced the club's long couches after agreeing to be interviewed by an entire U.T. journalism class.

doing stuff

Unless you like watching people work, Downtown from 9 to 5 is relatively boring. Outside of a few parks and limited shopping, there are few genuine points of daytime interest for locals, even on weekends. For tourists, the two must-sees are obvious: the State Capitol and the Governor's Mansion.

There are few quieter places or better museums in Downtown than **The O. Henry Museum** *(409 E. 5th St. 512/472–1903)*, the 19th-century cottage William Sydney Porter lived in with his family before heading to prison and starting his writing career. The house, which retains its original furnishings despite several renovations, contains artifacts and memorabilia from Porter's 13 years in Austin. Perhaps because the house has been a museum since the '30s, there's never a wait to get in. It's home to the O. Henry Pun-Off, an annual competition for amateur punsters. Also on Congress Avenue and 5th Street is the **Mexic-Arte Museum** *(419 Congress Ave. 512/480–9373)*, a center for traditional and contemporary arts in all media from Mexico, Latin America, as well as Austin. If you're lucky enough to be in town October and November, make sure to visit the *Dias de los Muertos* exhibit—it's so beautiful and scary it might even make you repent.

The Governor's Mansion *(1010 Colorado St. 512/ 463–5518)* is both home to the governor of Texas and a historical site. Built in 1856, the mansion houses a collection of mementos left behind by previous govs, plus a desk used by founding father and city namesake Stephen F. Austin. You can see those souvenirs on the popular tours, but the mansion is closed weekends and at the discretion of the governor. The odd schedule and the long waits are worth it, because the mansion has an open-door-mi-casa-su-casa tradition, which means there are no ropes or barricades stopping the public from sitting on the same couch the governor might have sat on earlier in the day.

After a major face-lift, the **Texas State Capitol** *(1100 Congress Ave. for guided tours, 512/463–0063)* is back in business for legislative sessions and tours. As clichéd as it may seem for a sightseer to head straight for the Capitol, it's wholly worthwhile. The impressive structure is seven feet taller than the U.S. Capitol and the grounds are beautifully landscaped, but the majesty of the grand rotunda and dome are best appreciated from within. Here you can also see democracy in action, of course, as the Senate and House proceedings are open to the public when in session. Mind you, the inner workings of the democratic process don't make for scintillating sightseeing, but it's comforting to see that somebody is showing up.

As for Downtown parks, there are just two worth visiting: **Woolridge Square** *(Guadalupe St. between 9th St. and 10th St.)* and **Waterloo Park** *(Trinity St. and 12th St.)*. The former, between the library and courthouse, is a peaceful bowl-shaped lot with green picnic-ready grass and a white gazebo. It dates back to Edwin Waller's original city plans and was used as a gathering point for political oratory before the University took over the rally concession in the '60s. Across Downtown, Waterloo Park is much larger—nearly 11 acres, big enough to host SXSW's largest outdoor performances. It's seen its share of picnics and community events over the years, and recently it's become a popular venue for small family-oriented concerts.

spectating... Somebody once said Downtown at night is the best spot in Austin for two things: alternative music and alternatives to music. Yes, Virginia, there is nightlife in Austin beyond live music. Both theater and cabaret establishments find a home on Congress Avenue—voted "Best Street for the Arts" in a recent Best of Austin poll—but there are also some great comedy, stage work, and cinema revivals on 6th Street and in the Warehouse District. Venues like the Paramount Theater and Esther's Pool are considered local institutions, and

Downtown revitalization has created a vibrant theater and performance-art scene. So, do call ahead for showtimes and ticket availability.

Congress Avenue has two must-visits: The Capitol is a no-brainer, but you may not know about the **Paramount Theatre for the Performing Arts** *(713 Congress Ave. 512/472–5411).* This classic vaudeville house, often called "The Grande Dame of Austin Theater," has been wowing visitors for the past 80 years. Designed in 1915 by noted theater architect John Eberson, the 1,300-seat room has hosted performances by everyone from Katharine Hepburn, Houdini, and the Marx Brothers to Tony Bennett, Lily Tomlin, and Mandy Patinkin. Today, this nonprofit theater hosts a full slate of dance, film, comedy, live music, Broadway shows, and children's theater. Whatever the quality of the particular show, the Paramount itself can only be described as "splendiferous," with a classic marquee, walk-up box office, balcony seating, proscenium arch, grand drapery, and angelic ceiling murals. For a room so pristine and steeped in tradition, it's tremendously comfortable. People like to get dressed up to see Paramount events, but it's rare that anybody would give an odd glance toward jeans and T-shirts. And all summer long you can wear shorts to the Paramount's classic movie double features, a bargain at $5.

State Theater Company *(719 Congress Ave. 512/472–5143),* formerly called the Live Oak Theatre, is just up the street from the Paramount, having recently relocated to the majestic space of the State Theater. The classic playhouse has been renovated into a veritable arts complex, with a 350-seat theater, a 120-seat second stage, an acting school and plans for a cafe gallery, and restaurant. The State

Theater Company hosts regional plays and musicals too small for the Paramount. For a full Saturday evening catch a Paramount performance, then head down to the State Theater for a late-night performance of live cabaret. From 10:30 p.m. to 1:00 a.m. on Saturdays, the State Theater's lobby becomes a cabaret space with a rotating selection of dance, jazz, comedy, and solo piano performances.

The Live Oak has become the model for staging moderately budgeted theater, and **Public Domain (807 Congress Ave. 512/474–6202)** has set similar standards within the progressive-theater community for its innovative and interactive productions, where the audience and aspiring actors are encouraged to join in. The space is also used for lectures, readings, and workshops, and the lobby gallery has rotating exhibitions—some of which rival those of larger galleries—from local artists.

Meanwhile, a new theater in the Warehouse District is proving that classic movies don't necessarily have to be shown in a classic theater. **The Alamo Drafthouse (409 Colorado St. 512/867–1839)** has quickly become the city's most distinctive movie house—and its only film/dinner venue. The regular menu features moderately priced salads, sandwiches, and cocktails, with special menus often planned to complement particular films: Quail with rose-petal sauce and Mexican hot chocolate was served at the screening of *Like Water For Chocolate*, while their *Dolomite/Superfly* blaxploitation series featured 40-ounce Schlitz Malt Liquors, a choice some considered to be of questionable taste on more than one level. Both the dinner and late-night screenings of big-name, second-run films are popular, and the Alamo has also featured several popular series of documentaries, cartoons, and "pre-code" flicks (racy '30s fare that predates the Motion Picture Producers and Distributors of America's conservative Production Code). And of course, this being Austin, the Alamo is even beginning to offer some live music: Recently they paired lounge sensation Mr. Fabulous and Casino Royale with a screening of the James Bond classic *Goldfinger*.

Though people may remember the Alamo as a great date spot, **Esther's Follies** (525 E. 6th St. 512/320–0553), in the Esther's Pool building, has been the city's preeminent low-risk get-to-know-ya place for far longer. It's the home of Esther's Follies, a sketch comedy showcase that for 20 years has consistently offered topical fare far funnier than the average edition of "Saturday Night Live." The cast is so well-rehearsed yet full of improv surprises that you'll want to keep coming back (note, though, that the show only really changes sketches and musical numbers once a month, so weekly visits are a bit redundant). On the other hand, some of the reappearing characters, like owner Shannon Sedwick's twisted take on Patsy Cline, have become such legendary pieces within the show, you probably won't mind seeing them more than once.

There are those who believe Monk's Night Out, Austin's best improv comedy troupe, rivals the laughs-per-minute ratio at Esther's. Appropriately, they play next door at **The Velveeta Room** (521 E. 6th St. 512/469–9116), an Esther's offshoot that offers moderately priced comedy. It's not nearly as distinct as Esther's, but it does host a ton of local up-and-coming talent (like the "Austin Stories" cast) as well as a fairly popular open mic night.

body

By the numbers, Downtown is the haircut and tattoo capital of Austin. In reality, there's very little to get excited about. Finding a hairdresser good for a basic perm or a tattoo artist capable of recreating the designs off his or her wall is relatively easy. Finding service that's above and beyond isn't. And not only do the stores tend to change hands frequently, but the hair and tattoo artists themselves tend to float from place to place. There are only three body shops in town that have reliable long-term staffs.

There's a reason why **Astarte's (318 Colorado St. 512/472–6357)** corner shop has been designed around big, wide-open spaces and giant picture windows: This is the Downtown salon people want to be seen in and it's also gossip central—so much so that columnists who can't afford a cut reportedly hang out here to eavesdrop anyway. Offering the basic hair-coloring, makeup, and manicures, Astarte's prides itself on preparing folks for everything ranging from cocktail parties to rockin' evenings at Emo's. They also offer what they call "Rock Star Hair Coloring"—apparently a collection of avant-garde hues—but don't be fooled: Co-owner Deborah Carter has a North American Hairdressing Award for Classic Hair. As such, a little window-shopping yields a peek at visiting supermodels and actresses—many of whom the stylists work with on set—but you may also find Mr. Lifto, the ultra-pierced freak from Jim Rose's Sideshow Circus. And just how far will Astarte go to make you feel special? They have on-site production facilities for shooting modeling portfolios and will help you find a photographer.

Aziz Salon & Day Spa (*710 W. 7th St. 512/476–4131*) constitutes Astarte's main competition for upscale "special event" haircutting. But while Astarte advertises a "salon environment," Aziz offers a "full day of beauty"—a massage, manicure, pedicure, hair and scalp stress relief, and yes . . . a light lunch.

On the other hand, eating much before wandering around at **Forbidden Fruit** (*513 E. 6th St. 512/476–4596*) is not recommended. It's a "Body Art Salon," and it's Downtown's premier spot for body piercing enthusiasts. They'll pierce anything here, and you might shudder at the sight of some of the anythings being pierced if you stroll through. As with haircutters, you can often judge a body-art specialist by his own appearance, and Bear, the store's in-house piercing legend, passes with flying colors. His earlobes, stretched to four inches, are a must-see. It's another good sign that the shop's other piercing expert, Geneva, recently spoke in front of a legislative subcommittee on the need to have the industry regulated. For tattooing, they've got a half-dozen artists at any point and advertise that while they specialize in custom work, they're also willing to do something "off the wall," meaning the wall of stock patterns everyone else offers, (rather than simply something unique and twisted).

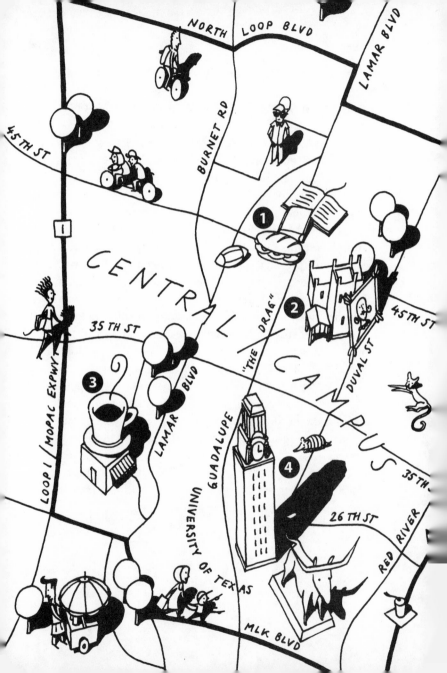

campus/central

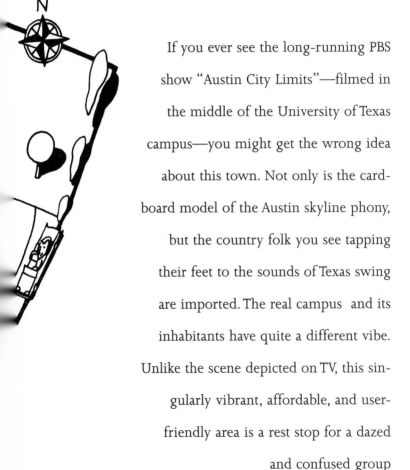

N

If you ever see the long-running PBS show "Austin City Limits"—filmed in the middle of the University of Texas campus—you might get the wrong idea about this town. Not only is the cardboard model of the Austin skyline phony, but the country folk you see tapping their feet to the sounds of Texas swing are imported. The real campus and its inhabitants have quite a different vibe. Unlike the scene depicted on TV, this singularly vibrant, affordable, and user-friendly area is a rest stop for a dazed and confused group

turn page for map key

of students, neighborhood characters, struggling musicians, and NEA-granted artists living in classic turn-of-the-century houses and arguing out local politics in funky coffee shops. If downtown's entertainment district feels like the heart of Austin, it's no secret that the Campus/Central area is its soul.

Of all the neighborhoods in Austin, Campus/Central is the one that is a must-see. Campus/Central comprises not only the hustling and bustling shopping strip and cultural center of university life on Guadalupe Street, known as "the Drag," but also Austin's first suburb, Hyde Park, located just north of Campus/Central. Although nearly 60,000 students fuel the area's economy and define the lifestyle, Campus/Central is not student-dominated. Young professionals, slackers, and starving artists all eat at the same mom 'n' pop restaurants, shop at the same record stores as the students (and in some cases buy from the same dorm-room dope dealers). Plus, two of the city's best groceries (Central Market and Wheatsville Co-Op), popular franchises such as Tower Records and Urban Outfitters, and the university's sports and arts offerings bring as many Austinites to the area as nightlife does to Downtown or shopping does to North Austin. And as more students enroll in the five-, six-, or even seven-year degree plan (some count their college time in dog years), it's harder to tell the students from civilian Austinites anyway.

map key

1 Thudercloud Subs	4 University of Texas
2 Elizabet Ney Museum	Campus
3 Kerbey Lane Cafe	

Officially, the Campus/Central area lies north of Downtown, bounded by Mopac and I-35 and Martin Luther King Boulevard to the south and 51st Street to the north. But the bulk of the area's activities are on the campus itself, the Drag (Guadalupe Street), West Campus (the area between Martin Luther King Boulevard and 30th Street), and in and around Hyde Park. Add some serious strip-mall shopping around Central Market and a collection of small shops and restaurants near the city's best all-night eatery, Kerbey Lane, and you've seen what you need to of Campus/Central.

Any tour of this area has to start at the base of the Drag, the intersection of Martin Luther King Boulevard and Guadalupe Street. It's the western border of campus and includes dozens of small shops and restaurants, plus the aforementioned big chain stores. And while there's no shortage of trendy hair stylists and houseware shops on the Drag that will be more than happy to max out your credit card, the area's shopping is mostly low-end and affordable. Better yet, you can walk toward the campus from the Drag and hit both a great museum, the Ransom Center, and the West Mall, home to the landmark Tower and the Texas (student) Union.

Any tour of the campus area is going to involve a lot of walking. Most of Campus is closed to non-student vehicles, and parking along the Drag is, well, a drag. On the other hand, local merchants have always had to cater to car-less students, so a decent amount of shopping, dining, and entertainment is really never far away. Note that when school is in session, there's a wait or line at nearly every restaurant, grocery, and major shopping center in the area. As such, there are jaded Austinites who go to Campus only in May and December, when most students are away.

Although North and West Austin have become popular places for students to live, most still attempt to live near Campus, a situation that has resulted in a lot of giant, faceless apartment complexes and condominiums in West Campus. Hyde Park, the area north of the University between 38th and 45th streets, has its share of students too, but is generally much quieter. Musicians, artists, and young families used to look to Hyde Park's Victorian and Craftsman-style homes for cheap rent, but prices have increased dramatically over the last 10 years (and should only increase further after 2000, when the airport, and its noisy flightpath, move out of the area). Even with higher prices and a recent battle between homeowners and a developer looking to add significant retail to the area, Hyde Park maintains a neighborhood feel, where kids play, garage bands jam, and people worry more about bicycle-helmet laws than crime statistics.

If you spend any time at all in Campus/Central you'll also see your share of homeless folk, referred to endearingly as "dragworms." They'll ask for spare change but are generally harmless and take rejection relatively well. In fact, according to the *Daily Texan*, the University's student-run paper, Austin's homeless are the most educated in the United States. Not only are many college-educated, says the paper, but they've specifically chosen Austin due to its reputation for intelligent conversation, not to mention the mild climate. Whether that's true or not (and it *does* make homelessness sound more like a lifestyle choice than a predicament), the *Texan* is a valuable resource for any trip to the area and may be the best college paper you'll find anywhere. But the pair of former *Texan* employees who founded the rival *Austin Chronicle* have given the daily a run for its money with what many believe to be one of the nation's finest independent weeklies.

The *Texan* and the *Chronicle* aren't the only media "empires" based in Campus/Central. "Beavis and Butthead" creator Mike Judge continues to produce his latest animated hit, "King of The Hill," from his office on Martin Luther King Boulevard. And since Richard Linklater's Detour Production offices are just east of campus along I-35 [see **east austin**], is it any wonder his film *Slacker* portrayed Campus/Central so realistically?

eating/coffee

Like restaurants close to any college campus, those that want to survive near the University of Texas must be four things: cheap, quick, reliable, and open. And specializing in any of the three major food groups in this part of town— hamburgers, coffee, and pasta—isn't bad for business either. Unfortunately, that means the Campus/Central area is the leader among Austin neighborhoods in chain restaurants, ranging from junk-food purveyors like Burger King, McDonald's, Mr. Gatti's, and Taco Bell to local outlets like Thundercloud, Double Dave's, and Little City.

In fact, of just two genuinely upscale restaurants in the area, one is a chain—Ruth's Chris Steakhouse. Even so, there are many reasons to neither make a run for the border—or visit the golden arches. For every generic Starbucks outlet there are five classic student cafes, such as Mojo's or Spider House, and for every Subway there is a branch of Austin's unmistakably local sandwich shop, Longhorn Po-Boys. Better yet, there's a thriving breakfast scene that draws customers from all over Austin, a Godzilla-sized gourmet grocery that doubles as a genuine tourist attraction, and the obligatory campus pizza wars that keep prices down and delivery time short. Sure, just about every restaurant in the area also happens to be impossibly busy all day long, head-achingly loud, and only moderately friendly, but these are restaurants catering primarily to hungry, impoverished students, not fine-food critics.

Cost Range per entree
$/under 10 dollars
$$/10–15 dollars
$$$/15–20 dollars
$$$$/20+ dollars

american... **The Hyde Park Bar & Grill** (4206 *Duval St.* 512/458–3168 $–$$) is the center of Hyde Park cuisine, and in truth, one of the city's best mid-priced restaurants. Finding it is easy—just look for the giant 20-foot fork with a rotating selection of items at the top. Getting a seat during lunch or dinner is a little trickier, given the fact that it's a small converted house with tables strewn throughout several cozy rooms—but it is well worth the wait. The food is all about big portions, and the Hyde Park fries are easily the most popular in Austin. In fact, the restaurant tears through 100 tons of potatoes a year, and the process is pretty complex: Each potato is peeled, sliced, dipped in buttermilk, tossed in a flour batter, and then fried in peanut oil. These fries also have somehow gained the reputation that green M&M's used to enjoy for their alleged aphrodisiac qualities. Any wonder this is one of the hottest date spots in town?

If the wait is too long at Hyde Park, you can't go wrong at **Waterloo Ice House** (1106 W. 38th St. 512/451–5284 **$**), which shares both reliable quality and an almost identical menu with the flagship restaurant on Lamar Boulevard [see **west austin**]. A big outdoor deck procures this location the nod in the spring and fall.

barbecue... **Ruby's Barbecue** (512 W. 29th St. 512/477–1651 **$**) serves hormone-free beef and has excellent ribs, but it will always be popular for two other things: its late-night hours and its proximity to the former Antone's location, which inspired Ruby's with its after-hours juke-joint look. (They hang lots of blues posters, play the blues, and even show off blues musicians in laminated photographs beneath glass tabletops.) Because this homestyle barbecue joint on Guadalupe Street is open until 4 a.m. on weekends, it was the pre-eminent after-hours hotspot for blues musicians and their fans coming from Antone's (which has since moved to Downtown). Ruby's still does a brisk business with both the dinner and late-night crowds.

breakfast/bagels... With the possible exception of Threadgill's, no restaurant represents Austin's traditional tastes better than **Kerbey Lane Cafe** (3704 Kerbey Ln. 512/451–1436 **$–$$**). It fits all the criteria for Austin flavor: converted house, hippie staff, Tex-Mex dishes, a large vegetarian menu, big breakfasts, and late hours. And while the lunch and dinner items are typically only slightly above average in quality, their all-day breakfast feeds hordes of students, musicians, and clubgoers. The menu is the closest thing you'll find to a classic old-fashioned East Coast diner anywhere south of the Mason-Dixon line. Try their rightly famous jumbo buttermilk pancakes.

The Drag has a few other early-morning quick fixes for students and faculty—**Einstein Bros. Bagels** (2404 *Guadalupe* St. 512/457–8722 $), **Private Idaho Potatoes** (2200 *Guadalupe* St. 512/473–2878 $), and **Ken's Donuts** (2820 *Guadalupe* St. 512/320–8484 $). Austin bagels in general aren't much to brag about, but at least Einstein Bros.' overrated bagels are hot and fresh in the morning. What used to be called The Bagel Manufactory is now called Private Idaho Potatoes, but The Bagel Manufactory still bakes the bagels on site and sells a limited number of bagels to earlybirds at a small counter inside Private Idaho. Rest assured it's worth the trouble, because these gems are the closest thing to a real New York bagel in town. As for Ken's, the donuts are the small, greasy type, more like Tasty Creme (not to be confused with Krispy Kreme) than Dunkin' Donuts.

coffee... **Captain Quackenbush's** (2120 *Guadalupe* St. 512/472–4477 $) is the crown jewel of the Drag and the standard by which all other Austin coffee shops are judged. *Slacker* made it famous, but decades of college students have kept it in business. The quality coffee and cheap meals (from ramen noodles to soups and muffins) are unmatched locally, although Quack's (as everyone calls it) is still mostly about atmosphere: a room full of comfortable couches and hardwood floors. As corny as it sounds, people come here to exchange ideas. Most patrons stay for hours, studying textbooks or just coffeehouse sociology—eavesdropping on students, professors, and artists/slackers who discuss politics or take chess or Trivial Pursuit a little too seriously. And while the tiny smoking room up front is always jammed, Quack's is the best high-profile spot on campus—and the perfect place to convince your friends that indeed you do crack a book occasionally.

Metro (*2222-B Guadalupe St. 512/474–5730 $*), just down the block, isn't as funky as Quack's, but it has its share of loyal individualists puffing away on their generic-brand cigarettes. Metro's large upstairs is the city's last bastion for indoor coffeehouse smoking (at least from 2 p.m. to 6 a.m.) Actually, scoliosis might be considered a bigger risk than secondhand smoke, since Metro's post-industrial motif and metal chairs define uncomfortable—but, hey, sometimes fashion hurts. For whatever reason, this place seems to attract a rowdy clientele of punk and gothic wannabes—best taken with a sense of humor and in small doses. But Metro's espresso is worthy of a double dose—a giant double—and cappuccino is a steal at $2.50.

Although both are a bit of a walk from campus, **Mojo's Daily Grind** (*2714 Guadalupe St. 512/477–6656 $*) and **Spider House** (*2908 Fruth St. 512/480–9562 $*) are clearly Quack's best student-driven rivals. Both are in converted houses and both are constantly crowded. Mojo's, which is open 24 hours Monday through Saturday and until midnight on Sunday, is famous for its fresh-squeezed juice, extra-large pastries, steamed coffeehouse eggs, and the mysterious Iced Mojo, a sweet and nutty coffee concoction that tastes different every time. The 19th-century home has a small patio and plenty of outdoor seating in the front yard; you'll want to go inside to check out the rotating installments by local artists. Some of the works—in all media—would be enough to send Jesse Helms into a tailspin, but they reflect Mojo's part alt-rock, part bohemian vibe well. Mojo's also hosts popular poetry showcases and is the official South by Southwest spoken-word venue.

Spider House—a cozy, yes, house with an insanely large patio—also hosts poetry readings, as well as live music on weeknights, but those are actually the times to avoid it. The quality of both the poets and musicians just isn't up to par, which is too bad because they've got a beer license and a great stage. In spite of the distraction, Spider House's patio—with its collection of mix 'n' match yard furniture—has made it the most consistently popular new coffeehouse in town. The clientele is a hodgepodge, too, an unlikely mix of studying students and happy-hour drunks. A great meeting spot for casual dates or book clubs.

In the Hyde Park area there are two coffee choices: **Flightpath Coffeehouse** (5001 Duval St. 512/458–4472 $) and **Dolce Vita** (4222 Duval St. 512/323–2686 $). Ignore the local hype, as neither is anything special. Flightpath is all about location—they've somehow turned the fact that they're in the middle of the Robert Mueller Municipal Airport's flightpath into some kind of airshow drawing card. (Try telling the neighboring homeowners that's something special.) In fact, when the airport finally moves, all that will be left here is an overpriced coffeehouse with decent hot chocolate, too little seating, a half-finished patio, and more attitude than necessary. As for Dolce Vita, an offshoot of Hyde Park Bar & Grill, it also suffers from too small a space and too big an attitude. Presumably, their upscale decor is a stab at sophistication, but it's out of place in this retro-bohemian neighborhood. Nonetheless, their gelatos and specialty ice creams are worth a to-go order.

Closer to campus, there are a couple of small chain off-shoots worth noting, **Texas French Bread** (*2900 Rio Grande St. 512/499–0544; 3211 Red River St. 512/478–8794* $) and **Little City** (*3403 Guadalupe St. 512/467–2326* $) in particular. Both locations of the former do a big lunch business in university traffic, while the latter—called Itty Bitty City by its fans—serves up excellent pastries and fine coffee in a shop considerably smaller than its downtown counterpart.

hamburgers... The three best hamburger joints in central Austin are all classic U.T. hotspots, if not outright traditions. **Nau's Pharmacy** (*2406 San Gabriel St. 512/476–1544* $), a 70-year-old family drugstore, is more old-fashioned soda fountain than restaurant, with a griddle that cooks up juicy hamburgers that go down well with a chocolate soda, cherry limeade, or some of the finest milk shakes in town. **Dirty Martin's Kum-Bak Place** (*2800 Guadalupe St. 512/477–3173* $) also dates back 70 years and griddle-fries its burgers—simple gems that have come to define the local dive burger. They've also got great chicken-fried steak and pork chops. However, the last couple of U.T. generations tend to prefer the sloppy hamburgers and fried vegetables at **Players** (*300 W. Martin Luther King Blvd. 512/478–9299* $). It's a cash-only sports bar that sits just outside Dobie—one of the campus' largest private dorms—and it has captured the lion's share of a student market desperate for a cheap late-night burger and milk shake.

italian/pizza... This isn't New York or Chicago, but don't tell Austin's pizza lovers—they're just students who don't know any better. That said, each of the dozen or so pizza joints and carryout chains in the central Austin area have virtues. **Mangia** *(3500 Guadalupe St. 512/302–5200 $–$$)*, a small local chain that's also popular with Austin's non-student population, specializes in Chicago-style deep-dish pizza, with more choices of toppings than their competitors. **Conan's Pizza** *(603 W. 29th St. 512/478–5712, 2606 Guadalupe St. 512/476–1981 $)*, another Austin-based chain with a student-dive atmosphere and a terrific Chicago deep-dish pie, has two campus locations with a popular (read: cheap) lunch buffet. They also have both whole-wheat and regular crusts. **Double Dave's** *(3000 Duval St. 512/476–3283, 415 W. 24th St. 512/472–3283 $)* has two locations that do well with the all-you-can-eat pizza and salad buffet. The most popular item is the patented pepperoni roll, a small stromboli-like concoction of cheese, bread, and pepperoni. And if you're walking through Dobie Mall, go to **Niki's Pizza** *(Dobie Mall, 2nd Floor, 2021 Guadalupe St. 512/472–8018 $)*, for the best New York–style thin-crust slice in town.

If you're looking for Italian other than pizza, **Milto's** *(2909 Guadalupe St. 512/480–8418 $)* is always a safe bet. Like Ruby's, it used to draw heavily from the neighboring Antone's blues crowd. Now it survives on traditional word-of-mouth, mostly due to its lasagna, a mushroom-heavy recipe that's among the best in the city. And speaking of bests, the best underrated date spot in the city may be the central area location of **The Brick Oven** (*1608 W. 35th St. 512/453–4330 $–$$*), a cozy converted house near Kerbey Lane that serves excellent brick-oven pizzas, fettuccine, and calzones, and has a better-than-average wine list.

mexican... El Patio (*2938 Guadalupe St. 512/476–5955 $*), a small West Campus Mexican tradition, doesn't have a patio, but it does have a wait most weeknights. The family that owns it has spent decades preparing classic Mexican food that both students and senior citizens can agree on. The enchiladas and tacos are excellent, but be careful not to fill up on salsa-dipped saltines, El Patio's patented and casual, but odd, substitute for chips.

While El Patio is all about ultra-traditional preparation, **Trudy's Texas Star** (*403 W. 30th St. 512/477–2935 $–$$*) has made a small fortune peddling (mostly mediocre) Tex-Mex, but their breakfasts, margaritas, and homemade hot sauce have been longtime award-winners. Unfortunately, there's always a wait and the service is spotty at best. If you're looking for something quicker, try **Chango's** (*3020 Guadalupe St. 512/480–8226 $*), a new offshoot from the owners of Manuel's [see **downtown**]. Its exterior fencing makes it look more like a prison than a restaurant, and the counter service is very fast-foodish, but their freshly made tacos and fajitas are easily the tastiest in town.

sandwiches... Thundercloud Subs (*705 W. 24th St. 512/495–9643, 1608 Lavaca St. 512/478–3281, 3204-B Guadalupe St. 512/452–5010 $*), the local mega-chain that

advertises "Fresh, fast and healthy food in a (pretty OK) atmosphere," has had the lock on the campus-area sandwich business for years. And for good reason: The service is fast, and the 12-inch sandwiches are freshly made, relatively cheap, and big enough to fill any student on a budget. Nonetheless, Thundercloud's found a real competitor in **Longhorn Po-Boys** (*2901-B Medical Arts 512/495–9228, Texas Union, 24th St. and Guadalupe St. 512/475–6518*), an unassuming local start-up that's vying to become the city's hottest new chain. They've already got two prime campus locations—one near the law school and another inside the Texas Union—and they offer a full lineup of 9-inch and 18-inch sandwiches on their own fresh-baked bread. But Longhorn's best asset may be its secondary menu—a selection of expertly prepared international favorites like spinach pies, tabbouleh, and baklava.

The campus area's other sandwich kings, the two locations of **Texadelphia** (*2422 Guadalupe St. 512/480–0107, Texas Union, 24th St. and Guadalupe St. 512/232–1785 $*), specialize in Philly cheesesteaks. They've recently added the Texas Union satellite and expanded their Drag location to accommodate their growing customer base. It's crowded, but veterans have learned to split up: One person orders while the others scout out a table. It's worth the trouble.

thai... The Drag location of **The Thai Kitchen** (*3009 Guadalupe St. 512/474–2575 $$*) has a loyal student following; many of them are actually from U.T.'s large Asian student population. It's kind of dingy, but they make up for lack of atmosphere with great service—they'll gladly substitute tofu for vegetarian customers and adjust the spice levels of any dish. The menu reaches far beyond typical pad thai into all kinds of exotica, like the whole filet of snapper prepared with anything from a fresh garlic and cilantro base to a dense curry sauce.

upscale... **Ruth's Chris Steakhouse** (3010 *Guadalupe St.* 512/477–7884 $$–$$$) makes a great splurge whenever the folks are in town to pick up the tab. Not surprisingly, the specialty here are the juicy steaks, which are excellent. Far and away, this is the Drag's swankiest eatery, dark and elegant. Besides Ruth's, the upscale market in these parts has just one entry, **The Granite Cafe** (2905 *San Gabriel St.* 512/472–6483 $$), and it's upscale only by campus standards. That's not to say that the Granite's not pleasant—it's got a large patio and adds a touch of class to an otherwise dull shopping center. And the fine Southwestern fare, fresh breads, and above-average wood-fired pizzas and quesadillas are good, but hardly fancy. Why Lyle Lovett reportedly drives in from Houston so often just to dine here remains a mystery.

vegetarian... After 17 years of "international vegetarian dining," **Mother's Cafe and Garden** (4215 *Duval St.* 512/451–3994 $–$$) is still the best place in town to play count-the-Birkenstocks. It's a vegan-hippie's paradise, complete with a shack-style garden room, egg-free pastas, and protein powder–enhanced smoothies. But even Austin restaurants can't survive catering to vegans alone. So Mother's has found ways to make its agenda palatable to the masses, which means cheese—as in jack-smothered versions of enchiladas, vegetable rancheros, and tofu lasagna. All that's much tastier than it sounds, plus the wait-staff is generally accommodating to mix 'n' match customers looking for substitutions and replacements. Even better, the popular weekend brunch is full of great equalizers like omelets, pancakes, French toast, and *migas*.

bars

For being a center of college life, Campus/Central has fewer real bars than you might expect. Bar owners say that since the drinking age changed to 21 in the late '80s, it's been almost impossible to rely solely on college crowds for business. Apparently, what it's taken to survive near Campus/Central is a willingness to cater to both current students *and* older crowds—faculty, alumni/alumnae, and regular neighborhood folk. The result is a small crop of bars that are both friendly and relatively inexpensive.

Like the Gingerman downtown, the German-style **Draught Horse Pub & Brewery** (4112 *Medical Pkwy.* 512/452–6258) is all about selection. They've got a tap wall full of domestic and imported choices, plus as many as nine house-brewed beers at any point in the season. But what sets it apart from the Gingerman is that it still feels like a neighborhood spot. Wednesday's famous "Pitcher Night" features a free barbecue or pizza buffet that's well worth the price of the beer alone.

Just a bit closer to the campus lie two more traditional student hangouts—**The Posse East** (2900 *Duval St.* 512/477–2111) and **Crown & Anchor Pub** (2911 *San Jacinto Blvd.* 512/322–9168). Both spots have greasy bar food, cheap pitchers, big decks, games, and large TVs for sporting events. Although regulars or the bar owners themselves might disagree, the differences between the two bars are so subtle that they're nearly indistinguishable from one another (kind of like the difference between good '70s disco and bad '70s disco). Both bars are so relaxed and friendly that most people just bounce back and forth between them until they find the right chess partner or conversation.

Trudy's Texas Star (409 W. 30th St. 512/477–2935) is the popular campus location of the Tex-Mex chain. After 5 p.m., the line at the bar for the phenomenal margaritas and jalepeño-infused Mexican martinis is as long as the wait for a table. And the bar is separated from the restaurant, so you can order appetizers and smoke inside the bar area or on the large patios anytime you like.

The Texas Showdown Saloon (2610 Guadalupe St. 512/472–2010) isn't as scary as it sounds, nor is it as scary as it once was when it was Raoul's, the stomping grounds for Austin's '80s punk scene. In fact, this big bar/amusement hall is friendly enough to reserve mugs for its regulars, organize pool tournaments and dart leagues, and run a happy hour that stretches from 2 to 7 p.m. every day. It's also the only bar in town with a "Happy Minutes Beer Special," a daily bargain offered only between 3 and 3:15 p.m.

The Texas Tavern (24th St. and Guadalupe St. 512/475–6520) inside the Texas Union, used to be a live- music hub but is now merely a mediocre bar. Even so, it's the only place to find a beer on the campus itself. Just make sure you have your ID with you—they're a bit suspicious, for good reason.

music/clubs

Fifteen years ago, the Campus/Central area was a live-music hotbed. With punk and new wave in full swing, it seemed like every student with or without an exam the next day was at the Texas Tavern, Cain & Abel's, or Raoul's, ground zero of Austin's punk movement. There were also dozens of yard parties and co-op gigs (co-ops in Austin are student housing) before many of the smaller West Campus houses were cleared out to make way for more apartments. Add Antone's decade-long run on Guadalupe Street and you had quite a scene. Today, the live-music

why an armadillo?

Within Austin's multi-genred musical history, no venue looms larger in memory or myth than the Armadillo World Headquarters. The legendary hippie music palace stood behind Threadgill's World Headquarters' present-day location on Barton Springs Road, and was a former National Guard Armory as well as the site of an early '60s Elvis performance. When current Threadgill's owner Eddie Wilson and his hippie friends threw open the doors one August day in 1970, it changed the course of Austin music history forever. In its day, the Dillo housed acts from Bruce Springsteen and Waylon Jennings to the Ramones. The Armadillo was so popular and its influence so pervasive that no one club could take its place after it closed in 1981.

But why an armadillo? Sixties legend and local under-focus has moved toward Downtown. In fact, in spite of the students, Campus/Central has just two regular live- music venues, albeit two of the best in town: The Hole in the Wall and Cactus Cafe.

As the name suggests, **The Hole in the Wall** (2538 *Guadalupe St.* 512/472–5599) is one of Austin's smallest clubs. It's also one of the most eclectic, often mixing punk, rock, country, and singer-songwriters on the same bill. It's always been the place where misfit and outcast Austin musicians are allowed to cut their teeth in front of intimate audiences. In fact, the club helped give a start to folks like Nanci Griffith, Timbuk 3, and Fastball. Although the main room holds only 100 or so comfortably—many

ground comic artist Jim Franklin divined a connection between the scrappy critters and the scruffy hippies (stoner epiphany?) and began to incorporate the animals—primarily known here for being dead on the side of the road—into posters and underground comics. Franklin's whimsical renderings of the beloved creature so inspired friend Eddie Wilson that he named his new music venue after the armored icon. The original Franklin logo for the venerable hall is incorporated into the Threadgill's sign at the restaurant's south location. The Armadillo's effect on this town has been so pervasive that numerous businesses adopted "armadillo" as a name—even a minibus system downtown is called the Dillo. And to think all of this hullabaloo came about because a bunch of long-haired, pot-smoking hippies in the '70s had an artistic obsession with funny-looking roadkill.

of them regulars who have been coming to drink at the bar for nearly 25 years—more popular acts like Alejandro Escovedo, Doug Sahm, and Mojo Nixon still book themselves here to perform in front of appreciative crowds. Nixon was once surprised by the audience member who came up to join him on "Don Henley Must Die"—Don Henley himself. But mostly "the Hole" is just a neighborhood spot whose walls are smothered with sports pennants and hundreds of commissioned caricatures of the regulars. While it's a popular lunch spot, and the pool room in back is actually bigger than the venue itself, it's still the music that matters. Nothing in town is a better bet on a Sunday night than the Rock and Roll Free-For-All, a long-running, no-cover showcase of new talent playing merely for exposure and free beer.

The Cactus Cafe (*24th St. and Guadalupe St.,* **Texas Union** **512/475–6515**) isn't much bigger than the Hole and was similarly responsible for launching Griffith and Lyle Lovett, but because it's in the Texas Union—and is an official part of the University—it's a lot less smoky. In fact, the club is Austin's only exclusively smoke-free music venue. It's mostly an older (non-college) crowd that shows up for the club's quiet and well-attended folk and singer/songwriter showcases. The talent rotates steadily between local upstarts and national touring acts, but regular performances by people like Jimmie Dale Gilmore and Townes Van Zandt have made the Cactus Cafe the scene's most important folk/acoustic venue. Occasionally, more popular acts like Ani DiFranco will move upstairs to the much larger **Texas Union Ballroom** (512/475–6636).

buying stuff

There is virtually nothing under the sun you can't buy somewhere within walking distance of the campus. The Drag is just a long, flat, homegrown version of the Mall of America. And with a car (a short drive will take you to the eye-popping Central Market), you can find a selection of whatever it is you're looking for—and perhaps a few dozen other things you didn't know you needed. For an area supposedly catering to money-strapped students, there are as many retailers specializing in luxury goods and services as there are discount shops and boutiques. The result is a thriving shopping scene that has appeal way beyond the student body. In fact, the best local shops, the vast majority of which are also locally owned, cater to alumni/alumnae—the folks who liked what they saw in college and now have money to burn (meaning those who studied something other than music or English or anthropology).

books... If you're a student, the textbook dealers on the Drag are good for one thing: overpriced textbooks. If you're not a student, they're still good for only one thing: overpriced U.T. paraphernalia and apparel. But ever since **The University Co-op** (*2244 Guadalupe St. 512/476–7211*) downsized a few years ago, telling the textbook players apart is almost impossible. That means you'll find a lot of the same T-shirts, sweaters, and pennants at **Texas Textbooks** (*2338 Guadalupe St. 512/478–9833*) and both **Bevo's Bookstore** locations (*2400 Guadalupe St. 512/*

476–7642; 2021 *Guadalupe St. in Dobie Mall*, 512/476–0013). As for the Co-op, they still do textbooks better than the rest, although the souvenir nod goes to their sister store, **The University Co-op East** (2902 *Medical Arts St.* 512/472–6156), a great source for fine-art supplies and law books. Unfortunately, it was the creation of a new three-level **Barnes & Noble** (2246 *Guadalupe St.* 512/457–0581) on the Drag that pushed the Co-Op down a store and out of the general book business. Although their selection and magazine rack are a big improvement over the Co-op's, it's as devoid of local flavor as any Barnes & Noble you've seen, with the exception of the upstairs coffee bar and deck that overlooks the Drag and the University of Texas Tower.

On the other hand, the independent specialty bookstore is still alive and well at both **Lobo** (3204-*A Guadalupe St.* 512/454–5406) and **Fringeware** (2716 *Guadalupe St.* 512/494–9273). The former is the city's premier gay bookstore, with thousands of titles and hundreds of greeting cards and novelty items. This was the first and only store in Austin to sell the controversial line of gay "Billy" dolls (as gay as any doll *can* be), an anatomically correct, leather-clad answer to the Barbie doll. But while Lobo is a large shop crowded with browsers, Fringeware is a small space and most of its customers are using the store's Netscape browsers to search Fringeware's online catalog of hard-to-find books on technology and counterculture. As an off-line entity, Fringeware started as one bookshelf in the back of a vintage clothing store while its creators attempted to build a "guerrilla media collective" for writers "marginalized or forgotten by contemporary mass media culture."

Whatever the case, they've become the premier shop in Austin offering books by writers like Susie Bright, Albert Meltzer, Ivan Stang, and William Gibson, while also hosting dozens of signings and software demonstrations.

Further down Guadalupe Street you'll find **News & Smokes** (3208 *Guadalupe St.* 512/454–9100), what appears to be a fairly generic magazine rack and cigar shop. But they've also got the most sextensive collection of pornography in town. Their magazine rack is also generally considered to be Austin's most comprehensive and up-to-date, but remember, although the porn and news sides of the store are separated, there is just one cash register. So keep a straight face as the guy in front of you buys a pile of both guns 'n' ammo mags and porn (or actually, maybe take a step or two back).

Everything's much more wholesome and straightforward at **Toad Hall Children's Bookstore** (1206 *W. 38th St., Ste.* 1101, 512/323–2665). Since 1978, this locally owned two-story shop has been selling children's books, educational toys and games, teaching resources, and parenting guides to just about every family in Austin. With a full slate of concerts, storytimes, field trips, and Saturday events, Toad Hall is the rare bookstore for kids that is both educational and fun. Their collection of children's audio- and videotapes, CDs, and puppets rivals even the best-stocked Toys 'R' Us.

Although it's part of a national chain and definitely lacks Toad Hall's charm, the children's section at the **Central Market Bookstop** (4001 *N. Lamar Blvd.* 512/452–9541) also does a brisk business. After all, Central Market [see **groceries**] is a "family grocer" and it's easier to keep a kid occupied during a meal on the outside patio with a new book or stuffed animal from Bookstop. For adults eating alone, Bookstop is also the best place near Central Market to buy a paperback, newspaper, or magazine to keep (or pick up) company with.

cards/gifts... The Central Market Shopping Center is ground zero for Austin gift-giving, and the best way to start (or perhaps end) a spree there is to indulge yourself at **The Three Chocolatiers** (4001 N. Lamar Blvd., Ste. 500, 512/454–0555), the city's best upscale chocolate shop. Displays of the sweet stuff in dozens of shapes, sizes, and themes (from golf balls to PC hard drives) are good for a browse and the occasional novelty gift, but it's the showcase of fudge and chocolate-covered fruit that's worth a look. The chocolate-covered Nutter Butters—who'd have thought?—are better than they sound and their mild, dark and white chocolate pretzel sticks can be had for less than a buck.

The staff at **The Paper Place** (4001 N. Lamar Blvd. 512/451–6531) generally prefers that you leave the chocolate outside, because they've got a lot of high-end paper, leather goods, picture frames, and greeting cards that are better left unsmudged. The card selection is impressive, and you can special-order any personalized stationery, calling cards, or invitations you can dream up.

Clarksville Pottery and Galleries (4001 N. Lamar Blvd., Ste. 200, 512/454–9079), the high-end hub of Central Market gift shops, will take special orders too, but their collection of crafts from local, national, and international artisans doesn't seem to be missing much. Some specialties are clay and "jewelry art," but they also do well with frivolous kitsch tortilla warmers and giant bird feeders (in case you have a giant bird). They also have one of Austin's largest collections of Judaica, besting all the city's synagogue gift shops in just a few display cases. Unfortunately, this isn't a place you can get out of cheaply, because most of the items are handmade and near museum quality.

Across the parking lot is **The Cadeau** *(4001 N. Lamar Blvd., Ste. 410, 512/453–6988)*, a smaller offshoot of this store's Drag location *(2316 Guadalupe St. 512/477–7276)*. Both stores routinely draw non-student shoppers, mostly because students can't afford much more than the novelty toys and games they keep near the registers. But in many ways, they are like Texas versions of Fortunoff's, where everybody complains about the prices but walks out with an armload of stuff anyway. Check out the Texas-size selection of glass, crystal, silver, candles, jewelry, women's clothing, and housewares.

The Renaissance Market *(23rd St. and Guadalupe St. no phone)* is much more affordable but also considerably more hit-or-miss. Since 1972, local artists have sold handmade woodcrafts, jewelry, pottery, clothes, and toys in an open-air market. The vendors themselves are friendly and quick to cut deals, but the market has lost the Grateful Dead parking-lot vibe it once thrived on. And now, even when more than a handful of dealers bother to show up, there's more generic jewelry and amateur hair-braiders than cool tie-dyes and freaky hand-painted hash pipes. Too bad about Jerry.

Fans of beaded necklaces generally skip the Renaissance Market and truck on down the Drag to **Nomadic Notions** *(2426 Guadalupe St. 512/478–6200)*, an eclectic shop that offers hundreds of ready-to-string beads imported from 60 different countries. Some of the store's voodoo masks, swords, Indonesian wall-hangings, and antique beads can set you back a bundle, but it's easy to throw together an ultra-cool self-serve necklace for less than a ten-spot (it's all about individuality, dammit).

Momoko (705-A W. 24th St. 512/469–0232), a tiny Japanese import shop in a West Campus strip mall, will have you turning Japanese in no time. It has the only authentic Japanese tea room where you can sit and sip or shop for imported toys, trinkets, and housewares. The good news is that everything seems suspiciously inexpensive, particularly for imported goods. The bad news is that a store this small, specialized, and affordable may not last long, so call ahead.

clothing... There are vintage stores all over Austin, but nobody turns over clothes like **The Buffalo Exchange** (2904 Guadalupe St. 512/480–9922) on the Drag. For students, the concept of cash for clothes within walking distance nicely complements their cash for books, cash for CDs, cash for blood, and cash for sperm options. This outlet of the nine-state chain is a great place for cowboy boots, southwestern wear, and funky period-vintage, and it's also good for affordable current clothes like dresses, T-shirts, and Levi's 501s. Unlike a lot of the other campus-area vintage stores, Buffalo Exchange's standards are pretty high, meaning they pay decent money for what they like and offer a sizable selection of quality clothes.

Tamarind Vintage (104-B E. 31st St. 512/469–5852) is a co-op of six dealers that specialize in secondhand clothing, furniture, and housewares in a charming garage-sale kind of atmosphere. But as far as pure vintage goes, few in town do better business than **Blue Velvet** (*3203 Red River St. 512/474–5147*), a campus-area hotspot specializing in men's and women's clothing dating from the '40s to the '70s. Perhaps in part because they carry nothing over $45, they've seemingly clothed every musician in Austin. And while they also appear to have the widest selection of '60s and '70s styles—from skinny ties and bell bottoms to leisure suits and psychedelic blouses—it's the timeless, unisex novelty stuff that makes for the best buys, like Hawaiian, bowling, and western shirts, *guayabaras* (aka Mexican wedding shirts), dashikis, and Chinese robes.

Speaking of gender-benders, **Garb-a-Go-Go** (*1906 Guadalupe St. 512/708–1556*) is designed for the whatever-rocks-your-boat crowd. Their motto is "flashy, classy, hip & trashy" and they live up to it, too, with a stunning and somewhat scary assortment of makeup, wigs, glitter, shoes, hair dye, and nostril screws (!!). They also have a small vintage department, but those duds of yesteryear are overshadowed by a selection of men's and women's clubgear available in PVC, latex, rubber, and velvet.

You'll find nothing so shocking at **By George** (*2905 San Gabriel St. 512/472–5951*), which is exactly what's made their three campus-area stores so popular with the natty, thin, and beautiful. On campus (*2324 Guadalupe St. 512/472–2731*) and in their larger San Gabriel Street store, it's all women's apparel, a lot in silk and velvet. The campus store caters a bit more to the young, trendy, and less expensive side; Austin hipstresses tend to prefer the San Gabriel St. spot, where they can pick up classy evening wear, upscale jewelry, and housewares. **By George for Men** (2346 *Guadalupe St.* 512/472–5536) is similarly upscale, with lots of Massimo and Calvin Klein, though there are more women shopping for their boyfriends at any given moment than there are men in the store. Meanwhile, the glut of celebrity shoppers like Lyle Lovett, Meg Ryan, Andie MacDowell, Nora Ephron, Sandra Bullock, and Shawn Colvin help separate By George from a close competitor, **Charles Edwin Inc.** (1512 *W. 35th St., Ste.* 100, 512/459–9077), a small women's boutique with similarly sophisticated clothing that carries a lot of the same lines, plus a popular shoe department (but, sorry, no plethora of celebs).

Josephine's (3709 *Kerbey Lane* 512/452–7575) is more moderately priced and on the conservative side. Neither trendy nor hip, Josephine's features women's clothing for older clientele—"mom clothing" as one competitor calls it. Meanwhile, the equally no-frills **CP Shades** (4001 *N. Lamar Blvd., Ste.* 580, 512/452–2275) has been doing brisk Central Market business with laid-back monochromatic outfits—what are essentially Garanimals for grownups. And speaking of things generic, it's worth noting that more students spend their money on the Drag at **Urban Outfitters** (2406 *Guadalupe St.* 512/472–1621) and **Gap** (2354 *Guadalupe St.* 512/482–0355) than anywhere else. Neither chain has made much effort to tailor their stock specifically to Austin clientele, but both do an amazing business anyway.

groceries... As odd as it may sound, a grocery has become one of Austin's best tourist attractions. Then again, not every town has a 63,000-square-foot specialty grocer. Since 1994, **Central Market** *(4001 N. Lamar Blvd. 512/206–1000)*, an offspring of the giant HEB (which stands for Herbert E. Butts, the founder) chain, has been Austin's best commercial spot for wowing out-of-town friends and family. Central Market has purposely positioned itself as a family store with a giant outdoor patio, a playground, and children's activities, and their clientele is the most diverse mix of age, class, and race in Central Austin. But what really makes Central Market the Disneyland of groceries are the numbers: 500 varieties of produce, 154 organic produce items, 200 varieties of fresh seafood, a meat market with 60 varieties of their own custom-made sausage, 300 domestic and imported beers, 2,500 domestic and imported wines, 40 loaf breads baked fresh daily, 700 cheeses, 55 varieties of freshly roasted coffee beans, and over 100 kinds of mustard alone. All that, and not a can of Budweiser, bottle of Heinz, or roll of toilet paper in sight. For those simple brand-name necessities, you have to go to HEB itself (this chain is too smart to leave bases uncovered). The store also houses the Central Market Cafe—an in-house food court with passable Tex-Mex, burgers, Italian, steaks, and seafood—the Central Market Cooking School, a large flower shop, and several coffee bars. A second Central Market due to open in spring of 1999 in South Austin should alleviate some of the congestion that can make this store's success a mixed blessing. Crowded or not, it's worth a look.

Without the **Wheatsville Food Co-op** *(3101 Guadalupe St. 512/478–2667)*, there would be no Central Market. It's

Austin's original organic grocery, and it proved that quality food could be a big business. Unfortunately, it's got small New York–style aisles and lots of products crammed into too few shelves. It's still relatively cheap and user-friendly, especially for co-op members who pay $15 a year for slightly cheaper prices than what's on the stickers. In that way, just think of it as a miniature, hippie alternative to Sam's Wholesale.

housewares... The widespread appeal of **Breed and Co.** (718 W. 29th St. 512/474–6679) is simple: houseware plus hardware, straight up, no twist. Everyone leaves here happy, because it's the only place in town where nails, caulking guns, and power drills share the spotlight with cookbooks, silverware, and coffeemakers. They also make keys, and have a great garden department.

music... If the success of the half-dozen record stores along Guadalupe Street proves anything, it's that college students have more disposable income than they let on. And those who don't—the scholarship types—must sell their textbooks mid-semester and use the cash for used CDs at **Technophilia** (2418 Guadalupe St. 512/477–1812) or **Duval Discs** (2928 Guadalupe St. 512/236–1655). The former actually introduced the notion of secondhand CDs to the campus in 1990, back when most people still wondered if used ones played as well as new ones. Since then, it's become the store of choice for students looking to trade in their Puff Daddy for Prodigy and vice versa. With thousands of choices—from hard-to-find trip-hop to dance music to new and used imports and bootlegs—you're just as likely to find an out-of-print funk or metal CD as you are an extra copy of the *Titanic* soundtrack (as a gift for your mom, we mean).

At Duval—which is now on Guadalupe Street rather than Duval Street—the secret of the stock lies with the rock critics and radio programmers who get free promo CDs from record companies and then turn them into cash here. In turn, folks from all around town have learned that this is the place to find new releases at nearly half the price. Duval also has an above-average collection of used jazz, classical music, and soundtracks, and its new partnership with Rolling Pin Music allows it to offer hard-to-find promotional items that aren't readily available elsewhere. So if you ever feel like you absolutely have to own an REM Viewmaster or an Everclear CD with five bonus tracks, this is the place to go.

Although **Sound Exchange** *(2100-A Guadalupe St. 512/476–2274)* files its used and new selections together, few seem to mind the confusing setup: The store has been a genuine U.T. tradition since the early '80s. In fact, Sound Exchange feels like a college radio station, with its piles of new stock sharing counter space with local 7-inch records, cassettes, and 'zines. And as if all the Frank Kozick poster art and the giant Daniel Johnston mural on the store's exterior wall weren't clues enough, the store specializes in hunting down releases from independent labels so small you couldn't find 'em with a magnifying glass. They also stock the usual pop drivel, even though clerks seem to delight in sneering at every sorority girl who walks out with a Mariah Carey or Counting Crows CD.

Further down the Drag, you'll find two more specialty

record stores—**Antone's Record Shop** (*2928 Guadalupe St. 512/322–0660*) and **Thirty-Three Degrees Records and CDs** (*4017 Guadalupe St. 512/302–5233*). Owned by the same folks who own the club, Antone's is the place for blues, perhaps selling more Albert and Freddy King records than any other store in the country. And because blues is all they do, if you come in looking for an obscure 45 or out-of-print CD, they'll at least know what you're talking about even if they don't have it in stock. You can also buy advance tickets here for shows at the eponymous club. Thirty-Three Degrees may not have an official affiliation with a club, but it's where all the club kids go to find the latest dance music and where all the indie-rock geeks go to find experimental noise, jazz, and industrial that's on the alternative side of alternative.

Tower Records (*2402 Guadalupe St. 512/478–5711*) is hardly alternative, but its Austin branch store is worth mentioning for its surprisingly large stock of locally released products and interesting imports. The magazines are current here too and it's the best spot in town to buy earplugs: A pack of ten flesh-colored Hearos will set you back only $4.99.

toys... You've got to figure that when the *Austin Chronicle* calls **Toy Joy** (*2900 Guadalupe St. 512/320–0090*) "like Toys 'R' Us on acid" it means it as a compliment. This independent toy shop is the last bastion for standards like hula hoops, MadLibs, Pop Rocks, Superballs, and hundreds of other affordable, but inane, distractions. Traditional toys are offered for infants all the way up to teenagers, but it seems most of Toy Joy's best customers are nostalgic grownup kids, if not just plain ol' college students latching on to a coolness they weren't alive for the first time around. Note that despite all of the store's inherent hipness, the hordes of parents looking for the latest Beanie Babies on weekend mornings can cause lines worthy of the DMV. They're open till midnight on weekends, but anytime after noon is safe enough.

Madame Alexander dolls and Muffy VanderBear stuffed animals may not be as fashionable as Spinner the Spider or Snort the Bull, but the customers at **The Kerbey Lane Dollshop** (3706 *Kerbey Ln.* 512/452–7086) seem to think they're a more dependable investment. This small shop in a converted house carries more than 100 different styles of dolls—not to mention a full universe of other doll accoutrements—dozens of stuffed animals, and an impressive assortment of doll stands, trunks, books, and magazines. Meanwhile, just down the block, in another converted house, is **Kerbey Lane Dollhouses and Miniatures** (3503 *Kerbey Ln.* 512/454–4287), a room of tiny furniture and homesteads that makes building a West Austin dream house for your doll easy.

miscellaneous... Austin has a host of oddball retailers, but none deserves the "miscellaneous" tag more than **Radio Ranch** (1610 *W. 35th St.* 512/459–6855). Specializing in everything and anything left over at unusual auctions, the Radio Ranch is the only place in town (perhaps in the country) where you can buy false teeth, eight-track players, obscure furniture, vintage electronic equipment, gravestones, and hundreds of items from science labs and medical-equipment wholesalers. Wanna play sensitive-guy actor? The Radio Ranch can provide enough military surplus items to let you rebuild the M*A*S*H set in your living room, right down to the operating tables.

Oat Willie's (*617 W. 29th St. 512/482–0630*) is your parents' headshop (of course, not your parents), straight-up Haight-Ashbury. And because nobody seems to outgrow their taste for hemp in this town—it's not *pot* for cryin' out loud!—Oat Willie's may have the most inclusive clientele in town: students, slackers, professionals, government workers, you, your mama, etc. And yet, in addition to the *tobacco*-smoking paraphernalia, there's eco-friendly clothing, pouch pillows good for hiding, uh, organic valuables in, and yes—Crumb comics.

sleeping

Because the Campus/Central area has some of the city's oldest homes, it also has the most bed and breakfasts. In fact, short of the run-down Days Inn at I-35 and 31st Street, B&B's are really the only option for campus lodging—not that any of the downtown hotels are far from Campus anyway. The Campus/Central B&B's are a mostly historic, popular, and affordable bunch where you're just as likely to find Austinites "getting away" for the weekend as you are visiting professors or real tourists.

> **Cost Range** for double occupancy per night on a weeknight. Call to verify prices.
> $/under 50 dollars
> $$/50–75 dollars

$$$/75–100 dollars
$$$$/100+ dollars

Like most of the Campus/Central B&B's, the proximity of **Brooks House** (*609 W. 33rd St. 512/459–0534 $$$*) to the University of Texas, the State Capitol, and Downtown draws a pretty even mix of parents, faculty, legislators, and businesspeople. The Brooks House drawing card is a country atmosphere: it's a 1922 home with a large porch, a gazebo, and a big backyard filled with post oaks and cedar elms. Three of the antique-filled rooms are in the house; a carriage house and cottage arrangement add another trio of rooms complete with secluded decks and kitchenettes. If you're on the road and miss your dog, they'll loan you theirs—Ernie, the house Labrador. But you'll have to give him back.

The Inn at Pearl Street (*809 W. Martin Luther King Blvd. 512/477–2233 $$$*), an 1896 Greek Revival–style estate surrounded by giant porches, seems to take itself a bit more seriously than its campus competitors. It refers to itself as "an exclusive bed and breakfast for the discriminating traveler," which translated into local English means "an expensive B&B for rich visitors." And while Brooks House chases a country atmosphere, The Inn at Pearl Street's three theme-furnished rooms (Far East, French, and European) go for the "other country" atmosphere. The Gothic Suite, with its medieval-style queen canopy bed and large bathroom, is the real winner of the lot. A stay in any of the rooms entitles guests to a weekday Continental breakfast and Sunday's overwhelming champagne brunch.

Far less ostentatious but not any less expensive is the Victorian-style **McCallum House** (*613 W. 32nd St. 512/451–6744 $$$–$$$$*), a former home of Texas Women's Suffrage Movement leader Jane McCallum that was restored and reestablished in 1983 as Austin's first B&B. Like the others, it has expansive porches and a selection of elms and oaks, but the five rooms succeed in being about charm *and* function: answering machines, irons, and large desks reside among Victorian antiques. And because each room feels so much like a quaint apartment, it's no surprise that academics and professors often take advantage of the extended-stay discounts.

The Woodburn House (*4401 Avenue D 512/458–4335 $$$*) gets its share of both long-term visitors and tourist walk-ins, because there's no better lodging in Hyde Park (just north of the campus) to give you a feel for the history of Austin's first suburb. This four-room 1909 house was actually moved six blocks in 1980, but it's been kept in classic condition, with hardwood floors, pine moldings, and a wraparound deck. Better yet, as the owner-operators of Hyde Park's only B&B, Herb and Sandra Dickson are experts at passing along breakfast table tidbits about Hyde Park folklore.

doing stuff

The University of Texas has the Austin market virtually cornered on unique recreational attractions and the arts. Not only do they own and operate two must-see museums, but they also offer a variety of sports venues and some great opportunities for self-guided walking tours of the campus. U.T.'s cultural offerings are not just for tourists—you'll see as many students and working-class Austinites touring the LBJ Museum or Ransom Arts Center. As for sports, a visit to Austin on any football Sunday will be proof that all life outside Longhorn fandom ceases for a few hours: Football is god, and guest worshippers are welcome as long as they're willing to pay homage by wearing at least one piece of burnt-orange clothing.

Of all the sightseeing options on campus, none is more popular than **The Lyndon Baines Johnson Library and Museum** (*2313 Red River St. 512/916–5136*)—and only partially because it's surrounded by one of the campus' rare public parking lots. Inside this tribute to the 36th president is a collection of 40 million administration documents, dozens of exhibits and displays, and two genuine showstoppers: a collection of ceremonial gifts given by our international allies and a $7/8$ths-scale replica of the Oval Office as it looked during Johnson's service. Best of all, there's a collection of Johnson-era political cartoons, many of which take cheap shots at Johnson himself (the nerve!). Although the overly friendly staff will try anything to push you into it, skip the films on Johnson's career, unless you've got a lot of dead time on your hands. Instead, while you're in the parking lot, use the extra time for a quick tour of the museum's neighbors: The **LBJ School of Public Affairs** (*Sid Richardson Hall 512/471–4962*), the **Texana Archives** (*Barker Texas History Center 512/495–4515*), and one of U.T.'s two visitors bureaus. The Archives possess a wealth of material such as documents of the Spanish period and Stephen Austin's original papers. The bureau also has some excellent panoramic photographs hung up that were taken over the many years of the University's development. And even if you never liked LBJ or don't think you can stomach the museum's revisionism, drive by anyway: With eight stories of travertine marble on a 14-acre hilltop, the LBJ's worth at least a glance.

The Harry Ransom Center (*21st St. and Guadalupe St. 512/471–8944*) is less of an architectural wonder, but represents the University's best cross section of art, history, and culture. The Center's collection of one million rare books, five million photographs, 3,000 pieces of antique camera equipment, 100,000 works of art, and 36 million manuscripts is actually divided into two buildings: the Ransom Center itself and the Leeds Gallery in Flawn Academic Center, just west of the U.T. Tower. Far and away, the high points of the collection are a display copy of an original Guttenberg Bible (one of 48 remaining, only five of which are in America) and the works of the Blanton Museum of Art, a collection of twentieth-century North and Latin American art. The Blanton Gallery also houses the Michener Collection, a formidable selection of modern art donated to the University by James Michener. The three prized pieces in this collection are Phillip Evergood's "Dance Marathon," Franz Kline's "Black and White #2," and Adolph Gottlieb's "Cadmium-Red Over Black." The majority of the Ransom Center's pieces are archived and reserved for University research, but the rotating displays on view to the public are changed at a dizzying speed and may include the world's first photograph (taken by Joseph Niepce in 1826), costumes from *Gone with the Wind*, Isaac

Bashevis Singer's handwritten notes, and original drafts of Arthur Miller's *Death of a Salesman*. Also on occasional display are pieces of the Theater Arts Collection, which includes the Burl Ives collection of folk-music recordings, a collection of Harry Houdini's correspondence, and marionettes, costumes, and general theater paraphernalia and collectibles. As if all that isn't enough, there's also the Willoughby-Blake room of 18th- and 19th-century silver and china, plus a display of 19th-century plaster casts of Greek and Roman sculpture.

The Ransom Center is just a short walk from the University of Texas' **Main Building and Tower**, the campus' center and one of the city's trademark sights. Most of the building dates from 1884, although the 300-foot tower was constructed in 1937. Until 1966, when Charles Whitman opened fire from its balcony, killing 16 pedestrians and wounding over 30 more, it was just another university tower. Stopping to see it now is like stopping at the scene of a car crash. While there's been some discussion of putting a coffee shop on the balcony and getting past "the incident," the Tower still mostly houses administrative offices and denies access to the balcony and bell carillon. (The incident also garnered further attention as the inspiration for Peter Bogdonavitch's first film, *Targets*.)

The Tower and main building separate the **East and West Malls** of campus. To the east, from the Tower's steps, is a view of the LBJ Library and an area where student protests raged in the '60s. The West Mall has also hosted its share of rallies, although the university has now added enough large planters, trees, and random shrubbery to both malls to make mass protests inconvenient. In the event that one does break out, perhaps a couple of times a semester, the university generally finds reason for additional landscaping, which means they leave an army of large trucks strategically parked to cut off a crowd.

Students are *encouraged* to congregate inside and outside the **Texas Union**, the hub of student life. It not only houses The Cactus Cafe, Texas Tavern, Texas Union Theater, and Union Ballroom, but also has its own bowling alley, campus store, and photocopying service. Within the union and on the patio there are plenty of places to study or sleep, although the university and its private food partners would rather you just ate from a food court that includes Taco Bell, Wendy's, and Chick-Fil-A. Wisely, the Union's privatization in 1994 also included plans for local businesses, including satellite shops for Amy's Ice Cream, Texadelphia, and Longhorn Po-Boys. The menus aren't as large as in their proper stores, but the food court has a nice array of local food.

There are a large number of University sports facilities near the LBJ Library. The centerpiece is **The Darrell K. Royal Texas Memorial Stadium** (*23rd St. and E. Campus Dr. 512/471–3333*), recently named for the coaching legend. It's the home of Longhorn football and track and field (all the teams at U.T. are called the Longhorns), and is one of the nation's biggest stadiums, even before a $50 million expansion that raised capacity to over 80,000 and created a line of luxury boxes to rival those of the Dallas Cowboys' Texas Stadium. If you're visiting on a Saturday game day, you'll likely get caught in the orange river of humanity flowing towards the stadium. (Also, beware, hot rivalries sometimes sell out.) If it's not a game day, there isn't much to see that you can't get from a quick glance while driving south on I-35. **The Frank C. Erwin Jr. Special Events Center** (*Red River St. and 15th St. 512/477–6060*), home of the University's men's and women's indoor sports events, is even less impressive to visit on non-game days. It's shaped like a drum. That's about all you need to know.

Off campus, and beyond the long arm of the university, there's yet one more essential museum stop in Campus/Central: the **Elisabet Ney Museum** (**304 E. 44th St. 512/458–2255**). The German-born Ney moved to Austin in 1892 and was Texas' first sculptor. Now her restored home and studio represent one of Texas' best small museums. The house itself, with stone columns and a tower study, is distinctive and tasteful, but the museum's real drawing cards are plaster models of her most known work. Not only will you find remarkable busts of giants such as Garibaldi, Bismarck, and Ludwig II of Bavaria, but also the life-size models for the sculptures of Stephen F. Austin and Sam Houston that Ney created for the Chicago Exposition in 1893. The original marble versions are now on display in the Capitol, but having the plaster models alongside her earlier and later work offers a more dynamic perspective. Best of all, there's a stunning plaster model of Lady Macbeth, a piece Ney considered her finest, in one of the home's large studio windows. Admission's free.

spectating... Any school the size of the University of Texas is going to have its critics, but few have ever charged that U.T. has failed to support the fine arts. In the Performing Arts Center—a massive collective of stages and concert halls—students and touring performers present dance, theater, and music in rooms that are state-of-the-art. That a room like the giant Bass Concert Hall hosts both Itzhak Perlman and Tori Amos just a few seasons apart says much about the school's commitment to both the students and the community. The only thing the school doesn't do well is present film, but you can get that a stone's throw away from campus at the city's must-visit art house, the Dobie Theater [see below].

Although most folks think they're seeing Texas' idea of dance in videos on TNN or CMT, Texans enjoy much more than the two-step. Austin actually lays claim to what are generally regarded as two of the state's best high-brow dance companies: **Ballet Austin** (3002 *Guadalupe St.* **512/476–9051**) and the **Sharir Dance Company** (3724 *Jefferson St. Ste.* **201, 512/458–8158**). The former was the city's first professional ballet company, and nearly thirty years later is still one of only three in the state. The company, housed in a converted firehouse at 30th and Guadalupe streets, has 24 professional dancers and presents 30 performances each season to a combined audience of over 70,000 people. At times the company has received criticism for being too conservative, but things seem to be changing under Artistic Director Lambros Lambrou, a Royal Ballet School graduate who's worked with the National Ballet of Cuba. He's helped incorporate more contemporary styles, like tap and tango, into both the company's classic and modern selections. In fact, the company's 1999 season will take its biggest leap yet, with an Agnes de Mille work featuring backing from Austin swing legends Asleep at the Wheel. (Okay, maybe you do see Texas dance on TNN.) Ballet Austin's season peaks every December with their annual performance of *The Nutcracker*, a hot and highly scalped ticket that fills every seat in U.T.'s giant Bass Concert Hall. The audience fills with proud parents, too, because the performance incorporates students from the Ballet Austin Academy's many dance and fitness programs.

The Sharir Dance Company, the University of Texas College of Fine Arts' company-in-residence, is more progressive, to put it mildly. The program is led by U.T. dance instructor Yacov Sharir, who regularly lectures on topics such as "Virtual Environments, Cyberspace, and the Arts." So with NEA grants in hand—another thing besides the right T-shirt that Austinites interpret as a badge of coolness—Sharir leads his group through a series of multimedia performances and Internet broadcasts that include computer-generated choreography. As with Ballet Austin, the company's four- to six-show season is presented at Bates Hall in the Performing Arts Center.

Like the local ballet companies it hosts, the **Performing Arts Center** (PAC) **(23rd St. at E. Campus Dr. 512/471–1444)** is itself a combination of both the old- and new-school approaches to Texas fine arts. Officially, it's a collective of U.T.'s theater spaces and recital halls, although the only real drawing cards for the average Austinite or tourist are **Bates Recital Hall** and the **Nancy Lee and Perry R. Bass Concert Hall (512/471–1444)**. Bates is the city's most prominent venue for chamber music, with room for 700 (as well as one of the world's largest organs, a Visser-Rowland powered by a combination of modern technology and more than 5,315 pipes). While Bates is typically reserved for smaller ensembles and soloists, the state-of-the-art Bass holds 3,000 and a stage big enough to host fully-staged Broadway extravaganzas—a rarity in Texas. With an orchestra pit that can be raised and lowered and computer-controlled lighting, it represents the bulk of the $41 million that U.T. spent constructing the PAC in 1981. Bates hosts **The Austin Lyric Opera** (512/472–5927) and **Austin Symphony** (512/476–6064) as well as a full schedule of shows from smaller touring Broadway shows to dance, jazz, and vocal companies. Its sheer size and postmodern grandeur make the room worth a look even when there's no show.

Most of the city's theater is presented on smaller private stages such as **The Hyde Park Theatre** (511 W. 43rd St. 512/419–7408), an intimate neighborhood space for contemporary plays and performance art pieces. The University's dramatic arts department has several lecture halls and a pair of stages in **The F. Loren Winship Drama Building** (23rd St. at San Jacinto St. 512/471–1444). The first, the 225-seat **Theater Room** (512/471–0679), is a thrust-style stage in a boxy room—the ideal space for student plays featuring rising stars. The larger room, and the theater non-students are most likely to frequent, is **The B. Iden Payne Theatre** (512/471–1444) a glitzier, more versatile theater space in the same building.

The University also owns and operates its own arena, **The Frank C. Erwin Jr. Special Events Center** (Red River St. and 15th St. 512/477–6060), a round building that hosts indoor U.T. athletics, the Ringling Brothers circus, and dozens of rock, country, and R&B roadshows. If you've seen one arena you've seen the Erwin Center—unlike Bass or Bates, it's architecturally unremarkable. And yet, compared to similar but larger arenas in Dallas or Houston, it's a joy, and with an average capacity of only 15,000, a great way to see superstars like Garth Brooks, Janet Jackson, Guns 'N' Roses, or TAFKAP (The Artist Formerly Known As Prince, or Whatever The Hell He's Called This Year).

Although the University also has **Texas Union Theater** *(Texas Union, 24th St. and Guadalupe St. 512/476–6666)* for art flicks, student films, film festivals and revivals, the coolest theater in town is an independent venue just a block from campus, **The Dobie Theater** *(Dobie Mall, 2021 Guadalupe St. 512/472–FILM)*. Inside Dobie Mall, the recently renovated theater shows first-run independent films on four screens. With a lively rotation of foreign language and nonmainstream cinema—not to mention the annual Spike & Mike animation festivals—the Dobie is at the center of the town's burgeoning film scene. It's virtually impossible to call yourself a film fan in Austin and not wind up here a couple of times a month. As such, the crowds are usually quiet and attentive, although the spaces are small enough that it's hard not to notice when someone exits for the bathroom or snack bar, an upscale pit stop with gourmet candy, fine ice cream, and coffee drinks.

body

The Campus/Central area's salons and hairstylists draw customers from all over Austin. And because there are nearly three dozen hair and/or nail salons in the neighborhood, there's genuine competition for the best service and most reasonable prices. Better yet, there's at least one great place to get a tattoo more challenging than a tired longhorn logo.

As a multiple winner in the *Chronicle's* Best Hair Salon category, **Avant Hair & Skin** (*3405 Guadalupe St. 512/ 458–5231*) seems like it's now one of those rare Austin businesses that can do no wrong. With a Manhattan hair-salon feel, Avant is the place to go for the trendy haircut you saw in *Vogue.* They offer a little hipper-than-thou atti-tude with their upper-salon prices, but folks swear by the complimentary head and neck massage as well as the cre-ative work of head stylist Kat Head, a woman whose trendsetting cuts are even catchier than her name.

Almost as popular, but at the other end of the high-end hair spectrum, is **Horsefeathers Salon** (*3404 Guadalupe St. 512/452–4099*), a collection of a dozen stylists in a house built on Guadalupe Street in 1910. Many of the styl-ists have their own rooms in this house of cowboy kitsch, which makes it feel less like Manhattan and more like a friend's living room. They also have one of the city's larger male clienteles.

Of the dozen or so haircutters on the Drag, at least three have solid enough reputations to attract a share of non-students: **Maximum FX** (*2326 Guadalupe St. 512/472–3331*), **Rick's Aveda Concept Hair & Nail Salon** (*2416 Guadalupe St. 512/476–6960*), and **Holly's Salon and Beauty Supply** (*2004 Guadalupe St. 512/478–3433, 2102 Guadalupe St. 512/479–0727*). All are constantly busy, but Maximum FX—despite its cruise-ship-lounge-band name—is the hippest of the bunch, with stylists that do a lot of movie and photo-shoot work and a huge selection of hair products. But some customers say you've got to be careful to rein in the stylists, or they'll give you the look *they* think you need, rather than the one *you* want. Rick's, on the other hand, will just take your instruction and tell you to lie back and enjoy a freebie beer—a trademark courtesy that's cemented their relationship with many a Shiner-loving student. Holly's two Drag locations also offer a relaxed cut and hair and skin care products, perfumes, and essential oils.

In Hyde Park, there's a salon as laid-back as the neighborhood itself: **4001 Duval Hair Salon** *(4001 Duval St. 512/451–4034)*. By design, it caters to average people with a staff of average cutters with a good sense of style. Meanwhile, there are at least two excellent salons and day spas in the area: **Bradz Salon** *(1822 W. 35th St. 512/454–0080)* and **Anne Kelso Salon** *(3018 N. Lamar Blvd. 512/467–2663)*. The former is a bit hipper and more popular with sorority girls spending Mom's money, while the latter offers great facials, pedicures, and manicures to a slightly older and more upscale crowd.

For the ultimate permanent makeover, how about a tattoo? According to ex-Austinite and master tattooer Rollo Banks, Chris Trevino at **Perfection Tattoo** *(4205 Guadalupe St. 512/453–2089)* is the city's best artist. Apparently, Trevino's work is indeed as good as tattooing gets: well-drawn designs and bright colors applied with precision and care (which those getting tattoos in intimate places will appreciate).

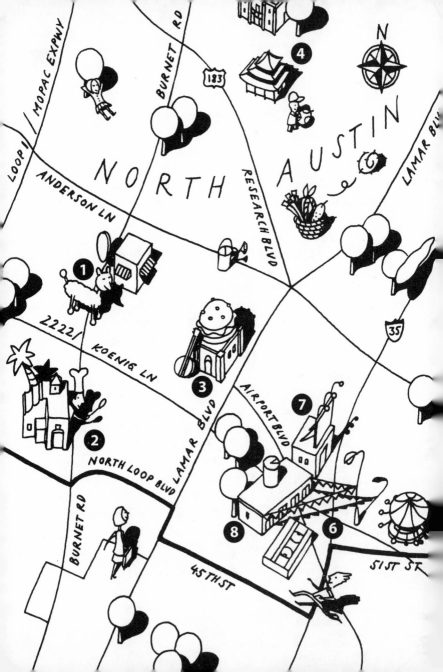

north austin

It's a truism that no matter how far down South you go, anything to the north is still regarded as Yankee turf. That's why even in South Austin, North Austin is seen as a carpetbagger of sorts: New businesses, new roads, new shops, new schools, new neighborhoods—most of this area didn't exist 15 to 25 years ago. North Austin's Anytown USA look can provide the same jolt of generic comfort you get when you're famished and lost at dusk, only to stumble on a familiar jumble of

turn page for map key

McDonald's and Denny's signs. Like it or not, as we head into the 21st century, you're home.

In the last 25 years, North Austin has spawned roads and businesses faster than Tribbles reproduced on "Star Trek." North Austinites, armed with their Suburbans and pickup trucks, have been busily merging little townlets and out-lying cities such as Cedar Park and Leander into a shiny new version of Austin. And along with street after street of cookie-cutter houses, more apartment complexes and condos seem to appear every week.

North Austin is not without personality, you just have to look a little harder for it. You won't find it in hip restaurants or cool stores. In fact, it's the refreshing lack of attitude in the people behind the counter, at the cash register, or waiting tables that sets North Austin apart. There is also a thriving Asian subculture, resulting from Vietnamese immigration in the late '70s when local church and service organizations helped many immigrating Asian families relocate to the affordable suburbs north of Highway 183. This has had a favorable effect on the community (and its restaurants), giving Austin's predominantly Hispanic flavor a further cosmopolitan spin.

This is also the right place if you are looking for mega-shopping, with the giant Highland Mall leading the pack. But be prepared to drive. North Austin is a public transportation no-man's-land; only a car can make you free.

map key		
1	Poodle Dog Lounge	5 Manor Downs
2	Fonda San Miguel	6 Carousel Lounge
3	Threadgill's	7 Tamale House
4	Ichiban	8 I Heart Video

Heading north on Interstate 35, take 183 west, and you speed across gaudy links of chain stores and fast-food joints into the hill country and the pricey Jester Estates subdivision. Or drive north on Lamar Boulevard, and follow the history of Austin's suburban growth outward. If you cut west onto North Loop Boulevard or Koenig Drive, you'll find another artery into the Great White North, Burnet Road (home to the triple-crown of bars: Lala's Little Nugget, the Poodle Dog, and Ginny's Little Longhorn). Pronounce it correctly or risk having some local in a baseball cap and a Willie Nelson T-shirt say, "It's Burnit, durn it, can't ya learn it?" And if this stretch looks vaguely familiar, that's because its '60s-style houses give off that have-a-nice-day feeling that director Richard Linklater capitalized on in his film *Dazed and Confused*. When "King of the Hill"'s LuAnne finally moves out of Hank and Peggy's house, she'll probably move here.

Farther west—but before you come to one of Austin's big attractions, nude swimming in Lake Travis—the mid-to-upscale neighborhoods of Northwest Hills and Balcones Woods feature some of the most elaborate Christmas light displays you'll ever see (an accurate barometer of any true southerner's affluence). If you move into Northeast Austin, the area's identity shifts uncomfortably from a suburb, to the closest Austin has to a somewhat dangerous inner-city neighborhood, only to glide into the gentle expanse of rolling farmland that follows Highway 290 east all the way to Houston. (Also east of town is one of Texas' few pari-mutuel betting horse tracks.)

Sound bleak? The miles and miles of concrete are daunting indeed, but if you're looking for soul in North Austin, keep looking. Watch the changing face of Burnet Road, for example, and see where the proximity of the Omelettry restaurant and Top Drawer Thrift Store (whose proceeds benefit a local AIDS group) makes for an inviting stop-n-shop combo. Or Airport Boulevard's hip strip mall, where you can pick up music at ABCD's, find something to wear at Sacks II, and attend happy hour at Amazonia fish store. It's the little touches like these that slowly but surely are giving North Austin something it has long needed: character.

eating/coffee

Finding a place to get something to eat in North Austin is easy. Finding someplace that's not junk-food or overpriced is a good bit harder. Fortunately, the Asian migration to North Austin in the '70s brought with it an explosion in the number of Asian restaurants that all congregate in the neighborhood phenomenon of the strip mall. They're generally inexpensive places that appeal to the entire population of the Northside, and many of the more than four dozen eateries have become neighborhood favorites—a novelty in the land of Tex-Mex. The owners of Satay, for instance, have gone on to successfully package many of their recipes for sale in places like Whole Foods. Vietnamese *pho*, that simple bowl of noodles, rivals the popularity of the almighty burger and the Mexican dinner for popularity.

Home barbecue pits apparently weren't high on the list of amenities when many of North Austin's houses were designed, but that's good for the local restaurant business. There are around two dozen barbecue restaurants fanned across North Austin. There are also about the same number of interior Mexican restaurants (meaning, food from the interior of Mexico, as opposed to border food) scattered about the northern part of the city. And North Austin *can* boast about a few of its dining possibilities—such as wild-game hot spot Hudson's-on-the-Bend—but the nightlife here (compared to livelier nighttime hangouts like Down-town and Campus/Central) is grim, grim, grim.

A note about trying to find some of these places: If the address is listed as Research Boulevard, you will want to be on Highway 183's access road. Research Boulevard is the name of the road below the highway punctuated by an endless stretch of discount stores, shopping centers, furni-ture outlets, and restaurants. Watch out though, because the part of 183 west which crosses I-35 is better known as West Anderson Lane, which then breaks off from 183 at Lamar Boulevard and continues west to Mopac. Research then picks up where Anderson detours and follows 183 west into the Hill Country. Similarly, when Anderson takes off on its own from 183 and crosses Mopac, it turns into Spicewood Springs Road. Got it? If you're driving, you may want to call for exact directions just to be safe.

Cost Range per entree
$/under 10 dollars
$$/10–15 dollars
$$$/15–20 dollars
$$$$/20+ dollars

24-hour/coffee... Breakfast is not as big a thing in North Austin as it is in other parts of the city, most likely

because it's mostly a bedroom community and not a haunt for night owls. "Let's do coffee" tends to happen near the main business districts of downtown and the University area, while "breakfast" is just as likely to be something you get after a club gig on the way home as the last meal of the day. **Triumph Coffeehouse** (*3808 Spicewood Springs Rd. 512/343–1875 $*) is technically in a strip mall, but its clean, modern design and new look don't have the lived-in comfort of Flightpath [see **campus/central**]. A good cup of joe and fresh pastries make up for the rather sterile interior, however. More **Texas French Bread** (*7719-A Burnet Rd. 512/419–0184, 10225 Research Blvd. 512/418–1991 $*) locations up this way offer their usual coffee, baked goods, bagels, and sandwiches. While you're there, pick up some of those yummy Texas-shaped butter cookies.

For a full Texas breakfast with all the fixins, North Austin has two of the best places in town: **Kerbey Lane Cafe North** (*12602 Research Blvd. 512/258–7757 $–$$*) and **The Omelettry** (*4811 Burnet Rd. 512/453–5062 $–$$*). Kerbey Lane's venture north has been thriving since it opened almost 10 years ago. This location is more family-oriented than Kerbey's slacker/yuppie haven in Central Austin, or the one frequented by bubbas and hippies in South Austin. Their belt-busting breakfasts include delicious, overstuffed omelets and buttery French toast. The Omelettry is the surviving half of an old popular local eatery—the original Omelettry became Magnolia Cafe on Lake Austin—but has always maintained its combination neighborhood cafe/veggie natural-foods restaurant appeal. The BLT has thick slices of creamy avocado, and the home fries are near perfect. Expect a wait on weekend mornings at both places.

asian... If you're a Thai-food lover, you'll do well at **Classic Thai** *(156 N. Lamar Blvd. 512/491–8856 $–$$)* which offers simple but varying Thai cuisine—saté, tom yum soup, pad thai—and many vegetarian dishes. The bonus of dining there on a slow Sunday afternoon is occasionally getting to watch some of the employees singing the likes of "I Only Wanna Be With You" along with the karaoke machine. The new kid in town is **Thai Spice Cafe** *(2501 Parmer Ln. 512/821–1522 $–$$$)*, overseen by femme chefs Vicki Vicha and Orasinee Ratana. The place is clean and attractively decorated—not too heavy on the kitschy Asian decor—and their green curry has just the right balance of coconut and spice.

Bangkok Cuisine *(9041 Research Blvd. 832–9722 $–$$$$)* and **Satay** *(3202 W. Anderson Ln. 467–6731 $–$$$$)* are rivals for those with more sophisticated taste buds. In an atmosphere that resembles a lush meditation garden, Bangkok lures the palate with such dishes as Thrilling Shrimp, sautéed with mixed vegetables and a searingly hot chili sauce. (If the hot sauce in Mexican restaurants makes you wary, steer clear.) Their weekday lunch buffet ($5.95) runs until 7 p.m.—something worth noting if money is tight. Satay is more exotic, with cuisine from Thailand, Singapore, Malaysia, Indonesia, and the Philippines. You have to look a little harder to find Satay, since it's tucked away on West Anderson Lane where it crosses over Mopac, but it's well worth the effort. The restaurant has its own garden of spices and vegetables, and friendly owner Foo Swasdee is serious about his diners enjoying their meals. The decor draws from the countries that inspire the menu without giving way to Chinatown cuteness. The Devil Fish (spicy Thai grilled catfish) and the Tiger Cry (grilled beef with Thai hot pepper and lime sauce) are worth the trip. While you're there, you can also pick up packaged foods like saté marinade.

Vietnamese fare comes in all shapes and sizes but the restaurants always seem to be located in the same generic strip mall. Happily, that doesn't keep them from offering sublime bowls of noodles at **Fortune Pho** (*5501 N. Lamar Blvd. 512/458–1792 $–$$*), where Vietnamese dishes grace the dinner menu, although Chinese fare dominates the lunch buffet. Fortune Pho has a very subdued atmosphere with little of the usual bric-a-brac, and a TV that's usually tuned in to the day's sports events. If you've never experienced **Mongolian Barbecue** (*9200 N. Lamar Blvd. 512/837–4898 $–$$$*), forget about any notions of Texas influence. Just stand before the buffet and choose what meat and vegetables you want grilled and ladle on the delicious sauces (which are varying degrees of hot!).

The most appealing self-promotion award has to go to **Korea House** (*2700 W. Anderson Ln. 512/458–2477 $–$$$*), whose web page boasts of "Chinese and Vietnamese food in strip mall environment" and that the "waiters net dinner from big tanks of fish." In reality, this quiet little restaurant is located in the not-unattractive Village Shopping Center, whose greenery and small ponds break up the shopping monotony. After the buildup, the fish tank is disappointingly small, but netted or not, the sushi is tasty and the *wasabi* lethal.

asian buffet... The two editors/writers of the local 'zine *Hey! Hey! Buffet* (the best place to find it is Sound

Exchange on the Drag in the U.T. campus area), relentlessly pursue and review buffets all around town. The HHB boys gave **Buffet Palace** (1012 *W. Anderson Ln.* 512/458–2999 **$–$$$**) a double thumbs-up for their Chinese, Japanese, Korean, and sushi selections. Editor Greg Steeb declares it "adventurous" and admires its anything-Asian-fits decorating scheme. You won't want to miss the hokey "floating sushi boat display." The more traditional **Ichiban** (7310 *Burnet Rd.* 512/452–2883 **$–$$$**) cooks a mean Korean barbecue. Their pagoda-style exterior is a welcome change from the anonymous strip malls that house most Asian restaurants on this side of town. **Korea Garden** (6519 *N. Lamar Blvd.* 512/302–3149 **$–$$$**) is more expensive, but many dishes are meant to feed two. You might want to check the ingredients so you don't get overwhelmed. *Dae Go Ki Chigae*, for example, is soup with "hot dog, ham, noodle, beef, and vegetables" ($17.95).

barbecue... Barbecue is one of the hot tickets in North Austin, in case you haven't seen the Visa commercial featuring the irritatingly named **Bo Knows Bar-B-Que** (10401 *Anderson Mill* 512/918–9544 **$–$$$**). But he *does* know barbecue, though not necessarily better than many others firing up pits around here. And mad-cow alarmists notwithstanding, chain barbecue joints have increased exponentially over the last few years. The locally owned and run **Pit Barbecue** (4707 *Burnet Rd.* 512/453–6464, 5423 *Cameron Rd.* 512/453–7866, 3815 *Dry Creek Dr.* 512/451–0000 **$–$$**) franchise and **Richard Jones Pit Barbecue** (9207 *N. Lamar Blvd.* 512/837–5013 **$–$$**) continue to dish up dependably good beef, chicken, and ribs.

Jones' Lamar location is the Northside outpost of his long-time South Congress Avenue restaurant, and what it lacks in personality inside is made up for by a menu full of inexpensive, tasty food that is easily packed to go if you're in a day trip mood. **Green Mesquite North** (13450 *Research Blvd.* 512/335–9885 $–$$$), one of the best local barbecue chains, brings the smoky flavor of their original Barton Springs Road location and their tradition of live music to all their locations. Just close your eyes and let your nose lead you to beef ribs big enough to knock over the Flintstones' car.

burgers and sandwiches... Although being seen at **Dick Clark's American Bandstand** (7522-B S. I-35 512/451–5160 $–$$$) may be worse than buying a Hard Rock Cafe satin tour jacket, visiting it is actually cool in a creepy way. The burgers are adequate if pricey for Austin at $4, but some of the items on display are hilarious. A recent rotating exhibit turned up an autograph from Jon Secada, Madonna's leather jacket, a guitar signed by Pink Floyd, and even a pair of Cher's boots.

Better burgers are to be found at places favored by locals, like **Airport Haven** (6801 *Guadalupe St.* 512/459–6859 $), whose silly sign of a nerdy 1920s lad in an old-fashioned airplane belies the old-fashioned luncheon-grill burger-n-fries menu inside. **Holiday House** (5201 *Airport Blvd.* 512/452–3136 $) grills its deliciously smoky "flameburgers" over an open fire, but the barbecue is unmemorable. Stick with the burgers—the one drenched in hickory sauce is a peculiarly Texas thing—and don't overlook their daily specials, including cafeteria-style (meaning not so fancy) chicken-fried steak and a choice of two vegetables for $2.99. You read right—that's a full (if starchy) meal.

Waterloo Ice House (8600 Burnet Rd. 512/458–6544 $–$$) has tried other neighborhoods in addition to the N. Lamar and 38th Street locations, but none have worked as well as this one, with its especially juicy, big burgers and large selection of beers (although they don't have live music here). Moreover, Waterloo Ice House has a friendly Texas roadhouse atmosphere, as if it were once a country burger joint and the city grew around it. **The Frisco Shop** (5819 Burnet Rd. 512/459–6279 $–$$) is easily identified by the beautiful neon hamburger out front, and it carries its big-city diner style with class. Many of the older staff here are slice-of-life characters you don't often meet anymore, so chat them up. You might even learn something. No guide to a Texas suburb would be complete without mentioning a bowling-alley restaurant: **The Dart Bowl Steak House** (5700 Grover Ave. 512/459–4181 $) is far better for people-watching than it is for cuisine, but you won't die from eating their burgers and the like. Real conversation overheard here: "Lura Mae done put a blonde rinse on her hair and Cletus liked to've had a fit." Response: "Wuz he mad?" You get the picture.

If you take the time to go inside and dine at **Top Notch Restaurant** (7525 Burnet Rd. 512/452–2181 $–$$), you won't necessarily send your compliments to the chef, but it's not so terrible either. What you want to do is pull up to the drive-in menus in the parking lot beside a car full of members of the opposite sex, do your best Matthew McConaughey Texas swagger, and say, "There's a fiesta in the makin' as we speak. Coupla kegs, you oughta come."

Silly, sure, but feel vaguely familiar? You have just reen-acted a scene from *Dazed and Confused* on location.

As always, the by-now-familiar red signs for **Schlotzsky's** (6921 Burnet Rd. 512/451–3208, 9616 N. Lamar Blvd. 512/837–0848 $) and blue ones for **Thundercloud Subs** (2300 Lohmans Crossing Rd. 512/263–1620, 13776 Research Blvd. 512/258–9145, 2521 Rutland Dr. 512/339–7827, 180 White Stone Dr. 512/259–2328 $) are welcome. Schlotzsky's is famous for its grilled sandwiches on bread resembling an English muffin. They will certainly cut that craving for some-thing hot and cheesy. And local chain Thundercloud beats Subway sandwiches cold. Don't mind the overly chirpy, cheery chain-store atmosphere of both places—the food is fresh and affordable.

indian... Both **Mr. India Palace** (9120 N. I-35 512/835–4447 $–$$$) and **Star of India** (2900 W. Anderson Ln. 512/452–8199 $–$$$) offer the traditional Indian fare well-prepared—curries, tandoori, etc., in mild and spicy degrees—with the usual kind of sitar-music floating around. Mr. India is a little more generic in taste and appearance (though priced inexpensively) but Star of India's low lighting makes their buffet seem a little more exotic. And the vegetable *pakora* and the *chana masala* are excellent. **Taj Palace** (6700 Middle Fiskville Rd. 512/452–9959 $–$$$) was one of the first Indian restau-rants in town, heavy on the decor. It's also famous for its buffet, the perfect way to introduce someone to Indian food. Taj Palace makes an especially good *saag paneer*, a cheese-and-spinach dish with curry spice ($5.50)—try it with the *naan* bread.

italian... Not much on the Northside for Eye-talian food lovers except **Pavarotti Italian Grill** (*3300 W. Anderson Ln. 512/453–5373 $–$$$$*). They somehow manage to strike a careful balance between bland/mall-ish and intimate dining. They carry more than 40 sauces on their menu, including Alfredo and classic marinara. Pizza fanatics rejoice: **Roppolo's Pizzeria** (*8105 Mesa Dr. 512/346–9800 $–$$$$*) is one of the town's critical favorites, known for its tasty, crispy crust and the fresh toppings they heap on the pies. Stuck in a hotel room or a friend's place in suburbia? Call **Double Dave's** (*11900 Metric Blvd. 512/719–3283, 9616 N. Lamar Blvd. 512/837–3283 $–$$$*) if Roppolo's doesn't deliver to your area. It's your basic delivery-style pizza; perfect at your hotel when other restaurants are closed. DD's chicken topping is particularly savory—try it with jalapeños if you're brave. **CiCi's Pizza** (*9717 N. Lamar Blvd. 512/873–8800 $–$$*) is only passable on a culinary scale, but their $2.99 all-you-can-eat buffet tastes great when funds are low.

regional... How do you know Southern cooking? It's usually the kind that makes no attempt to be PC or calorie- or cholesterol-conscious. Ladle on the gravy, fry up the chicken, put lots of butter on the corn, and pass the biscuits, please. If it looks like your grandmother (or somebody's grandmother) made it, that's Southern cooking. **Dot's Place** (*13805 Orchid Ln. 512/255–7288 $*) dishes out cafeteria-style food that smells and tastes like Sunday dinner. **Grace's Home Cooking** (*6601 N. Lamar Blvd. 512/583–0504 $*) also serves the grand-slam lineup of meat, potatoes, and dessert. The food is filling and hot and the atmosphere is cozy and friendly. There's nothing wrong with Grace's—nothing except being located across from the granddaddy of Austin homestyle cooking, **Threadgill's (6416 N. Lamar Blvd. 512/451–5440 $$)**. It's hard to imagine that 20 years ago, the original Threadgill's Restaurant was a gas station. Folkie, country singer, yodeler, gas station-bar-restaurant owner, Kenneth Threadgill is now best remembered for having established the first regular picking-and-singing jam sessions in Austin. His most famous alumna was a pre-acid-rock Janis Joplin, and Threadgill's walls today are full of old newspaper clippings and notices attesting to that. The menu? Along with the plate of mouthwateringly fresh biscuits and rolls and pats of real butter, it's fried, fried, fried, and—okay, a little broiled here and there. But let's not soft-pedal it: The affable chef, Wilson, refers to his fried chicken livers as "the heart-attack special."

seafood... Don't tell the crowds at **Pappadeaux (6319 N. I-35 512/452–9363 $–$$$$)**, another regional chain, that Austin isn't on a coast. They seem to buy into the contrived coastal-boathouse look and put up with hour-long waits for plates piled high with catch-of-the-day specials which are actually hard to resist. This is a good chain. **Pearl's Oyster Bar (9033 Research Blvd. 512/339–7444 $$–$$$)** is more intimate, and features live music on a regular basis, even though it's stuck in a nondescript shopping strip called the Colonnade. Those who know seafood swear **The Captain's Seafood & Oyster Bar (5700 N. I-35 512/452–1417 $–$$$)** is one of the best places in town. Their plump, tasty butterfly shrimp will tell you why. Never mind the cheesy look and interstate location.

tex-mex... While it's not quite the Tex-Mex heaven South Austin is, North Austin's Mexican restaurants run the gamut from the elegant interior cuisine of Fonda San Miguel to tacos for a buck at Tamale House. Both of **Chuy's** (**10520 N. Lamar Blvd. 512/836–3218, 11680 Research Blvd. 512/342–0011 $–$$$**) northern locations have pretty good chile rellenos. Both are also quite garish in style: The Research Boulevard spot is notable for the statue of Atlas bearing the world of Chuy's on his back, and Lamar is a kind of Arnold's Drive-In meets Taco Bell, with a '50s diner look on the inside, where hubcaps cover the ceiling completely. All locations are famous for potent margaritas.

If you want to take it up a level, **Casita Jorge's** (**2203 Hancock Dr. 512/454–1980 $–$$$**) has been dishing it out for almost 20 years at one location or another. Since moving here some 10 years ago, it's thrived on a menu composed of Tex-Mex favorites that are more freshly prepared than at other places. The creamy and flavorful guacamole is supreme—pile it on the vegetarian enchiladas. In nice weather, dining on the patio can be a dreamy experience, especially in the afternoon, when business is slow and the bartender has lined up a string of sensual Tejano songs on the jukebox.

El Mercado (**7414 Burnet Rd. 512/454–2500 $–$$$**) brings its South Austin panache north, with flashy, neon-decorated cantina-style decor, Pepto-Bismol colored walls and a raucous atmosphere inside. Try their flautas topped with guacamole, pico de gallo, and sour cream. Don't forget to keep plenty of their chunky hot sauce close by. The Houston-based regional chain **Ninfa's** (**214 E. Anderson Ln. 512/832–1833 $–$$$**) made its first appearance in town at this location; last year they opened another on 6th Street. The menu is passable, the chips are a little hard and greasy sometimes, but their tart and spicy green tomatillo sauce is divine: Put it on everything.

Two words: **Tamale House** (*5003 Airport Blvd. 512/ 453–9842 $*). It looks like a sweatbox. It is. See the sign? "If we buy air conditioning, you will pay more to eat here." Just smile, mop your brow, and wait for the food. It's so cheap here there's almost no reason to eat anywhere else again ever; what you pay for food here is the tax at other restaurants. For $1.50 and under you can get chalupas, tacos, and breakfast tacos with any fillings you like. Even the lunch plates are cheap, at $3 to $4. Take it to go, unless you like the views of patrons' butts as they line up.

upscale... Hudson's-on-the-Bend (*3509 Ranch Road 620 512/266–1369 $$–$$$$*) has long specialized in Texas wild game, with succulent results. Its upscale mountain lodge-like setting near the lake is the perfect atmosphere to savor such dishes as smoked quail with plum sauce. Call ahead for the current menu, and make reservations, since it's quite the drive.

Fonda San Miguel Restaurant (*2330 W. North Loop Blvd. 512/459–4121 $–$$$$*) is the standard by which Mexican cuisine is measured in Austin. The spacious, saltillo-tiled restaurant was once home to noted interior Mexican cuisine chef and cookbook author Diana Kennedy, and the superb menu is her legacy. You'll love the *anjitos*, bite-sized appetizers of crab, shrimp, and avocado. Try the *ancho* chicken, a highly spiced grilled dish served like fajitas, with tortillas and toppings. And savor the just-made corn tortillas.

Reservations are recommended, though a long wait at the bar is great for people-watching.

miscellaneous... Mykonos Greek Food (7329 **Burnet Rd. 512/451–0677 $**) is a welcome respite from a North Austin overload of Asian, barbecue, and Tex-Mex, serving inexpensive Greek food, including a particularly tasty veggie gyro, in a deli/strip-mall atmosphere.

We won't try to pass this off as nutrition, but if you can't remember the last time you had a snowball (snowcone, shaved ice, whatever), get thee to **Casey's New Orleans Snowballs** (808 51st St. 512/453–8123 $). Cheap, sweet, cold, and flavorful—what more can you ask for? They even offer a chocolate snowball. Try the Suicide if you dare.

bars/music/clubs

North Austin bars don't usually have live music. Here, it's more often found in restaurants, stores, and shopping centers; clubs have dancing with DJs. Also, if you do plan on bar-hopping, be sure to dust off your designated driver. In this part of town you have to do some driving to get from venue to venue. Given the convenience and availability of music elsewhere in Austin, this distance between places is not such a bad proposition for the businesses, as they're more likely to keep you in one place all night.

The following bars and clubs in North Austin usually observe a No Live Music policy; you can expect most of the recorded music to be of the pop country/urban cowboy variety. At **Dallas Nightclub** (7113 Burnet Rd. 512/

459–9009), **Avalon** (13800 *Dragline Dr.* 512/252–7600), and **Cowboy Nite Club** (9515 *N. Lamar Blvd.* 512/834–2640), it's lots of Shania Twain and no Patsy Cline, but you sure can't beat them for a slice-of-life look at modern country discos. Dallas is the grandaddy of them all, having been around when country wasn't really cool. The crowds at Avalon and Cowboy look like they watch too much Nashville Network. For something more fun, try **The Common Interest Karaoke Bar** (8440 *Burnet Rd.* 512/453–6796). Grunt like Michael Bolton or soar like Whitney Houston in the undistinguished confines of The Common Interest—you're only visiting, right?

The best two of the oft-referred-to "triple crown" of bars on Burnet Road are **The Poodle Dog Lounge** (6407 *Burnet Rd. no phone*) and **Lala's Little Nugget** (2207 *Justin Ln.* 512/453–2521). The Poodle Dog Lounge is kind of seedy, but the beer is cheap and no one cares if you're dressed right. Good pool tables, too. Lala's is another anomaly—it's Christmas 365 days a year here. Holiday decorations were put up years ago and never taken down. (Careful entering and exiting the men's bathroom; the little elves nearby are rigged to jump and jingle when the door opens.) You'll hear lots of gush stories about Tarantino, Linklater, Rodriguez, *ad nauseum* hanging out here, but the real draw has to be the great cry-in-your-beer jukebox playing everything from Bing Crosby to George Jones.

Sure, **ABCD's** (4631 *Airport Blvd.* 512/454–1212) is a record store, but don't pass up their regular in-store performances. "First Thursday" is a gathering plugged as "a monthly celebration of Austin music, carbonated intoxicants, and free shit." For 10 years, **The Arboretum** (10000

Research Blvd. 512/338–4437) shopping center has offered Blues on the Green, a weekly live music event held outside near a couple of somewhat grotesque marble cow statues. The music is kind of a crapshoot, though, with your standard bar-band fare.

North Austin's best live music can be seen at a handful of places. **Dessau Music Hall** (13422 *Dessau Rd.* 512/252–1123) was once the northern equivalent of South Austin's raucous Broken Spoke but today you might see anything from the early '80s metal-meisters Quiet Riot to the local Celtic band Two O'Clock Courage. **Ginny's Little Longhorn** (5434 *Burnet Rd.* 512/458–1813), the third of the Burnet Road triple crown, is a bar where you're more likely to hear, "What'd you say, boy?" than "Excuse me?" They have top-notch country music from players like heartbreak king Dale Watson. **Tejano Ranch** (7601 *N. Lamar Blvd.* 512/453–6615) is primarily a dance club, but once in a while they attract name Tejano acts on tour. This is the type of venue that is fostering the vibrant cross-cultural sound made popular by artists the likes of the late Selena and Ricky Trevino. **Ski Shores** (3301 *Pierce Rd., Lake Austin* 512/346–5915) is a strictly seasonal spot, and though they offer a grill menu, the real reason to go there is to drink beer, swim, and water-ski. The live music is sporadic at best, but the rustic location and spectacular vantage point on Lake Austin are the real charms. To get there, drive west on RM 2222 (stands for Ranch Market) to City Park (about 8 miles), turn into City Park and follow the short road to the water.

No tour of North Austin clubs would be complete without mentioning **The Carousel Club** (1110 *E. 52nd St.*

512/452–6790). With the lounge music revolution in full swing in Austin, the Carousel is the place to land. Solo keyboardist Jay Clark is the man, though you'll regularly find alternative and swing bands, too. Matt "The Cat" Jones leads dance lessons there weekly. The circus mural inside is especially psychedelic after a couple of happy-hour martinis.

buying stuff

North Austin is mall-and-shopping-center land. Highway 183 is nothing but block-to-block shopping, meaning if you want to buy it, it's probably here. The granddaddy malls are **Highland Mall** (6001 *Airport Blvd.* 512/454–9656) and **Northcross Mall** (2525 *W. Anderson Ln.* 512/451–7466), where the kids tend to hang on weekends. The new and shiny **Lakeline Mall** (11200 *Lakeline Mall Blvd.* 512/257–7467) and open-air **Gateway Shopping Center** (*Hwy. 183 at Loop 360 no phone*) join the very upscale **Arboretum** (10000 *Research Blvd.* 512/338–4437) in linking with the ever-popular strip malls, turning the area into one huge mall.

books/music... Austin is rumored to have one of the best-read populations in the United States, based on the ratio of bookstores to people. What's seldom noted is that religious bookstores make up a large proportion of that ratio, but there's no denying that the selection of bookstores in Austin is impressive. **Bookstop** (9070 *Research Blvd.* 512/451–5798), one of the first discount chain bookstores in the country, manages to retain its local flavor even while moving mountains of books cheaply. No surprise then that marketing giants **Barnes & Noble** (The Arboretum, 10000 Research Blvd. 512/418–8985) and **Borders Books & Music** (10225 Research Blvd. 512/795–9553) have moved into town, alongside the shopping-mall staples **B. Dalton Bookseller** (Northcross Mall 512/454–5125, Highland Mall 512/452–5739) and **Waldenbooks** (Lakeline Mall 512/257–1950). Borders has a literary discussion group and poetry readings. Barnes & Noble has weekly poetry workshops and monthly fiction discussions.

While corporate giants taking the place of mom-and-pop bookshops is becoming commonplace, places like **Earfull of Books** (9607 Research Blvd. 512/338–6706) survive the trend by focusing on a specialty: They sell books on tape and have titles by the hundreds. And don't let the name fool you, **Half Price Books** (8868 Research Blvd. 512/454–3664) is one of the places to shop for both new and used books. It's so comfortably carpeted and stocked it feels like a new bookstore. Their remaindered books (here's where to find out how quickly Elizabeth Wurtzel's latest book tanks) are as varied and interesting as their used titles.

The Book Exchange (7411 Burnet Rd. 512/454–6139) is a small, maze-like trade-in paperback bookstore. Sure, you can buy the used titles off the shelf, but if you're done with the latest Stephen King or Jude Devereaux, bring it with you and trade it in against another in the same genre. A delightful specialty bookstore is the intimate **Mysteries and More** (11139 N. I-35, Ste. 176, 512/837–6768), selling new and used titles. Owner Jan Grape is the merry-faced motherly type behind the counter. Besides being a published mystery author herself (ask for the Deadly Women anthology and you might get it autographed), she has an almost encyclopedic knowledge of mystery and suspense titles and authors.

In the Northside music market, **Camelot Music** (Northcross Mall Ln. 512/452–2916), **Blockbuster Music** (9607 Research Blvd. 512/837–8808), and **Best Buy** (10001 Research Blvd. 512/795–0014) have the usual mainstream offerings—perfect if you're looking for the latest MTV hits. But you'll find a more eclectic collection at **ABCD's** (4631 Airport Blvd. 512/454–1212), with a respectable selection of Austin and Texas artists. ABCD's often features live music and in-store record-release parties, so you'll never quite know what to expect there. The locally owned **Encore** (8820 Burnet Rd. 512/451–8111) is a favorite for CDs, but is also noted for its videos. Owner Chuck Lokey is proud of his business—that's usually him out stocking the shelves on the floor—which specializes in LaserDisc and DVD as well as music and videotapes. **I Heart Video** (4631 Airport Blvd. 512/450–1966, 11139 N. I-35 512/837–9510) has not only the usual new releases but also the kind of cheesy flicks (Poor White Trash, The Trip) that do the memory of Ed Wood proud. Decorated like a student film freak's dorm room and packed with videos, this place is well worth a stop because even if you're not renting, the employees are usually more than willing to share their knowledge of the cult-film genre.

Aaron's Rock & Roll Emporium (Northcross Mall 512/419–9866) carries posters, T-shirts, rolling papers, and other countercultural accessories. **Comic Castle** (6700 Middle Fiskville Rd. 512/451–4024) is home to

Austin's gamers and roleplayers. The store features Magic the Gathering tourneys, a big selection of action figures, posters, T-shirts, comics, and collector's magazines.

clothes/accessories...

Thrifty shoppers love **Ross Dress For Less** (8100 *Burnet Rd.* 512/452–5728) and **Loehmann's** (2438 *W. Anderson Ln.* 512/451–7908), both carrying designer labels and accessories; some local drag queens prefer Ross because they carry women's shoes in larger sizes. Some of the more popular consignment stores are: **A Time or Two Boutique** (1748 *W. Anderson Ln.* 512/452–6992), **Nouveau Options: The Designer Exchange** (7739 *Northcross Dr.* 512/452–0606), and **Fashion Exchange** (5114 *Balcones Woods Dr.* 512/338–0200). All handle resale fashion while avoiding the slightly pretentious phrase "pre-owned."

The recently expanded **Out of the Past** (5341 *Burnet Rd.* 512/371–3550) specializes in vintage clothing, accessories, household items, and collectibles. The bright pastel exterior colors of **Top Drawer Thrift Shop** (4902 *Burnet Rd.* 512/454–5161) take a more traditional secondhand-store approach, but say fun and funky, as do the wares for sale: A bright orange '60s-style ashtray here goes for $6. If you're over near ABCD's, I Heart Video, or Amazonia, stop into **Sacks II** (4631 *Airport Blvd.* 512/451–4108). Racks and racks of secondhand clothes and retro-wear reflect the tongue-in-chic approach. **Nomadic Notions** (3010 *W. Anderson Ln.* 512/454–0001) offers more than just beads and beaded jewelry, though their collection of exotic stones and silver jewelry is hard to pass up. Exotic masks, tapestries, crochet bags, bead curtains, and bronze statues round out their fancy beads. They also offer classes in beadwork.

computers... The **Dell Computer Outlet Store** (8801 *Research Blvd.* 512/728–5656) is much larger than a dorm room at U.T., which is where founder and Austinite Michael Dell began his computer empire. Today he's a a cyberspace mogul second only to Bill Gates, with an outlet store which is a boon to computer-literate Austin. Dell may well be the best deal in town.

household/antiques... If you're considering a move to Austin and want to check out inexpensive furnishings a cut above cinderblock-and-plank bookshelves, try **The Texas Futon Company** (5440 *Burnet Rd.* 512/450–1606). Their selection of futons, covers, and frames won't break you—a twin mattress with a frame that folds into a chair runs about $190. The cleverly titled **Eurway** (2236 *W. Braker Ln.* 512/835–4006) is among the latest in superstores featuring affordable furnishings. Don't let its enormous sprawl intimidate you; there are many good bargains to be found in its miles of aisles. For quality antiques and used furniture, the enormous **Antiques Marketplace** (5350 *Burnet Rd.* 512/452–1000) is a must-stop on your list. You could spend days poking through the tiny "rooms" of antique furniture, knick-knacks, artwork, glassware, and other items—and it's more quality than kitsch.

miscellaneous... A trip through **Amazonia** (4631 *Airport Blvd.* 512/451–0958) is the next best thing to being underwater—and you don't get wet. Owner Caroline Etter was part of Austin's original punk scene, and now it's her tanks of exotic fish with their splendid flowing fins and glowing colors that are getting the attention. A Fish Happy Hour on Friday nights offers discount prices! Might even encourage you to get an aquarium when you get home. **Aquatek** (*8023 Burnet Rd. 512/450–0182*) also carries a variety of fish, and they've made a show of "Feeding the Fish"—literally. On Mondays at 11 a.m. only, you too can feed a piranha. Just watch those teeth.

Like its south locations, **Planet K** (*9407 N. I-35 512/832–8544; 11657 Research Blvd. 512/502–9323*) is headquarters for all your pipes-posters-paraphernalia needs. You'll find plenty of comics, incense, and novelties to comb over.

If you're looking for vitamins, dying for some real ice cream, or want a massage, one trip to **Whole Foods Market** (*9607 Research Blvd. 512/345–5003*) will cure everything. Graze the salad bar, browse the aisle of their body shop with its fragrant soaps and indulgent toiletries, breathe deep in the fresh fruit and vegetable aisles, and indulge in their specialties, from locally made Pure Luck goat cheese to a nicely priced bottle of Italian Icardi Barbera.

sleeping

If you are staying in this part of town you probably have a very good reason, like work or relatives, or maybe because downtown and South Austin motels are full. Or maybe your car broke down here. North Austin's lodgings are affordable and convenient to the Interstate, Highway 183, and Mopac. Maybe that's the most one can say to recommend them.

> **Cost Range** for double occupancy on a weeknight. Call to verify prices.
> $/under 50 dollars
> $$/50–75 dollars
> $$$/75–100 dollars
> $$$$/100+ dollars

All the chain hotels along this part of the interstate will give you about the same generic quality of room and comfort at a decent price. You can expect clean rooms, telephones, and cable TV; amenities will increase with the price. It's always worth a call to ask about specials—and do so directly and not through the 800 numbers, which may not have the most current information on prices or occupancy. **Rodeway Inn North** (5656 N. I-35 512/452–1177 $–$$$), **La Quinta Inn** (5812 N. I-35 512/459–4381 $$–$$$), **Red Lion Hotel** (6121 I-35 N. 512/323–5466 $$–$$$), **Super 8** (8128 N. I-35 512/339–1300 $–$$$), **Austin North Travelodge Suites** (8300 N. I-35 512/835–5050 $$–$$$), and **Budget Inn** (9106 N. I-35 512/837–7900 $–$$$) will usually be priced competitively.

There's also a trend among larger chain hotels to offer a less pricey version of their quality services, such as **Courtyard by Marriott** (5660 N. I-35 512/458–2340 $$$$), **Sheraton Four Points Hotel** (7800 N. I-35 512/836–8520 $$$$), and **Holiday Inn Express** (7622 N. I-35 512/467–1701 $$–$$$). These places tend to cater to the business traveler. For more home-like digs, **Habitat Suites Hotel** (*500 Highland Mall Blvd.* 512/467–6000 $$$$) and **Embassy Suites Austin Airport** (*5901 N. I-35* 512/454–8004 $$$–$$$$) offer apartment-like lodgings with built-in kitchen facilities.

And if you've got the bucks to spend, **The Hilton and Towers** (*6000 Middle Fiskville Rd.* 512/451–5757 $$$$), **Doubletree Hotel Austin** (*6505 N. I-35* 512/454–3737 $$$–$$$$), **Holiday Inn** (*6911 N. I-35* 512/459–4251 $$$–$$$$), and **Renaissance Austin Hotel** (*9721 Arboretum Blvd.* 512/343–2626 $$$$) will provide more luxurious surroundings. For those who like to shop and stroll between meetings, the Hilton is within walking distance from Highland Mall, and the Renaissance Austin is located next to the Arboretum Mall.

doing stuff

Since North Austin lacks the historical character of the rest of town, activities are limited, but they are varied. As always, you will need your own transportation to get around to most of these places.

The Austin Country Flea Market (*Hwy 290 East*) is open weekends, and is one of the great places to pick up all the inexpensive Texas gimcracks you passed up at the retro store. (Recent example: A set of four drinking glasses shaped like cowboy boots cost $2.)

The Celis family brought its Belgian beer recipe to Texas and founded the successful **Celis Brewery** (*2431 Forbes Dr., off Hwy 290*, 512/835–0884). They've marketed a variety of beers to appeal to the Texas palate, but the Bock and the Pale Ale seem to be the favorites. Judge for yourself— the brewery offers free tours Tuesday through Saturday, of which beer-tasting is an important part. Call ahead for tour hours.

This might not be the hippest thing to do (more of a family thing than a date thing) but you can't beat it as a memorable way to spend an afternoon. **The Hill Country Flyer Steam Train** (FM 1431 and Hwy 183, 512/ 477–8468) makes daily round-trip treks from Cedar Park to the town of Burnet. The train leaves at 10 a.m. sharp and returns around 5 p.m., stopping in Burnet for about three hours of shopping, dining, and sightseeing. The train itself is beautifully restored, and the fields and towns flying past the windows on a sunny day are mesmerizing and won't soon be forgotten. The trip costs $24 per person; the air-conditioned lounge cars are $38, including snacks and drinks.

Speaking of refreshingly unhip, **Manor Downs Racetrack** (Hwy 290 East 512/272–5581) is only 10 minutes east of Austin on Hwy 290, costs $2 to get in, and offers fairly cheap beer in an air-conditioned setting. Heck, it beats any scene at the OTB! Starting time is usually 1 p.m., just about when the sun starts to beat down hard. Racing season is March through November, when quarterhorses race Wednesday through Sunday; there's simulcast racing from around the country the rest of the year. Trivia hounds please note: During the '80s, Manor Downs was also a major outdoor music venue that hosted FarmAid as well as the Grateful Dead. Thoroughbred racing takes place at **Retama Park** (1 Retama Pkwy. at I-35;

swimmin' nekkid

What better way to relax than feeling free like the day you were born? Here's the skinny on skinny dipping at **Hippie Hollow** on Lake Travis. (Take Koenig Drive/2222 west to RM 620 and turn left. Look for the Comanche Trail signs; Hippie Hollow is 2.5 miles down the road on the left.) Interestingly, establishing a nude swimming park may be one thing the punks never trashed the hippies for doing. Officially Hippie Hollow is known as Mac-Gregor Park, a county day-use park located 20 minutes west of Austin, but no one in these parts calls it that. It's a lovely park, with over 100 acres of trees, cliffs, and trails for hiking and exploring—and swimming naked, because let's face it, no one comes here to hike. You must be 18 to enter the park; there's a $5 admission fee per car, and no glass, pets, or fires are allowed. After you park, follow whatever sort of people you won't mind being naked beside down the trails—you'll know when you reach the gay beach. Beach is a relative term though, as rocks line the sides of Lake Travis, and getting down to the water is no easy proposition: Wear good hiking shoes and bring lots of drinking water and sunscreen.

210/651–7000) in Selma, about 45 minutes south of Austin on I-35.

If you're looking for something a little less genteel than horses, **Longhorn Speedway (6401 U.S. 183 South 512/243–1122)** has races April through October. The night races include stock and super stock cars, street stock and hobby cars, a monthly demolition derby, and assorted events, including women's racing. The crowds here are also likely to attend tractor pulls and curse the network that canceled "The Jeff Foxworthy Show."

spectating... Movies go where malls are, and there are now more than 50 screens spread across North Austin. For multiplex fans, the usual suspects include **Arbor 7 (The Arboretum, 10000 Research Blvd. 512/416–5700 ext. 3456)**, **Gateway 16 (Hwy 183 512/416–5700 ext. 3808)**, **Great Hills 8 Cinema (9828 Great Hills Trail 512/794–8076)**, **Highland 10 (6700 Middle Fiskville Rd. 512/454–9562)**, **Lakeline Starport (Lakeline 512/335–7138)**, and the **Northcross 6 (Northcross Mall 512/416–5700 ext. 3804)**.

Alternatives to the summer blockbuster can be seen at the **Village Cinema Theater (2700 W. Anderson Ln. 512/451–0352)**, whose art-theater sensibility is most welcome. **Discount Cinema (3407 Wells Branch Pkwy. 512/244–1114)** is worth noting if only because shows are only $1.50 before 6 p.m. Cheaper than renting!

The cast at **ComedySportz Playhouse (Northcross Mall, 2525 Anderson Ln. 512/266–3397)** works hard to be funny in the sobering environs of a mall. The touring comics at **Capitol City Comedy Club (8510 Research Blvd. 512/467–2333)** have better luck; this was the scene of the MTV talent search that launched the now defunct "Austin Stories." Watch for their annual Funniest Person in Austin contest as well as name comics. Big laughs, low cover.

body

Avant Salon (*901 N. Capital of Texas Hwy., Ste. 240, 512/502–8268*) has been chosen as a readers' favorite in Austin for four years running in the *Austin Chronicle*. Their north branch includes a body-pampering spa with massages and various beauty treatments. **Moonstruck Hair Salon** (*8133 Mesa Dr. 512/349–2499*) also offers the standard full line of hair-care services, but regrettably advertises that "Yes, Moonstruck was named after the movie. What an inspiration it was when Cher went into the salon an ugly duckling and emerged a princess!" Meanwhile, **Atomic Tattoo and Body Piercing** (*5533 Burnet Rd. 512/458–9693*) would doubtless be happy to tattoo and pierce Cher or anyone else who stops in. They're clean and licensed, but go to Perfection Tattoo if you want the best in town [see **campus/central**].

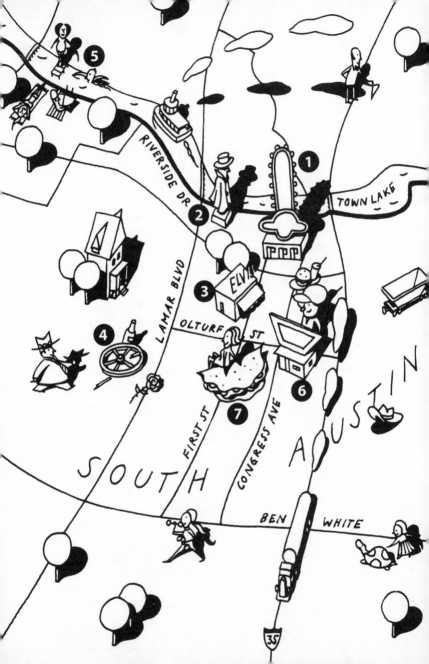

south austin

When you're driving along South Congress Avenue and you spot the Austin Motel's unintentionally phallic red neon sign like a beacon in the night, you may feel like you've crossed into another country. That's because you have— South Austin, 78704: Welcome, pardner, to Bubbaland. South Austin is a pair of used cowboy boots in a room full of Doc Martens and Nikes. It's beat-up pickup trucks, whirligigs, and pink flamingos in front yards. It's Hank

turn page for map key

Hill in a ten-gallon hat mowing the lawn and his rock 'n' roll neighbor smoking pot on the purple porch swing of his turquoise house. It's ice-cold Shiner beer and chicken-fried hospitality and Christmas lights up year-round. The baddest-ass swimming hole in the world is right here in South Austin. The South Congress shopping strip is the coolest in town, and the suggestive shape of the Austin Motel's sign is accidentally-on-purpose hilarious (and the longest running joke around). South Austinites are smug with the knowledge that there's no need ever to go across the river with all them highfalutin college kids, granola markets, and West Austin yuppies. The Continental Club and Back Room have long been premier nightspots in Austin's fabled music scene, and Threadgill's, the official bastion of Southern cooking in Austin, is on the corner where the venerable old hippie club Armadillo [see **campus/central**] used to stand. Even the national rock 'n' roll shrine to Stevie Ray Vaughan, a genuine South Austin guitar god, is on this side of the river. Who needs the rest of town?

South Austin is physically defined as the general area south of Town Lake (the Colorado River), west of I-35 and east of the suburb of Loop 1. Its southern border is more nebulous, but Ben White Boulevard is a good enough choice, since everything south of there is either suburbs or feels like North San Antonio, which has nearly grown into the outskirts of Austin. As with North and East Austin, this

map key			
	1 Austin Motel	4	The Broken Spoke
	2 Stevie Ray Vaughan	5	Barton Springs
	statue	6	Fran's Hamburgers
	3 Elvis Cafe	7	Guero's Taco Bar

delineation simply defines the heart of the business area and not its boundaries proper. South Austin's population is as racially mixed as East Austin's, but the old neighborhood lines are even more porous. Although the area does boast the cushy Travis Heights neighborhood, the South Austin lifestyle is not defined by it. Simply put, if Elvis were from Texas, he would've lived in South Austin.

Because South Austin has such a down-home mentality, the two main activities outside of keeping a day job are eating and whooping it up. The neighborhood bars here act more as gathering spots for locals than as stages for musicians, and those spots that do have live music manage to avoid the theme-park feel of 6th Street. South Austin's howdy-neighbor sense of community is more real than the politically motivated neighborhoods north of the river. People who live in the north's Hyde Park whip themselves into a lather protesting neighborhood development; people in South Austin apply the same effort to garage and yard sales.

The collection of kitsch and Americana that is South Austin is best experienced on foot or by bicycle or car since the buses here are confined to the three main arteries. They might as well be on tracks. The central artery, South Congress Avenue, continues Downtown's main street across the Congress Avenue Bridge and through the heart of South Austin. South 1st Street is the south-of-the-river extension of Guadalupe Street, snaking down across the South 1st Bridge and alongside Auditorium Shores and Palmer Auditorium. Lamar Boulevard continues across the Lamar Bridge and down through the western half of South Austin. Between I-35 and Ben White Boulevard, the only direct east-west thruway is Oltorf Street—but accessibility to it depends on whether a train is racing down the tracks, literally cutting off east-west traffic. One advantage of going by car is you can take in the yards. Watch for religious altars, truck carcasses, blast-from-the-past statuary, xeriscaped yards (landscaping done with indigenous plants rather than imported foliage), and houses painted Easter-egg colors in and around the neighborhood between South Congress Avenue and South 1st Street. And don't pass up the chance to stop at a garage sale, even if it just looks like clothing. You might find an old Willie Nelson T-shirt that will forever remind you of your trip to this quirky burg.

eating/coffee

Dining in South Austin offers the full range of authentic Austin experiences. At a place like Jovita's, the Cornell Hurd Band will ply its brand of left-wing Texas swing while your eyeballs roll back in ecstasy as you taste some of the best enchiladas in town. The Barton Springs Road restaurant row is flush with tacky theme joints overflowing with obnoxious groups of U.T. frat boys and their bowhead dates. That's not to say the food in these places isn't edible—it's just overpriced—but the inhumane waits for tables and the manic "Hi! My-Name-Is" waiters hell-bent on your great time are enough to make you lose your lunch (or dinner).

Despite Austin's reputation for famous homestyle Texas cooking, South Austin is the land of that culinary creature known as Tex-Mex. There are nearly 50 Tex-Mex eateries here, a number subject to change with the almost weekly restaurant closings and openings. Take a chance and try a breakfast taco at one of the lesser-known spots. But be forewarned: These hole-in-the-wall places sometimes fly under the radar of the health department. Most area restaurants are in the low end of the price range, and happy hour prices make the obligatory cold Mexican beer the perfect complement to your meal. While the better-known restaurants take plastic and traveler's checks, it's strictly cash at the small places.

Cost Range per entree
$/under 10 dollars
$$/10–15 dollars
$$$/15–20 dollars
$$$$/20+ dollars

24-hour... At **Kerbey Lane Cafe** (2700 S. Lamar Blvd. 512/445–4451 $–$$) the wait can be long, the din sometimes deafening, and the service lackluster, if friendly. But Kerbey serves up some of the best food in town round the clock, making it easily one of Austin's favorite spots. (Jello Biafra swears by their gingerbread pancakes.) *Migas* with verde or ranchero sauce, soft tacos with loads of black beans and veggies, and the grilled chicken breast sandwich with chipotle mayonnaise are all winners. The hamburgers are made from free-range beef, and the greens and tomatoes are locally grown. Yum.

The other perch for local night owls and early birds is **Magnolia Cafe** (1920 S. Congress Ave. 512/445–0000 $–$$). Like its sister cafe in West Austin, it serves good-for-you food round the clock. Their Super Nachos are a meal in themselves, and the Magnolia Club Sandwich is served with a side of chunky fried red potatoes. Magnolia is a favorite after-show spot for local and touring musicians.

asian... South Austin's Asian restaurants are hard to find among the dozens of Tex-Mex eateries that seem to sit on every corner, but that doesn't mean you can't get a crispy egg roll or a smoking rib here. You will find a growing number of affordable and demure restaurants on South Lamar Boulevard that cater to local Asian families. The food is consistently good and fresh, and a family atmosphere extends to make any traveler feel at home—in whichever haunt you choose.

Chinese and Thai make a nice, typical combo at **Asian Cafe** (1000 S. Lamar Blvd. 512/912–7788 $); ditto for **China Wok** (3001 S. Lamar Blvd. 512/445–6466 $). The popular **Hunan Lion** (Brodie Oaks Shopping Center, 4006 S. Lamar Blvd. 512/447–3388 $–$$$) has decent Chinese fare—the usual chow fun and smoked duck, with occasional skewered items like barbecued pork with a curry sauce. And when almost all Austin restaurants shut down for holidays, Hunan stays open. **Mandarin Chinese Restaurant** (212 E. Oltorf St. 512/445–2225 $–$$) is a delightful little gem of an eatery in an otherwise anonymous strip mall. The garlic shrimp is highly recommended for its spicy and tasty—but not too garlicky—sauce.

Công Ly (2121 E. Oltorf St. 512/448–4195 $) proves that a bowl of noodles can be special. Not only can you order pho, the standard broth-and-noodles dish of all Vietnamese restaurants, in all the traditional forms from veggie to meat, but for local flavor you can also add (you guessed it!) jalapeños.

Unfortunately, neither **Seoul Restaurant & Sushi Bar** (6400 S. 1st St. 512/326–5807 $–$$) nor **Shogun** (1007 W. Slaughter Rd. 512/292–1580 $–$$) is exactly convenient to inner-city fun, and their good but not outstanding fare may not be worth the trip. But if you're in the 'hood, Seoul is one of the few restaurants in Austin that will serve up traditional Korean fare, such as *bulgaki* (marinated beef with Korean-style vegetables).

barbecue... If you drive through any of the South Austin neighborhoods, you may wonder what in blazes so many oil drums are doing in so many backyards. The answer explains why South Austin isn't overrun with barbecue joints, as you might expect: South Austinites don't need them because they'd rather make their own. Of course, it is a little time-consuming, but it gives them plenty of time to argue about what really defines "barbecue"—the cooking method or the sauce? Fortunately, you can sample some of the good stuff for yourself *sans* the oil drum and hours of smoke.

Artz Rib House (2330 S. Lamar Blvd. 512/442–8283 $–$$), a longtime fixture on the pit scene, delivers zesty barbecue, amazingly greaseless sausage, and all the usual side dishes. The menu also includes regular and veggie burgers. Some nights they even have live music. A little over 10 years ago, **Green Mesquite** (1400 Barton Springs Rd. 512/479–0485 $–$$) inherited a spot that had been purveying barbecue for some 30 years, so you know there's good smokin' meat to be had from a grill with such a distinguished pedigree. Ribs, brisket, sausage, chicken—it's all here and it's all good. Musicians often play in the patio area, and old Austin music posters liven up the decor inside. **Richard Jones Bar B Que** (2304 S. Congress Ave. 512/444–2272 $–$$) will never be mistaken for a hip place, but with to-go "family packs" of meat and fixings that feed four people for $11.99, it's a good deal. It's also handy for picnic takeout if you're planning a day trip in the area.

burgers and sandwiches... Naturally, meat-and-potatoes South Austin takes its hamburgers seriously. Amid the McDonald's and Sonics and Dairy Queens (which are not half-bad), there's **Dan's Hamburgers** (4308 Manchaca Rd. 512/443–6131 $). Once the leading independent hamburger chain around town, the business splintered after the owners divorced and the South Congress Dan's Hamburgers became **Fran's Hamburgers** (1822 S. Congress Ave. 512/444–5738 $). But never mind the name game—at both places, the fried burgers are tasty and they're always easy to find under the familiar red-and-white signs. Fran's is particularly notable for the Girl Power (the pre–Spice Girls variety, mind you) statue on its roof, a little girl hoisting a guitar, a curious image for a burger joint in any other city, but not in Austin. Likewise, **Sandy's Hamburgers** (603 Barton Springs Rd. 512/478–6322 $) is practically a landmark, holding its own under a custard-yellow neon ice cream cone. The one-of-a-kind burger stand has weathered everything from hordes of hippies treating stoner munchies at the old Armadillo nearby to the invasion of the Whataburger franchise next door. But Sandy's just shows you that soft ice

cream cones and cheap cheeseburgers are forever (now there's a Jimmy Buffet lyric for you).

There are some other burger-type places, such as the forgettable **Filling Station Restaurant & Bar** (801 Barton Springs Rd. 512/477–1022 $) and the ludicrous **Hooters** (425 W. Riverside Dr. 512/478–9464 $–$$), where boneheads too cheap to patronize topless joints get served up greasy chicken wings by women (probably single mothers) sporting Farrah Fawcett hairdos and undersized T-shirts. Anybody capable of reading this would be better off fighting for a parking spot on the Barton Springs restaurant row. **Shady Grove** (1624 Barton Springs Rd. 512/474–9991 $$) does good by its sandwiches, chili, and burgers, which almost makes up for the long wait (margarita, anyone?). The decor is literally trailer park but the food is swell.

There are two franchises that are always good for a sandwich. You won't get much out-of-the-ordinary, but you will get a tasty, filling sub at **Thundercloud Subs** (201 E. Riverside Dr. 512/441–5331, 2021 E. Riverside Dr. 512/445–4163, 1010 S. Lamar Blvd. 512/443–0888, 2801 S. Lamar Blvd. 512/443–0960 $). They've rounded up the usual suspects—deli meats, cheese, and veggies—and almost all subs are under five bucks. **Schlotzsky's** (1301 S. Congress Ave. 512/444–8441, 4032 S. Lamar Blvd. 512/447–6943, 2205 E. Riverside Dr. 512/443–6518, 111 W. William Cannon Dr. 512/462–2222 $) and **Schlotzsky's Deli & Bread Alone Bakery** (218 S. Lamar Blvd. 512/476–2867 $–$$) is a more-than-decent chain. Their signature sandwich contains delectable slices of deli meat (turkey and vegetarian versions are available, too) and cheeses melted in a sourdough bun so delicious its recipe is a trademarked secret. Some locations offer pizzas, too, and the deli/bakery on Lamar Boulevard has irresistible baked goods.

coffee... While the coffeehouse mentality hasn't taken South Austin by storm, there are most definitely alternatives to the ubiquitous **Starbucks (5400 Brodie Ln. 512/891–9173 $)**. The **503 Coffee Bar** (519 W. Oltorf St. 512/462–0804 $) is one, with a variety of java choices to jumpstart your day. It's a sofa-comfy atmosphere where Ire-phile students groove on Celtic music night. You can get the caffeine jolt at **High Time Tea Bar & Brain Gym** (1501 S. 1st St. 512/445–5405 $), but stick around for lunch—this little cafe also serves sandwiches, veggie dishes, and goodies like yellowfin tuna nori rolls. Part juice bar, part Internet cafe (there are several terminals), part gaming parlor, High Time survived a move from its original Downtown location to its current spot, and thrives.

Flipnotics Coffee Space (1601 Barton Springs Rd. 512/322–9750 $) functions as a coffee joint, as one of Austin's more popular singer/songwriter venues, and as a retro-clothing boutique. It's small, but you can enjoy a cup of joe and the sounds of local faves Ana Egge and Jon Dee Graham.

italian... You won't find great Italian food around here. After all, we're in Texas, so get used to hearing about "Eye-talian," if it's mentioned at all. **Gino's Italian Grill** (730 W. Stassney Ln. 512/326–4466 $–$$) is pretty good and it does have decent local jazz for such a suburban setting, but the music is a long stretch from the quality you'll find downtown. **The Olive Garden** (3940 S. Lamar Blvd. 512/440–

0131 $–$$), part of a nationwide chain, is the Italian Bennigan's: predictable, affordable, palatable, forgettable. Like Shady Grove, **Romeo's** *(1500 Barton Springs Rd. 512/476–1090 $–$$$)* might be more hassle than it's worth if the margarita-guzzling crowd is out en masse. The inoffensive pasta is served up in a corny, checkered-tablecloth atmosphere. The more traditional plates like Pomodori and eggplant parmesan are good, and definitely the best bet here. A better choice might be **Pizza Nizza** *(1608 Barton Springs Rd. 512/474–7470 $–$$)*, one place on restaurant row that's worth taking on the U.T. masses and nonexistent parking for. Their excellent crust is unusually crispy, and their pizza sauces are hearty and spicy. Pizza Nizza delivers with a minimum order in the South Austin area and beats Domino's by leagues.

mexican... At the corner of South 1st and West Mary streets is one of the original neighborhood restaurants, **La Reyna** *(1816 S. 1st St. 512/447–1280 $)*. It's been quietly serving homestyle Mexican food with little fanfare to a steady clientele for three decades. An added bonus for the neighborhood is the Mexican bakery inside, which cranks out fresh sweets and bread daily. **La Mexicana Bakery** *(1924 S. 1st St. 512/443–6369 $)* is a newer entry, but its array of baked goods is a tasty alternative to bagels and coffee or the ubiquitous breakfast taco. Likewise, you won't go wrong with **Pulvos Mexicano** *(2004 S. 1st St. 512/441–5446 $)* or **Little Mexico** *(2304 S. 1st St. 512/462–2188 $)*. These tiny places—some with only five or six tables at best—have standard menus that vary little from one to the next, so you can get a taste of local flavor relatively easily. These mom-and-pop joints are also easy on the wallet, catering mostly to Hispanic families who are in search of great homestyle food at reasonable prices. At **Dos Hermanos Panaderia** (501 W. Oltorf St. 512/ 445–5226 $), just off South Lamar Boulevard, the plates are generous and cheap and tasty. It's one of Dash Rip Rock's favorite stops when the New Orleans trio plays town.

Another cluster of South Lamar's eating spots of note include **Maudie's Too** (1212 S. Lamar Blvd. 512/440–8088 $–$$), sister of the original on Lake Austin Boulevard [see **west austin**], **La Feria Restaurant** (1816 S. Lamar Blvd. 512/326–8301 $), and **Baby Compadre's** (1817 S. Lamar Blvd. 512/441–9789 $–$$). All of them are friendly neighborhood veterans that have no problem serving a hearty *plato* of your favorite dish. **Matt's El Rancho** (2613 S. Lamar Blvd. 512/462–9333 $–$$$) is among the best-known of Austin's Mexican restaurants, famous for having been Lyndon B. Johnson's local favorite. Suffice it to say that LBJ's assessment of Mexican culinary matters doesn't hold much *agua* around here. Anyway, the service is professional and snappy, but it would take either a horrifically undiscriminating patron or a dead president to pardon the unspectacular food.

El Sol y La Luna (1224 S. Congress Ave. 512/444–7770 $), in the shadow of the shaft of the Austin Motel, is one of those little gems of an eatery—unpretentious, good, filling. Being across from the Continental Club doesn't hurt either, especially if happy hour has gone on a little long. **Rosie's Tamale House** (102 E. Oltorf St. 512/440–7727, 2701 S. Congress Ave., 512/462–9484 $) offers cheap, tummy-filling Tex-Mex, as does another veteran, **El Gallo Restaurant**

(2910 S. Congress Ave. 512/444–2205 $). For a different twist on Tex-Mex, try **Curra's Grill** (614 E. Oltorf St. 512/444–0012 $–$$), which tests the waters with creative uses of red snapper and enchilada variations. A full bar makes it easy to cool down anything that gets too hot. But you can't get hotter (in another way) than **Guero's Taco Bar** (1412 S. Congress Ave. 512/447–7688 $–$$$), always brimming with celebs like Sandra Bullock, Matthew McConaughey, and some guy named Bill Clinton. This converted feed store is large and high-ceilinged. A painted-over brick wall still reveals some residue of its past, advertising "Old Feed." No question that Guero's is the see-and-be-seen restaurant in South Austin, and its food backs up its popularity with a menu that's more Mex than Tex. And if you think you see Grammy-winning singer/songwriter Lucinda Williams chowing down with her buddies, you're probably right.

The East Austin Tejano subculture crosses south on Riverside Drive east of I-35. It looks like Anytown, USA, with strip mall after strip mall punctuated by national fast-food places and taco stands. If you're low on bucks, these anonymous taco and fajita stands are as cheap as eating from the food carts on the Drag. For slightly more formal sit-down eating, **El Pastor** (1911 E. Riverside Dr. 512/442–8402 $) has a good menu and friendly service. It caters to the nearby Tejano club crowds and will stay open late unadvertised.

regional... It's a pleasure to see that the four main purveyors of homestyle cooking in South Austin all have warm and memorable atmospheres. That would suit Grandma just fine, and it's her cooking being used as the standard here, so the big question is, how well do these places do chicken-fried steak? Quite well, we're happy to report. Even **Good Eats Cafe** (1530 *Barton Springs Rd.* 512/476–8141 **$–$$**), in a traditional Southern diner environment, manages to escape the restaurant-row hype because it serves up a substantial crispy cutlet smothered in slightly floury cream gravy. Nicely prepared sides of new potatoes, fried okra, and corn on the cob are tasty, and the grilled catch of the day adds variety to the menu. **The Broken Spoke** (3201 *S. Lamar Blvd.* 512/442–6189 **$**) dishes up its plain old chicken-fried steak truck-stop style, with mashed potatoes or fries and iceberg lettuce with Kraft salad dressing. At $4.95, it's more than a steal. Besides, black-and-white photos of country stars stare back at you while you eat. Authentic live country and western music, along with some Texas two-steppin', will also be found on the premises. **The Texicalli Grill** (534 *E. Oltorf St.* 512/442–2799 **$**) is part unofficial visitor's center, part defender of classic Texas fare. Feast on owner Danny Young's chunky chicken-fried steak while enjoying a brief history of Austin music plastered wall-to-wall. The pictorial overview is pretty mind-boggling: You go from Willie Nelson to the Butthole Surfers in the time it takes to demolish your plate of biscuits and gravy.

It's a bit of a drive outside the South Austin interior, but the jaunt to **Catfish Parlour** (4705 *E. Ben White Blvd.* 512/443–1698 **$–$$**) will pay off handsomely for fans of fried fish. As the name suggests, catfish is heaped in all its fried glory on platters for big eating. No one pretends this is healthy or sophisticated, which is an integral part of its generic-fish-house charm.

A visit to South Austin simply isn't complete without a trip to either of the two locations of **Threadgill's World Headquarters** (*301 W. Riverside Dr. at Barton Springs Rd. 512/472–9304, 6416 N. Lamar Blvd. 512/451–5440 $–$$*). It's not just that the Texas cuisine here inspired a wildly successful cookbook. It's not just because you can star-gaze at Texas politicos and pundits while stuffing your face with amazing regional food (even the meat loaf is something to write home about). It's more that this haunt is an astonishingly naked salute to pot-smoking '60s counter-culture wrapped in the Lone Star flag. This location is heavy on memorabilia from owner Eddie Wilson's days as a founder of the Armadillo World Headquarters [see **campus/central**]. Wilson and his wife/partner Sandra O'Connor carry on the live-music tradition of the Armadillo here with classic roots-rock and alt-country. The mustachioed ex-hippie's favorite boast (aside from being featured in a national VISA commercial) is being stepfather to actress Renee O'Connor, who plays Gabrielle on "Xena: Warrior Princess" and makes appearances at the restaurant—without that leather bit. And yes, their chicken-fried steak may be the best in town, a big chunk of tenderized beef with a thick batter coating and creamy gravy atop it. Three- and five-vegetable plates are also available for herbivores, but don't expect a lot of health-conscious calorie-counting here.

The appeal of **Paggi House** (*200 Lee Barton Dr. 512/478–1121 $$–$$$$*) seems to be largely to older Austinites who like their nonthreatening Continental-style cuisine. Paggi House sat without incident for many years in its South Lamar/Riverside location until a Taco Cabana landed on the same strip of land in the '80s. Paggi fans squawked to no avail, so today the two sit side by side. But guess who's busier. **Si Bon** (801 *S. Lamar Blvd.* *512/326–8323* $$–$$$) is the latest to try its luck in what should be a good location on a hill with a view of downtown Austin, but which seems to be cursed for restaurants (sadly, there's no rhyme or reason why). While Si Bon is upscale, it remains affordable, and its adventurous Southwestern cuisine is encouraging. Chef Peter O'Brien, formerly of the Granite Cafe, skillfully prepares dishes like duck and roasted peppers, but the consensus is that they're trying too hard. When most people think of fine dining in South Austin, **Green Pastures** (811 *W. Live Oak 512/* *444–4747* $$–$$$$) is the name that comes to mind. The restaurant's pastoral neighborhood setting—complete with resident peacocks strutting about—is a popular backdrop for folks tying the knot, but it's the famous Sunday brunch that has kept locals faithful for years. The genteel Southern spread includes prime rib, classic seafood specials, cheeses, tropical and seasonal fruits, salads, and fresh vegetables. Reservations are recommended, and it's kind of dressy.

seafood... Seafood in Austin is a tricky business. Being in Central Texas just about guarantees most seafood is frozen or served up Red Lobster style, as it is in the faux-Louisiana ambience of **Old Alligator Grill** (3003 *S. Lamar Blvd.* *512/444–6117* $–$$$). **Landry's on the Lake** (600 *E. Riverside Dr.* *512/441–1010* $–$$$$) is run-of-the-mill, but their fried-shrimp platter is just fine. **Mariscos** (1504 *Town Creek Dr.* *512/462–9119* $–$$$) is more adventurous, with Mexican-style seafood dishes. This place is particularly great because it serves traditionally more expensive Mexican fare like *ceviche* (a light seafood dish with fish cooked in lime juice) at a low price.

tex-mex... What is Tex-Mex and how is it different from Mexican food? Mexican cuisine is as diverse as any national cuisine, with ingredients and styles of preparation varying from the interior to the coastal regions. But basically Tex-Mex is the result of putting an American spin on Sonoran border-style recipes, such as slathering sour cream on enchiladas and using Velveeta cheese food instead of queso. (Who cares—Velveeta makes great queso.) But beware those Tex-Mex establishments that are nothing more than Margaritatoriums, like **Chuy's** (*1728 Barton Springs Rd. 512/474–4452 $–$$$*) and both **Baby Acapulco** locations (*1628 Barton Springs Rd. 512/474–8774, 1705 S. Lakeshore Blvd. 512/447–1339 $–$$$*). Maybe the gimmicky decor at Chuy's—colorful plastic fish suspended from the ceiling, etc.—is supposed to distract customers from the mediocrity of the food. Distracted or not, you'll be downright baffled by the Elvis altar. (What does he have to do with Mexican food? He wasn't even Catholic. He wasn't even a cook!) Ditto for **Jalisco** (*414 Barton Springs Rd. 512/476–4838 $–$$*), where ordering a Slammer provides you with enough alcohol to kill a Russian wolfhound and hordes of waiters who cheer you on while you drink. The whole scene smacks of one of those outlawed fraternity hazing rituals. **La Vista** (*208 Barton Springs Rd. at S. 1st St. 512/477–1234 $–$$$*), the Hyatt Hotel restaurant, claims to have the best fajitas in Austin. In truth, they're mediocre, salty, and drowned in a surfeit of peppers and onions. And at $18.50 for two, they're also overpriced. The place has excellent hot sauce, though, which is rather baffling, since salsa quality is usually the litmus test for how good a Mexican restaurant is.

You're better off choosing from the array of restaurants stretching down South 1st Street, which could also be called the Tex-Mex Turnpike. These restaurants are usually neighborhood favorites, though some enjoy citywide reputations. Like East Austin Mexican restaurants, these spots sometimes close on Sunday or Monday, and smaller ones may not serve dinner or be open into the evenings. The beauty of these restaurants is that the meals are usually quite affordable and filling; rice and beans are staples served with most all dinners. **El Mercado** (1302 S. 1st St. 512/447–7445 $–$$) has been a South 1st Street fixture since the early '80s, serving up delicious fajitas, enchiladas, and flautas, not to mention cold beer and drinks. Its candy-pink interior is accented with bright plastic Tijuana parrots that hang from the ceiling. It can get crowded at times, but the wait is well worth it. One local writer was so addicted to their chunky salsa that when she moved to Hawaii she would have friends buy it in bulk from the restaurant, freeze it, and Fed-Ex it to her in the islands. **Jovita's** (1619 S. 1st St. 512/447–7825 $–$$) is another noted name in Austin Tex-Mex, famous for its tasty enchiladas and burritos with creamy guacamole, and a thin but lethal hot sauce, all served with fresh, crisp chips. Jovita's usually features live music in the evening, but spectating can be a challenge—this might be Austin, but it's still a restaurant. Imagine a plate of hot, cheesy enchiladas with rice and beans, an icy dark Dos Equis, the Texas-sized sun making its move on the blushing horizon while Don Walser's plaintive yodel brags about "Big Balls in Cowtown," and there you have it—the Austin experience.

miscellaneous... Puerto Rican food is the specialty at **Borinquen** (2728 S. Congress Ave. 512/443–4252 $–$$) while **Casa de Luz** (1701 Toomey Rd. 512/476–2535 $–$$) does a vegetarian variation of Mexican with their fresh and organic menu, which appeals to a crunchy art-student crowd. Middle Eastern fare is the order at **Phoenicia Bakery & Deli** (2912 S. Lamar Blvd. 512/447–4444 $) with inexpensive falafel sandwiches, baba ganoush, tabbouleh, and more. **Shaggy's Caribbean Grill** (1600 S. Congress Ave. 512/447–5375 $) tries its luck at Jamaican cuisine—jerk chicken and beef. It succeeds with the meat but sides like coleslaw are tasteless. Good thing they serve beer and drinks to wash it down. This is a true story about the **Juice Joint** (1625 Barton Springs Rd. 512/494–1767 $): "Do you have coffee?" someone inquired politely. "No! No coffee! Coffee bad! Try wheatgrass," answered one of the employees. "Wheatgrass a better buzz!" Hmmm.

bars/music/clubs

If you're down with country music, good. If you're not, too bad, because Austin has been the home of subversive country music ever since Willie Nelson thumbed his nose at Nashville and grew his hair like a good (or bad) Catholic schoolgirl's. Doug Sahm, another Austin legend, never stopped plying his brand of country music, which sounds as fresh and original at the end of the century as it did in the late '60s when he topped the charts with "She's About A Mover" and "Mendocino" as the frontman of Sir Douglas Quintet. Likewise, old country kings and cosmic cowboys like Jerry Jeff Walker, Billy Joe Shaver, and Rusty Wier often play in Austin among the likes of Don Walser, Cornell Hurd, Dale Watson, and the Derailers. All of this is just a long-winded way of recommending **The Broken Spoke** (3201 S. *Lamar* Blvd. 512/442–6189) for the authentic country music experience in Austin. This is no Nashville-butt-kissin' hole full of ersatz cowboys and their giddy admirers. It's a pure Texas country music joint that has never laid eyes on a mechanical bull.

The Continental Club (1315 S. Congress Ave. 512/441–2444) is the best club in South Austin. If the vaguely loungey atmosphere seems authentic, it is: Up until the mid-'70s, the Continental was a leftover-from-the-'60s working-class cocktail lounge. After it got revamped with a rock 'n' roll heart and had its delightful, tacky original wall murals restored, it became home to roots-rock bands, much as Antone's nurtures blues or Emo's does punk. Owner Steve Wertheimer is a dapper gentleman with Buddy Holly glasses and silver hair. He's always looking for an excuse for a Continental occasion, which is why Elvis' birth and death are celebrated with blowouts, as well as Buck Owens' birthday, which, unlike Elvis', actually attracted the birthday boy one year. Catch vocalists like Toni Price and Junior Brown at the Continental's happy hours and early Sunday night shows. The beer's cheaper and there's still time left to see more music around town.

The South Austin base for most of Austin's singer/songwriter culture is at **The Saxon Pub** (1320 *S. Lamar Blvd.* 512/448–2552), not a hard place to find since it sets up an enormous suit of armor outside. Inside it's a guitar-picker's paradise with players like Rusty Wier and Steven Fromholz—leftover cosmic cowboys from Austin's progressive country glory days in the '70s. The music at **Flipnotics Coffee Space** (1601 *Barton Springs Rd.* 512/322–9750) downshifts toward a younger songwriter crowd, Ana Egge and Seela being popular names here.

At **The Filling Station Restaurant & Bar** (801 *Barton Springs Rd.* 512/477–1022), lesser-known hopefuls ply their songs 'n' guitars to a burgers 'n' beer audience. Since aggressively moving into the live-music circle, the saloon at **Threadgill's World Headquarters** (301 *W. Riverside Dr. at Barton Springs Rd.* 512/472–9304) has attracted more and more fans of the rootsy country music so popular in Austin; even Jimmie Dale Gilmore and Joe Ely occasionally sit in. Champ Hood & the Threadgill's Troubadours play every Wednesday. Look for other kinds of music at Threadgill's, too, such as the bayou lure of the Gulf Coast Playboys or the swing of Hot Club of Cowtown. The joys of **Jovita's** (1619 *S. 1st St.* 512/447–7825) are many, as outlined previously [see **eating/coffee**]. Even if Don Walser's conservative country doesn't move you, the likes of Cornell Hurd's wisecracking Western swing or Ponty Bone's West Texas accordion are harder to resist than another cold cerveza. **Artz Rib House** (2330 *S. Lamar Blvd.* 512/442–8283) is best known for barbecue, but on Sunday afternoons there's Central Texas Bluegrass Jam, and on Tuesdays it's the Texas Olde Time Fiddlers Jam. While you have to pay to eat, the music is free. Restaurants in

seven musicians you must know

Alejandro Escovedo—This critically acclaimed singer/song-writer has never had much commercial success nationally but can do no wrong locally. His original punk band, Rank & File, were local favorites, while his late-'80s follow-up, the True Believers, spurned a movement called "New Sincerity" that helped put Austin back on the musical radar.

Gibby Haynes—He's the son of a Dallas kiddie-TV legend, Mr. Peppermint, but the frontman for the Butthole Surfers is Austin's most public bad boy—both by parading around town with Johnny Depp and Kate Moss and by refusing to hide his reported mid-'90s heroin addiction.

Daniel Johnston—Anybody who was in Austin in the early '80s will delight in telling you about how they used to buy brilliant homemade cassettes from a young pop upstart named Daniel Johnston. But the same twisted genius that made his songs so quirky and appealing has landed him in many an institution—making his rare live appearances special.

Jimmie Vaughan—Sometime during your first conversation with an Austinite about Stevie Ray Vaughan, they'll tell you "But man, his brother's even better." Whether he actually is or not, he's certainly the town's guitar standard and best overall example of a player with grace and class.

Jerry Jeff Walker—Walker, the inventor of "Gonzo Country," has spent over three decades touring and recording as sort of the working man's Jimmy Buffet, but he's best known for writing "Mr. Bojangles," singing "London Homesick Blues," and writing and performing that "home with the armadillo" theme song from "Austin City Limits." His real name is Ron Crosby and he's from New Jersey, but damned if he doesn't make a decent good ol' boy Texan.

Kelly Willis—When this beautiful redhead appeared in *Bob Roberts* and on the cover of the *National Enquirer*—apparently sneaking out of a then-married Lyle Lovett's Austin hotel room—few Austinites were surprised. Willis always seems to have had genuine star potential—mostly, as an edgy country songstress with the perfect Texas twang in her voice. Her frequent live shows are extremely popular.

Miles Zuniga—Until 1998 and the breakthrough of Fastball's "The Way," Zuniga was just another struggling Austin rock-star-in-waiting—showing obvious talent as a pop singer, songwriter, and guitarist, but enduring a series of bad breaks that included major-label failures with both his band Big Car and the first Fastball record. Now, with some success, the outspoken Austinite has managed to embrace MTV and *Rolling Stone* without losing any local credibility.

general are a good source of music, usually free. Look for it at **Eats Grill** (1530 *Barton Springs Rd.* 512/476–8141), **El Sol y La Luna** (1224 *S. Congress Ave.* 512/444–7770), **Trophy's** (2008 *S. Congress Ave.* 512/447–0969), **Gino's** (730–A *W. Stassney Ln.* 512/326–4466), **Borinquen** (2827 *S. Congress Ave.* 512/443–4252), **Polvo's** (2004 *S. 1st St.* 512/263–1055) and **Shaggy's Caribbean Grill** (1600 *S. Congress Ave.* 512/447–5375).

The Back Room (2015 *E. Riverside Dr.* 512/441–4677) is an anomaly on the music scene, a hardy cactus of a club that's survived all of Austin's musical trends and thrives in the midst of the Tejano nightclub scene. It's the only real hard-rock club in Austin, and has been actively in business for most of a quarter-century. In that time, it's seen the likes of the Ramones and Ice T's Body Count while supporting local acts such as Dangerous Toys, Pariah, and the KISS cover band SSIK. One side of the huge hall has video games and pool tables with a bar. The other side is metal-band city. The Tejano club crawl begins with whatever club is located at the corner of East Riverside Drive and South Congress Avenue, currently **The Realm** (110 *E. Riverside Dr.* 512/326–5277), but continues on across I-35 to the main strip and one of Austin's Tejano showcases, **Club Carnaval** (2237 *E. Riverside Dr.* 512/444–6396). Tejano is exuberant Mexican pop music, a common ground where old and young meet and celebrate life through song. Sadly, its most vibrant voice, Selena, was silenced in 1996 when the young singer was shot to death by her fan-club president in a Texas coastal town. Current Tejano acts to watch for include Reben Ramos and La Mafia.

Ego's (510 *S. Congress Ave.* 512/474–7091) is practically in a class of its own, as befits Austin's love of lounge music. This is one of the original lounges, the South Austin version of North Austin's Carousel Lounge. Blind jazz singer Bobby Doyle holds court on Thursdays in the early evenings, but look for "cocktail & Western" from Ted Roddy's Tearjoint Troubadours for that weep-in-your-martini sound. In a way, you shouldn't even classify Ego's under "live music,"since this sort of music was never really meant to be listened to—it's more of a soundtrack for the human drama that unfolds in a smoky bar. Ego's has that kind of swingin' Rat Pack ambience where you might expect to see Sammy Davis Jr. waltz in and join Ted Roddy on stage.

Good country music in Austin has way more wry humor than your average alt-angst rock and is often thoughtfully presented in a restaurant setting. You can stuff your face and cry in your beer afterward and no one will care as long you don't leave whiskey dings on that shiny Ford pickup parked next to you. And remember, if a country-music club or band plays more Garth Brooks and Clint Black than George Jones and Willie Nelson or more Shania Twain than Patsy Cline, they're not real country, just pop. Also, you're better off at a non-music joint like **The Horseshoe Lounge** (2430 S. Lamar Blvd. 512/442–9111), where the Pearl beer is cold and the lights dim, than at **The South 40** (629 W. Ben White Blvd. 512/444–9329), **The Chaparral Lounge** (5500 S. Congress Ave. 512/441–9008), or **Dance Across Texas** (2201 E. Ben White Blvd. 512/441–9101), where line dancing and hat acts still rule and you might just come face-to-face with a hard-living, beer-breathing stereotype. The Horseshoe is in a little limestone building between Blackmail and Amelia's [see **buying stuff**] in an otherwise nondescript horseshoe of antique shops. The place is so real and resolutely free of artifice, you'll never forget it.

venues... The Back Yard (13101 Hwy. 71 W 512/263–4146) pulls in everyone from k.d. lang to Willie Nelson to Jimmie Vaughan to Sarah MacLachlan. The large, attractive venue is set on a hillside under oak trees and the sky, so the only bummer is that concerts sometimes get rained out. The same folks that run La Zona Rosa and the Austin Music Hall oversee The Back Yard. The tours go to **Southpark Meadows** (8600 S. I-35 512/280–8771). Lollapalooza, HORDE, B-52s, NIN, Lilith Fair, and Phish all have played the spot. The faithful will always make the trek to the grail and are guaranteed to forget sunscreen and appropriate clothing.

buying stuff

National scribes who write about the local music scenes regularly comment—sometimes with great amusement—that Austin has a fashion sense of its own. And it's true: Austin put long hair and jewelry on cowboys in the '70s during the progressive country scare, and when the black leather fury of punk fireballed into Texas, it was outfitted with cowboy hats and boots and cowpunk was born. But it was the local blues scene that really defined Austin's fashion in the '70s and '80s—a kind of Elvis meets the Blues Brothers in the barrio—and that love of vintage clothing, kitsch, and furnishings is still reflected in the number of resale stores that have flourished since. Fashion in Austin today usually means a wardrobe that includes not only contemporary clothes but a selection of vintage clothes and accessories as well. A Gap T-shirt looks like a Gap T-shirt regardless of what city you're in, but it's the suspenders decorated with dice that really dress it up in Austin.

clothing... Austin's quirky fashion sense might be a little puzzling to outsiders because it's one of the most dressed-down towns you'll ever see. The 9-to-5 set has **Barton Creek Square Mall** *(Hwy. 71 at Loop 1)*, with department stores, Victoria's Secret, Ann Taylor, Gap, Banana Republic, and the predictable like. And outlet malls in neighboring San Marcos cater to the Coach leather goods and Donna Karan dress set, but the general look of Austin is a variation on the classic T-shirt and jeans or shorts. Dressing up often simply means wearing a black T-shirt, but you know how that goes—it ain't what you wear, it's the way you wear it. It's usually too hot for men to wear a jacket to restaurants most of the year, so the ubiquitous cotton dress shirt is a practical alternative.

There are two good reasons to shop the outskirts of South Austin. Both the **Bazaar** *(1605 E. Riverside Dr. 512/448–0736)* and the **Bazaar Back Stage** *(1609 E. Riverside Dr. 512/448–1079)* next door are southern versions of the former Guadalupe Street location, a longtime staple on the dressed-to-kill scene. This is a better setup: ultra-cool new clothing and luscious lingerie at the Bazaar; makeup, jewelry, and hair accessories at the Back Stage. If there's a holiday anywhere nearby, plan to wait in line—both places will be packed.

Austin's upscale shopping isn't quite on the Dallas or Houston end. Neiman Marcus is the original Big Texas

Money store, but it's a little rich for most local blood. Austin is just as pleased with **Neiman Marcus's Last Call** (*W. Ben White Blvd. at S. Lamar Blvd.* 512/447–0701) outlet store, where all those chi-chi designers get marked down to more Austinite prices, generally from 40 percent to 75 percent off the retail price.

Located in the rear of Eco-Wise [see **miscellaneous**] is **Therapy** (110 *W. Elizabeth St.* 512/326–4474), a tiny women's boutique of attractive designer labels with a rather limited selection of styles and sizes. **Simply Divine** (1606 *S. Congress Ave.* 512/444–5546) knows its demographic a little better, making all-cotton clothing for women and children, just the thing for the often-humid weather in Austin. The nearby **Allen's Boots** (1522 *S. Congress Ave.* 512/447–1413) is a place to stop if you prefer new boots, cowboy hats, and Western wear. Not much in the way of originality, but a better choice than the vintage stores if you've got big feet, for example.

clothing, vintage... South Austin's secondhand

clothing stores are highly competitive—even cool people have to make a living—but the owners enjoy the friendly competition and won't hesitate to recommend another store if what you're looking for isn't on their particular premises. Most of these shops are located in easily canvassed clusters along Lamar Boulevard, South 1st Street, and Congress Avenue and usually carry more than just clothes. You may be ready to puke after seeing your fourth velvet Elvis, but you'll walk out of at least one store with something you never dreamed you'd want: a string tie decorated with a cow skull or perhaps sequined opera gloves.

The stores listed below offer a variety of the usual retro clothing, jewelry, accessories, and collectibles. Like the hipper shops in most cities, they carry one-of-a-kind items and tend to specialize in particular areas. You can even stop in for coffee and music at **Flipnotics** (*1601 Barton Springs Rd. 512/322–9750*) while you check out their line of vintage wear. Remember, too, that Austin has an extensive selection of Western-style and Mexican clothing, the result of savvy local buyers and proximity to Mexico. Here's your chance to complete your wardrobe with a stylish pair of cowboy boots, a tooled leather belt, or a secondhand Stetson. Hint: People are still snatching up '70s Qiana shirts, bell-bottoms, flowered dresses, etc., so be smart and start collecting '80s clothing. Anything Adam Ant or Cyndi Lauper wore—skinny ties, flirty miniskirts, torn old-time punk T-shirts, anything black and white—will do. Look for retro New Wave in the next millennium.

The bland-looking shops in the 1000 block of South Lamar Boulevard are worth a stop if only because of **Champagne Clotheshorse** (*1030 S. Lamar Blvd. 512/441–9955*). This eclectic store specializes in new and resale fashions of a rather contemporary nature, but their collection of vintage Japanese kimono, *obi*, and *koto* coats is splendid and reasonably priced. The craftsmanship that goes into the material alone is breathtaking. This same generic-looking strip mall also houses **Big Bertha's Bargain Basement** (*1050 S. Lamar Blvd. 512/444–5908*), a great spot for a fun dig through clothes, wigs, and furnishings. It's the kind of place that could cause you to take up smoking simply because you found an ivory cigarette holder. Another trendy selection of '50s, '60s, and '70s items can be found across the parking lot at **Let's Dish** (1102 S. Lamar Blvd. 512/444–9801). Let's Dish reaches as far back as the '20s and '30s for some of their vintage wear, and the jewelry is divinely eclectic. Take the time to see what other shops may have opened in this slightly seedy, U-shaped bit of real estate: Its location is likely to attract more subculture shops in the future.

South Lamar is also the first stop for two of the oldest vintage stores in Austin. **Amelia's Retro-Vogue and Relics** (2024 S. Lamar Blvd. 512/442–4446) is located in the native limestone strip mall affectionately dubbed "the Horseshoe Krewe." Amelia's has grown into a sprawling collection that includes retro clothing and jewelry as well as period housewares and knickknacks from the mid-1800s to the present. Amelia's also has lots of accessories like leopard-print cateye sunglasses for $10. Next door is **Blackmail** (2040 S. Lamar Blvd . 5 12/326–7670), so named because everything for sale is black, from clothes to art to furnishings.

Right across the street, **Flashback** (2047 S. Lamar Blvd. 512/445–6906) is a wildly painted (purple and yellow when last checked) fixture on the shopping scene. Owner Marcia Laine hangs out at the Continental Club [see **bars/music/clubs**] and her cool-kitty sense as a clothing buyer has made her store a required stop for more than 15 years. Hats, purses, gloves, lingerie, scarves, belts, shirts, slacks, dresses, jackets, shoes, vintage furs—Marcia can dress you like Elvis, Jayne Mansfield, Frank Sinatra, or Marcia Brady, or simply offer the perfect accessory for the look you want. Good stuff under $10: KISS buttons, Farrah Fawcett trading cards, ties, comics, cuff links. The real steal: a half-price dress rack with dresses from $5.

The grande dame of Austin kitsch is **Electric Ladyland** (**1506 S. Congress Ave. 512/444–2002**) and **Lucy In Disguise With Diamonds** (which is located within Electric Ladyland) costume store and rentals. No wonder it attracts the likes of Bob Dylan, who turned wearing a beat-up vest into a fashion statement. Electric Ladyland will charm the pants off you . . . and then put you into something more comfortable, like a studded leather number. Walls of jewelry are sorted by colors, a remarkably intelligent solution. Tiaras, turbans, ties—this place is an alliteration of tacky, trashy, and torchy things to wear. Hawaiian shirts, dashing ties, scrumptious satin shirts, black leather jackets, snazzy trousers, and black cocktail dresses add to the fashion fun. Step through a threshold into Lucy In Disguise, and behold the world of skeleton masks, pirate hats, devil tridents, vampire capes, and all manner of makeup. Go ahead—buy that red foam clown nose (it's only a buck) or the rhinestone shirt, pearl necklace, or the feather boa. Owner Jenna Radke is one of Austin's most famous vintage purveyors, regularly seen at the crack of dawn at estate and yard sales, and her store reflects her total dedication.

collectibles, retro...

Kitschy Western, Southwestern, and Texas-themed souvenirs might include drinking glasses, knickknacks, beer-label trays, ostentatious belt buckles, and ashtrays shaped like Texas. You'll also see collectible items from less enlightened times—racial slurs and humor in art, postcards, decals, and business signs. The little Jim Crow statues and mammy dolls are startling and fascinating in their various manifestations . . . and quite collectible, bringing in a pretty penny for those who are willing to part with them.

The patron saint of secondhand shopping is **St. Vincent de Paul** (1327 S. Congress Ave. 512/442–5652), located on the same block as the Continental Club. St. Vinny's is revered for its longevity and complete lack of trendiness, but it's not exactly a good neighbor. They long ago fenced off their parking lot to keep out late-night clubgoers, and they don't participate in any of the neighborhood merchant efforts. They do carry cheap appliances and furnishings though, and it's amazing what kind of cool junk still ends up there even with all the eagle-eyed buyers around.

Aqua (1415 S. Congress Ave. 512/916–8800) is more than just another stop on Congress. A strictly 20th-century modern, a kind of "from Bauhaus to your house" approach, and the shop is by far the tidiest of the whole strip of stores. It's also pricier than its neighbors—a 25-piece set of George Nelson–designed dinnerware is $250—but every item on display is in top condition—not so with most other shops. Really cool junk has been the domain of **Under the Sun** (1323 S. Congress Ave. 512/442–1308), another collectibles mainstay of Austin, recently relocated from North to South Austin. Take time to rummage through the racks of Westernwear and check out the cool furniture—and the stellar collection of rock 'n' roll memorabilia.

Across the Avenue, **Rue's Antiques** (1500 S. Congress Ave. 512/442–1775) is another longtime neighborhood resident and packed enough to chew up at least an hour or so of your time. Good buys there include real horseshoes ($4) and iron seals of the State of Texas ($12). It's also the place to point out a few caveats about buying reproductions.

Some authentic-looking '60s concert posters printed on cardboard were priced as repros ($5.25) but were really badly faked posters for shows that never happened. (One poster for a 1965 Rolling Stones tour featured a large photo of the band lineup, including Ron Wood, who didn't join the Stones until 1974. Hmmmm.) Discerning shoppers will want to check out the Mexican and South American *objets d'art* available at **Antigua** *(1508 S. Congress Ave. 512/912–1475)*: neat little ceramic light-switch plates for only $9, Guatemalan wood carvings of the sun and the moon for $12 and $18. **Uncommon Objects** *(1512 S. Congress Ave. 512/442–4000)* has what are actually common objects, but some funky little folk-art pieces too. Recently, a set of two soda-shop-style chairs with a tiled table sitting on the sidewalk in front of the shop was priced at $45. **Tinhorn Traders** *(1608 S. Congress Ave. 512/444–3644)* carries both Mexican and American folk art native to the region in its shop full of collectibles. A turquoise Mexican chair with a woven straw seat was going for $45.

The entrance to **Mi Casa** *(1700-A S. Congress Ave. 512/707–9797)* is rather hidden on this side street, but its selection of Southwest art and gifts deserves a peek. Mexican tin crosses were running about $10. Around the corner, **Off the Wall** *(1704 S. Congress Ave. 512/445–4701)* is true to its name, carrying shelf after shelf of wall tchotchkes and knickknacks: More pedestrian fare than Mi Casa, but then those damn harlequin dolls have to come from somewhere. **Armadillo Market** *(1712 S. Congress Ave. 512/443–7552)* has trays of old jewelry to paw through. A nicely rendered framed pencil sketch of Willie Nelson was fetching as much as the portrait of . . . who else . . . Elvis: $40. **New Bohemia**

(1714 S. Congress Ave. 512/326–1238) has a quirkier approach to retro. Didn't think you'd ever need a bolero hat—but for $7, why not? Never thought you'd start a 50-cent collection of swizzle sticks shaped like mermaids, palm trees, and monkeys either, did you? Bonus points for being open until 10 or 11 at night if business warrants. **Pieces of the Past** (1718 S. Congress Ave. 512/326–5141) is a different kind of resale trim shop for home and garden, kind of the Bob Vila of vintage shops. Look for carved moldings, birdbaths, crystal doorknobs, small marble statuary, stained glass, vintage iron fencing, mantlepieces saved from destruction and other architectural details you probably never thought much about.

Over on South Lamar Boulevard, two neon stores call each other neighbor. Check out **The Neon Jungle** (2026 S. Lamar Blvd. 512/448–2787) next to The Horseshoe Lounge and **Hayward Neon** (2038 S. Lamar Blvd. 512/440–0005). You never know when you might need a little light in your life.

miscellaneous... The smiley-faced-sounding **Eco-Wise** (110 W. Elizabeth St. 512/326–4474) specializes in hemp products from paper to wearables—even hemp baby clothes! (Has anyone ever seen a hemp baby?) Pick up books on how to think globally and live "green," along with environment-friendly paint, garden products, cards, T-shirts, advice, and more. It's right next to **Vulcan Video** (112 W. Elizabeth St. 512/326–2629) whose cheap (sometimes free) movie posters are worth a look. Vulcan Video's name, incidentally, doesn't come from "Star Trek," but is a tribute to the original underground '60s club in Austin, The Vulcan Gas Company, whose performers included the

Velvet Underground and Big Mama Thornton. In case you haven't noticed, Austin has an almost biblical reverence for its past and its dead.

Like Eco-Wise, **Dragonsnaps** (*1700 S. Congress Ave. 512/445–4497*) has kids' natural-fiber clothing. But, not long ago, adults started buying Dragonsnaps' "baby blocks," tiny sterling-silver alphabet blocks, and stringing them on necklaces and leather thongs. Sometimes you see just initials, sometimes an entire name. And **Terra Toys** (*1708 S. Congress Ave. 512/445–4489*) is also purportedly a kids' toy store, but hey, all those grownups in there sure look happy. A tiny $2 kaleidoscope with a faceted glass lens can turn South Congress Avenue into a psychedelic wonderland (and with no aftereffects). It's a good stop for souvenirs (a mood ring for $2 or a windup panda drummer for $4.50) or just a journey back to childhood in its notable kids' books section.

sleeping

Cost Range for double occupancy per night on a weeknight. Call to verify prices.
$/under 50 dollars
$$/50–75 dollars
$$$/75–100 dollars
$$$$/100+ dollars

The Hyatt Hotel (*208 Barton Springs Rd. 512/477–1234 $$$$*) on Town Lake is the modern behemoth sitting by the South 1st Street Bridge. During the South by Southwest

Music Conference this hotel is a madhouse, though not nearly as bad as in years past when the conference was held within the hotel itself. Its view of downtown Austin is without peer, especially from the higher floors at night. The comparably priced **Embassy Suites** (300 S. Congress Ave. 512/469–9000 $$$$) offers its standard suite arrangement. Both places will give you a very comfortable night's stay but are light on substance and character. **Omni Southpark** (4140 Governors Row 512/448–2222 $$$$) is down near Ben White Boulevard on I-35 and also on the pricey side. You may want to consider the following chain hotels (think wrapped plastic water cups and cable): **Quality Inn** (2200 S. I-35 512/444–0561 $$$), **La Quinta Inn** (4200 S. I-35 512/443–1774 $$$) or the **Ramada Limited** (2915 S. I-35 512/444–8432 $$). **Homegate** (1001 S. I-35 512/326–0100 $$–$$$) offers not only more affordable suites, but weekly and monthly rates, good if you're going to hunker down for more than a few days. The local **Hostelling International Austin** (2200 S. Lakeshore Blvd. 512/444–2294 $) is not far from I-35, either, just off East Riverside Drive. Not a bad sleep at $13 a night!

But there are numerous places to stay in South Austin besides the strip of motels along I-35. Because the bulk of South Austin dining, shopping, clubbing, and recreation is located along three main avenues, inner South Austin makes an excellent base, especially if you are depending on the bus. Options include the **Bel-Air Motel** (3400 S. Congress Ave. 512/444–5973 $); the **Classic Inn Motel** (4702 S. Congress Ave. 512/445–2558 $–$$); **Village Inn** (3012 S. Congress Ave. 512/443–8383 $); and the **St. El-Motel** (4419 S. Congress Ave. 512/442–2331 $). If you don't like the looks

of a motel along Congress by its parking lot or its guests—
and they do sometimes attract unsavory business transac-
tions (i.e., expect to see the stray hooker or two)—head to
I-35, move a little closer to town at the **San Jose Motel**
(*1316 S. Congress Ave. 512/444–7322 $*), or read on.

You'll get a decent night's rest at any of the above places,
but only the **Austin Motel** (*1220 S. Congress Ave.
512/441–1157 $$–$$$$*) adds that special ambience, and
it's not just because of its sizable phallus of a sign. The Austin
Motel is Austin's most unique motel—relatively cheap, and
no two rooms are alike. Ask for a single and you'll be
assigned to the 1938 wing of individually furnished, com-
fortable rooms. Upward from that, doubles, poolside, and
king rooms feature different murals—scenes such as the
Great Wall of China, tulips in Holland, and Mount Fuji—
plus refrigerators in some rooms. You can even splurge on
their Executive Suite, with jacuzzi and Saltillo tile floors. The
pool is inviting year-round, situated on a ledge overlooking
the avenue. Located catercorner to the Continental Club
[see **bars/music/clubs**] and within walking distance of
the South Congress shopping strip, the Austin Motel's
adjoining restaurant, El Sol y La Luna, is so good with its
gooey Tex-Mex that even regular Austinites go there to eat.

doing stuff

swimming... The in-town swimming is better in South
Austin than anywhere else in the city. No, make that in all
of Texas. First, there is **Barton Springs** (*2201 Barton Springs
Rd. Zilker Park 512/867–3080*), an aquifer-fed, 1,000-foot-

long pool open March through October. Recently it made the news as the site of a Texas-size political tug-of-war that pitted the city council against the all-powerful salamander lobby. Environmentalists were so adamant that a routine cleaning of the pool would kill the slimy but endangered little species that the pool didn't get cleaned for months in early 1998. Finally, the court ordered a sala-mandatory scrubbing, noting that they hoped for the best for the harmless reptile. At last report, the salamanders were thriving and the pool was once again clear. And cold. The pool is a constant 68 degrees, which might be a tad chilly for shrinkage-prone humans, but it seems to suit the crawfish, ducks, freshwater bass, and other longtime residents just fine. You'll probably have better luck pretending to be a duck than trying not to stare at the nonchalantly topless sunbathing section, yet another stubborn remnant of Austin's hippie days. Thank heaven for RayBans. And hippies.

Although it's free to get in, **Stacy Pool (800 E. Live Oak 512/476–4521)** always seems to take a backseat to Barton Springs. Actually, it's more like Barton Springs' blue-collar double. While Barton Springs stays a cool 68 degrees, Stacy is heated by a warm spring, which still makes for a refreshing dip on a hot Austin afternoon. It was set up in the '30s by Roosevelt's WPA and is very much a neighborhood favorite despite its small dimensions and lack of trees or shade. It gives the pool a scrappy air, daring you to take on its unforgiving surroundings. Take the bus from Downtown.

walking/tours/outdoor fun... The irony of the first-rate **Town Lake Hike and Bike Trails** along both

shores of the lake is that Austin's crummy public transportation system forces people to drive somewhere just so
they can go for a walk. Parking areas at the Lamar Boulevard and South 1st Street bridges where Riverside Drive
cuts across are a good place to start if you're looking to
walk or jog. On Town Lake's south banks between the Lamar
Boulevard and South 1st bridges, you'll find the infamous
Stevie Ray Vaughan statue, deemed "tacky" by *Spin* magazine's travel guide, and with some merit. For all his cult-
following and national guitar-slinging image, Stevie was a
consummate proto-slacker, plugging away in the shittiest
of dives and couch-surfing for years before fame and drugs
came en masse, followed by the inevitable heroic rehab.
But to a certain breed of South Austinite, the SRV statue,
like Threadgill's and topless bathing at Barton Springs, is
the ultimate anti-establishment statement. The loading
dock for the **Lone Star Riverboat Tour** **(S. Congress Ave.
and S. 1st St., on the south shore of Town Lake 512/327−1388)** is
nearby, just west of the Hyatt. It doesn't answer the age-old
question as to why Town Lake is called a lake when it's part
of the Colorado River, but it's an interesting way to while
away 90 minutes ($9). You'll doubtless find yourself among
the most touristic of tourists—this is one of those faux,
old-timey paddle-wheelers—but you'll get to look at
Austin the way few locals do. There are daily cruises March
through September, but try the 10:30 moonlight cruise on
a weekend; its midnight docking time still gets you to the
headliner at a club.

The area just south of the Congress Avenue Bridge is the
"official" spot for that most bizarre of Austin rituals—bat
watching. Every evening, hordes gather to witness hundreds

austin for next to nothing...

You can spend a full day in South Austin for as little as $25 if you fill up your water bottle and have no expensive addictions. Try an itinerary like this :

Morning: Have spectacular breakfast tacos at the **Tamale House** or pastry at **Texas French Bread** ($3 to $4). Late morning to mid-afternoon: Walk along misnamed **Town Lake** or play a rousing round of disc golf at **Zilker Park**, then cruise the shopping strips and promise yourself you'll spend no more than $5 in $1 increments to see how imaginative you can be. (One such trip's loot yielded a jeweled letter opener, a sandalwood bookmark, some plastic ants, a florid Saint's Prayer card, and a wooden bead bracelet.) Lunch: Go directly to **Fran's Hamburgers**—the place with the guitar-wielding waif on top—and give in to your most carnivorous tendencies ($3 to $4). Mid-afternoon: Swim at **Stacy Pool**—it's free, but there are no topless bathers as at Barton Springs. Late afternoon: Clean up a bit and hit happy hour at the **Continental** with good music, beer, and tip ($3 total). Before dusk: Head to the **Congress** or **South 1st** bridge and watch the bats for free. Finally: Have a swell dinner at **Threadgill's** or **Jovita's** for 10 bucks, tip included. At some point later when someone wants to know just what the hell it was you did down in Texas, of all places, you can just smile. No need to destroy the illusion for the folks back home.

of thousands of bats in their evening rite of swooping out from under the bridges in dark ribbons and swirling upward into the sky. No kidding. As far as anyone can tell, the flying mammals became an attraction back in the early '80s when a colony of Mexican Freetail bats nested under the Congress Avenue and South 1st Street bridges, and the party has grown steadily ever since. The critters have become such a tourist draw that a nonprofit group called **Bat Conservation International** *(P.O. Box 162603, Austin, TX 78716 512/327–9721)* watches over these intriguing non-vampires. These natural exterminators are also civic-minded creatures, darkening the sky nightly to do battle with Austin's never-ending supply of insects. Well over a million bats live under the bridges, and the high-octane smell of bat guano, the scientific name for batshit, is proof [see **bats** in **downtown**].

Do observe those speed-limit signs when in **Zilker Park** *(2201 Barton Springs Rd. 512/472–4914)*, as the laws are strictly enforced by government workers carrying sidearms. Still, there's much to do slowly in the almost 500 acres. Jock types can enjoy swimming, canoeing, volleyball, soccer, hiking and bike trails. There's even a course set aside for disc golf (Frisbee-golf), taking sports to a whole other level. More sedentary types can relax by picnicking, enjoying a performance in the outdoor amphitheatre, or taking the tots on the playscape or the kiddie train that runs throughout the park. Tree huggers make for the **Botanical Garden Center** *(Zilker Park 512/477–7273)* and the **Austin Nature Center**. Given Austin's mild climate, these activities are available most of the year. At Christmastime, a 165-foot Tree of Lights glows colorfully near the Trail of Lights, a drive-thru mile of brightly-lit holiday scenes. The Trail of Lights is a cornball deal but you can spin around in the center of the tree and feel like you're five (or tripping) again. Zilker Park is open daily 5 a.m. to 10 p.m. and is free (admission to swim at Barton Springs). If parking is crowded, and it will be on weekends and during the summer, there are shuttles ($1) from the City Coliseum lot at Riverside Drive and Bouldin.

And if you are considering outdoor activities, don't pass up the chance to play a round of mini golf. The **Peter Pan Mini Golf** (1207 Barton Springs Rd. 512/472–1033) course with its Brobdingnagian namesake standing watch is another one of those places ostensibly for kids where adults abound. It's $4 to tee off among the giant whale, dinosaur, turtle, and skull holes.

galleries/spaces... If you've ever considered collecting original art, **Yard Dog** (1510 S. Congress Ave. 512/912–1613) could be the place to start. For a mere $50, you can own the unframed limited-edition print "Bob Wills Signs His Contract," rendered by Mekons brainman Jon Langford, who brings his alt-country outfit the Waco Brothers to the gallery's patio every South By Southwest music festival. Fifty bucks will also buy you an original drawing by Austin songwriter/manic genius Daniel Johnston. For $100 upward, you can choose from regional folk artists like the late Prophet Royal Robertson, whose demented rantings in felt-tip pen on cardboard mix vibrant biblical imagery with rage at a wife who left him, or Lamar Sorrento, the Memphis musician who pays tribute to Robert Johnson and others in his apocalyptic

earth-tone paintings. For something a little lighter on the wallet, there's usually a tin washtub in back filled with odd little murmurings and scribblings on shingle-sized planks by anonymous artists. There are no prices, but putting a $5 to $10 donation in the box (the artist simply shows up occasionally and collects it) buys good karma as well as original and unusual folk art.

Over on South 1st Street, an unofficial arts collective has sprung up, with **Alternate Current Art Space (2209 S. 1st St. 512/443–9674)** and **Resistencia Bookstore (2210 S. 1st St. 512/416–0944)** as anchors. Both collectives reflect the vibe of this supportive, cheap, friendly, and artsy neighborhood. Alternate Current offers art shows, exhibits, and occasional music performances on an irregular basis. A while back AC had a Barbie show where local personalities and artists were invited to create their own dream Barbie, with predictably wild results. **Laughing at the Sun (2209 S. 1st St. 512/442–7055)** and **Stuffola (2209 S. 1st St. 512/444–1188)** share space beside Alternate Current. Stuffola's Ed Kilford specializes in refinishing and restoration of fine furniture. He even replaces cane seats and chairbacks. Laughing at the Sun houses the permanent collection of Daryl Colburn's metal sculpture art. **Primordial Expressions (2209 S. 1st St. 512/462–9041)** is the studio of Ross de la Garza's raku-fired clayworks, but is open for appointments only. Artist Tony Romano cobbles together unusual frames made from found objects at his **Just Say Cheese** studio **(512/892–6464)**, open by appointment only.

But South Austin's political heart beats across the street in a tiny space that houses Resistencia Bookstore. It's the domain of dashing poet Raul Salinas. Inside the small bookstore are volumes of poetry, essays, calendars, Indian art, a jar collecting for the Free Leonard Peltier fund (remember *Incident at Oglala* or even *Thunderheart*?). Salinas will sometimes throw a parking-lot party with local bands to raise money for the oppressed of Chiapas, Mexico, or hold readings in the stores. Always a presence at the store, he can often be found clipping news stories of political unrest—ever the voice that won't be silenced.

Next to Resistencia is the one-room **Blue Road Studio (512/326–8909)**, featuring the oversized, splashy oils of Joyce DiBona. DiBona loves to paint but she really specializes in sculptural robotics. At any given time she may be dismantling a mannequin and rewiring it for art's sake. DiBono and Salinas are also collaborating on some mixed-media projects. In **Raindog Studios (512/416–9245)** next door, Colly Krieder specializes in stone and steel sculpture, and shares the space with several other artists including people from the **Art Gazer Gallery (512/924–1761)**. In the same strip of studios is **La Menagerie (512/326–4090)**, an open studio with artists Mark Matlock and Casey McKee, two local sculptors.

south by southwest (SXSW)

For the past twelve years, the annual South by Southwest (SXSW) conference has turned Austin into an international center for the entertainment business. And into a five-day multimedia party. The March event is packed with film screenings, panels of entertainment experts, musical performances, and trade shows.

The Film Conference and Festival is considered one of the most important film forums in the country, and at the separate but simultaneous Interactive Festival, computer and Internet-heads find their niche, but it's the Music Conference and Festival that attracts hundreds of performers and thousands of visitors to Austin.

Previous performers at the conference have included Sonic Youth, Son Volt, The Fugees, and Beck. But folks other than alternative rock gods attend; Tony Bennett and Johnny Cash just to name a couple. The *New York Times* has called this "the reigning meet-and-greet of the rock business," and while groundbreaking business certainly does take place here, it's been deemed the spring break of the music industry, as well.

If you're interested in attending SXSW, be sure to call hotels way ahead of time for reservations. To register for the conference or to get your name on the SXSW mailing list, visit their web site at www.sxsw.com. Or call 512/466–SXSW.

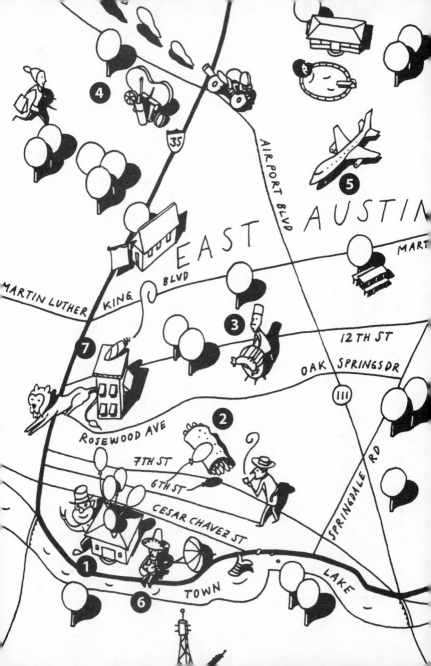

SPRINGDALE RD

LUTHER KING BLVD

183

east austin

As pre-production work began in 1997 on *The Newton Boys*, director Richard Linklater's valentine to the way things wuz, the normally sedate East Austin neighborhood where his office is located was overrun by movie stars. Mixed among the regular old neighborhood hoi polloi were the likes of Matthew McConaughey, Julianna Margulies, Vincent D'Onofrio, Skeet Ulrich, and Ethan

turn page for map key

Hawke. But students living across the street and families in the small clapboard houses nearby were unfazed, unimpressed by the perpetual Oscar bash in their front yard—they had tests to take and lives to live, movie stars or not.

Linklater's 1990 film *Slacker*, a tribute to Gen-X sloth, put his hometown in America's face, and his ensuing success brought credibility to Austin as a film base. When he went looking for office space, affordable and colorful East Austin beckoned. Those who choose to live east of I-35 like the fact that it's more down to earth than South Austin or West Austin. You don't have to be hip or rich to live here, and all the Mexican restaurants are worth the trip in their own right. The neighborhood is perfect for both struggling artists and entrepreneurs since rents are low and there are plenty of affordable stores and restaurants nearby. Linklater shares his Detour Film Production's east side digs with the Austin Film Society, an arrangement that has attracted considerable industry traffic, with directors like Robert Rodriguez and Quentin Tarantino often dropping by for screenings, and Third Coast Extras Casting and other video/stage/screen companies sprouting up nearby.

East Austin entrepreneurs are definitely thriving, but that hasn't upstaged the area's predominantly Tejano character—a hybrid of Mexican and Texan culture. You can count on a host of great Tex-Mex eateries and huge, shiny, low-riding cars that are meticulously maintained (be care-

map key		
	1 Piñata Party Palace	5 Robert Miller
	2 El Azteca Restaurant	Municipal Airport
	3 Sam's Bar-B-Cue	6 Juan in a Million
	4 R. Linklater's office	7 The Liberty Grill

ful opening your doors if you're parked next to one). East Austin is home to the city's largest concentrations of Latinos and African-Americans. The heart of the area is a triangle formed by Town Lake (the Colorado River) on the south and I-35 on the west, with Airport Boulevard connecting the two (northwest to southeast). The interstate, built in the '60s, has become a not-so-great wall separating the east side from the rest of the city. A lot of visitors—and locals—avoid East Austin because they perceive it as an insulated ghetto where they might not be welcome. Nothing could be further from the truth. East Austin is mercifully free of the self-conscious hipness that permeates the Drag and University area. While the U.T. campus echoes with the clamor of drunken frat boys and tipsy "bowheads" (sorority girls) yakking in the bushes, the predominantly black East Austin neighborhood of Rosewood is peaceful and friendly. This area is home to Huston-Tillotson College and the oldest public-access television network (three channels) in the country as well as some of the best barbecue on the planet. On weekends, the legendary Victory Grill comes alive, filling the area with sweet jazz. Head east on East 12th Street to Sam's Bar-B-Cue, grab some ribs to go, and continue east for a picnic in green belts as lush and inviting as the best parks in West Austin. The coolest graveyard in town is just south of Martin Luther King, Jr. Boulevard and east of I-35. Even a cursory stroll among the headstones will reveal names instrumental to Austin's history, such as the architect Major George Washington Littlefield, of U.T. fountain and Downtown building fame. The Latino art studios that line East 6th and East 1st streets put snootier West Austin galleries to shame. Poke through the flea markets and second-hand stores while you're there, and by all means, don't leave town without trying the *migas* (Mexican scrambled eggs) at Cisco's and collecting an El Azteca calendar for a souvenir.

eating/coffee

Visitors to these parts have to forget what they learned in health class about grains, fruit and legumes and their places in that ridiculous nutritional pyramid: In Texas, the three major food groups are barbecue, Mexican, and down-home Southern cookin' (the fourth food group is cold beer). You'll find more of them all on the east side than anywhere else in the city, and, unbelievably, there are no chain or theme restaurants in the area. The east side triangle has three restaurant rows—East Cesar Chavez Street, East 6th Street, and East 7th Street—four, if you count the mini-strip along Manor Road (pronounced MAY-ner). There are nearly two dozen Mexican restaurants, not to mention barbecue, soul-food, regional, and even vegetarian establishments. Most of them are mama-and-papacito joints that serve authentic, inexpensive food and don't take plastic. So make sure to bring cash and brush up on your Spanish. The mainstay of the slacker diet is a little Tex-Mex gem called the breakfast taco, found just about everywhere in East Austin. They are cheap ($1 to $1.50), portable, spicy, and available with a variety of ingredients. Delicate tummies might protest the influx of spicy food in the morning, but don't let that scare you. Do what Texans do in August: Get used to the heat.

Cost Range per entree
$/under 10 dollars
$$/10–15 dollars
$$$/15–20 dollars
$$$$/20+ dollars

american... If the mark of a good restaurant is how well it draws people from other neighborhoods, **Eastside Cafe** (2113 Manor Rd. 512/476–5858 $–$$$) is a winner. Head chef Ruth Carter—who, along with her husband, co-wrote many of Stevie Ray Vaughan's hit tunes, including "Crossfire"—has created a delightful setting for diners in the restaurant's gardens. They grow their own vegetables, and the gardens are beside the dining area, so you can admire what you might order the next time. Considering most dishes run about $6 to $11, it's a steal. The raspberry vinaigrette over their garden-fresh lettuce is like a taste of heaven.

breakfast... Though Mexican breakfasts are the norm at most East Austin eateries, few are as colorful or as memorable as **Cisco's Restaurant Bakery & Bar** (1511 E. 6th St. 512/478–2420 $–$$). Patrons at this longtime favorite of politicos and wheeler-dealers don't care if the menu is limited—they come here for the *migas*. When cigar-chomping owner Rudy Cisneros died, he took part of the restaurant's character with him, but look for Cisneros' caricature painted on the side of the building with a sign that reads: "We have no No-Tipping area" (which beats the "Tipping is not a city in China" alternative). **Lucy's** (1628 E. Cesar Chavez St. 512/457–0337 $) is a traditional coffee shop set in a Mexican bakery—its unassuming exterior and limited seating make for a short-but-sweet breakfast. The goofily named **Juan in a Million** *(2300 E. Cesar Chavez St. 512/472–3872 $)* also features the standard breakfast offerings of huevos rancheros, migas, and breakfast tacos in a cozy atmosphere. The food is so heavy, though, it may make you forget about lunch.

barbecue... Barbecue is required eating in Texas—only hard-core vegetarians get off the meat hook. **Ben's Long Branch BBQ** *(900 E. 11th St. 512/477–2516 $)* overlooks downtown and serves till 3 a.m. It's not barbecue to brag about, but there's no such thing around here as bad barbecue. Ben's does something right—he's been in the same spot for over 20 years. But if there's a holy land of barbecue joints, it's **Sam's Bar-B-Cue** *(2000 E. 12th St. 512/478–0378 $)*, a favorite haunt of musicians and the late-night set (open until 3 a.m. weeknights, Fridays and Saturdays till 4 a.m.). Dan Mays—whose family has run the joint since the 1970s—is a genuine barbecue god. Let his spicy sauce lap over onto your beans and potato salad if you want to taste real local flavor. Most of the restaurant's souvenir autographs, posters, and photographs went up in smoke in a 1992 fire, but Sam's is still a classic, whether you eat on the side porch or buy by the pound for a picnic in a nearby park.

caribbean/soul food... While it's not truly Southern "soul food," the Caribbean-style fare at **Calabash** *(2015 Manor Rd. 512/478–4857 $–$$$)* is certainly food for the soul. Your soul will be torn, however, when you have to choose among the waffle and eggs, the jerk chicken and the fried plantains. **Miss Flo's** (1209 E. 11th St. 512/482–9840 $) is one of the most popular home-style restaurants around, but only open 11 a.m. to 4 p.m. The menu? Think Sunday dinner at Grandma's, with equally large portions. Flo Williams is something of a legend in these parts for her hearty cooking; her Deep South dishes such as butterbeans and ham will make you drool long after you've left Austin.

ice houses... Just like San Antonio, East Austin has "ice houses"—a term that survived the invention of the refrigerator in this part of Texas. **The Texas Ice House** (913 E. Cesar Chavez St. 512/322–9330) is little more than a standard beer-and-cigarettes convenience store, but six short blocks away is **The House** (1510 E. Cesar Chavez St.), where you can drive up to the window and get a six-pack in a plastic bag of ice. This is especially handy if it's July and you are on your way to buy barbecue at Sam's.

late night... **Star Seeds Cafe** (3101 N. I-35 512/478–7107 $), attached to the Days Inn University [see **sleeping**], is open 24–7, which is the main reason it is East Austin's central magnet for the late-night post-club crowd, musicians and lay people alike. Aside from that, the place, well, sucks. The menu is boring, the food is worse, and the service is typical slacker-style (slow and indifferent). On the other hand, it's cheap and the jukebox is sublime.

tex-mex... In the heart of East Austin alone, you could eat at a different Mexican restaurant three meals a day and it would take you a week to get to all of them. Almost all are muy bueno and tend to be open only for breakfast and lunch. (They are often closed Monday or Tuesday too.) Some of the best—and cheapest—Mexican eats are at weekend bazaars in church parking lots, where tacos, fajitas, and barbecue plates cost about $3.

Every March, **El Azteca Restaurant** (2600 E. 7th St. 512/477–4701 $$) is packed with SXSW-goers, who waddle back to the coasts stuffed with primo Tex-Mex and carrying Austin's best $2 souvenirs—full-color wall calendars featuring macho Mexican heroes and buxom maidens in outfits Cher would kill for.

If you watched "Austin Stories" on MTV (read: if you were watching that day) you've seen **Hernandez Cafe** (1201 E. 6th St. 512/472–0323 $), with its institutional green walls and ever-patient waitress Chloe. There's no Chloe in real life, and there's nothing out-of-the-ordinary about the menu, but the hot sauce is hot and the beer is cold—what else do you need? At **Nuevo Leon** (1209 E. 7th St. 512/479–0097 $$), a classic Tex-Mex joint a block away, it has become a matter of honor to see how much hot sauce you can consume before dying.

Closer to the University area, the red-and-white exterior of **Mi Madre's** (2201 Manor Rd. 512/480–8441 $) attracts people for its cheap, hearty Tex-Mex dripping with cheese and chunky salsa. A little north, near MusicMania [see **buying stuff**], try **Pato's Tacos** (1400 E. 38 1/2 St. 512/476–4247 $). This neat little working-class beer garden serves brewskis the way Texans like them best: in aluminum cans packed in ice. There are also pool tables, shuffleboard, a jukebox packed with local music, occasional live music—and a proliferation of pickup trucks in the parking lot.

vegetarian... You can get your daily fix of tacos and tamales at **Mr. Natural** (*1901 E. Cesar Chavez St. 512/477–5228 $*), but they'll be the veggie and tofu varieties. Mr. Natural heaps on huge servings of healthful fare in a cafeteria setting. The bakery offers lots of take-out possibilities, from *empanadas* to fruit breads. Although tofu tamales are not authentically Mexican, these are good enough to avoid ridicule. Too much.

bars/music/theater

Club-hopping on the east side can be a tricky business and few visitors ever get it right. It used to be a place where white boys played blues in Mexican restaurants, but now most of the neighborhood bars are strictly local hangouts without music, and usually without white boys. On the other hand, there are still a few great *conjunto* bars like **Happy Days Lounge** (*2712 E. 2nd St. 512/474–1834*) that welcome newcomers and are often packed with a diverse crowd. Since *conjunto* is the equivalent of Mexican country music, with lots of pumping accordion, you may not be able to resist the urge to dance.

East First Garden Theatre (*4822 E. Cesar Chavez St. 512/386–8686*), **The Victory Grill** (*1104 E. 11th St. 512/474–4494*), and even **Vortex Repertory Company/ Planet Theatre** (*2307 Manor Rd. 512/478–5282*) all encourage and support cultural performers and the occasional spoken-word artist. The East First Garden Theatre is a large outdoor venue sporadically in use for touring acts. The Victory Grill is one of Austin's oldest nightspots, a stop in the '60s for acts like the Ike & Tina Turner Revue. Various free-form theater groups make use of the space within Planet Theatre—the *Austin Chronicle* will usually have the current program.

The Crazy Lady (3701 N. I-35 512/478–2444) is Austin's oldest topless bar, an unassuming working-class hangout where Pato's dinner crowd often ends up. Last year, a group of veteran Austin musicians formed a band called The Esquires and began playing old-timey strip-club rock there. Cool retro or female exploitation with a hip patina? You decide. Call to check show times.

venues... If you pay attention, you just might stumble into some of the most down-home music in Austin at **Doris Miller Auditorium** (2300 *Rosewood Ave.* 512/476–4118), across from the ACAC studios, and at **Fiesta Gardens** (2101 *Bergman St.* 512/480–3036), right on Town Lake. Doris Miller often features gospel revues; Fiesta Gardens hosts a variety of events. Call for information, as these shows are rarely advertised outside the neighborhood.

buying stuff

Shopping in East Austin is a bit of a treasure hunt—and a welcome contrast to Central Austin's pricey galleries, West

Austin's imported-soap emporiums, and South Austin's calculated retro-hipness.

cds/records/videos...

You'd have to go shopping in San Antonio for a better selection of Tejano music than the one at the granddaddy of East Austin record stores, **Maldonado's Record & Video Shop** (2207 E. 7th St. 512/478–0020). Since it moved from its original Cesar Chavez Street location, it has flourished as the Austin source for Tejano, *conjunto*, *norteno*, *orquesta*, and other Latino music. Longtime owner Henry Maldonado will happily answer questions and make recommendations. **Acapulco Video & Audio Tapes** (2009 E. 7th St. 512/482–0215) is more like a Kmart of Spanish-language music and videos. You have to know what you want before you walk in the door unless you speak Spanish. **Musicmania** (3909-D N. I-35 512/451–3361), Austin's No.1 source of hip-hop and rap music, is a lovingly cultivated independent business. The vinyl selection is well worth the effort of looking through the bins.

vintage/miscellaneous...

You can find great secondhand bargains at garage and church sales all over the neighborhood, as well as at the **Remar USA Christian Thrift Store** (1410 E. Cesar Chavez St. 512/482–0797) and the **flea market** (2326 E. Cesar Chavez St., no phone). The flea market doesn't have a sign, so it's a bit hard to find. The dollar stores and yard sales can also produce great finds, from Virgin Mary nightlights to used cowboy boots. **City General Store** (2605 E. 7th St. 512/474–6819) carries herbs, incense, oils, crystals, and other odd little items that seem vaguely voodooish despite the bland name. For something a little less mystical, the **Piñata Party Palace** (*2017 E. Cesar Chavez St.* 512/322–9150) is a hoot, though stuffing that Bart Simpson piñata in the plane's overhead compartment could be a prob, dude.

The spots to hit for cool little items that won't empty your pockets are **Green & White Grocery** (*1201 E. 7th St.* 512/472–0675) and **Fiesta Mart** (*3909 N. I-35* 512/406–3900). Both are prime candle and knickknack turf. Any place that sells both love potions and root beer must be seen to be believed. **Pitchforks & Tablespoons** (*2113 Manor Rd.* 512/476–5858), also known as the Eastside Cafe Store, is a little oasis. Grab a salad and some juice from the cooler while you pick through garden supplies, various herbs, T-shirts, and Austin bat-watching souvenirs.

sleeping

Cost Range for double occupancy per night on a weeknight. Call to verify prices.

$/under 50 dollars

$$/50–75 dollars

$$$/75–100 dollars

$$$$/100+ dollars

They may not be fancy, but the fact that there are only three places to stay in East Austin makes decision making much easier. Choose from the new **Club Hotel** (*1617 N. I-35* 512/479–4000 $$$–$$$$), the **Days Inn University** (*3105 N. I-35* 512/478–1631 $$–$$$$), or the **Super 8**

the portable austin

Looking for a take-home souvenir party pack? Try a combination of these items:

Shiner Bock beer (Lone Star and Pearl are okay, but we don't recommend them. Celis beer is fine, too.)

A bottle of hot sauce (Try Wheatsville or Whole Foods for food items.)

A bag of chips (Any local variety, baked or fried, will do— except blue corn. Blue-corn chips are not "Austin.")

Bottled queso and/or black-bean dip

An Emo's T-shirt

A gimme cap from Antone's

A Stevie Ray Vaughan statue postcard

A suntan around that Band-Aid you forgot to take off when swimming buck-nekkid at Hippie Hollow

An *Austin Chronicle*

A hot-sauce stain from Jovita's on your favorite shirt

A CD by any of the following: The 13th Floor Elevators, Don Walser, Butthole Surfers, Kacy Crowley, Fabulous Thunderbirds, the True Believers. (Note: Publisher is not responsible for any major life changes caused by listening to these albums.)

Motel (1201 N.I-35 512/472–8331 $$–$$$$). Super 8 and Days Inn are inexpensive; Club Hotel is proof that not everything in East Austin is cheap. The Super 8 is strictly utilitarian, but if you like a seedy rock 'n' roll atmosphere, Days Inn is a great deal. The Club Hotel is much more upscale and tends to be full of parents of university-bound students, especially in the summer and fall.

doing stuff

Unless you're a history fanatic, **The French Legation Museum** (802 *San Marcos St.* 512/472–8180) will bore you silly. For those who appreciate the intricacies of Franco–Texan relations: In 1841 the French liaison to the Republic of Texas built himself a dandy little pine museum right by a cemetery. (Okay, the cemetery wasn't there then and the Daughters of the Republic of Texas made the place a museum later on.) The cottage claims to have the only authentic Creole kitchen in the United States. Take that, Louisiana! Open afternoons; closed Mondays.

galleries... The oldest glass-blowing studio in Texas, **Fire Island Hot Glass Studio, Inc.** (3401 E. 4th St. 512/389–1100), demonstrates the art between 9 a.m. and noon on Saturdays (September through January and March through May). Noted painter Sam Coronado is one of over 50 Latino artists represented in the collection of contemporary Tejano art at **Coronado Studios and Gallery** (1707 E. 6th St. 512/322–0109). The gallery is open only on Saturdays, but it's worth a visit. You might get a mini-lesson in how limited-edition prints are made. **Holy Eight Ball Studio** (*2206 E. 7th St. 512/474–2570*) is not open to the public unless it's throwing a party or hosting an exhibition. The space is now used by photographer Bruce Dye. If it looks like there's something happening there, go on in. If not, don't even knock—Bruce will be crabby and you probably don't want to catch him in his undershorts. **BB Studios** (*2211-A Hidalgo St. 512/477–3157*) is one of those funky warehouse-to-arthouse renovation stories. It hosts dance programs, art exhibits, films, and theatrical performances from October through May (it's closed during the summer).

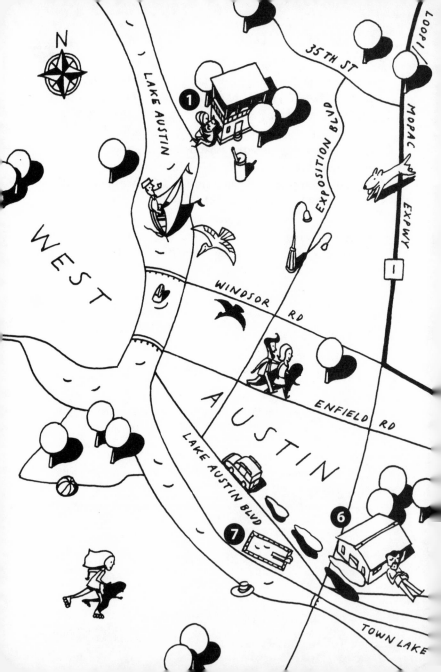

west austin

It would be easy to dismiss West Austin as just another upscale neighborhood—if you've seen one, you've seen them all. And it's true—life in Austin west of Lamar can be unbearably sterile, homogeneous, and downright b-o-r-i-n-g. But if the hidden character of West Austin escapes you, do as the locals do—think of it as "old-school," a Texan term of endearment for an old-fashioned, genteel,

turn page for map key

good ol' boy lifestyle. While the rest of the city's hip music scene screams *Rolling Stone*, West Austin quietly murmurs *Better Homes & Gardens*. It's the seat of the town's old money. West Austinites can name a blue-chip stock more readily than they can a Stevie Ray Vaughan tune, and successful real estate agents there achieve the local celebrity status generally reserved for musicians. Nevertheless, the area is home to a few choice gems that most tourists—and even some snooty locals—have not yet discovered. Although their names should be giveaways, it's not immediately obvious that famous Shoal Creek Saloon's patio actually does back up to beautiful and historic Shoal Creek, for example, or that the Deep Eddy Saloon really is right in front of Deep Eddy, the best workout pool in town. Because of the often relentless heat in Texas, Austinites truly savor their swimming retreats, as well as the cool shelter of the bars that tend to cluster around them. Neighborhood watering holes (yes, bars and pools alike) actually begin to seem like cultural centers. And West Austin's old-money trail has spawned some of the city's finest hiking and biking trails as well. If the squeaky-clean streets and manicured lawns start getting to you, escape to the comparatively wild outdoors of Lake Austin and Mount Bonnell.

To get your bearings, picture West Austin as a Texas chili pepper (with the wide end of the pepper facing north). The right (east) edge of the pepper is Lamar, a huge thor-

map key			
	1	Dry Creek Cafe and Boat Dock	4 Waterloo Records
	2	Whole Foods Market	5 The Tavern
	3	Book People	6 El Arroyo
			7 Deep Eddy Pool

oughfare. The top (north) of the pepper is 24th Street, the bottom (south) is West 5th, and running down the left (west) side is the Mopac Expressway, which follows the path of the Missouri-Pacific railroad. (Okay, if this pepper image escapes you, just look at a map.) East of Lamar is Downtown; north of 24th is the campus area. The gated communities of the Lake Austin area and posh Tarrytown are in the northern section, just west of Mopac; Clarksville is midway down, on the east side of Mopac. A historic district settled by emancipated slaves during Reconstruction and now home to a sizeable student population, Clarksville is the neighborhood closest to Campus and Downtown.

As a rule, the closer a west side neighborhood is to the campus or Lamar, the more affordable the homes and shopping. The difference between 12th and Lamar and 5th or 6th and Lamar is noticeable. The corner of 6th and Lamar houses one of the city's most popular natural grocers, Whole Foods, as well as Austin's landmark Waterloo Records. It's no accident that Austin's newest Land Rover dealer set up shop on W. 5th—the "right side of the tracks"—where the big-bucks status symbols can be sold by the boatload.

You may need one of those Land Rovers if you head very far west of Mopac and want to navigate the poorly lit and semi-treacherous roads that lead to some of Austin's best views of the Hill Country. Overlook the touristy development that is rooting itself in the area, a sore subject for locals who feel that neighborhood values have taken a backseat to tourist interests. One such drive—worth the risk or the rental fee on a Rover—is a straight shot west, out 35th toward Mount Bonnell, where a 100-step hike offers a spectacular view of the Hill Country and Lake Austin. This vista is better than a trip to the lake itself, mostly because the west side's approach to the lake, where Enfield (15th) dead-ends, is crammed with tourists, tacky theme restaurants, and pricey coffeehouses.

eating/coffee

The best thing—some say the only thing—about West Austin is its food. Three of the city's schmanciest restaurants are here, plus a few classic Austin hangs and a thriving—if expensive—coffee culture. For such an otherwise sterile area, there's an amazing selection of restaurants here, and almost every notable eatery is an independent enterprise. West Austin has somehow developed an immunity to the chain-restaurant virus that infects most other suburban areas, but this clean living comes at a price: Most folks can't afford West Austin restaurants like Jeffrey's or Zoot more than once or twice a decade (for college graduation and marriage proposals).

West Austin lacks a distinct restaurant row, but the area around 5th and 6th has a number of coffeehouses, barbecue joints, and Mexican eateries, along with Whole Foods. But outside of the smaller joints, almost everything you'll need to know about the atmosphere of west side dining can be summed up in three phrases: "converted house," "nice patio," and "moderate to expensive."

Cost Range per entree
$/under 10 dollars

$$/10–15 dollars
$$$/15–20 dollars
$$$$/20+ dollars

american... Like Austin Java Company across the street, **The Austin Land & Cattle Company** (*1205 N. Lamar Blvd.* *512/472–1813 $–$$*) compensates for its old-money west side ambience of delicate white linens and candles with moderate prices. The real deal here is meat and potatoes. A large rib-eye steak will leave you begging for a doggy bag. Note: Do not confuse this locally owned and operated restaurant with the Texas Land & Cattle Company, a bland chain restaurant on the north side of town.

For meat and potatoes without the frills, go to **Waterloo Ice House** (*600 N. Lamar Blvd. 512/472–5400 $*), a down-home burger joint, bar, and live-music venue. The perfect meal here is a Texas Philly steak sandwich smothered in queso, chased with a frosty cinnamon-chocolate shake. If you're low on cash, drop by during happy hour for half-price appetizers. Or, if cash is bulging out of your wallet, tell your driver to take you to **Jake's Steaks & Seafood** (*3826-B Lake Austin Blvd. 512/477–5253 $–$$$$*), a brand new surf 'n' turf place with huge windows facing the lake. Jake's has three separate venues—casual, fine dining, and club (which includes live entertainment)—and the classic fare and selective wine list are excellent.

breakfast/late night... You can't talk "old school" without talking **GM Steakhouse** (*626 N. Lamar Blvd.* *512/472–2172 $*). This tiny west side luncheonette, open for two decades, is less legendary than its original

Guadalupe Street location, but from breakfast to dinner, they've got every greasy item from pork chops to pancakes, plus attitude galore—getting insulted by the wait staff is actually part of the charm. Their T-shirts warn: "How do you want your eggs . . . not that it matters." The crowd that can tolerate the "charm" is definitely local and looking for blue-plate specials at early-bird prices. Call ahead for their most current hours of operation.

The diner fare at **Magnolia Cafe (2304 *Lake Austin Blvd.* 512/478–8645 $–$$)** comes with half of GM's grease and none of the attitude. It's Austin's best late-night hang, open 24 hours, just minutes from Downtown. Their "Popeye" omelet is popular, with spinach, onion, sour cream, bacon, mushrooms, and cheese. Expect a 30- to 45-minute wait every night and most of the weekend, although once you're seated they'll let you stay and consume as much coffee and as many breakfast tacos (sort of an omelet wrapped in your choice of a flour, corn, or whole-wheat tortilla) as you can stomach. Magnolia is most popular for being one of the few West Austin eateries where nicotine freaks are in heaven: In half the restaurant, you can smoke 'em if you got 'em.

chinese... Unlike the glitzy Tarrytown strip mall that houses it, West Austin's only real Chinese restaurant—**Formosa (2414 *Exposition Blvd.* 512/322–0344 $$)**—is inexpensive and very casual, if not actually dull in atmosphere. But there is nothing bland about the Hunan, Szechuan, and Mandarin menu which serves the usual suspects like almond chicken and beef and broccoli. Big portions and super-quick service turn customers into regulars.

coffee... At the corner of 12th and Lamar, the **Austin Java Company** (1206 *Parkway* 512/476–1829 **$**) is the crossroads for Campus, Downtown, and west side coffee connoisseurs. Sitting in one of the casual, dog-friendly patios with a throng of smiling locals, you'd never guess that this same spot once housed the gases of Terminex, an exterminator. The company's sign sported a giant papier-mâché insect that was stolen repeatedly by packs of unimaginative fraternity pranksters. Ironically, the coffee's the least impressive item on the menu, ringing in at a consistent "mediocre." Many come for the outstanding French toast and spinach omelets (served until 11 a.m. weekdays and 2 p.m. on weekends), or the soup and pasta. Try the chicken penne pasta with sun-dried tomatoes.

The best place to go for salads is also a somewhat sterile local coffee-joint franchise: **Tarrytown's Texas French Bread** (3112-*A Windsor Rd.* 512/478–8845 **$**), where the coffee is unbeatable and Caesar salads with a loaf of fresh-baked bread have become a local lunchtime tradition.

It may not be high on Jenny Craig's list of acceptable treats, but the Philadelphia Sticky Bun, a gooey sweet roll with caramel and pecans, is the favorite to-go item at **Sweetish Hill Bakery** (1120 *W. 6th St.* 512/472–1347 **$**), a chic and comfortable coffee shop that has been a regular meeting spot for local press and government officials since 1975. The large patio is a great spot for lounging or pretending to study.

If in Texas bigger is better, then nobody has a better patio than **Mozart's** (3826 *Lake Austin Blvd.* 512/477–2900 **$–$$**), a midsize coffeehouse with a ridiculously large series of decks perched on the edge of Lake Austin. The coffee is mediocre and a bit expensive, but the panorama of the lake and its docks is absolutely fantastic if—and only if—you beat the evening crowds and weekend traffic. In an effort to meet the needs of some of their loyal customers, Mozart's added a small bookstore/magazine rack/smoothie stand.

family... **Amy's Ice Cream** (*1012-B W. 6th St. 512/ 480–0673 $*) is now available in your local grocer's freezer, but you owe it to yourself to try the original—where the flavors and the optional crush-ins regularly rotate. Kids love Rocky Brown—not a flavor, but a legendary local punk who works behind the counter. For years, west side parents have used the **Holiday House** (*2425 Exposition Blvd. 512/478–2652 $*) as a treat/bribe for their restive kids. It's Tarrytown's version of McDonald's, but the burgers are closer to the backyard-grill variety and the appetizer selection says "restaurant," not fast food.

italian... **Basil's** (*900 W. 10th St. 512/477–5576 $$–$$$*), a homespun Italian classic just off Lamar near Shoal Creek, is a great dinner-date stop. It's cozy and romantic, with five small dining rooms and candlelit tables. The Northern Italian fare is consistently good, with a signature dish of Pesce Florentine (fresh fish in a spinach sauce). The award-winning wine list is even better, though many of the wines cost a fortune, even by the glass. **Mangia** (*2401 Lake Austin Blvd. 512/478–6600 $–$$*), a Chicago deep-dish pizza franchise, puts a fairly hefty price on their pies—but each slice is so dense that one pie goes a long, long way. In an unusually Southern twist, salsa sometimes replaces marinara sauce. This Mangia location is just steps from Deep Eddy Pool, so don't forget the "wait an hour before swimming" mantra.

mexican/tex-mex...

The Hula Hut (3826 Lake Austin Blvd. 512/476–4852 $–$$) serves the standard line of nachos, flautas, and fajitas, but this is no ordinary Mexican joint. First, there's the odd Hawaiian/Mexican-style entrees, like mango cream-cheese quesadillas. Then there's the fact that the food is consistently awful. The thing is, nobody cares about the food—people come for the meat-market atmosphere. (Dennis Rodman—that kooky millionaire—once pulled up to the dock with a boat full of strippers.) Undeniably, the lush Lake Austin setting makes the Hut a guilty pleasure, but too often its *au naturel* beauty is negated by long waits and drunken frat boys. The latter also tend to hang out at **Maudie's Cafe** (2608 W. 7th St. 512/473–3740 $), but only because this inexpensive "Tex-Mex Heaven" is close to some rather purgatorial student housing. Nonetheless, youthful energy and ultra-friendly service make Maudie's a high point of West Austin. Cheap beer and alliterative menu items like Rockin' Ruthann's Smothered Burritos and the Fajita Fanatic's Chalupas guarantee its continuing popularity.

El Arroyo (1616 W. 5th St. 512/474–1222 $–$$) rebounded from a devastating fire that leveled the dining room and brought down the patio overhangs, but even a fire couldn't keep customers away from the always-good Tex-Mex menu and succulent margaritas. It's a popular after-work stop, and a low-key joint where you could bring Grandma for a taste of local culture—as long as she never got a look at the sign out front. The message changes each day and is sometimes, well, a tad off-color. Some of the better ones fit for family consumption? Try our favorite, "Body by queso."

El Rinconcito (1014-E N. Lamar Blvd. 512/476–5277 $–$$) is a cut above the rest of the Tex-Mex haunts. Chef/owner Lalo Garland's menu goes far beyond chips and salsa: In addition to great Mexican food, El Rinconcito is also Austin's only source for other authentic Latin American cuisine. The Monday-night Peruvian tasting dinners are wildly popular. Specialties include *ocopa peruana*, a dish of sweet potato and yucca topped with a chilled sauce of spicy roasted peanuts, feta cheese, *aji* (a Peruvian pepper), and parsley.

southwestern...
Like El Arroyo, **Z Tejas Grill** (1110 W. 6th St. 512/478–5355 $$) has also survived a major blaze and come back better than ever—this time with a private party room and expanded waiting area. The food style covers the border from Louisiana Cajun to California Southwestern, and is very flavorful, but not too spicy. A tree-lined patio that serves up 2-for-1 breakfasts has made Z Tejas one of the most popular west side eateries, so expect to wait. (It's worth it.)

upscale...
If you go to **Jeffrey's** (1206 W. Lynn St. 512/477–5584 $$$), plan on eating a great meal and spending a great deal. The romantic atmosphere is enhanced by its division into four smaller rooms, where candles and flowers prevail. The paintings are by local artists, and are changed every six weeks or so. Chef David Garrido constantly changes his Southwest/New Texas menu; local epi-

cures lust after his Cervena venison with chayote walnut salad, pineapple, and brandy cascabel pepper sauce. Jeffrey's is the ultimate in service, intimacy, and high-end fare (elk, foie gras, and caviar), but **Zoot** (*509 Hearn St., 512/477–6535 $$–$$$*) has become almost as famous for its haute New Texan cuisine at more moderate prices. The house specialty may sound rather unexotic—roasted chicken with corn custard—but it's the chicken against which all Austin chickens are measured. They also use locally grown organic produce, making for tempting vegetarian selections.

Wine snobs say nobody offers more Bordeaux for your buck than **Castle Hill Cafe** (*1101 W. 5th St. 512/476–7218 $$*). Simply put, they have it all and they sell it for less. But bring your reading glasses: It takes longer to peruse the over-annotated menu than it does to eat the food itself. The menu changes every two weeks or so. Try the grilled tenderloin with garlic-mashed potatoes and asparagus. Or, join the savvy business types who opt for the lunch special—big Caesar salads and individual pizzas.

vegetarian... It took Texans a while to warm up to the idea of health food, but the **West Lynn Cafe** (*1110 W. Lynn St. 512/482–0950 $–$$*) was among the first to recognize that there is a fortune to be made in an environmentally correct cafe. The secret to their success in the heart of cattle country is that the atmosphere is comfortable even for those who lean toward the more politically incorrect end of the spectrum. No militant vegetarians humming "Meat Is Murder" will harangue you about your past or present eating habits.

bars

You can get a drink at most West Austin restaurants, but if you feel like hanging out in a real bar, your choices are limited. Still, they're all truly neighborhood bars, and definitely worth checking out. Each of them has been open for at least two decades and has a solid core of loyal regulars from all walks of life, but they are also inviting to newcomers. It's too bad the rest of West Austin isn't as intimate, friendly, and immediately appealing as its bar scene.

The Tavern (922 W. 12th St. 512/474–7496) is 12th and Lamar's most interesting building, if only because it looks like Tim Burton's twisted model of a gingerbread house. Originally a grocery store (it opened in 1915), it became one of Austin's first air-conditioned public spaces, advertised with a classic "Air Conditioned" neon sign. Most locals call the spot the "Air Conditioned Tavern." It's still chilly and dark, illuminated mostly by the glow of satellite television sports events. It's not really a sports bar, though, but more of a big happy-hour hangout—lots of great finger food and a wide selection of beers—and a popular haunt for local musicians who want to avoid the music scene on their nights off. Many of them moonlight as Tavern bar staff. Just down Lamar, the **Shoal Creek Saloon** (909 N. Lamar Blvd. 512/477–0600) is more of a dive, with a slightly older clientele. A lively happy-hour and Sunday-football spot, it's more like two bars in one: The down-home saloon in front has sports on the TV, hard liquor, and smoked-duck gumbo, while the more relaxed back patio overlooking Shoal Creek and Duncan Park is a fine place for a nature lover's happy hour. Warning: On the patio, you're encouraged to drink, but in the park ten feet away you'll be arrested for it.

Although the **Deep Eddy Cabaret** (2315 *Lake Austin Blvd.* 512/472–0961) is named after Deep Eddy Pool, it's not really a cabaret and it doesn't get much of the post-swimming crowd business, either. It's the home of 20-year regulars, where the bartender not only knows your name, but pastes your obituary on the wall once you're gone. You'll get a few curious glances on your first couple of trips, but if you tip well and come back daily, your kids will have a place in which they can forever read about your exploits. The **Dry Creek Cafe and Boat Dock** (*Mt. Bonnell Rd.* 512/453–9244) seems a bit less friendly, but it is just as classic. It's about a half mile from Mount Bonnell, past a couple of snobby gated communities, yet the vintage Coke signs are real and the bottled beer is cheap—and stored in classic coolers. Patsy Cline's voice can usually be heard wafting from the jukebox—that is, if the vociferous proprietress, Ms. Sara, isn't holding court: She's been here forever and will rip you a new one should you fail to bring your empty bottles back down from the deck upstairs.

music/clubs

On every piece of city letterhead that declares Austin the "Live Music Capital of the World," an asterisk ought to exclude West Austin. There are just two regular stages in the neighborhood—one worthy and the other bizarre—and both must operate as restaurant/bars to survive.

Waterloo Ice House (600 N. Lamar Blvd. 512/472–5400) is one of the better burger joints in town and its music offerings are similarly dependable. Sure, the Cactus Cafe [see **downtown**] is a better-established room for national talent, but Waterloo has become one of the premier showcases for local singer/songwriter talent such as Jimmie Dale Gilmore, David Halley, Jo Carol Pierce, Sara Hickman, and Kris McKay. The room is fairly large and actually has seats, and the cover and beer prices are reasonable.

Donn's Depot (1600 W. 5th St. 512/478–0336) is equally affordable, but the music often isn't as colorful as the club's owner. Donn bought this train depot, its cars, and the red caboose in 1972, decorated them as an old saloon, and has since used a small stage as a showcase for his band (Donn and the Stationmasters) and for hundreds of other country and blues outfits. Although he offers an ambitious calendar of music—every night except Sunday—most of it is mediocre at best. But Donn is the owner, so he gets to play a set with every band he books. If you've never stopped by at closing time to see this Freebird struggling through Skynyrd's "Sweet Home Alabama," you haven't seen West Austin music.

buying stuff

Diversity isn't West Austin's strength, to put it mildly, and that fact becomes most apparent when you go shopping. It's as if Martha Stewart authored some nutty city ordinance requiring every merchant to carry imported soap, furniture, and jewelry and prohibiting the sale of men's clothing, period. And the glut of mediocre folk art borders on nauseating. Virtually all the shops on Lamar, 5th, and 6th are homegrown and family-operated, but their merchandise never strays far from homogeneous, overpriced tourist-trade fare. CDs and books are West Austin's only truly dependable retail items.

books/music... For two decades, **Waterloo Records (600A N. Lamar Blvd. 512/474–2500)** has been hailed as Austin's—if not Texas' or America's—best record store. Many music-industry insiders consider Waterloo to be the national model for independently owned record stores. They've got every title you could ask for (in stock virtually all the time); there is always at least one clerk on hand with an encyclopedic knowledge of each genre; and they let you listen to whatever you want before you buy it. But wait, there's more: If you get home and decide you don't like something you just bought—like that ridiculous Yoko Ono CD—they'll let you return it! Waterloo also stocks the city's best array of local music and has become a pre-gig stop for almost every touring band of note, many of whom play in-store gigs (which often include free beer).

Locals love Waterloo so much that some won't even set foot inside **Cheapo (914 N. Lamar Blvd. 512/477–4499)**, a new shop just down the street. In truth, it's not a bad store, and it's not just a knockoff of Waterloo. The majority of the stock is used—which is good because it's easy to find used copies of recent releases for $9, and bad because their "buy anything" policy means they'll buy any ol' CD for a quarter and throw it in the vaguely alphabetical bins.

You'll have no trouble finding Ani Difranco discs at

hometown heroes

They're not primarily musicians—although a few are, part-time—but in Austin these names inspire respect and admiration, or at least, they're notorious for a variety of reasons.

Kerry Awn—The longtime poster artist and performer with Esther's Follies is also leader of the Uranium Savages, an aging-hippie parody band that still manages to get off plenty of good jokes that skewer the vaunted Austin lifestyle and music scene.

Lars Eighner—The once-homeless author of *Travels with Lizbeth* still has Lizbeth and is probably homeless again. The Bacchanalian figure he cuts belies his utterly exquisite prose—don't miss hearing him read. In his increasingly rare outings, you might catch him reading at Book People.

Richard Garriott—Better known as Lord British, the eccentric founder of Origin Game Systems is known for the lavish parties he throws at his castle on the outskirts of West Austin, as well as for creating popular Origin game titles like "Ultima Online" and "Wing Commander."

Jen Garrison—She's everywhere, she's everywhere! One of the most high-profile women in Austin is one half of the popular 101X morning show with Sara Trexler, and TV host of the Austin Music Network's weekly entertainment show "Check This Action." At last glance she was repping for Sony.

Harry Knowles—The originator and writer of "Ain't It Cool News"—the anarchic on-line entertainment review which can make Hollywood moguls quake—is low profile in his actual, as opposed to his virtual, location. The media sensation matters so little here it's bizarre—earning him a special mention.

Carlyne Majer—She's been called a "pretty tough customer" (to put it mildly) by some, but the ex-hippie who went from artist management to making Austin a player in the Grammys gets the job done.

The Prince—One of the most hardcore defenders of the punk faith is old enough to be your grandfather, owns the coolest toy store in town, and sports one of the most famous tattoos in the Western world. He's usually behind the counter at Atomic City, but he's likely to be crabby about showing his full-body, Japanese-style tattoo suit of movie monsters with Godzilla as the centerpiece.

Paul Ray—He'll flinch at being thought of as the grand old man of Austin blues musicians, but that's what he is. He's the voice of the brilliant Saturday night blues program on KUT-FM, emcees the annual Austin Music Awards, played with both Vaughan brothers, and ain't going away.

Wammo—Poet and rubboard player with the Asylum Street Spankers, Wammo is best known as a member of Austin's Poetry Slam Team and for his spoken-word rants, including the video "There is Too Much Light in This Bar."

Roland Swenson—Another former band manager, this one parlayed his rock 'n' roll savvy into heading up that most prestigious music symposium, the South by Southwest. Along with partners Louis Black and Nick Barbaro of the *Austin Chronicle*, Swenson and Co. own Austin for two weeks every March.

Eddie Wilson—Yet another ex-hippie success story, Wilson went from being founder of the Armadillo World Headquarters to restaurateur nonpareil with his Threadgill's restaurants.

Book Women (918 W. 12th St. 512/472–2785), the city's best gender-specific bookstore. Because DiFranco plays in town often, records here, and has always struck a chord with the local gay community, the store has a prominent display/shrine for DiFranco's records alongside all the lesbian fiction, women's studies, and parenting titles. And if you've ever wondered where to get that "Congratulations on coming out" greeting card or a "This is what a feminist looks like" T-shirt, Book Women's gift shop is the place. **Book People's** (603 N. Lamar Blvd. 512/472–5050) 300,000 titles are sensibly arranged and the selection is terrific. A smart staff and a huge roster of guest authors makes it the Waterloo, as it were, of bookstores.

clothes/accessories... Emerald's [see **gifts** below] is the west side's leader for young and trendy women's *apparel* (a distinctively west side word), but a growing number of loyal locals swear by **Croft's Originals** (1101 W. Lynn St. 512/472–4028), a small and reasonably priced boutique that hangs clothes outside and specializes in business/casual and "Austin hippie" lines. An Emerald's spin-off, **Fetish** (1112 N. Lamar Blvd. 512/457–1007), is the hands-down favorite for funky shoes in all varieties: lifts, pumps, and platforms. The place sells clothes, too, but most of their stuff isn't nearly as sexy as the name might make one hope. **N8** (1014-B N. Lamar Blvd. 512/478–3446), on the other hand, sells explicit "body conscious clothing"—mostly to gay men and club-scene types. Body self-conscious might be a better description, considering the bare-butt thongs, sex-play harnesses, and show-it-all hot pants that are N8's specialty.

On a completely different note, **Lambs-E-Divey** (2415-B Exposition Blvd. 512/479–6619) is undeniably the west side's coolest yuppie baby store. They've got furniture, toys, and all the Ralph Lauren shirts and pants a four-year-old Tarrytown tyke will ever need.

gifts... If you hit only one folk art dealer in West Austin, make it the **Eclectic Ethnographic Art Gallery** (700 N. Lamar Blvd. 512/477–1816). Close to the corner of 6th and Lamar, this store puts the rest of the street to shame with a huge selection of authentic tribal, folk, and ancient art. And lots of stuff costs less than $20. If that's pocket change for you, have your personal shopper choose some flashy furniture by David Marsh—this store is the exclusive dealer for the legendary Houston architect-cum-designer. **Wildflower** (908 N. Lamar Blvd. 512/320–0449) isn't as much of a gas, but if you're in mortal danger of running out of traditional oils, soaps, and cotton clothing, you're saved here. Check out the cool baby furniture.

Further down Lamar is **Emerald's** (624 N. Lamar Blvd. 512/476–3660), the retailer of choice for sorority girls and soccer moms clinging to the hipness they never had. Their selection of "new" vintage clothing and shoes is growing, but the place is still mostly a gift shop, with the same overpriced picture frames, candles, and knickknacks you'll find all over the west side. Around the corner, **Sparks** (1014 W. 6th St. 512/477–2757) is like a homegrown Hallmark store, with hundreds of locally inspired and handmade cards. **Miguel's Imports** (524 N. Lamar Blvd. 512/481–0815) is to lawn ornaments what Sparks is to birthday cards, with thousands of ceramic vases—some tasteful, some god-awful, but you have to be from the South to gauge the difference. If you just can't take the Nativity statues, escape to **Pecan Street Emporium** (1122 W. 6th St. 512/477–4900), a busy European-style shop in a 1910 building. Their year-round world of Christmas is tacky but oddly alluring, with German collectibles, nutcrackers, and even barbecue smokers—the ultimate Austin Christmas present.

grocery/takeout... Although they're in separate Tarrytown strip malls, both **Food! Food!** (2719 Exposition Blvd., Ste. 112, 512/474–8515) and **The Grocery** (3102 Windsor Rd. 512/478–8582), cater to their upscale neighborhood. Food! Food! is adored by local retailers for its quick! quick! lunches, particularly fresh lasagna and homemade lemonade. The Grocery is small but interesting, and jam-packed with a surprisingly wide variety of fresh produce and fish for shoppers unwilling to fight the crowds at the granddaddy of all upscale groceries, **Whole Foods Market** (601 N. Lamar Blvd. 512/476–1206). This is the mothership of the multimillion-dollar chain, relocated from its original store a few blocks away on Lamar (now Cheapo Records). It is a natural-food paradise—fresh produce, poultry and fish, bulk spices, and the latest in vitamin supplements. And while it's pricier than the average grocery, the knowledgeable staff and the freshness of the food turns what could have been a contrived concept into a friendly and healthy wonderland that reflects Austin's natural-first values. Parking is impossible and the tiny aisles are tough to navigate, but this is one of West Austin's cultural hangouts, full of musician/cashiers and celebrity shoppers (Mike Judge, Sandra Bullock, Molly Ivins).

new age... New Age doodads are for sale all over town, but the smallest New Age shop in West Austin is probably the city's best. **Crystal Works** (*908A W. 12th St. 512/472–5597*) has all the standard paraphernalia—crystals, incense, candles, *feng shui* books, and astrology accoutrements—but they don't sneer at you if all you want is some fossils for the kids or a small fountain to decorate your garden.

sports/sportswear... The University Cyclery (*2901 N. Lamar Blvd. 512/474–6696*) is a good place to start your shopping day. Rent a mountain bike and pedal around the neighborhood completely immune to the headaches and hassles of finding a parking spot at Whole Foods, Waterloo, Lake Austin, or anywhere on 6th. The Cyclery is a member of a near-extinct species of mom 'n' pop bike operations, with friendly service and flocks of Mongooses (Mongeese?) and Schwinns.

Whole Earth Provision Co. (*1014 N. Lamar Blvd. 512/476–1414*) is another parking hell, but it's one of Austin's most useful outlets. They've got everything you need to navigate the Hill Country [see **off the edge**]—backpacks, luggage, tents, climbing gear, boots, and outerwear—at reasonable prices.

sleeping

West Austin's anti-corporate ethic applies equally to food and clothing choices as well as hotels. There's not even a Marriott or Holiday Inn in West Austin, although with so many downtown hotels nearby, it's not really an issue. The west side does have a couple of good homegrown alternatives, though: pricey bed-and-breakfasts in the heart of some ultra-swanky neighborhoods.

Cost Range for double occupancy per night on a weeknight. Call to verify prices.
$/under 50 dollars
$$/50–75 dollars
$$$/75–100 dollars
$$$$/100+ dollars

Although it'll set you back a pretty penny, the chance to stay in relative quiet on the banks of Lake Austin and within Tarrytown at the **Inn at River Oaks Farm** (2105 Scenic Dr. 512/474–2288 $$$$) might be worth it. Both of the inn's two stone cottages are secluded and feature a morning meal along with great views of the lake. Or try **Southard House** (908 Blanco St. 512/474–4731 $$–$$$$) for a rare opportunity to spend the night in a historic landmark without forking over a fortune. Built in 1890 and restored in 1985, this two-story Greek Revival town house features pine floors, high ceilings, marble fireplaces, and a swimming pool.

doing stuff

The interior of Texas is known for being mostly dry and flat, so any real estate that is either lakefront or elevated is much sought after. Because so many people want to live near one of their favorite parks or city views, popular attractions such as Mount Bonnell and Pease Park not only draw a steady stream of locals and tourists year-round, but also serve as community centers. In fact, many tourists take the Mount Bonnell Road drive just to gawk at the fancy houses that have popped up in this desirable area. And the views of the Hill Country and Lake Austin can take your breath away.

The easiest and most rewarding West Austin drive starts at W. 35th and Lamar and ends at Mount Bonnell. **Mayfield Park** (*3505 W. 35th St. 512/327–5437*) is a relaxing 22-acre spot with gorgeous gardens, bridges, and peacocks. The preserve and spectacular homes you'll pass on the mile drive toward **Mount Bonnell** (*3800 Mt. Bonnell Rd.*) are even more impressive from the top of the mountain. It's 785 feet, or 100 steps, to the highest point, and day or night this climb 'n' look is both the city's best postcard view and most popular tongue-tanglin' romantic hot spot. And yet, rather than becoming a cruising spot or a place for underagers, Mount Bonnell has maintained an atmosphere in which families can go for an after-dinner trek. If your date goes really well on Mount Bonnell, you might want to backtrack and check on the availability of a wedding date inside **Laguna Gloria** (*3809 W. 35th St. 512/458–8191*), home of a superb west side arts institution. The Mediterranean-style villa, built in 1916 on a 28-acre palm-lined tract, contains the **Austin Museum of Art**, a nationally recognized showcase for 20th-century painters, sculptors, and photographers. If the museum's calendar of films, lectures, and continuing education is too overwhelming, May's weekend Fiesta is a good lowbrow alternative, with jugglers, clowns, Mexican food, and general carousing for the whole family.

Whatever you do, leave enough time to walk through Laguna Gloria's grounds. They are to landscape lovers what Mount Bonnell is to the binocular set, and they make for a better picnic spot than Mount Bonnell itself. The cobbled paths are well-worn and the shady sections are among Austin's best low-key hangs. Note for history buffs: **The Treaty Oak** (503 *Baylor St.*) lost a third of its trunk to a 1989 poison attack but is still very much a West Austin must-see. The 500- to 600-year-old oak tree has been owned by the city since the '30s, and was reportedly where Stephen F. Austin signed the settlers' first peace treaty with the Native Americans. Now the historic spot is a great place for a shady picnic.

Eiler's Park and Deep Eddy Swimming Pool (401 *Deep Eddy* 512/472–8546) is another popular family stop and official Texas historical landmark. What began as a turn-of-the-century bathing spot reopened as a swimming pool in 1936, with a cold spring–fed swimming area for both general use and semi-pro lap swimming. It's free, it's just a block off Lake Austin Boulevard, and the park has plenty of hiking trails and barbecue pits—one of those rare West Austin spots that's entirely unpretentious and easily accessible. The pools at **Pease District Park** (1100 *Kingsbury*) are student favorites for final-exam procrastination. Pease, recognized as the city's first official park in 1876, is a textbook example of an "old-school" park: playgrounds, basketball, volleyball, swimming pools, and a prized section of the three-mile Shoal Creek Hike and Bike Trail. All that has always been good enough to drag students away from school—and professionals away from Downtown—but the addition of a 12-hole disc golf course (aka Frisbee golf) a decade ago brought a whole new daytime crowd that's deemed Pease the premier Texas grounds for this slacker-friendly "sport."

body

West Austin is the last place to go for a tattoo or body piercing. The only "skin art" in this neighborhood is body waxing—a feature available at almost all neighborhood spas. Most West Austinites consider their American Express Platinum Card bill incomplete without a long list of spa, personal-fitness, and New Age therapy charges.

There are several small spas and aromatherapy shops, but almost all of the praise for uniquely West Austin self-pampering is about one place: **Bella** (1221 W. 6th St. 512/474–5999). There are folks in West Austin who know Bella like they know their own bathroom. It became Austin's most popular salon—and the subject of a *Vogue* feature— by offering everything in personal coddling from advanced massage, hydrotherapy, and aromatherapy to more basic skin care and hairdressing. Its laid-back staff will flash the same smile for a newcomer buying a bar of soap or a candle as they will for their regular escape artists. Even if you can't afford to stay for a facial, it's the West Austin hot spot for a peek at how the other half lives.

off the edge

San Antonio

If the only thing you can think of when you hear the name San Antonio is "Remember the Alamo!," take heart—everyone else thinks that too. If you're a stickler for such things, the Alamo is properly called the Misión de Valero, and it's one of five Spanish missions still standing in the San Antonio area.

Since San Antonio is a little over an hour south of Austin on the I-35, there's a lot of concert and sports traffic between the two cities: Austin has the music; San Antonio has the NBA Spurs. It's a quick drive down to the Alamo City, though, outside of peak traffic times. Just go south on I-35 until you reach downtown and see the Hemisfair Tower, then turn in and park. Like most Sunbelt cities, San Antonio has experienced massive growth in the last three decades—it's now the ninth-largest city in the U.S.

There's much to do in San Antonio, one of the nation's most cosmopolitan cities, much more than can be crammed into a few paragraphs. For general information, contact the **San Antonio Visitors Bureau (P.O. Box 2277, San Antonio, TX 78298–2277, 800/447–3372)**. But assuming you're just doing the day trip thing, here are a few suggestions:

eating/coffee... There are many places to eat, but if you have time for only one, experience **Mi Tierra El Mercado** (*218 Produce Row inside the market square 210/225–1262 $$–$$$$*). The long-established 24-7 (even Christmas) eatery has caved in to yuppie demands on its menu, but the huevos rancheros are still spicy enough to make women sprout hair on their chests. The huge, drippy plates of enchiladas and the fresh, tasty hot sauce are also good any time of day. The wandering groups of mariachi singers will know just about anything you might want to request. They even respond to something as arcane as, "Do you know how to play 'Down the Road and Far Away'?"

sleeping... Hey! You're visiting Austin, remember? If you must stay overnight in San Antonio, however, there are zillions of cheapie hotels on Broadway, Interstates 10 and 35, and the city loops. Vintage San Antonio elegance can be found at **The St. Anthony Hotel** (*300 E. Travis St. 210/227–4392, 800/355–5153 $$$$*), a short walk to downtown. Need something cheaper? Try the **Super 8 Motel** (*1614 N. St. Mary's St. 210/222–8833 $–$$$*) Cheaper than that? Head back to Austin—it's only an hour away.

doing/buying stuff... If you've wandered around downtown San Antonio at all, you've seen the many stairs leading down to the San Antonio River Walk, better known as the **Paseo del Rio** (*210/227–4262*). While the San Antonio River is a questionable presence—it looks about three feet deep and has skanky water—shops and restaurants line it for miles. Flatboats will take you on a guided tour of the river for $4—worth it if you just want to kick back and look at the tourists instead of tromping around in the heat.

San Antonio has some notable museums. Both **The Witte Museum** (3801 *Broadway* 210/357–1900) and **San Antonio Museum of Art (SAMA)** (200 *W. Jones Ave.* 210/978–8100) offer regular and touring exhibits. SAMA is located in the old Pearl Brewery and often has quality exhibits of Spanish, Latin-American, and pre-Columbian art. **The Hertzberg Circus Collection** (210 *W. Market St.* 210/207–7810), with its rare circus memorabilia, is one of the coolest museums around, period. This isn't the most comprehensive or largest of such collections, but it's a fascinating way to pass the time. You'll see Colonel Tom Thumb's parade carriage, costumes, photographs, and a replica of the circus in miniature. Not bad for $2.50.

Many people miss it the first time they drive by, but that unassuming fortress-like structure on Commerce Street with the security guards and people imitating John Wayne is **The Alamo** (300 *Alamo Pl.* 210/225–1391). Established by the Spanish sometime in the 1720s, this is indeed the place where fewer than 200 scrappy Texans and supporters, including Davy Crockett, Colonel William B. Travis, and Jim Bowie, battled it out for almost two weeks against Mexican General Santa Ana's thousands of soldiers. The death toll was 189; the only survivors were slaves, women, and children. (Please note that Ozzy Osborne did not actually pee on the Alamo itself but on the stone walkway. He apologized for it in 1992.) So go ahead. Do your best John Wayne. Those security guards have seen it all.

Brackenridge Park (940 E. Hildebrand Ave. 210/207–3000) is the largest park in San Antonio, and includes a skyride, riding stables, the Brackenridge Park Eagle miniature train, **The Japanese Tea Gardens** (3500 N. St. Mary's St. in Brackenridge Park 210/821–3120), better known as the Sunken Gardens, and **The San Antonio Zoo** (3903 N. St. Mary's St. in Brackenridge Park 210/734–7183). Its spacious grounds are located just a few miles north of downtown near Trinity University. The amphitheater next to the gardens often hosts touring rock acts like White Zombie and Pantera. The zoo and gardens are the park's main attractions—the elephants, the African Plains exhibit, and Monkey Island are among the most popular features—but don't miss a trip to the petting zoo, even if you think you're too grown-up for that. The little animals are really lovable and will melt hearts of all ages.

Hemisfair Park (600 Hemisfair Park 210/207–8590) stands in the middle of downtown on the site of the 1968 World's Fair. Exhibits include those at the **Instituto Cultural Mexicano** (210/227–0123), featuring talks and exhibits detailing Mexico's rich history, and **The Institute of Texan Cultures** (210/558–2300), a multi-media exhibit focusing on the varied cultures that make up Texas. Standing 750 feet tall in the center of Hemisfair Park is **The Tower of the Americas** (210/207–8615), worth the $3 admission for its expansive, 360-degree view of San Antonio. Skip the revolving restaurant, since the food's dreadful and the prices alone are enough to make your head spin. Across Commerce Street from the Tower is **Market Square—El Mercado** (514 W.

Commerce St. 210/207–8600), the biggest Mexican market in America. You can buy imported, handmade arts and crafts, souvenirs, clothes, purses, and leather goods, and there's a farmer's market bustling from 10 a.m. to 6 p.m.

Hill Country

No, we're not talking about "King of the Hill" country. We're talking about Texas in the springtime, when the wild-flowers are in bloom and the roadsides are blanketed with bluebonnets, red Indian paintbrush, and bright yellow black-eyed Susans. Even if you're here another time of year, an afternoon or overnight in the Hill Country can be a welcome respite from the city.

The Hill Country of central Texas was formed by what is commonly known as the Balcones Fault, the same geological force that created Barton Springs, the cliffs along Lake Austin, and Lyle Lovett's gravity-defying hairdo (as good an explanation as any). The rolling hills, winding roads, and panoramic vistas make for spectacular touring. This is also LBJ country—the former president is buried at his Johnson City ranch. In the heart of the Hill Country is the town of Fredericksburg, which trades on its German heritage and attractive setting. Highway 290 west takes you straight there.

eating/coffee/sleeping... Being a touristy little town, Fredericksburg has plenty of motels as well as lots of bed & breakfasts with the word *haus* in the name. **The**

Fredericksburg Brewing Company Bed & Brew (245 E. Main St. 830/997–1646 $$$) offers accommodations, beer, coffee, and food under one roof. Since most of Fredericksburg is located within walking distance of here, this is a handy place to stop for a look around. Or you can drive back to Austin—it's just 80 miles.

doing/buying stuff... Driving around the hills is the most popular pastime here; wandering through Main Street shops is another. The shops are all pretty much the same, but they do offer charming handicrafts. One thing you will want to know is that the peaches grown locally are spectacularly delicious (move over, Georgia). Buy some and you won't be sorry. The best souvenir is also the cheapest, since **Fredericksburg** has a bizarre local ritual that involves adults dressing up in rabbit costumes at Easter. It seems the original settlers here told their children that the fires of the Indians in the hills were caused by the "Easter Rabbit preparing Easter eggs." There are postcards of the grownups in bunny suits enacting this "scene." The cards are cheap and hilarious.

The Backyard (13101 W. Highway 71 512/263–4146) boasts that it's "just three songs from Downtown," (Austin, that is, but what a difference three songs makes). The 3,000-seat Live Oak Amphitheater (owned by the same company that runs La Zona Rosa and the Austin Music Hall) is literally Austin's live-music oasis. Not only is it located at the foot of Hill Country, but the venue is dotted with large grassy knolls for seating and a series of huge oak trees that don't obstruct the view of the stage. A slightly older clientele usually gathers here to see the likes of Willie Nelson, The Allman Bothers, Bonnie Raitt, k.d. lang, Widespread Panic, and Little Feat. But even on nights when the talent is dragging, The Backyard revels in its Hill Country atmosphere.

Also, about 20 miles west of Austin on Highway 71, in the town of **Bee Cave**, is what many consider to be the area's most peaceful swimming hole: **Hamilton Pool (24300 Hamilton Pool Rd. 512/264–2740 $5 per vehicle).** With its 65-foot waterfall and sandy shores, the site's huge rock formations circling the pool were created several centuries ago when a grotto collapsed. The park and pool accommadate only a few hundred people, so the early birds get the swim. And after heavy rains the pool is closed, so call ahead.

transportation

airport: **Robert Mueller Municipal Airport**, 3600 Manor Rd., 512/472–5439; **Airport Paging**, 3600 Manor Rd., 512/472–3321.

buses out of town: Greyhound, 916 E. Koenig Ln., 512/231–2222; **Kerrville Bus Co.**, 916 E. Koenig Ln., 512/389–0319.

public transportation: Capital Metro (2910 E. 5th St., 512/474–1200) serves Austin, Cedar Park, Leander, Lago Vista, Jonestown, Pflugerville, Manor, and San Leanna, as well as southwest Travis County and Anderson Mill. Buses run Monday through Saturday, 5 a.m. to midnight, and Sunday 6:30 a.m. to 10:30 p.m. Call for current fare. Special services include van pools and transit services, which provide "door-through-door" service, where the driver will accompany a passenger to the door at the destination. The **Dillo Express** (512/474–1200, downtown-only service) is free. **University of Texas Shuttle**, 512/474–1200.

taxis: American Cab, 512/452–9999; **American Yellow Checker Cab**, 512/476–2124; **Roy's Taxi**, 512/482–0000; **Austin Cab Company**, 512/478–2222; **Yellow Checker Cab Co.**, 512/472–1111.

train: **Amtrak Intercity Rail Passenger Service**, 250 N. Lamar Blvd., 512/872–7245.

emergency/health

fire department: For emergencies call 911, for non-emergencies or information call 512/477–5784.

police: For emergencies call 911, for non-emergencies or information call 512/480–5000.

pharmacies: Walgreen's Capital Plaza (24 hours), 51st St. at I-35, 512/452–9452.

hospitals: St. David's, 919 E. 2nd St. at I-35, 512/397–4240; **Brackenridge,** 601 E. 15th St., 512/476–6461.

media/information

newspapers: *Austin American Statesman,* daily, 512/445–3500; *Daily Texan,* UT student daily, 512/471–5083; *Austin Chronicle,* alternative weekly, 512/454–5766.

radio stations for emergencies, traffic and weather: KLBJ AM (590 AM); KVET AM (1300 AM) [see **your 5 pre-sets** in **downtown**].

tv stations: CBS: KEYE 42, cable 5; ABC: KVUE 24, cable 3; NBC: KXAN 36, cable 4; FOX: KTBC 7, cable 2.

convention & visitors bureau: 512/478–0098.

January: Red Eye Regatta—50 keel boats compete in this New Year's Day race at the Austin Yacht Club on Lake Travis 512/266–1336. **Elvis's B-Day Party**, Continental Club—A wildly popular Elvis tribute show 512/441–2444.

February: Carnaval Brasileiro, City Coliseum—An Austin spin on Fat Tuesday, complete with conga lines and elaborate costumes 512/452–6832.

March: Austin Music Awards, Austin Music Hall—Local award presentations and performances that kick off the South by Southwest Music Conference 512/469–SHOW. **South by Southwest Music Conference**—Nearly 1,000 bands and five times as many industry insiders and fans hit Austin for four rockin' days 512/467–7979.

April: SpamORama—An odd, enduring and strangely compelling cook-off, party, and demonstration for Spam fans 512/416–9307. **Eeyore's Birthday**—A hippie tribute, with music and beer, to the world's most famous donkey 512/912–5080.

May: Cinco de Mayo, Fiesta Garden—An all-out Mexican freedom celebration 512/499–6720. **O'Henry Pun-off**—A battle among local punsters 512/ 472–1903.

June: Juneteenth Freedom, Fiesta Garden—Week-long party celebrating African-American heritage 512/472–6838. **Clarksville/West End Jazz Festival**—A local jazz festival 512/477–9438.

austin calendar

July: Austin Symphony 4th of July Concert & Fireworks, Auditorium Shores—40,000+ Austinites attend this two-hour concert and fireworks display 512/476–6064.

August: *Austin Chronicle* Hot Sauce Festival—Salsa and live music 512/454–5766.

September: Old Pecan Street Fall Arts Festival, East 6th St. from Congress Ave. to I-35—A giant arts and crafts fair 512/478–1704.

October: Austin Heart of Film Festival, Driskill Hotel—A festival for film buffs and screenwriters 512/478–4795. **Halloween**, 6th St.—50,000+ people circle the entertainment district in elaborate costumes.

November: Día de los Muertos (Day of the Dead), Mexic-Arte Museum—A showcase for Mexican art 512/480–9373.

December: Yulefest 1998: Zilker Tree Lighting Ceremony and Trail of Lights, Zilker Park—A huge tree and a mile of lights 512/397–1468. **New Year's Eve**, 6th St.—A faux ball drop 512/478–1704.

eating/coffee

Airport Haven, 118
Amy's Ice Cream, 210
Arroyo, El, 211
Artz Rib House, 147
Asian Cafe, 146
Austin Java Company, 209
Austin Land & Cattle Company,
    The, 207
Azteca Restaurant, El, 194
Babe's, 18
Baby Acapulco, 157
Baby Compadre's, 152
Bangkok Cuisine, 115
Basil's, 210
BB's, 23
Ben's Long Branch BBQ, 192
Bo Knows Bar-B-Que, 117
Boiling Pot, The, 25
Borinquen, 159
Brick Oven, The, 73
Broken Spoke, The, 154
Buffet Palace, 117
Calabash, 192
Calle Ocho, 24
Captain Quackenbush's, 68
Captain's Seafood & Oyster Bar,
    The, 122
Carmelo's, 19
Casa de Luz, 159
Casey's New Orleans Snowballs,
    125
Casino El Camino, 18
Casita's Jorge's, 123
Castle Hill Cafe, 213
Catfish Parlour, 154
Chango's, 73
Chez Nous, 17
China on the Avenue, 15

China Wok, 146
Chuy's 123, 157
CiCi's Pizza, 121
Cisco's Restaurant Bakery & Bar,
    191
City Grill, 25
Classic Thai, 115
Conan's Pizza, 72
Công Ly, 146
Curra's Grill, 153
Dan's Hamburgers, 148
Dart Bowl Steak House, The, 119
Dick Clark's American
    Bandstand, 118
Dirty Martin's Kum-Bak Place, 71
Dolce Vita, 70
Dos Hermanos Panaderia, 152
Dot's Place, 121
Double Dave's, 72, 121
Eastside Cafe, 191
Einstein Bros. Bagels, 68
Feria Restaurant, La, 152
Filling Station Restaurant & Bar,
    149
503 Coffee Bar, 150
Flightpath Coffeehouse, 70
Flipnotics Coffee Space, 150
Fonda San Miguel Restaurant,
    124
Formosa, 208
Fortune Pho, 116
Fran's Hamburgers, 148
Fredericksburg Brewing
    Company Bed & Brew, The,
    232, 233
Frisco Shop, The, 119
Gallo Restaurant, El, 152
Gilligan's, 25
Gino's Italian Grill, 150
GM Steakhouse, 207

Good Eats Cafe, 154
Grace's Home Cooking, 121
Granite Cafe, The, 75
Green Mesquite, 147
Green Mesquite North, 118
Green Pastures, 156
Guero's Taco Bar, 153
Hernandez Cafe, 194
High Time Tea Bar & Brain Gym,
    150
HighLife Cafe, 19
Hoak's, 22
Holiday House, 118, 210
Hooters, 149
Hot Jumbo Bagel, 14
House, The, 193
Hudson's-on-the-Bend, 124
Hula Hut, The, 211
Hunan Lion, 146
Hut's Hamburgers, 18
Hyde Park & Grill, The, 66
Ichiban, 117
International House of Pancakes,
    22
Iron Works, The, 15
Jaime's Spanish Village, 24
Jake's Coffee, 17
Jake's Steaks & Seafood, 207
Jalisco, 157
Jazz, 26
Jean-Luc's French Bistro, 18
Jeffrey's, 212
Jovita's, 158
Juan in a Million, 192
Juice Joint, 159
Katz's Deli & Bar, 20
Ken's Donuts, 68
Kerbey Lane Cafe, 67, 145
Kerbey Lane Cafe North, 114
Korea Garden, 117

Korea House, 116
Kyoto, 20
Landry's on the Lake, 156
Little City, 16, 71
Little Mexico, 151
Longhorn Po-Boys, 74
Louie's 106, 26
Lovejoy's, 17
Lucy's, 191
Magnolia Cafe, 145, 208
Mandarin Chinese Restaurant,
    146
Mangia, 72, 210
Manitas, Las, 23
Manuel's, 23
Mariscos, 156
Mars, 18
Matt's El Rancho, 152
Maudie's Cafe, 211
Maudie's Too, 152
Mercado, El, 123, 158
Metro, 69
Mexicana Bakery, La, 151
Mezzaluna, 19
Mi Madre's, 194
Mi Tierra El Mercado, 229
Miguel's La Bodega, 24
Milto's, 72
Miss Flo's, 193
Mojo's Daily Grind, 69
Mongolian Barbecue, 116
Mongolian BBQ, 26
Mother's Cafe and Garden, 75
Mozart's, 209
Mr. India Palace, 120
Mr. Natural, 195
Mykonos Greek Food, 125
Nau's Pharmacy, 71
Niki's Pizza, 72
Ninfa's, 123

Nuevo Leon, 194
Old Alligator Grill, 156
Olive Garden, The, 150
Omelettry, The, 114
Paggi House, 155
Pao's Mandarin House, 15
Pappadeaux, 122
Pastor, El, 153
Patio, El, 73
Pato's Tacos, 194
Pavarotti Italian Grill, 121
Pearl's Oyster Bar, 122
Phoenicia Bakery & Deli, 159
Pit Barbecue, 117
Pit, The, 15
Pizza Nizza, 151
Players, 71
Private Idaho Potatoes, 68
Pulvos Mexicano, 151
Reyna, La, 151
Richard Jones Bar B Que, 148
Richard Jones Pit Barbecue, 117
Rinconcito, El, 212
Romeo's, 151
Roppolo's Pizzeria, 121
Rosie's Tamale House, 152
Ruby's Barbecue, 67
Ruta Maya, 16
Ruth's Chris Steakhouse, 75
Sam's Bar-B-Cue, 192
Sandy's Hamburgers, 148
Satay, 115
Schlotzky's Deli & Bread Alone
    Bakery, 149
Schlotzsky's, 120, 149
Seoul Restaurant & Sushi Bar,
    147
Serrano's Symphony Square, 24
Shady Grove, 149
Shaggy's Caribbean Grill, 159

Shogun, 147
Shoreline Grill, The, 27
Si Bon, 156
Sol y La Luna, El, 152
Spider House, 69
Star of India, 120
Star Seeds Cafe, 193
Starbucks, 16, 150
Stubb's Bar-B-Q, 14
Sullivan's, 26
Sweetish Hill Bakery, 209
Taj Palace, 120
Tamale House, 124
Tarrytown's Texas French Bread,
    209
Texadelphia, 74
Texas French Bread, 71, 114
Texas Ice House, The, 193
Texicalli Grill, The, 154
Thai Kitchen, The, 74
Thai Spice Cafe, 115
Threadgill's World Headquarters,
    155
Threadgill's, 122
Thundercloud Subs, 73, 120. 149
Top Notch Restaurant, 119
Triumph Coffeehouse, 114
Trudy's Texas Star, 73
Vista, La, 157
Waterloo Ice House, 67, 119,
    207
West Lynn Cafe, 213
Z Tejas Grill, 212
Zoot, 213

bars/music/clubs

ABCD's, 126
Antone's, 34

Arboretum, The, 126
Artz Rib House, 161
Austin Music Hall, The, 36
Avalon, 126
Babe's, 37
Babe's Stageside, 37
Back Room, The, 164
Back Yard, The, 166
Bates Motel, The, 40
Bitter End, The, 29
Black Cat, 37
Borinquen, 164
Broken Spoke, The, 160
Cactus Cafe, The, 80
Carousel Club, 127
Casino El Camino, 32
Cedar Street Courtyard, 34
Chain Drive, The, 43
Chaparral Lounge, The, 165
Charlie's, 43
Club Carnaval, 164
Club Deville, 32
Common Interest Karaoke Bar,
    126
Continental Club, The, 160
Copper Tank, The, 29
Cowboy Nite Club, 126
Crazy Lady, The, 196
Crown & Anchor Pub, 76
Dallas Nightclub, 125
Dance Across Texas, 165
Deep Eddy Cabaret, 215
Dessau Music Hall, 127
Dog & Duck Pub, The, 28
Donn's Depot, 216
Doris Miller Auditorium, 196
Draught Horse Pub & Brewery,
    76
Dry Creek Cafe and Boat Dock,
    215

Eats Grill, 164
Ego's, 164
Electric Lounge, The, 36
Elephant Room, The, 35
Emo's, 41
Fadó Irish Pub, 29
Fiesta Gardens, 196
Filling Station Restaurant & Bar,
    161
Flamingo Cantina, The, 41
Fliptonics Coffee Space, 161
Forum, The, 43
Gingerman, The, 29
Ginny's Little Longhorn, 127
Gino's, 164
Happy Days Lounge, 195
Hole in the Wall, the, 79
Horseshoe Lounge, The, 165
Iron Cactus, The, 31
Jovita's, 161
Lala's Little Nugget, 126
Liberty Lunch, 35
Lovejoy's, 31
Lucky Lounge, 30
Maggie Mae's, 31
Mercury Lounge, The, 41
Oilcan Harry's, 43
Polvo's, 164
Poodle Lounge, The, 126
Posse East, The, 76
Rainbow Cattle Co., The, 44
Realm, The, 164
Ritz Lounge, The, 40
Ruta Maya, 34
Saxon Pub, The, 161
Scholz Garten, 28
Shaggy's Caribbean Grill, 164
Shoal Creek Saloon, 214
Ski Shores, 127
Sol y La Luna, El, 164

South 40, The, 165
Southpark Meadows, 166
Speakeasy, The, 30
Steamboat, 40
Stubb's, 42
Sullivan's, 35
Tavern, The, 214
Tejano Ranch, 127
Texas Showdown Saloon, The, 77
Texas Tavern, The, 77
Texas Union Ballroom, 80
Threadgill's World Headquarters,
    161
Top of the Marc, 35
Trophy's, 164
Trudy's Texas Star, 77
Victory Grill, The, 195
Waterloo Brewing Company, 28
Waterloo Ice House, 216
Zona Rosa, La, 36

buying stuff

A Time or Two Boutique, 131
Aaron's Rock & Roll Emporium,
    130
ABCD's, 130
Acapulco Video & Audio Tapes,
    197
Adventures in Crime and Space,
    49
Allen's Boots, 168
Amazonia, 132
Amelia's Retro-Vogue and Relics,
    170
Antigua, 173
Antiques Marketplace, 132
Antone's Record Shop, 92
Aqua, 172

Aquatek, 133
Arboretum, 128
Armadillo Market, 173
ArtPlex, 46
Atomic City, 45
B. Dalton Bookseller, 129
Barnes & Noble, 82, 129
Barton Creek Square Mall, 167
Bazaar Back Stage, 167
Bazaar, 167
Best Buy, 130
Bevo's Bookstore, 81
Big Bertha's Bargain Basement,
    169
Blackmail, 170
Blockbuster Music, 130
Blondie's, 45
Blue Velvet, 87
Book Exchange, The, 129
Book People's, 220
Book Women, 220
Bookstop, 128
Borders Books & Music, 129
Breed and Co., 90
Buffalo Exchange, The, 86
By George, 87
By George for Men, 88
Bydee Arts & Gifts, 48
Cadeau, The, 85
Camelot Music, 130
Central Market, 89
Central Market Bookstop, 83
Champagne Clotheshorse, 169
Charles Edwin Inc., 88
Cheapo, 217
City General Store, 197
Clarksville Pottery and Galleries,
    84
Comic Castle, 130
CP Shades, 88

Croft's Originals, 220
Crystal Works, 223
Dell Computer Outlet Store, 132
Dragonsnaps, 175
Duval Discs, 90
Earfull of Books, 129
Eclectic Ethnographic Art Gallery, 221
EcoWise, 174
Electric Ladyland, 171
Emerald's, 221
Encore, 130
Eurway, 132
Fashion Exchange, 131
Fetish, 220
Fiesta Mart, 198
Flashback, 170
flea market, 197
Fliptonics, 169
Food! Food!, 222
Fringeware, 82
Galeria Sin Fronteras, 46
Gap, 88
Garb-a-Go-Go, 87
Gateway Shopping Center, 128
Green & White Grocery, 198
Grocery, The, 222
Half Price Books, 129
Hayward Neon, 174
Highland Mall, 128
I Heart Video, 130
Josephine's, 88
Kerbey Lane Dollhouses and
    Miniatures, 93
Kerbey Lane Dollshop, The, 93
Lakeline, 128
Lambs-E-Divey, 221
Let's Dish, 170
Lobo, 82
Local Flavor, 49

Loehmann's, 131
Lucy In Disguise With
    Diamonds, 171
Lush Life, 46
Lyons Matrix, 47
Maldonado's Record & Video
    Shop, 197
Mi Casa, 173
Miguel's Imports, 221
Momoko, 86
Musicmania, 197
Mysteries and More, 129
N8, 220
Neiman Marcus's Last Call, 168
Neon Jungle, The, 174
New Bohemia, 173
News & Smokes, 83
Nomadic Notions, 85, 131
Northcross, 128
Nouveau Options: The Designer
    Exchange, 131
Oat Willie's, 94
Off the Wall, 173
Out of the Past, 131
Paper Place, The, 84
Pecan Street Emporium, 222
Pieces of the Past, 174
Piñata Party Palace, 198
Pitchforks & Tablespoons, 198
Planet K, 133
Radio Ranch, 93
Remar USA Christian Thrift
    Store, 197
Renaissance Market, The, 85
Ross Dress For Less, 131
Rue's Antiques, 172
Sabia, 47
Sacks II, 131
Simply Divine, 168
Sound Exchange, 91

Sparks, 221
St. Vincent de Paul, 172
Tamarind Vintage, 86
Technophilia, 90
Terra Toys, 175
Tesoros Trading Company, 48
Texas Futon Company, The, 132
Texas Textbooks, 81
Therapy, 168
Thirty-Three Degrees Records
    and CDs, 92
Three Chocolatiers, The, 84
Tinhorn Traders, 173
Toad Hall Children's Bookstore,
    83
Top Drawer Thrift Shop, 131
Tower Records, 92
Toy Joy, 92
Uncommon Objects, 173
Under the Sun, 172
University Co-op East, The, 82
University Co-op, The, 81
University Cyclery, The, 223
Urban Outfitters, 88
Vulcan Video, 174
Waldenbooks, 129
Waterloo Records, 217
Wheatsville Food Co-op, 89
Whole Earth Provision Co., 223
Whole Foods Market, 133, 222
Wild About Music, 47
Wildflower, 221
Women & Their Work, 46

sleeping

Austin Marriott at the Capitol, 51
Austin Motel, 177
Austin North Travelodge Suites,
    134
Bel-Air Motel, 176
Brooks House, 95
Budget Inn, 134
Classic Inn Motel, 176
Club Hotel, 198
Courtyard by Marriott, 134
Days Inn University, 198
Doubletree Hotel Austin, 135
Driskill, The, 50
Embassy Suites Austin Airport,
    135
Embassy Suites, 176
Four Seasons, The, 52
Habitat Suites Hotel, 135
Hilton and Towers, The, 135
Holiday Inn Express, 134
Holiday Inn, 135
Homegate, 176
Hostelling International Austin,
    176
Hyatt Hotel, The, 175
Inn at Pearl Street, The, 95
Inn at River Oaks Farm, 224
McCallum House, 96
Omni Austin Hotel Downtown, 52
Omni Southpark, 176
Quality Inn, 176
Quinta Inn, La, 51, 134, 176
Ramada Limited, 176
Red Lion Hotel, 134
Renaissance Austin Hotel, 135
Rodeway Inn North, 134
San Jose Motel, 177
Sheraton Four Points Hotel, 134
Southard House, 224
St. Anthony Hotel, The, 229
St. El-Motel, 176
Super 8 Motel (Austin), 134,
    198

Super 8 Motel (San Antonio),
     229
Village Inn, 176
Woodburn House, The, 96

doing stuff

Alamo Drafthouse, The, 56
Alamo, The, 230
Alternate Current Art Space, 183
Arbor 7, 138
Art Gazer Gallery, 184
Austin Country Flea Market, 135
Austin Lyric Opera, The, 104
Austin Museum of Art, 225
Austin Nature Center, 181
Austin Symphony, 104
B. Iden Payne Theatre, The, 104
Backyard, The, 233
Ballet Austin, 102
Barton Springs, 177
Bass Concert Hall, 103
Bat Conservation International,
     181
Bates Recital Hall, 103
BB Studios, 201
Bee Cave, 234
Blue Road Studio, 184
Botanical Garden Center, 181
Brackenridge Park, 231
Capitol City Comedy Club, 138
Celis Brewery, 135
ComedySportz Playhouse, 138
Coronado Studios and Gallery,
     200
Darrell K. Royal Texas Memorial
     Stadium, The, 100
Deep Eddy Swimming Pool, 226
Discount Cinema, 138

Dobie Theater, The, 105
East First Garden Theatre, 195
Eiler's Park, 226
Elisabet Ney Museum, 101
Esther's Follies, 57
F. Loren Winship Drama
     Building, The, 104
Fire Island Hot Glass Studio,
     Inc., 200
Frank C. Erwin Jr. Special Events
     Center, The, 101, 104
Fredericksburg, 233
French Legation Museum, The, 200
Gateway 16, 138
Governor's Mansion, 53
Great Hills 8 Cinema, 138
Hamilton Pool, 234
Harry Ransom Center, The, 98
Hemisfair Park, 231
Hertzberg Circus Collection, The,
     230
Highland 10, 138
Hill Country Flyer Steam Train,
     The, 136
Hippie Hollow, 137
Holy Eight Ball Studio, 201
Hyde Park Theatre, The, 104
Institute of Texan Cultures, The,
     231
Instituto Cultural Mexicano, 231
Japanese Tea Gardens, The, 231
Just Say Cheese, 183
Laguna Gloria, 225
Lakeline Starport, 138
Laughing at the Sun, 183
LBJ School of Public Affairs, 97
Lone Star Riverboat Tour, 179
Longhorn Speedway, 138
Lyndon Baines Johnson Library
     and Museum, The, 97

Manor Downs Racetrack, 136
Market Square, 231
Mayfield Park, 225
Menagerie, La, 184
Mercado, El, 231
Mexic-Arte Museum, 53
Mount Bonnell, 225
Nancy Lee and Perry R. Bass
    Concert Hall, 103
Northcross 6, 138
O. Henry Museum, The, 52
Paramount Theatre for the
    Performing Arts, 55
Paseo del Rio, 229
Pease District Park, 226
Performing Arts Center, 103
Peter Pan Mini Golf, 182
Primordial Expressions, 183
Public Domain, 56
Raindog Studios, 184
Resistencia Bookstore, 183
Retama Park, 136
San Antonio Museum of Art, 230
San Antonio Visitors Bureau, 228
San Antonio Zoo, The, 231
Sharir Dance Company, 102
Stacy Pool, 178
State Theater Company, 55
Stuffola, 183
Texana Archives, 97
Texas State Capitol, 53
Texas Union Theater, 105
Theater Room, 104
Tower of the Americas, The, 231
Town Lake Hike and Bike Trails,
    178
Treaty Oak, The, 226
U.T. East and West Malls, 99
U.T. Main Building and Tower,
    99

U.T. Texas Union, 100
Velveeta Room, The, 57
Village Cinema Theater, 138
Vortex Repertory Company/
    Planet Theatre, 195
Waterloo Park, 54
Witte Museum, The, 230
Woolridge Square, 54
Yard Dog, 182
Zilker Park, 181

body

Anne Kelso Salon, 107
Asarte's, 58
Atomic Tattoo and Body
    Piercing, 139
Avant Hair & Skin, 106
Avant Salon, 139
Aziz Salon & Day Spa, 59
Bella, 227
Bradz Salon, 107
Forbidden Fruit, 59
4001 Duval Hair Salon, 107
Holly's Salon and Beauty Supply,
    106
Horsefeathers Salon, 106
Maximum FX, 106
Moonstruck Hair Salon, 139
Perfection Tattoo, 107
Rick's Aveda Concept Hair & Nail
    Salon, 106

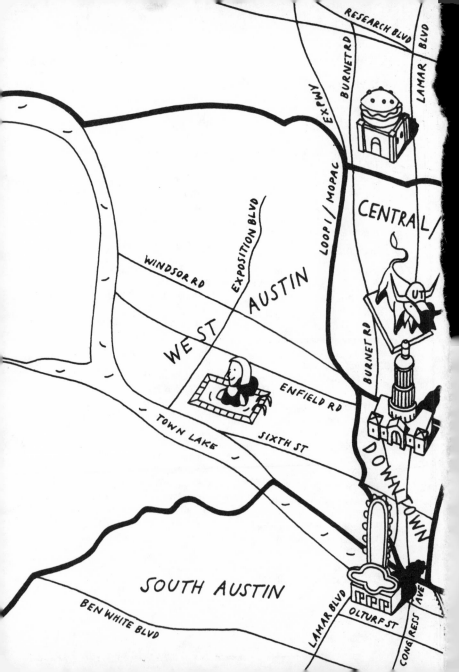